D0408483

VORTEX

S. J. KINCAID

KATHERINE TEGEN BOOKS
An Imprint of HarperCollins Publishers

ALSO BY S. J. KINCAID
Insignia

Katherine Tegen Books is an imprint of HarperCollins Publishers.

Vortex
Copyright © 2013 by S. J. Kincaid
All rights reserved. Printed in the United States of America.
No part of this book may be used or reproduced in any manner
whatsoever without written permission except in the case of brief
quotations embodied in critical articles and reviews. For information
address HarperCollins Children's Books, a division of
HarperCollins Publishers, 10 East 53rd Street,
New York, NY 10022.
www.epicreads.com

Library of Congress Cataloging-in-Publication Data
Kincaid, S. J.
  Vortex / S. J. Kincaid. — First edition.
    pages cm
  Summary: "While serving as a superhuman government weapon during World
War III, teenager Tom Raine's loyalties are tested by corruption and nefarious
enemies"— Provided by publisher.
  ISBN 978-0-06-209302-8 (hardback)
  [1. Science fiction. 2. Virtual reality—Fiction. 3. Video games—Fiction. 4. War—
Fiction. 5. Conduct of life—Fiction.] I. Title.
PZ7.K61926Vor 2013   2012051722
[Fic]—dc23   CIP
                                                                       AC

Typography by Carla Weise
13 14 15 16 17   LP/RRDH   10 9 8 7 6 5 4 3 2 1
❖
First Edition

To Meredith
For inspiring me to start writing as a kid
And for being the voice of reason

1 1 1 1 1 0 0 0 1 0 0 0 0 1 1 0 1 0 1 0 1 0 1 0 0 1 0 0 1 1 0 1 1 0 0 1 0 0 1
0 0 1 0 1 0 1 1 0 1 1 0 0 0 0 0 0 1 0 0 1 1 1 0 0 0 0 0 1 0 1 1 0 1 0 0 1
1 0 0 0 0 0 1 1 1 1 1 0 1 0 0 1 1 1 1 1 0 1 1 0 0 1 1 0 1 0 0 0 1 0 1 0 0 0
0 1 0 1 1 0 0 1 1 1 1 1 1 1 0 0 1 1 1 0 1 0 1 1 0 0 0 0 0 0 1 0 0 1 1 1 1
1 0 0 0 1 1 0 1 1 0 1 1 1 0 0 1 1 1 0 0 0 0 0 0 0 1 0 1 1 0 1 0 0 1 0
1 1 0 1 0 0 0 0 0 1 1 1 1 0 0 1 0 0 1 0 1 1 1 0 0 1 1 1 0 1 1 0 0 1 0 1 1
0 1 0 1 0 0 0 1 1 0 1 1 0 1 0 0 0 0 1 0 1 1 1 0 1 1 0 0 0 0 1 0 1 1 1 0 0 0
1 0 1 1 0 0 1 1 0 1 0 0 0 0 0 1 0 1 1 1 0 1 1 0 0 0 0 0 0 1 0 1 1 0 0 1
1 1 0 0 0 1 1 0 0 0 0 0 1 1 1 1 0 1 0 1 1 0 1 0 0 0 0 0 1 0 0 1 1 0 0
1 1 1 1 1 0 0 1 1
1 0 1 0 0 1 1

THE COALITION OF MULTI

THE INDO-AMERICAN ALLIANCE:

European-Australian Block • Oceanic Nations •
North American Alliance • Central America

MULTINATIONAL CORPORATIONS
(and sponsored Combatants):

Dominion Agra
SPONSORED COMBATANTS: Karl "Vanquisher" Marsters

Nobridis, Inc.
SPONSORED COMBATANTS: Elliot "Ares" Ramirez,
Cadence "Stinger" Grey, Britt "Ox" Schmeiser

Wyndham Harks
SPONSORED COMBATANTS: Heather "Enigma" Akron,
Yosef "Vector" Saide, Snowden "NewGuy" Gainey

Matchett-Reddy
SPONSORED COMBATANTS: Lea "Firestorm" Styron,
Mason "Specter" Meekins

Epicenter Manufacturing
SPONSORED COMBATANTS: Emefa "Polaris" Austerley,
Alec "Condor" Tarsus, Ralph "Matador" Bates

Obsidian Corp.
SPONSORED COMBATANTS: None

0 1 1 1 1 1 0 0 0 1 0 0 0 0 1 1 0 1 0 1 0 1 0 0 1 0 0 1 1 0 1 1 0 0 1 0 0
0 0 0 1 0 1 0 1 1 0 1 1 0 0 0 0 0 0 1 0 0 1 1 1 0 0 0 0 0 1 0 1 1 0 1 0 0
1 0 0 0 0 0 1 1 1 1 1 0 1 0 0 1 1 1 1 1 0 1 1 0 0 1 1 0 1 0 0 0 1 0 1 0 0
0 1 0 1 1 0 0 1 1 1 1 1 1 1 0 0 1 1 1 0 1 0 1 1 0 0 0 0 0 0 0 1 0 0 1 1 1
0 1 0 0 0 1 1 0 1 1 0 1 1 0 1 1 0 0 1 1 1 1 0 0 0 0 0 0 0 0 1 0 1 1 0 1 0 0 1
1 1 1 0 1 0 0 0 0 0 1 1 1 1 0 0 1 0 0 1 0 1 1 1 0 0 1 1 1 0 1 1 0 0 1 0 1
0 1 0 1 0 1 0 0 0 1 1 0 1 1 0 0 0 0 1 1 0 1 0 0 1 1 0 0 0 1 0 1 1 1 1 0 0
0 1 0 1 1 0 0 0 1 1 0 1 0 0 0 0 0 1 0 1 1 1 0 1 1 0 0 0 0 0 0 0 1 0 1 1 0 0
1 1 1 0 0 0 1 1 0 0 0 0 0 1 1 1 0 1 0 1 1 0 1 0 1 0 0 0 0 0 1 0 0 1 1 1 0

NATIONAL CORPORATIONS

THE RUSSO-CHINESE ALLIANCE:

*South American Federation • Nordic Block •
Affiliated African Nations*

MULTINATIONAL CORPORATIONS
(sponsored members unknown):

Harbinger

Lexicon Mobile

LM Lymer Fleet

Kronus Portable

Stronghold Energy

Preeminent Communications

CHAPTER ONE

"**Y**OU'VE GOTTA SEE this watch, Tommy. The inscription says 'Property of Sanford Bloombury, 1865.' Imagine that. Some guy was wearing this thing before we even had electricity."

Tom slid off his virtual reality visor and blinked as his eyes adjusted to the dimness inside the bustling casino. The bright lights of the nearby video displays flashed over the smile cracking Neil's worn face—and glinted across the gold watch dangling from his hand.

"Huh." Tom didn't really get why his dad was showing it to him. "Is this watch thing worth a lot or something?"

"Worth a lot? Tom, this watch has been passed down from father to son for generations. It's a precious family heirloom, and it's got a lot of sentimental value. Not to *our* family, of course, but definitely to that banker's." He jabbed his finger over his shoulder toward the bald man he'd beaten at poker a few minutes earlier. "So I hope it means something to you when I say that I want you to have it. Happy fifteenth birthday."

It took Tom a moment to process his words. "You're giving it to me?"

He couldn't remember his dad giving him a present for his birthday . . . not *on* his birthday or anywhere near it, at least. He seized the watch eagerly. The VR visor slipped from his hand, and Neil caught it before it could clatter to the floor.

"This is fantastic, Dad!" Sure, he had absolutely no need for a watch, what with the precise, satellite-tuned chronometer in his brain that measured time down to one two-thousandths of a second. . . . It was one of the many perks of having a computer in his head. Getting a present was still awesome, though.

Neil clasped his shoulder. "Come on, let's grab some steak."

Steak. That was even more awesome.

Tom leaped up and followed Neil through the bustling crowd in the casino. They brushed past the vanquished banker, who greedily eyed the watch in Tom's hand. Tom had no scruples about fastening it on in front of the guy, but it might've been a mistake being so brazen about it, because he swore he saw the banker's face tighten into a mask of hostility—and Tom saw the banker wave over some large man who looked suspiciously like some sort of bodyguard or thug.

Tom darted a last glimpse over his shoulder before he and Neil swept around the corner. Then they plunged through the door into the enveloping, dry heat of the Nevada evening, the startling neon lights of the Las Vegas strip bombarding them from all sides.

Neil surveyed the casino they'd left. "Think the banker's going to send his manservant after us?"

So he'd noticed the ominous gesture, too. Tom shook his head. "I dunno yet."

"Walk fast."

Tom didn't need Neil to tell him that; Tom *did* still have

some survival instincts from the first fourteen years of his life he'd spent following his dad from one casino to another. As soon as Neil got money, on the rare occasions when he won, *keeping* that money became the biggest task.

The question was, how alert was Neil right now? Tom threw a careful glance down at Neil's legs, and he saw that his dad was moving steadily, no swaying or shuffling. Good. Sober. Or at least, as close to it as he ever got.

Tom turned his watch to and fro as they threaded through the crowd, the gleaming lights of the Las Vegas skyboards playing over its surface. The mile-wide screens in near-Earth orbit bombarded ads down at anyone within a hundred-mile radius below them—but their reflections in the watch shrank to tiny slivers of light. Then in the shiny surface, he spotted a figure weaving through the crowd behind them. One glance back confirmed it: the banker's manservant was tailing them.

Great.

Tom's eyes snapped back to the front. "Yeah, Dad. We're being followed. Your banker's a leecher."

Neil gave a disgusted snort. "Figures. It's always the Wall Street guys."

There was this practice in the poker circuit now called "leeching," where men would hire a few thugs and play the game to win, even if they lost. If they legitimately won, they kept the spoils of victory, and if they lost, they dispatched their thugs to take back the money they'd gambled away. It ruined the game for everyone, because leechers didn't seem to understand the concept that gambling meant accepting your losses as well as your winnings. They seemed to think that win or lose, they were entitled to the spoils.

He elbowed Tom. "You remember how we deal with leechers?"

"I've only been gone six months," Tom protested. He tugged off his watch and let the thug see him giving it back to Neil. "Back of the head?"

"Back of the head," Neil agreed.

This was the sort of incident Tom hadn't missed while living at the Pentagonal Spire, training to be an Intrasolar Combatant. There, life was about routine, abiding by regulations, and Tom generally knew what would happen one day to the next.

Life with his dad was like this: chaotic, unpredictable, sometimes dangerous. Tom was almost relieved they were running into trouble, because the first two weeks of his legally mandated time away from the military's custody had been going so smoothly, he'd half expected a meteor to crash onto their hotel to make up for it. Getting pursued by a hired thug who was planning to rob them, take everything Neil had won tonight, and maybe beat them up, well . . . that was familiar enough. Tom knew how to handle it.

"Go in there," Neil directed, jabbing his finger toward the storefront of the next restaurant.

Tom saluted him. "See you soon, Dad." He veered from his father's side and headed on into the restaurant, leaving Neil to continue down the street in the press of the crowd.

They'd done this enough to have a basic routine down. Tom waited as the thug trailed to a stop in the midst of the crowd streaming around him, considering which of them to follow. Then he made up his mind and began stalking after Neil again. Tom scanned the room to make sure no one was looking his way, then swiped a heavy napkin holder from a nearby table and plunged back out onto the sidewalk. He began tailing the thug, who was so busy tailing Neil, he didn't notice. They never did.

Through the crush of the crowd, Tom saw the guy swerve

after Neil into an alleyway. Tom broke into a flat run. He reached the lip of the alley as the thug closed in for the kill. "Hey! Hey, you!" the man bellowed at Neil.

Neil made a show of spinning around coolly, primed for a confrontation, his eyes glinting with challenge. He gave a small smile, seeing Tom drawing up on the man from behind. "What can I do for you, buddy?"

Tom raised the metal napkin holder for a devastating blow, waiting for the guy to make the first move and officially render it self-defense when Tom whacked him over the back of the head, and Neil jumped forward to pummel with his fists. Tom watched the man reach into his coat pocket, and he knew it was time. He lunged forward, but Neil must've seen something other than a gun in the thug's hand, because his eyes shot wide open and he thrust up a splayed palm. "Tom, no! Don't!"

The man spun around, and Tom saw what he'd taken out.

A police badge.

Tom felt a dropping sensation, realizing he'd almost clubbed a cop. The napkin holder danced out of his fingers and clattered to the ground. The cop tore out his gun and leveled it at Tom. Tom's mouth went dry. He raised his hands and backed away. "Sorry. We thought you were . . . Sorry."

Neil raised his hands, too. "My kid and I thought you came to rob us."

The police officer snarled at Neil, "I'm going to need that watch back. And that money you pocketed tonight."

They both stared at him, realizing they'd been right: he *had* come to rob them. Neither of them had expected the leecher to hire an actual cop to do his dirty work.

Neil gave a derisive laugh. "Private detail duty, eh, Officer?"

Like most everyone else nowadays, cops couldn't really

live on their salaries, especially now as automated machines replaced them in standard patrolling and crowd control. An unscrupulous few of them took side jobs like this, acting as badge-carrying servants to the same men who'd given themselves bonuses with what used to be the cops' pensions.

This cop holstered his gun, satisfied he'd established his legal right to steal Neil's winnings. "We all do what we gotta do. Now hand it over."

"You don't seem to get how this works," Neil spat, his hands curling into shaking claws. "Your patron wagered and he lost. He lost to me fair and square. Maybe he's never gotten the memo, but when you gamble and you lose, you actually *lose*. It's a bargain you make for the money you get if you win. He can't just send a pet cop to take it back because the game didn't go his way!"

The cop was unmoved. "Do you want to give me a problem tonight, sir? Do you want this to turn ugly? Because I've got no issue with that. Just from the look of you, I'm betting you have prior offenses. That'll be helpful later when I say you were resisting arrest, or maybe that you were aggressive and left me no choice but to defend myself with force. And maybe your kid came after me, which will be good reason to lock him up, too." He smirked at Tom. "I don't think you want this nice-looking boy of yours in there with that bunch. I think you should play nice and give me what I was sent here for, and we'll all walk away."

Every muscle in Neil's body tightened.

Anger simmered in Tom's gut, too, but he knew there was no standing up to a cop. This guy could beat them both up and charge *them* with the felony. His word would always be taken above theirs in a court. For that matter, even if Tom hooked into a census device and uploaded this memory to the Spire's systems so someone could view it, and he could *prove* the cop was in the wrong, he and Neil would still end up the ones in trouble for illegally recording a police officer.

Tom reached out and nudged his dad. "Just give it to him."

With a noise of disgust, Neil delved into the pockets of his worn suit and hurled down the watch and a wad of cash, letting it all litter across the broken concrete of the alleyway. "You're no better than a common hoodlum."

The officer swooped down and snatched the roll of bills. "We've all gotta feed our own."

Neil gazed at the man with a burning rage in his eyes, and Tom knew this bomb would explode if he didn't intervene now. He reached forward and grasped Neil's rigid arm, then jerked his dad back toward the street with him. But Neil couldn't resist a parting shot.

"You're next, you know!"

The cop swung back up to his feet. "Are you threatening me?"

Oh no. Tom tightened his grip on Neil. "Dad . . ."

But Neil had that reckless light in his eyes, a crazed grin twisting his leathery face, and Tom knew this was a lost cause. "My boy and me, yeah, the corporate overlords already see us as surplus people breathing their air, living on their planet, but you know what? You're a worthless cockroach to them, too, buddy. They *used* to need you to keep your boot on our necks while they emptied our pockets. . . ."

"Dad, let's just go!"

Neil forged on. "But I hope the next time you look up at a drone in your sky or a patrol unit on your street, you'll realize you're nothing to them, too, and if you don't like it, they've got an automated boot to shove up your—"

The cop crossed the distance between them in two strides,

and cracked the butt of his gun across Neil's face, slamming him to the ground. Neil started laughing, raising himself up on his elbows, blood dripping from his nose in dark globs.

"Too close to the truth, *Officer*?"

The cop ripped forward for another blow, and Tom didn't even think about it—he shoved the man back. He knew a moment later that he'd made a mistake, and the cop's Taser jammed into his side, sending an electric jolt tearing through his muscles, locking them up, hurtling a mass of stars before his eyes. The entire world became a vibrating mass of prickling needles, and his body slipped out of his own control, thrashing to the ground. . . .

Tom came to sprawled on the ground, his palms stinging, his knees burning. He became aware of Neil shaking him persistently.

"Tommy . . . Tommy! You're starting to scare me. Come on. Wake up, kid. Wake up."

Tom forced his eyes open, a groan escaping his lips. "Dad?"

"Oh, thank God. I don't know what that was you just had." Neil's face was washed of color, a stark gray. "A seizure or something."

"I'm okay." His voice rang strangely in his own head. Everything seemed very far away.

"Well, you sent the banker's pet running." Neil hoisted him to his unsteady feet. "I guess he didn't want to get blamed for killing a kid."

They began the slow, difficult journey back to the hotel, Tom half draped over his dad's shoulder. His nose was buried against Neil's jacket, the smell of stale smoke and alcohol filling his nostrils. Numbers danced meaninglessly over his vision.

Tom woozily tried to sort out what had happened. He'd

definitely lost a few minutes, or maybe his chronometer was messed up.

He'd been tased before, back when he was a lot younger and had started gambling in VR parlors. He lost to this grown man, and he didn't have the money he'd bet against the guy, so he tried to run away. He wasn't fast enough. The man caught him, hauled him into this empty bathroom, and tased him over and over again until he was sure Tom had lied about having money. Then he tased Tom for losing a bet with money he didn't have. He said it was to "teach him a lesson."

Tom had learned his lesson: he stopped losing.

He'd also learned what a Taser felt like, so he knew it wasn't normal feeling this weak, feeling the strange buzzing in his skull, seeing the strange numbers dancing over his vision. It had to be the computer in his head, registering its objection to that electric jolt. He hoped he hadn't messed it up too much.

The neural processor didn't calm its strange seizure of flashing numbers until Tom was lying on his bed in their hotel room, the AC pumping a jet of icy air at him, the television buzzing. Tom could hear Neil muttering where he sat, drinking on the other bed.

Tom lifted his head blearily to see the screen was graced by the newly public Camelot Company Combatants. The Indo-Americans and the Russo-Chinese had worked out a temporary cease-fire, allowing the CamCos to go on publicity tours, where they touted their efforts in the war and their sponsors from the Coalition of Multinational Corporations. The military was also taking advantage of the absence of the younger trainees to open up certain areas of the Spire for a bunch of media events.

Ever since CamCo's identities had leaked, they'd become famous. Tom saw strange rumors about them all over the internet, too. "Britt Schmeiser's Weekend of Debauchery"; "Alec

Tarsus's Dark Past"; even headlines about the old favorite: "Elliot Ramirez's Forbidden Love."

Now Tom watched the screen hazily, seeing the handsome face of Elliot Ramirez, the Pentagonal Spire's longtime public CamCo. The dark-haired boy sat easily in the center of the massed CamCos, graciously assuring the reporters that he was pleased to share the spotlight. Snowden Gainey was preening in the chair next to his, and Cadence Grey kept darting nervous glances toward the camera. Everyone was there but . . . Someone was missing.

Huh. Heather Akron.

That gave Tom a dull sense of surprise, because he'd seen a lot of the gorgeous brunette from Machiavelli Division the first few days of vacation. Now that he thought about it, though, she'd virtually disappeared from the public radar the last few days. It struck him as strange. Photogenic and charming as she was, Tom expected her to be one of the foremost CamCos trotted out and shown off to the public.

"Look at those kids." Neil glared at the TV over his drink. "They look like a bunch of plastic puppets. Ever notice how they don't blink so much? Eh, Tom, ever notice that?"

Tom managed, "No, never noticed it." He'd asked his friend Wyatt Enslow to write up a program for his neural processor to randomize his blink rate. He was pretty sure that was one reason Neil hadn't noticed anything too off about his face—Tom had made an efffort to act as normal as possible. Between that and the hair he kept swept down over his neural access port, he'd been careful so far.

Now the focus of the press segment shifted to the CEOs of corporations sponsoring the CamCos. The show flipped to an interview with Reuben Lloyd, CEO of Wyndham Harks. The weedy little man with an unfortunate resemblance to a rat smiled toothily and spoke into a microphone.

"Just look at Reuben Lloyd here, playing up the PR so Wyndham Harks can angle for its next taxpayer bailout." He sighed, his voice growing strangely flat. "You know, Tommy, you're the only reason I've got any stake in this dump. Otherwise, I'd be glad to watch this whole world burn. I'd rather burn it than let them take it all from us."

Tom sensed danger in the air: Neil working himself up into a rage after the indignity of being robbed. He tried to think of something to say to distract him, but the screen filled with a glowing image of Joseph Vengerov, CEO of Obsidian Corp.

Tom's muscles froze.

The news report was fawning, because Vengerov had been named CEO of the Year by the *Institutional Investor* for the fifth time. All Tom could think of was the census device. Those three syllables that had nearly doomed him rolled through his mind, *Ven-grr-ahv*. . . . As soon as Lieutenant Blackburn realized Tom knew him, terrible things ensued. Tom almost lost his mind, his place at the Spire, everything. . . .

He was still shaken by the reminder several minutes later, after a hasty shower. He swiped the fog from the bathroom mirror, water still dripping from his thin face, matting his blond hair to his skull. The strange little flashes of numbers across his vision center were mostly gone now, so Tom figured there was no real need to do anything about it, even though technically, very technically, he was supposed to contact Lieutenant Blackburn if he had any problems with his neural processor over vacation.

Blackburn had even given all the trainees a remote-access node to hook into the port on the back of their necks. It was there to connect their processors with the Spire's server so Blackburn could examine their hardware from across the country.

Tom fished the remote-access node out of his backpack and

weighed it in his hand, considering it, then disregarding the thought. He was about to flick it away again when he noticed the marks on his torso, the bruises over his ribs where he'd gotten tased. Something dark boiled up inside him, his mind flashing over the face of the banker's pet cop. He'd probably handed the money back to the bald banker, who was probably counting it up somewhere.

Tom's fist contracted around the remote-access node.

Maybe he had a use for it, after all.

ALL THE MAJOR government servers were linked, so as soon as Tom jolted out of himself into the stream of data leading to the Pentagonal Spire's server in Arlington, Virginia, it didn't take long to find his way into the server of the Department of Homeland Security.

For a disconcerting moment, he felt strange, detached, a free-floating signal in a void. He was never entirely sure what he was doing when he interfaced like this. It seemed to come so much more naturally to the only other person he knew who could enter machines like this, the Russo-Chinese Combatant and his sort-of ex-girlfriend, Medusa. But today, Tom focused on his anger at the cop, and it sharpened his wits. He delved into the vast chain of zeros and ones, searching for the pipelines between the DHS and the domestic police drones flying over the United States.

When he located those, his neural processor sorted through an array of rapid-fire coordinates, and he latched on to the armed drone nearest to him.

A quick scroll through the database of registered gun owners in the area brought a familiar image to mind: Sergeant Erik Sherwin, the cop who'd robbed them. All registered gun owners had tracking chips in their skin, so he zeroed right in on Sergeant Sherwin's frequency.

Thousands of feet above Sherwin, in the darkened skies between Las Vegas and the overhead skyboards, the drone's mechanized gaze captured images of the cop just outside the casino, tailing the banker like an obedient puppy. Tom's vision center registered the images like he was seeing through mechanized eyes of his own.

His plans changed.

Tom felt an evil little thrill, because he'd intended to wreak some havoc on the cop, but now that he thought about it, he really should ignore the hired thug and focus on the mastermind: the bald banker the DHS's biometric database identified as Hank Bloombury, who worked for a subsidiary of the Matchett-Reddy Corporation.

Tom homed in on Hank and stalked him from the casino to his private car, the drone far overhead cutting a lethal path through the sky. Hank's car began to pull out of the strip, but Tom was in control of a police drone—which could link remotely into vehicle auto navigation systems and tamper with them at will. Tom enjoyed messing with Hank's autonav, steering the car back around and directing it toward the hotel he and Neil were staying in.

Hank must've finally realized what was happening, because he engaged the emergency shutoff. The car jerked to a halt; and the bald man popped out from inside it, rubbing at the back of his neck, obviously trying to figure out where he was.

Then Tom pulled off his next trick: he plunged the drone through the night sky, and settled it mere meters before the stunned Hank Bloombury. Tom leveled its Tasers straight at the guy's bald head, and enjoyed the sight of the banker standing frozen in place, his mouth hanging open.

Thanks for sending that cop, Tom thought, and sent a talon of the drone's Taser lashing out, shocking Hank just enough to knock him to the ground. Hank scrambled back to his feet, but when he tried to dive back into the car, Tom sent another flare of electricity that way to block him. Hank tried to run in the other direction, but Tom steered the police drone after him, a relentless pursuer, and zinged him again. Then again.

Hank threw up his hands in surrender and stood there, defeated, as Tom circled the drone around him like a vulture. Certain Hank was good and scared, Tom accessed the drone's text screen and gave the banker an order, knowing it would be relayed via communication screen and a mechanized voice.

"TAKE OFF YOUR CLOTHES."

Hank shook his head, his face flushed like he was outraged. He leaped for his car again, so Tom sent more electricity lashing out. That stopped Hank.

"TAKE OFF YOUR CLOTHES," Tom had the drone order again. *"RIGHT NOW."*

Hank seemed to get the message this time, and he stripped down. Tom decided it would be worth his eyes bleeding for the payoff.

"NOW RUN. RUN FAST."

Hank hesitated, so Tom launched the drone toward him, zapping the ground at his feet. The banker began running away, and Tom dogged his steps awhile, zapping behind him every so often, making sure the words "KEEP RUNNING, KEEP RUNNING" were displayed on the drone's communication screen. Tom kept it up until his drone corralled Hank onto the street near their hotel, then he released the drone from his control, launching it back into the sky.

He jolted back into himself, yanked off the transmitter, and popped out of the bathroom.

"Dad, you have to come outside." His voice throbbed with excitement. "Right now!"

Neil gave a grunt of acknowledgment but nothing more. His melancholy stare was fixed on the TV like he was in some sort of trance.

"Dad, come on, get up." Tom seized the remote and flipped off the TV, and then tore Neil's drink from his hand. *That* got his attention. "Believe me, you want to see this."

"Give me my drink back," Neil slurred.

Tom reluctantly handed it back. "You're going to miss it. Then you're gonna be sorry."

"Fine. Fine, I'm up." Neil was visibly irritated, but he followed Tom outside. That's how he walked out of the hotel in time to see the naked man arrive on their street, gazing up into the sky, searching for the rogue drone.

"Hey." Neil straightened a bit. "Hey, isn't that . . ."

Tom's lips blazed with a grin. "What a coincidence. It's your favorite leecher." He shoved past Neil to access one of the strip's emergency phones. Tom informed the dispatcher, "There's some crazy naked man running down the street. He's flashing kids and selling drugs and . . . and shouting about a holy war." He figured all three threats would get a hasty police response.

"What are you doing, Tom?"

Tom shrugged. "I figure he's so fond of cops, let's bring him a whole bunch."

The banker was busy haranguing people for clothes when the armada of cops arrived to deal with the drug-dealing, pedophiliac terrorist. Hank Bloombury had never learned to respect the men and women he regarded as his private goons, and he'd never been on the other end of their wrath. As soon as the cops piled out of their cars, he started bawling them out over their rogue drone, but the police didn't see any fancy suit, and they had no way to realize this guy was important. All they knew was, he was naked and aggressive, so they swarmed him, nightsticks flashing, Tasers flickering.

As the police brutality began in earnest, Tom raised his eyebrows at his dad. "Well? What do you think?"

Neil scratched at his unshaven cheek, blinking like he was trying to be sure he was actually seeing this. "I think I have no idea how you pulled this off."

"Let's just say that the military's taught me a lot of tech skills. That's all I can tell you. Classified."

Neil leaned closer, his voice a whisper. "Is there *any way* someone can trace this back to you?"

"Nope," Tom assured him breezily, even though he wasn't sure. "They'll probably figure out I put in the call to the cops, but the rest is a mystery."

Even to Tom. He wasn't sure why he was different from other trainees with neural processors or why Medusa was different, too. He had no idea why they could interface with machines other trainees could not. . . .

He just knew he had a particular skill at something, and his mind danced with possibilities about how he could use it.

"Tech skills, huh?" Neil marveled. "Those military guys are really doing right by you, after all. It blows me away when I think about that." He chuckled quietly. "My kid, actually having a shot in life . . . I never knew it was possible."

There was something different in his dad's face, in his voice now, and Tom swore, Neil seemed almost *happy*. The cops cleared the scene, and Tom felt a deep sense of satisfaction. Obviously his terrible vengeance on the leecher had done its job.

THE FINAL NIGHT Tom spent with his dad, he couldn't sleep. He ventured out onto the balcony into the neon embrace of Las Vegas. Lights bombarded him from every direction: the streets below, the buildings around, and even from skyboards overhead. Over Las Vegas, there were dozens of the mile-wide screens, all competing for attention from the tiny people so far below them.

Tom gazed upward, ignoring the ad from the DHS about hearing a whisper, giving them a whisper, and the ad from Nobridis about how its efforts to get rich off the war were actually beneficial to Americans. All he could think about were the possibilities ahead of him. He planned to be an Intrasolar Combatant who controlled the drones fighting the war in outer space, but now he was thinking he could also be a vigilante or maybe even a superhero.

Why not? He had the power to strike back at people like Hank Bloombury. He wasn't traceable, and everything was digitized now.

Medusa and I could even team up. Tom leaned his elbows onto the rail, thinking of his greatest foe, his sort-of ex-girlfriend, and the deadliest warrior on the Russo-Chinese side . . . the single person he knew who could've pulled off the same revenge on Hank Bloombury that he himself had.

Oh, and Tom grinned at the thought of what he could do to his mom's awful boyfriend, Dalton Prestwick, if he wanted to. Yeah, he'd find the guy in his Manhattan home and have some fun with that. Or maybe he'd do something to that George-town mansion of Dalton's. There were so many possibilities, they made Tom's head whirl in giddy circles.

He'd even get Karl Marsters.

No. No, wait. Maybe this was abusing his power. It probably was. So how about he only went after Karl once? After all, if he did the world-justice-vigilante stuff, he probably earned himself the right to follow up on a personal grudge *just once.*

At that moment, a loud roaring mounted in his ears, and with shocking swiftness, a black shape descended from the sky, blotting out the skyboards. Tom's entire body grew rigid, and he stood there frozen in place, as one of the Centurion-grade drones used in outer space began to hover, right in front of his balcony.

It wasn't a measly little police drone like the one he'd controlled. This wasn't for surveilling individual suspects and subduing them; it wasn't for breaking up crowds. This was built to blow things up in space. And it was close enough to touch.

Tom gaped at it, amazed. He'd never seen one of these suckers up close, not through his human eyes. The sharp, scythelike missile turrets curved toward him in open men-ace, their blackness stark against the skyboard light streaming about them. After a moment of looming there, the drone's optical camouflaging activated, shimmering its mass into invis-ibility, leaving only one visible aspect: the pinpoint camera eye, glaring right at him. Optically camouflaged ships were only detectable when they moved—and only if a person knew to look for the telltale wavering of the air. The camera seemed to float in space.

Then the instant communication program in his neural processor activated, and words were net-sent right into his vision center: *I know about your drone, Mordred.*

Tom was overjoyed, realizing who it was. If there was one person he'd want to share his triumph, it'd be Medusa. "You saw that?" he spoke, knowing she'd hear him. "Awesome. I've gotta admit it, though: yours is bigger. Where did you get this guy? I want one."

Are you an idiot?

Tom blinked. That wasn't the reply he'd expected. Or hoped for.

Unless you are actively trying to give us away, you need to stop messing around like this!

Tom ignored his sudden, sinking disappointment at her reaction and made a show of shrugging his shoulders. "I know you want to keep what we can do a secret. So do I, okay? But I had to do that thing yesterday. It was a matter of honor. I had to right a wrong. And honestly, Medusa, it's kind of rich calling me a moron for using that drone when you flew in a Centurion right over Las Vegas, of all places."

This Centurion was optically camouflaged when I flew it down. It disappeared off the grid years ago. No one will miss it. You tampered with the navigation of an active-duty police drone. Someone will notice. That is not acceptable.

"What, so I should do nothing, then?" Tom leaned forward, irritated. "I should wait until I'm a Combatant and use what we can do as a *cheat* like you do?"

The drone drew menacingly closer at the implication. Tom knew he'd made her mad, but he stood his ground.

"Don't you get it?" he said. "This ability we've got—we could do anything. We could make the world better. We could be like . . ." He faltered a moment, knowing this would make him sound like a dumb eight-year-old, but it was the only word he could think of. " . . . superheroes."

This is not a comic book, Mordred. We are not untraceable, and we are not invincible. We only operate in safety now because no one knows to look for us. The next time you pull something this stupid, I will come back and make sure you can't do it again.

"Like how? You'll kill me?"

He'd thrown that out there carelessly. He hadn't been serious.

Suddenly, the drone swept toward him, the optical

camouflaging peeling up enough to reveal the guns Medusa was leveling at his head, and something triggered instinctively in Tom as the red laser–targeting scanners crept over him, the massive machine searing the air around him. He scrambled back until he hit the door to the balcony, and found himself plastered there, staring right down a gun barrel, his heart pounding furiously, cold sweat prickling all over his body. For a timeless moment, they were suspended like that, her missile turret leveled right at his head.

Satisfied she'd made her point, her drone gave a taunting wave of its body, and Medusa planted a gibe in his vision center: *That's the idea.*

Tom found himself vividly remembering the moment at Capitol Summit when he'd used her disfigurement just to win. They'd liked each other before that.

He'd changed everything.

"Would it help if I said I'm sorry?" Tom asked her. He wasn't referring to what he'd done today.

No. Apologies are a waste of air, Mordred. Don't do this again.

And then her drone roared up and shrank away. Soon he couldn't even see the drone's telltale shimmer in the night sky, just a blinding ceiling of skyboards.

CHAPTER TWO

Two DAYS LATER, the morning sky gathered a purple light as his plane tilted up its rudders, shifted into helicopter mode, and lowered itself onto the Pentagon. Tom stepped onto the roof below the chrome tower of the Pentagonal Spire.

Two armed marines approached, and he flipped his Challenge Coin out of his pocket, raising it up so they'd see the eagle insignia. "Thomas Raines, trainee, US Intrasolar Forces." The coin flashed green as it simultaneously verified his voice-print, his fingerprints, and his DNA. One final step, the sweep of a retina scanner, and Tom had officially confirmed his identity for access to the Pentagonal Spire. An elevator swept him into the Pentagon.

Minutes later, duffel bag slung over shoulder, Tom walked into the Spire's lobby. He paused beneath the massive golden eagle with its outstretched wings, then set off down the corridor to the Patton mess hall.

There, he saw returning trainees, a handful of newly

promoted CamCo Combatants, and a dazed-looking new plebe with spiky, short-shorn red hair. She was sitting by herself next to the elevator and mournfully brushing her palm over her scalp. His neural processor immediately pulled up her profile information:

NAME: Madison Andrews
RANK: USIF, Grade III Plebe, Genghis Division
ORIGIN: Connell, Utah
ACHIEVEMENTS: Chairman of the Utah Federation Young Debater's Society, member of the Fairness in Voting Youth Committee
IP: 2053:db7:lj71::369:ll3:6e8
SECURITY STATUS: Top Secret LANDLOCK-3

Tom caught her eye and flashed her a grin. "Don't worry. Hair grows way faster than it did before the processor."

She offered him a shaky smile, and he headed onward toward the massive oil painting of General Patton. There he found what he was looking for. Even though it had only been two weeks, Tom felt a rush of joy at seeing Vikram Ashwan, his best friend. Vik launched himself up from the bench where he'd been waiting; strode over to Tom; and they dropped their bags on the floor between them with simultaneous, decisive thumps.

"Tom," Vik announced, his dark eyes dancing crazily, "we are no longer plebes."

"We are no longer plebes."

Vik gave a solemn nod. "It is time."

THE ELEVATOR DOOR parted to admit them to the plebe common room on the fifth floor. Tom and Vik stalked out. They saw all the suddenly nervous plebes, then he and Vik did what they'd been waiting to do since coming to the Spire.

"All of you," Vik shouted, "GET OUT!"

Tom started running around at the plebes, waving his arms in a shooing gesture. "Move, move, move!"

The plebes jumped to their feet and scrambled out of their own common room, scurrying through the doors of their divisions.

Tom and Vik slumped down, satisfied, into the now-empty chairs. Tom reflected fondly upon the times he, as a plebe, had been booted from the plebe common room by older trainees. It gave him an incredible sense of accomplishment, realizing he was no longer at the bottom of the Spire's food chain.

Vik rubbed his hands together wickedly. "So . . ."

"So?" Tom said eagerly, hoping Vik had some awesome idea about what to do now that they had the place to themselves.

They sat there a few seconds.

"I don't have any ideas about what we should do now," Vik finally confessed.

"Yeah, my thinking only went as far as booting the plebes out."

"I want to go stick my bags upstairs. The plebes will come back as soon as we're gone. Maybe we can kick them out again later once we've figured out something we want to do in here."

They retrieved their bags, then headed up to the Middle Company floor and into the door with the sword, marked ALEX-ANDER DIVISION. As they started down the corridor, something astounding happened: they received their assignment to their new bunk. Or rather, *bunks*.

Tom and Vik realized it when they started off in opposite directions down the hallway. Tom stopped and whirled around. Vik stopped, too, and raised an eyebrow at him.

They had *different* bunks.

"This can't be right," Tom blurted.

"It happens."

Tom stood there, rooted in place. Vik had been his room-mate since his arrival at the Pentagonal Spire. He was the first trainee Tom met after his neural processor was installed. It had never occurred to him that they might get split up.

"I'm just down the corridor, Tom."

"Yeah, I know." Tom made sure to laugh, too, even though it sounded strange to his ears. "Whatever. You know. See you." He started off again, but the change threw him a lot more than he wanted to let on. Tom did not like change.

He was almost at his door when Vik's earsplitting shriek resounded down the corridor. Tom was glad for the excuse to sprint back toward him. "Vik?"

He reached Vik's doorway as Vik was backing out of it. "Tom," he breathed, "it's an abomination."

Confused, Tom stepped past him into the bunk. Then he gawked, too.

Instead of a standard trainee bunk of two small beds with drawers underneath them and totally bare walls, Vik's bunk was virtually covered with images of their friend Wyatt Enslow. There were posters all over the wall with Wyatt's solemn, oval face on them. She wore her customary scowl, her dark eyes tracking their every move through the bunk. There was a giant marble statue of a sad-looking Vik with a boot on top of its head. The Vik statue clutched two very, very tiny hands together in a gesture of supplication, its eyes trained upward on the unseen stomper, an inscription at its base, WHY, OH WHY, DID I CROSS WYATT ENSLOW?

Tom began to laugh.

"She didn't do it to the bunk," Vik insisted. "She must've done something to our processors."

That much was obvious. If Wyatt was good at anything, it

was pulling off tricks with the neural processors, which could pretty much be manipulated to show them anything. This was some sort of illusion she was making them see, and Tom heartily approved.

He stepped closer to the walls to admire some of the photos pinned there, freeze-frames of some of Vik's more embarrassing moments at the Spire: that time Vik got a computer virus that convinced him he was a sheep, and he'd crawled around on his hands and knees chewing on plants in the arboretum. Another was Vik gaping in dismay as Wyatt won the war games.

"My hands do not look like that." Vik jabbed a finger at the statue and its abnormally tiny hands. Wyatt had relentlessly mocked Vik for having small, delicate hands ever since Tom had informed her it was the proper way to counter one of Vik's nicknames for her, "Man Hands." Vik had mostly abandoned that nickname for "Evil Wench," and Tom suspected it was due to the delicate-hands gibe.

Just then, Vik's new roommate bustled into the bunk.

He was a tall, slim guy with curly black hair and a pointy look to his face. Tom had seen him around, and he called up his profile from memory:

NAME: Giuseppe Nichols
RANK: USIF, Grade IV Middle, Alexander Division
ORIGIN: New York, NY
ACHIEVEMENTS: Runner-up, Van Cliburn International Piano Competition
IP: 2053:db7:lj71::291:ll3:6e8
SECURITY STATUS: Top Secret LANDLOCK-4

Giuseppe must've been able to see the bunk template, too, because he stuttered to a stop, staring up at the statue. "Did you really program a giant statue of yourself into your bunk template? That's so narcissistic."

Tom smothered his laughter. "Wow. He already has your number, man."

Vik shot him a look of death as Tom backed out of the bunk.

As it turned out, Tom had no assigned roommate of his own. He'd never had his own bunk before, not by himself. He spent about twenty minutes sitting in there, trying to figure out what to do with all the new space, wondering what he'd do if Giuseppe replaced him as Vik's best friend somehow.

Tom grew annoyed with himself and headed downstairs to the Middle Company primer meeting. As he stepped into the Lafayette Room, he delved into his pocket for his neural wire and upgrade chip. Row after row of benches filled the lecture hall, leading to a massive stage with a podium, a US flag, and a flag with the logos of the Coalition companies that were aligned with Indo-American interests: Epicenter Manufacturing; Obsidian Corp.; Wyndham Harks; Matchett-Reddy; Nobridis, Inc.; and Tom's least favorite of all, Dominion Agra.

He glared at that one as he took his place in the row before the stage, where Wyatt Enslow was already waiting.

"Tom, you didn't brush your hair today," she greeted him.

"Nice to see you, too. How was break?"

But Wyatt was too distressed by the messy hair issue to answer him. "General Marsh won't be happy if he sees you. He might yell."

"We should wait and see."

"Tom, no! Yuri didn't even get promoted with us, but he brushed his hair today. I saw him."

"Maybe that's why he didn't get promoted with us. He brushes his hair too much."

Wyatt frowned, genuinely perplexed. They both knew Yuri

hadn't gotten promoted because he was suspected of being a Russian spy and consequently had a lower security clearance than everyone else.

Tom surrendered. "Fine. Okay. Happy?" He pawed at his head, but he was clearly messing it up even more, since Wyatt reached up to claw at his head, too.

"No, you have to smooth down this right here. . . ."

"Ow!" Tom exclaimed as she tugged. "Don't pull it out!"

Vik swept over to his place beside them. "Enslow, stop assaulting Tom."

"I'm not assaulting Tom." Wyatt smiled wickedly at Vik. "Speaking of assaults, how did you like your bunk?"

"Glorious," Vik said dangerously. "I am going to retaliate, you realize. After all, I'm not Tom. I am far from terrible at programming."

Tom realized Vik was mocking him. "Hey!"

"*I* can actually write a program every so often," Vik went on, "a program with no nulls, no infinite loops."

"I can write programs."

"He means programs that actually work," Wyatt told Tom helpfully. It wasn't an intentional insult; it was more the Wyatt-type of insult she tended to do by accident. A lot.

Then the stern-faced, older general Terry Marsh assumed the podium on the stage. His blue eyes surveyed them over his bulbous nose, and all the new Middles lapsed into silence.

"Trainees." Everyone snapped to attention at the sound of Marsh's voice. "First of all, congratulations on your promotions. You are one step closer to Camelot Company. Hook into your neural chips and prepare to download your upgrades."

Everyone connected neural wires between their brain stem access ports and the chips they received at their promotion ceremony. Code flashed before Tom's vision, and an executable file installed itself in his neural processor. A password prompt appeared in the center of his vision.

Marsh pulled a slip of paper out of his pocket, and propped a pair of reading glasses on his nose. "It says here the password to activate the programs is 'I can see everything twice! Eleven, twenty-two, thirty-three, forty-four, sixty-six.'"

Tom thought it out, and code whirled before his vision and abruptly ceased. *Content unpacked* flashed across his vision center. Tom braced himself for the mental confusion that tended to follow a binge download of too much data without enough processing time, but he found his head completely clear.

Marsh nodded crisply, seeing that they were all done. "You'll notice there wasn't much to that upgrade. There's a simple reason: Lieutenant Blackburn installed the upgrades before you left for vacation. This password unlocked them. Now, trainees, take a moment to look at the map of the installation and chuck those chips into this bin here for reuse." He kicked a small box out from behind the podium. All the new Middles tossed their upgrade chips into the container. None missed.

Then Tom called up a map of the Pentagonal Spire in his neural processor. The familiar blueprint of the installation glowed across his vision center, showing fifteen floors of chrome and steel launching up from the dead center of the old Pentagon, but when he zoomed in to gaze inside the building, Tom found himself shaking his head. That couldn't be right.

The Spire had changed. The Calisthenics Arena encircling the interiors of the second, third, and fourth floors now contained a massive room labeled ARMORY.

That wasn't possible. He'd seen the upper floor of the

Calisthenics Arena dozens of times. There was no armory there. He was sure of it.

And then he looked over the other new sections: entire wings for military regulars stationed in the Spire, an observation deck on the twelfth floor, sections of wall containing power relays or processor parts, and below the basement level of the Spire, there was a brand-new floor labeled Mezzanine.

Wait. He couldn't have overlooked an *entire floor* for the last six months!

"You'll notice there are new areas to the Spire," Marsh noted. "These aren't actually new. They were always there. Your eyes saw them, your ears heard about them, but we blocked them from your conscious brain—rendered them in a sort of stealth mode in your processor. Certain sensitive personnel are also locked out of your processors. As plebes, you hadn't earned liberty of these areas of the installation. Now you have. This is a sign of our confidence in you."

Tom found his eyes straying over the Mezzanine, seeing the passageway leading to the fission-fusion reactor. So that's where that was. Another passage led to something labeled INTERSTICE.

"You Middles may not all progress," Marsh said, "and you may not all become Combatants, but you didn't wash out as plebes and get those processors removed, so congratulations, you're already a step ahead. You got promoted as plebes because you didn't prove yourselves unsuitable for life here. You will get promoted as Middles if, and only if, we think you belong in Upper Company."

Wyatt raised her hand, then dropped it quickly, remembering this wasn't like a classroom. At Marsh's nod, she blurted, "Sir, if we've had areas blocked from our processors, how do we know there aren't other things in the installation we can't see?"

Sniggering from the other side of the room. General Marsh gave a stern head shake, then said to Wyatt severely, "If there are, Ms. Enslow, you will find out in due time when we decide we want you to see them."

Wyatt fell silent.

Then Marsh went on, "You'll all have your first meet and greets with Coalition executives this Friday. Even those of you who don't become Combatants down the road will find this a useful networking opportunity if you play your cards right."

Tom's thoughts flickered to Dominion Agra. He'd flooded sewage on their entire executive board, so that was one company that would never sponsor him. He could use this chance to make a better impression with the other companies.

As soon as they were dismissed, Tom's mind turned back to that armory. His gaze shot to Vik's. Tom could see the same eager spark in his eyes.

"Guns?" Vik asked him, obviously ready to go to the armory right away.

"Weapons," Tom agreed.

They realized only when they neared the door that Wyatt wasn't with them.

"Wyatt?" Tom called to Vik.

Vik spun around, looked behind them, then answered that question with a single name. "Blackburn."

One word, but it was enough to send an unpleasant jolt through Tom's body like he'd been shocked by another Taser. His gaze swung around to see Wyatt and Lieutenant James Blackburn. Tom's heart began thumping, adrenaline and hostility surging through him as he saw the large, hard-faced lieutenant with close-cropped hair and a scarred cheek leaning over Wyatt, saying something to her. He wasn't sure when Blackburn had slipped into the Lafayette Room, but he'd obviously called Wyatt over for a quick talk by the opposite doorway.

Tom's vision tunneled into a single focus point.

This was the man who'd tried to rip his brain apart. Tom's every survival instinct began blaring an alarm. Blackburn and Wyatt had had a falling out of sorts when Blackburn thought she'd hacked his personnel file and told people private things the trainees weren't supposed to know about him.

Now they were talking again. Tom's head spun. When had this happened? How had he missed it? Blackburn reached down and clasped Wyatt's shoulder with a big hand. Tom didn't like this. Not at all.

Vik lightly whapped the back of his head. "Doctor, guns!"

"Right, Doctor." Tom grinned at his fellow Doctor of Doom. They weren't real doctors, of course, but they'd called each other this ever since the war games. "Weapons."

It was hard to force himself toward the door when all he wanted to do was charge over and shove his worst enemy away from one of his best friends.

CHAPTER THREE

I T WAS GLORIOUS.

The armory stood like some miniature fortress in the middle of the track, obstacles, climbing walls, and shallow pools. When they crossed through the door into the armory's depths, they found themselves in a narrow corridor. Each step carried them past racks dangling armor and other accessories such as optical camouflage suits to render a soldier invisible. There were guns of all types, some that Tom's neural processor identified, some it would not. At the end of the hall, a massive platform rested at shoulder height on top of it. Tom and Vik saw row after row of aluminum-and-steel machines that resembled exoskeletons, like a small army of headless androids ready to go all artificial-intelligence-doomsday scenario on them.

Tom and Vik gazed up in mute reverence, vaguely aware of other newly promoted Middles walking in, exclaiming over the sight, then leaving again. Soon no one else remained, leaving them to contemplate the wonders around them. Tom wanted to test shoot every one of the guns, don all the armor, and go all out against an alien invasion, or maybe against those metal skeleton things.

Vik gingerly lifted a small cylinder that resembled some sort of handheld cannon. "Look at this."

"I'm not sure what that sucker is, but I'm going to call him 'Big Bob,'" Tom said approvingly.

"Your head could fit in the muzzle of this thing," Vik said, awestruck. "Seriously. Come on and let's see."

"I'm not sticking my head in a cannon thing. Stick your own head in."

"I have highly temperamental hair. It'll get nestlike. You don't care when your hair gets nestlike, Tom. You can't possibly."

Tom wasn't listening, because he was reaching out to pick up another intriguing weapon of terrible death. His neural processor informed him it was a miniature electromagnetic pulser. For some reason, the knowledge this thing could fry a neural processor made it all the more exciting for him. Visions of firing it at Karl Marsters danced through his head.

Then Vik lifted a small, rounded object with a flattened base that Tom recognized from the infirmary. "What do you suppose this thing does? It was on the floor, not on any of the racks."

Tom quashed his smile. "Oh, I know what it is. Press that button on top."

Vik pressed the button. Confusion furrowed his brow when the device started beeping.

Tom drew a deep breath, then bellowed, "IT'S A GRE-NADE!"

Vik gave an earsplitting shriek and jumped so high, he crashed back into the wall, sending the device clattering to the floor. Tom cackled gleefully and scooped the device up, then flipped off the beeping. "Just kidding. It's a timer thing. I've seen them in the infirmary."

Vik snatched the rounded timer from him and peered at it suspiciously. "I am going to put you in the infirmary now, you gormless cretin. Find something we can duel with in here so we can launch eons of dynastic Raines-Ashwan warfare."

Joy filled Tom, and he scoured around, hoping for some knives or something similar, but just as he claimed his gun, Wyatt joined them. She looked at Tom with one gun, Vik with another, and halted in her tracks.

"Are you guys seriously messing around with real weapons?" she exclaimed. "It's like you want Darwin Awards!"

Tom flushed, and set his gun back on its hook. "It's not like we were going to start a dynastic war or something."

"Yeah," Vik said guiltily, returning his own weapon.

Wyatt bit her lip. She threw an uneasy glance around them, looking daunted by the sight of all the weapons, right there for the taking. Tom spoke as casually as he could. "What did Blackburn want?"

Wyatt reached out and poked at a piece of armor with a finger, like it was some animal that might snap at her. Then she poked it harder when nothing bad happened the first time. "He found out about something I did during my vacation, and he said it was good work."

"What?" Vik said.

Wyatt shrugged mysteriously. "He also said he knew I didn't hack his profile and he tends to assume the worst about people, so he apologized for getting so upset about the Roanoke thing and discontinuing my programming instruction."

"And, what, you forgave him?" Tom blurted. "After he yelled at you like that and ignored you for weeks, he just has to say sorry and you're over it?"

Her eyebrows drew together in her long, solemn face. "He said he was *really* sorry."

"You saw what a psycho he was, Wyatt. He turned on you for no reason before. You think that can't happen again?"

"It was only because you said that Roanoke thing. That's the only reason he acted that way. Obviously it was a sore point."

"No. No, you don't get it," Tom said, agitated. "It's not a sore point. It's the *only* point. That guy you saw that day? *That's* the real Blackburn. Trust me on this."

"I know him way better than you do, Tom."

"No," Tom said, raking his fingers through his hair, frustrated. "You *think* you do. You see the way he *pretends* to be. He pretends to be reasonable; he pretends to be sane. He's not."

He stopped talking, since Wyatt and Vik were both looking at him strangely.

The thing was, they knew Blackburn had tried to "fry his brain in the census device," in those exact words. Tom had never told them much more than that. He hadn't told them Blackburn had set out to tear his mind apart when Tom had refused to show him his memory of Vengerov; they didn't know Blackburn had threatened to wipe out the Spire's systems, just to stop Marsh from freeing Tom; they didn't know Blackburn had a vendetta against Joseph Vengerov, since Vengerov had intentionally implanted him with a neural processor that he knew would kill him or drive him insane. They didn't know that during his psychotic episode, Blackburn had accidentally killed his own kids, and as a consequence, he'd thought nothing of destroying Tom in search of something he could use in his vendetta against Vengerov, the man he held responsible.

But Tom couldn't even begin to tell his friends about this.

Not any of it, because there were too many secrets, not all of them his, and they were all tied into the memories Blackburn had discovered in his brain. Blackburn miraculously turning around and forgiving Wyatt felt like a direct threat to Tom. Sure, he might've been the one who told Blackburn that Wyatt never hacked his profile, that she didn't even know about Roanoke, but Tom hadn't done that to *reconcile* them. . . . He'd done that to rub Blackburn's mistake in his face.

He regretted it now.

They headed out of the armory to join the rest of the Middles who were trickling into the Calisthenics Arena for their morning workout. Tom, Vik, and Wyatt waited outside the armory along with the other four new Middles—Makis Katehi, Kelcy Demos, Jennifer Nguyen, and Mervyn Bolton. They all nodded at each other, but no introductions were needed; they'd been plebes together.

Soon Tom realized who they were waiting for. His fists clenched.

Lieutenant Blackburn ascended the stairs from the lower floor of the arena, then halted before the armory. With a tap on his forearm keyboard, he caused eight of the machines that resembled headless, metal skeletons to step down from the platform and march out to stand before them.

Blackburn turned to them. "Let's get started, Middles. You'll find Calisthenics much like it was when you were plebes— exercising, simulated images to motivate and direct your actions, that sort of thing. There's a notable exception: the armory. Each Monday, simulations are programmed to expose trainees to a variety of weapons that military research and development plans to give to future, neural processor–equipped soldiers. Since muscle memory is vital, we physically give the trainees weapons without ammunition. Not only does this enable you to learn how to use them, but it enables our researchers to study how well you're *able* to use them solely from the downloads installed in your processors. One of these weapons is particularly dangerous. Since they can only be controlled by someone with a neural processor, I'm the lucky guy stuck teaching you how to use them without killing yourselves or anyone else. What's the first rule of this lesson you're going to have with me?"

No one answered him. Tom had no idea.

Blackburn held up a finger. "Rule number one is: my time is infinitely more valuable than yours. Don't waste it by messing around or ignoring your instructions. I will tell you once, and I expect you to remember. You have photographic memories and superhuman brains. You have no excuse for inattention, and no excuse for forgetting what I've said. Now, let's discuss these exosuits."

He thumped his palm on the nearest metal machine.

"There are your basic strength-enhancement tools. You see, top brass believes that every armed en terra—Earthbound—conflict in the future will be handled by a small number of soldiers. There's a compelling reason for scaling down the number of soldiers in the armed forces: it's easier to find *one man* willing to fire upon civilian insurgents than it is to find a few thousand. It's cheaper to pay one soldier than it is to pay thousands. So these individual soldiers have to be walking arsenals. They need to be in command of heavy machinery that one person can't possibly handle unless he has inhumanly superior strength and stamina. That's where exosuits come in."

Blackburn inserted his legs into the wide, leg-shaped frames of an exosuit, then shoved his arms into the exosuit arms. When he clenched his fist, the metal mesh fingers contracted with his, and the metal frame closed around his arm, shortening so the metal joints aligned with his elbows and shoulders.

Then Blackburn reached back and pulled up the metal neck of the exosuit, hooking the prong on the end of the neck into the access port of his own neck. Immediately, the rest of the exosuit mimicked the actions of the arms, contracting to fit around his body, the joints of the exoskeleton lining up with his joints. Soon, Blackburn was wearing what resembled a metal mesh frame from neck to toe.

"Right now I have forty-two times an average man's strength." Blackburn held his arms out to the sides, displaying the way the thin metal even encased his fingertips. "Give me a pair of goggles with infrared and night vision; some high-density steel armor with fiber-optic cloaking capability to render me invisible; maybe a ceramic, medicine-secreting vest to clot up and heal any wounds I receive; some built-in air-conditioning to regulate my body temperature; a few mechanized drones to be my scouts; some overhead satellites to be my eyes and ears; a couple rocket launchers for my arms; a distant carrier ready to launch cruise missiles at my command, and . . . well, kids, give me all that, and I become a supersoldier, the decision maker at the center of a vast nexus of automated weapons and armaments. Theoretically, one supersoldier could travel back in time and obliterate the entire Third Reich. This is the future of warfare. Now"—his gray eyes roved over them—"what is the most important thing to remember when you're wearing these?" His gaze snapped over to Vik. "Ashwan. Guess."

Vik blinked. "Is this the your-time-is-infinitely-valuable thing again?"

"That was rule one, Ashwan. This is rule number two." And then Blackburn grabbed Vik in one swift movement and hoisted him over his head, causing Vik to give a startled yelp. Then, to Tom's shock, Blackburn hurled Vik up into the air a good twenty meters.

Tom's heart leaped as Vik's kicking body sailed toward the ceiling and plummeted back down. Blackburn caught him easily and set him gently back on his feet.

"Care to guess now, Ashwan? What is the next rule we are going to discuss?"

"The s-strength." Vik raised his wide eyes up toward the ceiling.

"Thatta boy, Ashwan. Superstrength. The human body is a frail, weak, easily ruptured thing. These exosuits are not. Rule number two: respect the power of these machines. Mess around in these and you will kill someone. The prototypes for these machines were around when I was a cadet. Those versions were only seventeen times an average human's strength. I got to witness one cadet jump up as high as he could in an exosuit. Before he smashed into the ceiling, he had a head. Afterward, he had something that resembled a smashed watermelon on top of his neck."

Tom looked up at the ceiling, intrigued. He figured if he jumped too high, he'd try to punch straight through the ceiling before his head got smashed. That would work. He was sure of it.

"That's why I'm teaching you the old-fashioned way how to use these," Blackburn finished, "working on muscle memory with you, not programming exosuit use into your brain. There's a fundamental difference between a human being and a machine. Human beings think in imprecise terms. 'A bit' means something to a person. If I told him to jump thirteen point seven centimeters, however, he would estimate and be wildly off because precise numbers don't mean much to the standard human brain. Machines, on the other hand, are precision instruments. They don't understand 'a little.' They *do* understand thirteen point seven centimeters. Using an exosuit properly means learning to be precise with your movements. The sole reason you can use these exosuits safely is because your brains are already part machine, but these are only safe if you're careful. So pick a suit, hook in, and wait for my instructions."

After Blackburn's intro, most trainees approached the exosuits with trepidation. Except Tom. He was excited to give it a shot. He eagerly hopped into his suit, flipped up the neck to connect it with his neural access port, and felt a thrill all over as the machine seemed to awaken around him, the metal legs and arms shrinking down to clasp around his limbs at the joining points. He stood there a beat, wondering if he should wait for everyone else, and he decided not to. He took a great, bounding step forward.

He sailed eight meters with the first leaping stride, six meters with the second, eleven meters with the third. Another couple steps, and Tom realized he was at the other side of the arena. He wanted to *live* in one of these.

And then he heard several loud clanks of exosuited legs pounding toward him. Before he could whirl around to see who it was, a steel-and-aluminum grip closed around the aluminum band across his collar and jerked him to a complete standstill.

"What do you think you're doing, Raines?" Blackburn's voice was furious.

Dread pervaded Tom. He dragged his gaze back to meet Blackburn's.

"Didn't you hear a word I said, trainee? These are *dangerous*. I didn't give you permission to move. You could have killed someone! Now hold still." He seized Tom's wrists and slammed them to his sides with a mighty clang that traveled all the way up the exosuit. Blackburn leaned in close so his gray eyes bore right into Tom's and whispered, "This is not a game."

Then Blackburn hoisted him up by the collar plate of the exosuit and carried him step by careful step across the arena. Tom hung there, arms at his sides, the eyes of the other trainees fixed on them every clanking step of the way. He got a mental image of a cat carrying a kitten by the scruff of its neck, and the giggles and sniggers of the other trainees stung his ears and confirmed that he looked as ridiculous as he thought.

Blackburn set him down carefully, then led them through exercise after exercise, working on finely tuned control, giving specific heights to jump to, specific stride lengths to walk. By the end of the lesson, Blackburn had progressed them at that same snail's pace to the point where they could perform some basic marches. Some made less progress than others. Wyatt was reluctant to move at all, even though when she did move, she was much smoother than people like Vik, who seemed unable to walk without flailing jerks of his limbs.

Tom tried to do the precision thing, but it made him feel awkward, the way thinking about breathing too much could make it difficult to breathe. The truth was, he found exosuiting easy. Very easy, actually—as natural as walking but a hundred times more thrilling. Since the very sound of Blackburn's voice made him want to do something violent, Tom decided to tune him out altogether and go with his instincts whenever Blackburn was turned away. At one point, Tom glanced behind him and felt a surge of certainty he could do something awesome here. He crouched down then shoved off into a backflip.

He wasn't sure he could've landed one in real life, but now he clanked back to the ground on his feet with perfect ease. Kelcy Demos and Jennifer Nguyen were both staring at him, wide-eyed.

He shrugged his shoulders. "I'm awesome at this."

They rolled their eyes.

Tom was disappointed. He'd hoped they'd be more impressed. He noticed Vik struggling with his own exosuit, so Tom made sure to saunter over to him and rub in his face how good he was with it by doing a jig right in front of him.

"I get it. You're good," Vik grumbled.

"Good? I'm like the Einstein of exosuiting. This is so easy. I even did a flip a minute ago. Seriously, I'll take any challenge you wanna throw down, buddy."

"Will you?" Vik said, a crazy glint in his eyes. He cast his gaze about, and his dark eyes drifted upward toward the ceiling. "Thirty bucks says you can't touch one of those lights."

Tom followed his gaze to the lights hanging from the ceiling thirty meters above them, thinking of Blackburn's watermelon anecdote.

Vik raised his eyebrows challengingly. "Well? Or do you want to revise your statement, Dr. Einstein?"

Tom threw him a ferocious grin. "No way."

Blackburn was standing in front of Wyatt, trying to coax her into taking a step toward him, arms out like he was braced to catch her. "You're doing great, Enslow. Move your leg."

Wyatt bit her lip. "What if I try to lift my foot, but my leg swings up and caves your head in?"

He chuckled. "I'll take my chances. Come on, Wyatt, you can do this."

Blackburn was busy. Good. Tom turned to face Vik, excited. It was now or never. "Adios, Doctor!"

Tom sprang into the air, excitement surging through him as he soared upward, higher than any human being could hope to leap. He raised his fists, ready to punch through the ceiling if he seemed in danger of getting his head smashed, but he'd calculated the height perfectly. His head was well clear of the ceiling when he began arcing down, and he reached forward to tap the light as he passed it.

That's where it went wrong.

His exosuited hand exploded against the light, shattering it, sending fragments of glass sprinkling toward the floor of the Calisthenics Arena.

Oh no, Tom thought as he plunged downward, stomach in his throat, glass raining on the ground as his metallic feet clanged against the dirt.

Tom found himself standing there, the exosuit bruising his joints, everyone staring at him in the sudden, enveloping silence.

Including Lieutenant Blackburn.

"Wow," Tom tried desperately. "These exosuits, man. I wasn't even trying to jump. I swear. That happened by accident. It must've malfunctioned." In a flash of inspiration, he added, "Shoddy Obsidian Corp. craftsmanship, huh?"

But the smear against Joseph Vengerov's company didn't appease Blackburn. He advanced on Tom and loomed over him like he was fighting the urge to hit him. All Tom could think was, *He is going to murder me,* and for a moment, he felt trapped back under the census device, questions he couldn't answer pounding into his ears. His chest grew tight, and he was only half aware of Blackburn craning his head back to survey the rest of the trainees.

"All of you, take those suits off. You'll be pulled into the workout with the other trainees. Raines, don't you move a single inch."

Tom stood there, full of dread, as everyone around him yanked out the connection between their neural access ports and the exosuits. As soon as they stepped out, their faces grew oddly blank, the Calisthenics workout program sweeping them into the exercise scenario. Soon, they'd all gone bounding off to climb up a wall with the rest of the trainees, leaving Tom and Blackburn to face off amid the exoskeletons.

Blackburn folded his arms, his shoulder stretching his uniform. A vein flickered in his forehead. "Disconnect and take the exosuit off."

Tom's heart pounded so loudly, he could hear it thundering in his ears. He reached up, knowing he should obey the order, but he couldn't do it. He couldn't. He knew something awful was going to come of this, he did, and adrenaline was surging through his veins. And rage. So much fury he felt like he was choking on it. "No," he said. "You first. *Sir.*"

Blackburn leaned menacingly closer. "I'm sorry. Did I articulate clearly enough for you, Mr. Raines? Disconnect from the exosuit. Now."

But Tom shook his head, his blood beating in his head so hard his vision seemed to be tunneling in, leaving the man in front of him the single, stark, clear focus. He wanted nothing more for an instant than to tear him limb from limb. "I don't think so. I kind of like you not having a forty-two-fold strength advantage on me. *Sir.*"

"You're that afraid of me?"

"I'm *not* afraid of you!"

Blackburn considered him, then the exosuit, and Tom could almost see his brain working over the hazards of an enraged trainee hooked into a machine he might not have full control over. The lieutenant reached up and pulled back the neck of his own exosuit, disconnecting. Tom's heart still thundered in his ears, anger like a poison inside him. Then the man stepped free of his exosuit, the fragile, "easily ruptured" human frame all that remained.

"Your turn, Raines."

Livid, Tom reached up, his sweaty hands slipping over the

neck of the exosuit. He'd just disconnected it when Blackburn snarled, "You really think I need an exosuit to deal with you?"

He closed the distance to him in two strides. Tom's hand flew up to jam the connection port back in, but it was too late. Blackburn's large hands seized him, and in one motion, he hauled him clear of the suit.

"Now, you listen up, Raines, because I'm only going to say this—"

But an unthinking anger surged through Tom, and as his feet met solid ground, he lashed out wildly with his fist. Pain shot up his arm as his knuckles hit Blackburn's jaw. Blackburn reeled back, but he spun around at once and hooked Tom's ankle, flipping his foot out from under him.

The world upended, and Tom's back slammed the ground hard enough to drive the air out of him. He doubled over, desperate to breathe, but Blackburn pinned him, crushing him into the ground. Tom struggled for several frantic seconds, but there was an unbearable weight on his throat, heavy legs pinning his, and the hand he thrust up to jab at Blackburn's eyes got captured and twisted around painfully.

"Stop this, Raines. Right now."

Tom yanked their arms closer and sank his teeth into Blackburn's hand. He took malicious pleasure in the pained cry, and punched the soft cartilage of Blackburn's throat. Tom jerked to flip them both over, then tried to bolt to nullify the strength and weight advantage Blackburn had over him. He didn't get far. Arms snared his midsection, and he was bowled over to the ground. Blackburn dug his knuckles into a pressure point on the back of Tom's neck, and he yelled out in shock, the pain driving him down.

"That one's not in your processor," Blackburn remarked. "I know it isn't, because I never installed it." Then he delivered a short, ringing blow to the back of Tom's neck.

Tom found himself on the ground, his head reeling. It came to him dully that he'd attacked a superior. And worse, he lost. His heart raged at Blackburn and he wished he'd hurt him more. In the corner of his vision, he saw Blackburn, seated on the ground, too, examining his hand and tiredly brushing off his uniform.

"I know what this is about," he said at length.

"No, you don't." Tom tried to surge back up, but Blackburn reached out and knocked him back to the ground, almost casually.

"Of course I do. I've been waiting for this since the census device."

"It's not . . ." *The census device.* But even as the heated words ripped from his throat, Tom choked off. His hands clenched into fists, and he screwed his eyes shut, a terrible, lingering sense of humiliation twisting through him when he thought of all those things Blackburn had torn right out of his mind—all those things he knew about him and the way he'd started fraying over those two days, puking over himself—and he wanted to tear him apart, shred his skin, stamp his guts. . . .

He shook with fury, wishing to kill him, hurt him, make him pay, and even the satisfaction of holding his threat over Blackburn's head, knowing the guy feared what Tom could do if he went to Vengerov, wasn't enough to cool the hot rage inside him.

Tom tangled his fingers in his hair, because he was so angry he didn't feel in control of himself. And he was painfully aware of Blackburn watching him fight to contain himself.

"You had your moment, Raines," he said after a bit. "You got in a good punch, and I'm even letting you get away with it. You get that." He leaned closer. "What you do *not* get to do is toy around with the exosuits. Do you hear me? That anger at me you've got pent up in there does not get to come out when you're dealing with machines that can kill people."

"Fine."

"We're clear here?"

"I told you, I get it! What else do you want?"

"I want you to *think*. You looked around today and you saw that every other trainee was having trouble controlling those exosuits, and your first impulse—your first one—was to show off to your friend. Didn't you step back for one microsecond and consider that ability you have with machines, and wonder if maybe you should keep it to yourself?"

"That has nothing to do with this. This was just exosuiting."

"It was hooking into a machine, Raines, *interfacing with a machine* and commanding it. Think. About. It." He jabbed his finger into Tom's forehead to punctuate each word.

Tom jerked back from him, his stomach churning. The truth was, he hadn't realized he was doing something so bizarre. He'd assumed he was good at exosuiting.

"Thatta boy. It's starting to make sense to you now, isn't it? You're going to have to be more careful in the future. No more showing off, and no more stunts like the one in *Las Vegas*."

Tom's mouth went dry. His eyes flew to Blackburn.

"Yes, you didn't think I knew about that." Every line stood out on Blackburn's face. "Do you honestly believe the Department of Homeland Security missed some ghost crawling around their server? I am betting there is a crack team of NSA agents trying to trace the source of that drone hijacking as we speak. You know what that means?"

"I'm sure you're going to tell me," Tom said.

Blackburn stabbed his thumb at his chest. "It means *I'm* the one stuck mopping up all traces of what you did. I'm not going to condescend to explain to you why my time is of utmost value around this dump. I can't afford to spend the next few years covering your tracks. You simply have to avoid leaving them. See, Raines, your threat to go to Joseph Vengerov and share what you can do with him if I 'mess with you' again? You have some devastating leverage there, but it's a hydrogen bomb. You only get to use it once. That means if the DHS ever notices your existence, your leverage is null and void, and there is nothing to stop me from taking another crack at extracting every secret from your head. And that's only if you're lucky and I get to you first."

"That's lucky?" Tom repeated bitterly. "Lucky now means 'worst case scenario ever,' then. That's great. Good to know."

"Sir," Blackburn corrected.

"You outrank me. You shouldn't call me 'sir.'"

"Raines, you'll address me as 'sir' or I will stick you back down in that cell next to the census device until 'sir' is the only word you remember."

Tom bristled. He'd never hated someone so much. "Sir, yes, sir. I'll use 'sir,' sir. Is that all, sir?"

"Oh, I'd say that's all. Get into the simulation with the others." Blackburn jabbed at his forearm keyboard. "It irritates me just looking at you."

Back at you, Tom thought, but then a tingling sensation shot up his neck, and the Calisthenics simulation cranked to life in his vision center. The Japanese army charged toward Tom in the simulated, World War II–era China, and Tom threw himself into the workout. But however fast he ran, he couldn't escape his lingering fury at the man who'd nearly ripped his mind apart.

He imagined every single fake enemy wearing Blackburn's face.

CHAPTER FOUR

Tom cheered up a bit when he arrived in the mess hall, because there was meat loaf for lunch and his friend Yuri Sysevich was waiting at a table. He was still a plebe, since he hadn't been promoted with the three of them. They mostly avoided talk about Middle Company so they wouldn't rub it in too much. As it turned out, Yuri had had a far more interesting vacation than they had, anyway. He'd signed up for a relaxing wilderness survival excursion, led by a former Green Beret, where he'd eaten bugs and climbed mountains and fended off wild animals.

"It is remarkable, truly remarkable, how many edible bugs there are to sustain you in the wilderness!"

"How many did you eat?" Tom wondered.

"Five different insects," Yuri answered proudly.

"Ew," Wyatt said, rubbing the spot on her head where he'd kissed her in greeting.

"Yeah, don't elaborate," Vik urged him, shoveling rice into his mouth.

"Were the bugs you ate like beetles or more like those rice-like mealworm things?" Tom said, watching Vik. Vik had the weakest stomach Tom knew, and it amused him endlessly.

Wyatt caught on to what Tom was doing. "Ooh, you mean the maggoty bugs from festering wounds that start like rice and sprout into full-blown intestinal parasites?"

Vik shook his head. "This won't work, guys. I know you're just making stuff up."

"No, the insects I consumed bore no resemblance to rice," Yuri answered seriously. "You are thinking of those parasites that grow in rice. They have very gooey, putrid innards, and they are slightly off-white, like the contents of Vikram's plate right now."

Vik finally tossed down his fork. "I'm done with lunch because I'm full. That's why. I'm not stopping because of you three. You have not won this."

Tom, Wyatt, and Yuri cackled, because they didn't believe him.

It turned out Tom and Vik were in the same simulation group, led by blond-haired, round-faced Combatant Snowden Gainey. Tom pulled up his profile from memory.

NAME: Snowden Gainey
RANK: USIF, Grade VI, Camelot Company, Napoleon Division
CALL SIGN: NewGuy
ORIGIN: North Westchester, Connecticut
ACHIEVEMENTS: Junior world squash champion, member of the Future Financial Innovators of America Society
IP: 2053:db7:lj71::224:ll3:6e8
SECURITY STATUS: Top Secret LANDLOCK-6

Within minutes, Tom realized that Snowden had a totally

different leadership style than his previous simulation group leader, Elliot Ramirez.

Elliot had always waited at the edge of one of the cots, visibly a part of the group, yet he'd also greeted them as they came in, which reminded everyone who was the boss. Snowden sort of hung out in the back corner, dread glimmering over his pale features as the number of trainees sitting on the cots with EKG monitors grew and grew. Only once everyone was there did he finally perch himself on a cot.

"Well, as you newbies have probably heard," Snowden ventured meekly, "Applied Scrimmages as a Middle involves scenarios similar to the ones you faced as plebes, but instead of facing simulated opponents, we directly face other groups of Middles, and we rotate every week. Today we're fighting Yosef Saide's group. So, do you guys want to start?" It was posed like a question, like he needed their permission.

Everyone dropped back to sprawl across their cots, and Tom twisted his head to the side to exchange an excited grin with Vik. "Got your back, Doctor."

"You, too, Doctor." Vik's eyes gleamed crazily.

And then Tom hooked in his neural wire and his senses dimmed as he was sucked into the simulation.

He found himself surrounded by chaos, World War II–era sailors screaming and rushing past him, the ship they were on jolting violently, fires flaring, seawater gushing into cracks in the hull.

Tom shouted for Vik, and they met up on the rocking deck, gasping for air, seeing a German U-boat in the distance slinking away.

"We're done for. Already," Tom said, incredulous. They hadn't gotten a chance to fight. The sim started this way.

"Life rafts!" Vik gestured toward a crush of frantic sailors, all eager to evacuate.

Tom gave a quick nod, realizing this must be the scenario: they'd get in those life rafts and fight Yosef's group. Maybe the Nazis would double back and attack again? Or maybe they'd face off with pirates or something?

Tom and Vik grabbed their place in the last life raft that dropped from the ship. A powerful wave tossed them from the main vessel as it sank into the churning ocean.

Soon, the water grew calm. Awe filled Tom as he marveled, not for the first time, that this was his life. He was sitting here on a rescue ship with his best friend, witnessing a devastating shipwreck like it was real. The raft was supposed to have two wooden oars, but it only had one. Tom and Vik steered their raft as best they could with it, and helped soaked, shivering trainees into it as they encountered them. Soon, they were sitting with Lyla Martin of Genghis Division, as well as two other Middles Tom had seen around: Walton Covner and Marrion Trout of Hannibal Division.

When Snowden Gainey appeared in the life raft with them, Tom realized the guy had actually been sitting out of the scenario until now, letting them undergo it by themselves. That was another huge change, because Elliot was a lead-by-example type.

"So," Snowden said nervously, "is this it?"

"I saw some of our group drown," Walton noted. He was a large kid with very dark skin, thick black hair, and an air of stoicism about him.

"Well." Snowden rubbed his palms together. "Well, that's unlucky for them. I should tell you, Yosef and I agreed together to run this scenario with the pain receptors on."

Tom shrugged, but he heard Lyla sputter with outrage. "Why? Why would you do that?"

"Well, it's a time-compressed scenario—" Snowden began.

Lyla seemed ready to punch him. Marrion groaned, too.

"What's the catch here?" Vik asked them.

"Time-compressed scenarios," Lyla explained. "Space combat takes place at machine-fast speeds, so the neural processor can be used to speed up your perception of time to keep up with it. Some training programs use that function to give you an artificially extended scenario."

"Really?" Tom sat up, fascinated. "So wait. We could spend days doing this scenario?" Awesome. Fighting pirates for days on end . . .

"Weeks," Lyla said. "And you're not going to be happy about that soon."

That's when Snowden announced, "Looks like everything's in order here. I'll pop in later." And his avatar vanished, leaving them all together in the life raft, bobbing listlessly on the ocean.

Tom stared at the empty space where he'd been. Lyla's last words rang in his ears and it occurred to him that there might be a reason Snowden wasn't participating in the sim.

As time passed and Tom grew dreadfully thirsty, he became certain of it. The problem with the scenario was, it felt true to life—like they were all on a life raft, floating in the middle of the ocean with no supplies but a canteen of water Walton salvaged that was rapidly being depleted. The worst thing was, they knew they could be stuck out here for weeks.

Tom swished the canteen grimly, hearing only a bit of water sloshing. "What happens now?"

"We'll die of dehydration. It will be slow and painful," Walton answered. He sounded very calm about it.

Tom scanned the horizon for pirates or Nazis or anything,

but no one came and attacked them. What was holding up Yosef's group?

When Snowden appeared in the life raft again to check on them, they were ready. They all turned on him and demanded an explanation for the scenario.

Snowden nodded pleasantly. "It's a survival scenario. You win if you survive."

Tom gaped at him. "Wait, that's it?"

"That's it. You're fighting the most dreadful enemy of all here. Impatience. Ooh, is that water? I'm parched." And then he did the unthinkable—Snowden plucked the canteen from Walton and swigged down the last of their water.

They all sat there, watching his Adam's apple bob. Disbelieving rage surged through Tom. Snowden had just arrived. He couldn't possibly be as thirsty as them, but he drank their water!

Marrion Trout couldn't take it anymore. The slight, black-haired girl declared that she was bored and "totally over this," then she threw herself overboard. For a few minutes, she treaded water, working up the courage to drown herself even though the pain receptors were on. And then fins cut through the water, and Yosef's group finally revealed themselves by tearing her apart.

"Impatience?" Walton pointed to the blood blossoming in the water. "Sure it's not about sharks?"

"Oh. Yes," Snowden said. "It's about surviving the sharks, too. Actually, it's mainly about the sharks. Good luck!" And then with a wiggle of his fingers, he disappeared again, leaving them with an empty canteen and a whole bunch of ravenous sharks.

Three days dragged by in scenario time. They grew desperate with thirst, terribly sunburned, and achingly hungry.

They'd managed to splinter the wooden oar into a makeshift spear, but as soon as they killed the first of Yosef's group, the sharks began steering clear—waiting for the humans to break down and come to them.

Walton gave up during the night and gulped a bunch of seawater.

Tom woke up to the sound of Walton's frantic slurps. "This is not going to end well for you, man." Tom's voice was so scratchy he barely recognized it.

Walton nodded, his mouth dripping with seawater. "It's very salty."

Vik shivered where he was sprawled out next to Tom in the raft. They all had oozing boils on their skin from exposure and saltwater, but one of Vik's had become infected, and the tell-tale red marks of blood poisoning were creeping up his limbs.

Tom was completely restless. He wanted to do *something* other than fantasize about tall glasses of water and hamburgers. He tried to figure out what this scenario was testing. Reactions under pressure? Under intolerable thirst and boredom? What?

As the sun rose, and grew higher in the sky, Tom's skin began to burn in the spots where he wasn't already blistered. Meanwhile, Walton announced, "I am the king of Mars."

Tom forced his eyes open and saw Walton standing in the middle of the raft. The saltwater had finally kicked in and started killing his brain, so now he was hallucinating.

Lyla was across the raft from Tom, her muscular arms folded listlessly over her body, blond hair tangled around her shoulders. "No, you're not the king of Mars. Sit down."

Walton raised his arms and held them outstretched. "Beep, beep."

"Stop that," Lyla snarled.

"Beep, beep."

"Stop that!"

"I am an antenna to signal the coast guard."

"Walton, sit down, man," Tom urged him.

Walton shrieked, "BIRDS LIVE ON YOUR HEAD!" He flung himself over and began tugging on Tom's hair, the sudden shift in weight rocking the raft violently, nearly capsizing them.

"Aah! Stop!" Tom fended him off with the oar end of their spear, and Walton retreated to the other side of the raft. Tom's scalp felt hot and sore, and he pressed his hand up to discover a bald spot. "Come on, man! You tore out some hair!"

"It's okay. I'm a doctor," Walton replied.

Vik stirred from where he'd fallen into a delirious sleep. "Doctor?"

"Yes?" Walton said, perking up.

"No!" Tom said, holding up the spear end this time to keep Walton back. He leaned over to nudge Vik. "Hey, Doctor. I'm here."

"Not you." Vik's voice was as hoarse as Tom's. "Real doctor. Think I'm sick. Water."

"We don't have water. This is a sim. It's not real, remember?"

"Right. Sim." Vik heaved himself up painfully. It took him several moments to get enough energy to say, "I hate this sim."

"We'll win or die and it'll be over." Tom knew that was optimistic, though. He wasn't sure how to win.

"Hate it," Vik moaned.

They'd all gone over it a bunch of times. This whole sim was ultimately rigged against them. Yosef's group, playing sharks, were in their natural environment. They had stuff to eat, plenty to drink, and they could survive the ocean elements. Their group had nothing. They'd bunched some seaweed up to try luring down seagulls, but the birds kept their distance. Vik dragged his shirt in the water, then tried some of the plankton he caught, but it made him violently vomit over the side of the boat, which was really counterproductive when they were all dying of dehydration.

The most water they could get was from the condensation on the raft first thing in the morning, and even that tasted like salt. And Walton's madness wasn't helping anything. He was reaching into the air now, swatting at something only he could see. Lyla sighed and asked what he was doing.

"Bats," Walton said, agitated.

"You should jump in the water and let the sharks eat you," Lyla suggested. "You're basically dead already. Worse, you're annoying me."

"No, I'll survive. I have gnome minions. Just nearby. They'll rescue us."

Lyla sighed. "Walton, you do not have gnome minions."

"You'll see. I'll go get them."

Then Walton hurled himself into the water with a resounding splash. Tom, Vik, and Lyla all waited for his scream, but it never came. Soon, he'd swum so far Tom couldn't see him. For a delirious moment, Tom marveled at the clean escape Walton had made. His water and food-deprived brain tried to wrap around it, and all Tom could think for a long moment was that Walton truly did have gnome minions out there, helping him.

Then fins cut their way through the water, and Walton's scream rose in the distance, killing that fanciful idea.

"Ugh." Vik threw his hands over his eyes. He leaned back on the raft, tugging at his shirt like he was hot, even though his teeth were chattering. "This is awful. So we have to live through getting eaten by sharks, or we die slowly and painfully of dehydration. Guys, there's only one option here." Vik rallied his strength and sat up. "We can't win. Let's all . . . you know. Kill each other somehow."

"It's bound to hurt less than the sharks," Lyla muttered.

Tom found his eyes riveted to the bloody spot in the water where Walton had been, the way the sharks were frantically swarming over it. All simulations as animals involved a battle between the powerful instincts of the creature they played and the deliberate human mind. Yosef's group was staying clear of their raft because their human minds told them they'd get stabbed.

Tom could see how frenzied the blood had made them. What if they did something to create that frenzy on purpose, so those animal instincts would truly take more control over them?

"Guys, I have an idea." Tom was excited. "What if we wait till Snowden reappears, we kill him, and we use his body as shark chum, and stab Yosef's group when they get lured in?"

"I'd pay to see Snowden killed," Vik exulted.

Lyla cackled evilly. "Shark chum made of Snowden. It would be so perfect."

It sounded like a plan to Tom.

When Snowden reappeared, Tom was ready. He gutted Snowden with one brutal thrust of his spear. Then he seized the thrashing blond kid before he could tumble overboard, and pinned his body to the floor of the boat, rancid water sloshing around them. "Okay, he's bleeding out fast. We should tilt him over the water or something—"

Tom blinked at her. "Are you crazy?" Lyla shouted at him.

"What? We talked about this." He looked at Vik. "You said you'd pay to see it!"

Vik's eyes were wide. He appeared torn between laughter and horror. "I didn't think you'd actually do it."

"Oh my God," Lyla exclaimed. "I thought you were joking, you psycho!"

"What? What's the big deal?" Maybe dehydration was frying his brain, but Tom was truly bewildered now.

"You're not supposed to kill our group leader, you moron!" Lyla exclaimed.

"We're supposed to kill all the sharks, and we need shark chum for that." Tom scooped up a handful of the bloody water and tossed it overboard. "This is great shark chum." He could see fins cutting through the water toward them. "See? They're already going for it."

"The big deal," she growled, "is that the shark chum is made of *Snowden*! If you were so eager for shark chum, you should've been the chum yourself, or I could've thrown you in! You can't kill our instructor."

"Why should *I* jump in?" Tom said disbelievingly. "*Snowden* got us into this. He wasn't helping us, and he drank our water!" That infuriated Tom the most. "He didn't even need it, and he drank it anyway. He was far and away the most expendable, useless person here, leader or no."

Lyla groaned. "Karl is right: you are such an idiot. Do you even realize the whole point of these sims is to impress people *in the military*?"

"I think winning will impress the military more than losing," Tom retorted.

Vik was shaking with a tired, giddy, delirious sort of laughter. "Tom, I love you."

Lyla punched Vik's arm. Hard.

Vik kept laughing. "This is so great. I'd cry with the joy of it if I could."

Lyla punched him again. This time, it really must've hurt, because Vik scuttled away from her to the other side of the raft. "Hey! No being violent to me unless you want me hitting back."

"Oh, please do. I was going easy on you, but I'd love a

chance to let loose. These are registered lethal weapons, you know." She held her fists up menacingly.

"Uh, you know, I'm over it," Vik said uneasily. "I'm glad we had this chance to talk out our differences and reconcile."

She dropped her hands, disappointed.

Tom turned away from them. He didn't care what Lyla had to say—he thought he'd done the right thing. He hoisted Snowden's body over the side of the raft to lure the sharks closer. As the first shark fin cut through the water by his raft, Tom whooped in glee and plunged his spear into its rough body, tearing the spear out before the shark could dart away and unbalance him. The next shark got the same treatment, then the next.

It was extremely cathartic, and Lyla snatched the spear from him so she could gore the next one, an animalistic growl coming from her lips that Tom was delirious enough to find painfully alluring. Vik even rallied his strength to kill a shark of his own. The water was saturated with blood, appealing to the shark instinct, overwhelming the trainee human instincts, so one after another, they grew excited and went into a frenzy by the raft, bringing them in reach of the spear.

Soon, they'd slaughtered all Yosef's trainees. But the lure didn't work on Yosef Saide himself. He was too self-disciplined. After his trainees were finished, Yosef became crafty. He began circling the raft at a distance, a dark shadow shimmering through the water. He dared not come within reach of their spear, and he didn't need to: they were going to die in due course without any actions on his part.

"What now?" Lyla said. "We don't have another instructor to murder. Maybe we should use you this time, Tom."

The suggestion was snide, but it gave Tom an idea. "Actually, that's a great idea."

Vik raised his head blearily. His voice was so hoarse and faint, Tom barely recognized it. "This does not sound like a great idea."

"No, it is. I'll jump in the water, swim far enough from the raft that Yosef will know I can't save myself by swimming back, and he'll come for me. I'll kill him."

"Or he'll kill you," Lyla said hopefully.

"That is a possibility," Tom admitted. "I'm going for it."

He threw himself into the cold water with a resounding splash and began swimming, spear in hand, the ocean dragging at his legs, Yosef hanging at a distance. A few times the shadow shimmered its way toward him, the lethal fin cutting a path through the water, but Yosef always veered off. He was feinting, testing whether Tom would flee to safety.

And then Yosef must've realized Tom had reached the point of no return. This time, he committed. His fin sliced through the water toward Tom. For a moment as that black shadow mounted upon him, a creeping horror grew inside Tom, realizing this was going to hurt, realizing what he'd done, what he'd invited upon himself. . . . Even if he got a spear thrust in, he was probably about to get chomped by a shark.

But then a crazed sort of euphoria swept over him, and Tom whooped in glee and thrust his spear forward as Yosef's razor-sharp teeth flashed right in his face—

And then his eyes snapped open in the training room. For a moment, Tom felt a profound relief, realizing his death had been painless. Then Snowden leaned over him, and Tom realized he'd been unplugged.

"We need to have a chat."

Tom sat bolt upright. "You unplugged me."

"I don't appreciate being killed by my own troops," Snowden informed him. "George Washington's troops didn't stab him to death. That's why we're not speaking British. . . . I mean, we are speaking British," he amended, "but not with a British accent."

Tom kept staring at him. Snowden had unplugged him at the most critical moment of the sim. He couldn't believe it. He'd been seconds from winning!

"Maybe someone should talk to you about the chain of command," Snowden decided. "Who was your old sim group leader?"

That's how Tom ended up waiting on his cot for Elliot Ramirez to come. He looked inward at the chronometer, his neural processor swiftly calculating the ratio between simulation time and real time. In the hours from Snowden's time of death to the time of his confrontation with Yosef, less than thirty seconds had passed, real time.

His head throbbed. It hadn't felt like thirty seconds at all. He rubbed at his temples. He couldn't believe all those days at sea had happened in mere hours.

"You get a time dilation hangover the first few extended sims." Walton's voice drifted over from a nearby cot. "You'll get used to it."

"I can't believe he pulled me out," Tom complained. What would happen to Vik and Lyla in the simulation now? He'd had the spear, and he'd been taken out of the sim. They had no weapon.

Walton sidled over to him and turned to keep his side to Tom while he spoke, like he was trying to fool a casual observer into thinking they weren't talking. "So, Raines, you killed Snowden, I hear?"

Tom eyed him, wondering if he'd react like Lyla. "Yeah, I kind of did."

Walton nodded crisply. "This pleases me."

"Sorry you got eaten by sharks, man. If it makes you feel

better, I was so dehydrated, I actually thought you had gnome minions."

Walton stared at him intensely until Tom's smile faded away. Then the other boy leaned forward and propped his elbows on the cot. "Tom, I don't really have gnome minions."

He said it so seriously that Tom grew confused. "Uh, yeah, I figured that."

Walton eyed him dubiously, like he doubted it. "It would be better if you kept quiet about what I said in the sim while my judgment was impaired. I'd hate for people to get the wrong idea and think I really do have gnome minions."

Tom grew bewildered. "Gotta tell you, Walt, I really don't think that's gonna happen."

"Yes, but rumors can take on a life of their own, and even a completely false rumor about gnome minions I don't have might give people the idea there are gnome minions I do have."

"No one's ever, ever gonna believe you have gnome minions!" Tom exclaimed.

Walton nodded grimly. "Let's make sure of it. Discretion"—he held up a single finger and let the word hang there in the air a moment, then finished—"is the better part of valor." And with that, he left Tom alone on his cot.

Tom grew very certain that Walton was trying to mess with his head—and doing a very good job of it, with that straight face and stoic bearing that gave away nothing. He sat there, perplexed and pondering gnome minions, until Elliot Ramirez appeared in the doorway to the training room and beckoned him over with a crook of his finger.

Tom sighed.

ELLIOT SIGHED.

Tom sat in the chair in Elliot's bunk, ready for a dressing-down by the unofficial leader of Camelot Company—and the person Snowden had enlisted to explain to Tom the importance of respecting those of higher rank.

"Snowden's a little insecure," Elliot said, surprising Tom. He turned from where he'd been gazing out the window. "He's not a natural fit for a position of authority, and I think he knows it."

"Wait. You're siding with me?" Tom was startled. And pleased.

"I am saying, I don't blame you, and I'm trying to give you advice about avoiding a repeat of your dispute in the future." Elliot folded his arms, leaning against the wall. "Can you acknowledge that what you did was unwise?"

"I almost won the scenario," Tom protested, thinking of the message Vik had net-sent him a few minutes ago when Yosef finally won the sim. "Yosef only managed to rip open the life raft and kill Vik and Lyla because Snowden yanked me out."

"You weren't about to win, Tom. Do you know what it's called when soldiers kill their leader? It's called 'mutiny.'"

"But Snowden was a burden on us. He was the most expendable."

Elliot shrugged. "You're in a hierarchical, top-down organization right now. Do you really think the people at the top will approve a victory you won by killing someone who outranks you?"

Tom remembered something Lyla had said, about how he should've thrown himself in instead. "So what if Snowden had beaten me to death to use as chum?"

"That's a different matter." He must've picked up on Tom's irritation, because he went on, "That's simply the way it works around here."

"But we're *not* training to run into the line of fire at

someone's command," Tom argued. "We're training ⸺r Intra-solar Combat. We don't risk our lives, and we don't get orders to direct us while we fight—we have to plan for ourselves. I thought initiative was a good thing."

"Mutiny is never considered a good thing, Tom. It's considered *too much* initiative. A threatening degree of initiative. You have to respect authority."

"I respect authority," Tom insisted, and he did.

General Marsh, for example. Yeah, he knew General Marsh would leave him in the dust in a second if he decided Tom wasn't useful to him, but Tom owed him a lot for giving him a chance in the program and at Capitol Summit, so he respected the guy. . . . Also, there was his father. Neil wasn't all that authoritative, but he was sort of looking out for him. He respected that, even if he didn't trust his dad to make the right decisions or use good judgment ever—his dad at least loved him and wanted the best for him. Oh, and there was Olivia Ossare, who would definitely have his back, but he also didn't fool himself. She was doing her job. Still, she'd saved him from the census device, so he owed her a huge debt, and he wouldn't forget that.

Those were three authority figures he basically respected right there. More or less.

Even Elliot, he could kind of respect sometimes. He knew now that Elliot was an okay guy who meant well, at least. So he tried to listen as Elliot urged, "You need to change your approach and learn to *show* respect, whether or not you feel it. Every aspect of your life from here on out will work this way. People in charge want the sense that other people are subordinate to them. Let's take your Coalition meet and greets Friday. You're going to be interacting with potential sponsors, men and women who are above you in a hierarchy. You're going to have to show respect, whether or not you really feel it; and if you can't, you'll be in trouble. If you can't even manage to show respect for Snowden, how are you going to handle Friday?"

"I'll handle Friday," Tom assured him.

And he would. Somehow. He was sure of it.

After all, he had to. Those executives were his only shot at being a Combatant, his only shot at sponsorship for CamCo. He couldn't screw it up—he couldn't afford to.

CHAPTER FIVE

THE NEXT MORNING meal formation, Tom was far too pleased to learn that Vik and his new roommate, Giuseppe, weren't getting along.

"There is something seriously wrong with that kid. All he talks about are the hotels he's stayed in," Vik whispered hastily to Tom as they stood by their chairs at the Alexander male Middle table, waiting for their cue to snap to attention. "Plus, he collects antique boot buckles. He showed me a bunch of them. He made me look at them, and he talked about each one at length. . . . Do you know what's so great about antique boot buckles?"

"What?" Tom said as they all snapped to attention.

"Nothing, Tom." Vik shook his head vigorously. "Nothing is great about them."

Tom's laugh split the dead hush as trainees marched in with the flag, so he muffled it quickly with a fake cough, then tried to appear neutral and stoic again as everyone darted glances his way, wondering who had penetrated the solemnity of morning meal formation.

Evidently, Vik's dislike of his new roommate was a mutual thing, because as Tom was stashing his tray on the conveyer belt, he overhead Giuseppe Nichols ranting to Jennifer Nguyen, ". . . and he actually programmed a giant statue of himself into our bunk template. Who does that?"

Consequently, Giuseppe didn't sit with them in Programming. The trainees from all levels gathered twice a week in the Lafayette Room so Lieutenant Blackburn could teach them how to write code for their own processors; the reason the class was so tedious was they had to use their human brains for it. The neural processor couldn't do the work for them. There was a law against self-programming computers.

Because human brains were needed, Tom knew he was hopeless at programming and didn't really bother much with the class. He'd never been that great in school. So instead of concentrating, Tom kept searching for excuses not to focus on his work. He found his attention on Yuri, slumped over the bench in front of them, pretending to zone out like he was still scrambled. Wyatt had removed the program that used to hide classified information from Yuri, including all the names of his friends, but Yuri had to pretend to zone out whenever certain things were mentioned or whenever he was in Programming.

While fake zoning out, Yuri still heard Blackburn's lectures. Apparently he'd been learning from them, too, since he startled Tom by nudging him and net-sending: *You made an error in your code.* One of his blue eyes peeked at Tom.

"How do you know?" Tom whispered, careful to turn his head toward Vik so no one would realize he was addressing Yuri. "You don't even see what I'm writing."

Yuri typed again: *I can discern what you are writing from*

the movement of your fingers. Look at line ten.

Tom indulged him and scrolled back up the program.

Oh. Oh, okay. Yeah. He'd mistyped a segment of the code.

I will show you the correct code, Yuri wrote, then crooked a finger at him. Tom sneaked a glance up toward Blackburn at the front of the room, and casually flopped his arm over his thigh to hang in Yuri's direction, giving Yuri access to the keyboard. Yuri leaned toward him and his fingers began dancing over the keyboard now between their bodies and the back of the bench in front of theirs. He typed from memory, modifying Tom's code.

Sure enough, when Tom tried compiling it, it worked perfectly.

Tom was tempted to be frustrated that Yuri was already way better than him at the Zorten II programming language and that was from being able to hear, not see, Blackburn's lectures for a couple months . . . but he was too intrigued by the possibilities. Yuri could potentially be an awesome cheat.

Tom was careful not to look at him. "Thanks, man," he said softly. "Can you tell me what to write next?"

Yuri wrote, *Thomas, I will not do all your programming for you, or you will not learn.*

"What are you talking about, 'or I will not learn'?" Tom murmured, head turned in the other direction like he was talking to Vik. "I won't learn anyway. I suck at this stuff. And, hey, this way, you can actually get your work critiqued. You and me, Yuri, we can have a mutually beneficial arrangement. How about it, buddy?"

Yuri seemed pleased with that, and he happily started doing Tom's programming for him. Tom was extremely satisfied with this for a half hour or so. But then something alarming happened—Blackburn assigned them another algorithm and strolled down the aisle, straight toward them.

"Get up, Raines." Blackburn gestured for him to move. "I need access to Sysevich's processor."

Tom felt a jerk of alarm. Yuri now had his eyes screwed shut. Had they been too obvious?

"Why?"

"What did we talk about yesterday, *trainee*?" Blackburn put emphasis on the last word.

"Sir, why, sir?" Tom said more respectfully. He didn't like this. At the lethal look Blackburn sent him, Tom realized he'd been given an order. He didn't move, aghast at the very idea Blackburn was going to do something to Yuri's processor and perhaps figure out Yuri wasn't scrambled. He looked at Vik; and Vik's lips were a thin line, his eyes dark hollows.

Tom sprang to his feet and nearly tripped over Vik, trying to get past him into the aisle. There, he hovered, sweat prickling his palms, as Blackburn settled next to Yuri and seized the back of his neck, then shoved his hand down so he could hook a neural wire into his access port. He stuck the other end of the wire into a small, portable screen.

Vik had stopped typing. His hands were balled into fists.

Tom remembered vividly how unhappy Vik had been when he'd learned Tom and Wyatt had unscrambled Yuri. It was treason. Vik hadn't even wanted to know about it.

Relax, Tom net-sent him. *Wyatt had to have thought of this, right?*

Vik drew a deep breath that lifted his shoulders, and seemed to hold it.

Tom searched Blackburn's face for any reactions. "What are you looking at? Sir?"

"Not that it's your business, Mr. Raines," Blackburn said, gaze trained on the screen flashing text at a rate too fast for anyone without a neural processor to follow, "but Trainee Sysevich has a particular filtering program installed in his processor. Whenever he leaves the Pentagonal Spire, his processor switches to an alert mode. It logs any attempts that are made to tamper with his software. I would've run this scan as soon as he got back"—his eyes flashed to Tom's—"if some trainee hadn't been an idiot over break and created a cleanup job for me."

Tom felt a surge of hope. They'd tampered with Yuri's software well *before* vacation, while he was *at* the Spire, so Blackburn shouldn't pick up anything.

And indeed, he didn't. Blackburn tapped his forearm keyboard to shut off the scanning, then reached out to grab Yuri by the shoulder and pull him upright. "Carry on," he ordered them, and headed back to the front

Tom slumped into his seat, soaked with sweat. He gave a relieved laugh when he was sure Blackburn was out of earshot and elbowed Vik. "Hey, man, it's okay. We're good."

"Yeah, we're good." Vik slouched down in his seat. "*This* time."

TOM'S SKULL BEGAN to throb during lunch, but it had less to do with Blackburn's scan of Yuri and more to do with Walton Covner's attempt to mess with his head. Tom was halfway through his cheeseburger when Walton strode past him, trailing a group of tiny gnomes. Tom gaped at him. Walton caught his eye and pressed a finger to his lips.

"No way," Tom said flatly, shaking his head. "No, no, no. I was dying of dehydration, Walton, and that is the only reason I believed for a second that you had gnome minions. I'm never gonna buy it when I'm feeling fine!"

Walton gave him a decisive nod. "Keep that up, Raines.

The more people hear it, the more they'll believe it." Then he continued onward.

Tom settled next to Wyatt and put his head on the table. She struck him several times, jolting his vision, and it wasn't until Tom sat up, rubbing the back of his head, that he realized she'd been trying to pat his head comfortingly.

"Is everything okay?" she asked him.

He explained the gnome minion situation. She tapped a few buttons on his keyboard to give herself remote access to his processor, then she ran a flash scan. The words flickered before his eyes all the rest of lunch, and the results finally came when they were all gathered for Intermediate Tactics in MacArthur Hall, the planetarium on the fifteenth floor. Tom saw the scan complete, and straightened up from where he'd been gazing at the massive screen that curved overhead and the roof that could retract to reveal the sky.

"Yes, you've got a virus." Wyatt tapped on her forearm keyboard as she examined the results. "The program's called Gnomes. Looks like it tampers with your vision center."

"Walton Covner," Tom grumbled.

"He must've slipped it into your homework feed."

"Can you block it out? I don't wanna see gnomes all day." He could see them even now, right across the room, hanging out near Walton.

"I'll patch your firewall tonight. You have to endure the gnomes in the meantime."

The tiny gnomes were obviously on to the fact that Tom was trying to get rid of them, because they began shaking their fists at him. Tom almost returned the gesture, then he caught himself and shoved his hands in his pockets instead. No. He refused to exchange angry fist shakes with nonexistent gnomes.

Tom surveyed the crowd as Wyatt studied the program's

code again. Middle Company had the most trainees. It was a bottleneck, because it was unlikely to be breezed through in six months, the way many could change through plebe company, but it was also too late for most trainees to get a phased removal of the processor and wash out altogether. That fact was a comfort to Tom. After the initial six months or so, their brains grew more and more dependent on the processor to carry out vital functions. Tom figured that, whatever happened, his brain's growing dependence at least ensured he'd never get threatened with removal of his processor again . . . well, not unless someone outright planned to kill him.

The chatter died as Major Cromwell strode into the room. She reached the podium and leaned against it. "One of the weaknesses of this training program is the lack of experienced veterans," she said in her hoarse voice. "You are the first generation with successfully implanted neural processors. The first generation to become Intrasolar Combatants. So we rely upon our current, active Combatants to assist with your training far more than we should. This is simply something we *have* to do because soldiers like me do not have the direct experience you require. One of these training exercises you need the Combatants for is the fly-along experience."

She typed something out on her podium keyboard, and immediately, an interactive illustration of the solar system popped up. Tom could see that it was split into the same zones Combatants sometimes referenced when they were discussing battles. The zones were partitioned according to their distance from the center of the solar system. The space between the sun and Mercury was labeled the Infernal Zone. The section from Mercury to the outer edge of the asteroid belt was marked the Prime. From Jupiter to Saturn was the Fallow, the closest orbit of Neptune through the Kuiper Belt was the Reaches, and a stray bit of text labeled the entire rest of the universe BEYOND SECTOR. The words acknowledged the unlikelihood that human beings would ever move beyond the confines of the solar system, and therefore, the rest of the universe's utter irrelevance to the war.

Tom felt a twinge, thinking of the constraint everyone had simply accepted, but then the image faded, a list of names appearing over it, some new Middles, some veteran Middles.

"To begin the fly-along experience, you'll work with the Combatants on some exercises in mental discipline," Cromwell said. "The names up here will be today's cohort to report to the Butler Room. The second group will stay for the lecture, and report downstairs on Thursday."

Tom sat up straighter, seeing his name on there. Wyatt's was, as well. Vik slumped a bit in his seat, realizing he was stuck hearing the lecture.

"Right now, those of you on this list will report to the Smedley D. Butler Conference Room on the twelfth floor. You'll come back for the lecture on Thursday. Dismissed."

TOM AND THE rest of his group met the CamCos in the large briefing room. There was a large oil painting of General Butler, who'd foiled a fascist coup against President Franklin D. Roosevelt in the 1930s, and a long table covered with decagonal devices. The Middles sat down, and Elliot Ramirez strolled in. He grinned broadly, and then Heather Akron trailed in behind him and cleared her throat.

The other CamCos striding inside sent her chilly looks, but Elliot dipped his head and gestured for her to take the lead.

The beautiful brunette perched at the head of the table. "Some of you are new to Middle Company, so I'll explain the basics of what we're doing here." Heather's amber eyes glittered. There was a certain brittle gaiety to her smile. "These decagons are group internet relay chat nodes. They let you hook in and communicate with each other using a thought interface. That's what we're going to practice today."

Thought interface? Tom grew alarmed.

"Why is Heather in charge?" Wyatt murmured. "I'm surprised they're letting her, after . . ." She trailed off.

Tom didn't press her on the subject. Heather had caught his eye and winked, so Tom nodded back, knowing she'd probably wear that same dazzling, so-happy-to-see-you look on her face while she slipped him poison if she had to. . . . Still, there was something about her that got to him sometimes. He followed the sway of her body as she strolled around the table and picked up a decagon.

"You may or may not know this, but there's a function in your neural processors called net-send that allows you to send messages to each other, either by typing or using a thought interface. The net-send thought-interface function isn't suitable for battle, though, because net-send directly captures the stray thoughts in your head. . . ."

Tom slouched in his seat a bit, remembering thinking to Vik over net-send, *How do steak boobs function?* He wasn't very good with thought interfaces. He had stuck to net-sending with his forearm keyboard ever since.

"Plus, net-send has a lag time—microseconds, but that might as well be hours during space combat. These decagons, however, facilitate instantaneous group communication, and the messages sent are the dominant concerns in your head at any one time. There is no lag time. Before you do your fly-alongs with us, you need to gain some basic mental discipline so you can communicate the way we do during combat, and do so in an effective manner. Today, we're going to have two to three CamCos at each decagon.

You guys pair up, and let's try this out together."

Tom and Wyatt paired up. The first decagon they reached was the one in front of Heather and Elliot. Tom's stomach contracted as he watched Karl come over to join them.

"Ready?" Elliot said, pulling out a neural wire. Then Heather raised her eyebrows, and he smiled. "Oh. Of course. Sorry, H. I know you need to take the lead."

"Why, thank you, Elliot." Heather turned to Tom and Wyatt. "Stick your neural wires into the ports on the decagon, sit down, then hook in like you would to any other machine."

Tom dropped into one of the cushy chairs, aware of Karl still standing, glowering at him. He stuck his neural wire into a port on the decagon, then plugged the other end into the back of his neck, and the world grew utterly dark around him.

I'm blind! He tried to say it, but his voice didn't come out. Tom flailed out his arms to alert someone, terrible suspicions flying through his brain that this was some plot of Karl's or even . . .

Footsteps drew toward him, and Tom jumped when hands grabbed his shoulders.

"Relax, Tom." Heather's breath tickled his ear. He felt her hands brush the back of his neck, sending goose bumps down his skin. He was disappointed when her fingers slid away. "We've programmed it to disable your eyesight and vocal cords while you're hooked in. It's to help focus your concentration these first few times. . . . Enslow, you look upset." Her voice grew vaguely threatening, "Do you want to join Tom or would you rather sit this one out?"

"I'll do it," Wyatt snapped, and Tom could see her name listed against the darkness in his vision.

After another moment or two, Heather's name appeared.

Is this on? Tom and Wyatt both thought, and the words

appeared right there before his eyes.

Then Heather thought, *I wonder which one of them will think something embarrassing first?* The words scrolled across Tom's vision.

Don't think about Heather's boobs, Tom thought to himself, and to his mortification, the words appeared there.

Yay, it wasn't me! Wyatt thought. Then after the words appeared, she thought, *Sorry, Tom.*

Tom. Wyatt. Try to focus, Heather thought. *You can control your thoughts.*

Boobs, Wyatt thought. *Aah! Where did that come from?*

It's called word contagion, and it's normal, Heather thought. *You can break it by occupying your thoughts with something else. Try times tables.*

2 x 2 = 4, 4 x 4 = 16, 11 x 11 = 121 . . . Wyatt thought. *This works. Send. I'm surprised she had good advice.*

Excuse me? Heather thought.

Elliot's name appeared in the IRC. *Hello, everyone! Don't worry, I'm here now! Just some technical difficulties. What did I miss?*

Riding in to save the day, Heather thought.

Tom thought, *Hi, Elliot. Send. Elliot's an okay guy.*

At least Elliot won't think about . . . Wait, I'm thinking this, Heather thought.

Can someone tell us what we're supposed to think about? Send, Wyatt thought.

Looks like there's a leadership deficit, Elliot thought. *I came just in time.*

Ugh, Heather thought.

So what now? Send, Tom thought.

Yes, why won't someone tell me what to think about? Send, Wyatt thought.

You guys don't need to think send, Heather thought. *I want you all to stop thinking send.*

Send, Tom thought. He couldn't help it.

Just then, Karl's name appeared in the IRC. *Stupid Fido.*

I hate Karl. Die horribly, Karl, Tom thought. Then, feeling a malicious glee, *Send.*

I want to jam a gun barrel down Raines's throat and see him choke on it, Karl thought.

God, Karl, Heather thought. *Issues?*

Ha-ha-ha-ha, appeared as Tom's text, since the laughter wasn't coming from his lips.

Hate him, hate him, gonna kill him . . . Karl thought.

Hates me so much and yet he can't pull off a single threat, Tom thought gleefully. *Ah-ha-ha-ha-ha . . .*

A string of swearwords was Karl's response, and for a moment they drowned out all the other text in the IRC. Tom laughed harder and harder as they went on and on, and soon Karl's swearing kept getting punctured by random "ha's."

This is degenerating into chaos, Heather thought.

Elliott thought, *I need to talk to Karl later. I find this rather disturbing.*

I'm not a little kid, Karl thought. *Elliot acts like we're all five.*

Karl's frequent, noisome farts, Tom thought.

That launched another long string of profanity, interspersed only by Wyatt's idle thought: *I made that program work,* and Tom's, *Ha-ha-ha-ha.*

Lieutenant Blackburn patted me on the back when he saw it, Wyatt thought. *He said I'm smart. My parents never say nice things to me.*

How sad and pathetic, Heather thought.

Bash his smug face, break his teeth out. Blood dripping out instead of that big, self-satisfied grin, Karl thought.

But I said you looked pretty that time you wore makeup, Karl, Tom thought.

More swearing from Karl.

And then Elliot: *Tom must know he's provoking him. Clever kid but I swear he'd prod a sleeping bear with a stick.*

Elliot thinks I'm clever, Tom thought, surprised. *Or stupid.*

High-spirited, but needs guidance and some table manners, Elliot thought. *Sorry, Tom, musing here. Ignore me.*

Table manners? Tom wondered.

Karl really hates Tom. He doesn't get Tom. Tom's a lot deeper than he seems, Wyatt thought. *Wait. Don't think about Tom. Tom. Tom. Why isn't there a send button so I can choose not to press send?*

Send, Tom thought again. He still couldn't help it. *What are you thinking about me?*

Stop it. Stop it. You're not allowed to do that, Wyatt sent. *Don't send. Don't send. Don't send.*

Send, Elliot thought.

1 . . . 1 . . . 2 . . . 3 . . . 5 . . . Wyatt thought.

Very clever focusing her thoughts on the Fibonacci sequence, Elliot thought.

I hate her, Heather thought.

I want Raines to die and stop being here, Karl thought.

Just needs guidance to channel some of that restless energy into something productive, Elliot thought. *So much potential but he sabotages himself.*

Nigel was right. He always said Elliot acts like a day camp counselor, Heather thought.

34 . . . 55 . . . Wyatt thought. *Boobs. No!*

Boobs, Tom thought.

Raines choking, Karl thought.

Jesus, Karl, Elliot thought.

These people are wasting my time, Heather thought.

She ended the connection abruptly. Tom felt a moment of shock when his vision flooded with light again and he could see the others blinking around him, pulling out the neural wires connecting them to the decagon. Wyatt ducked her head and made herself as small as possible. Karl was flushed bright red. Only Elliot was smiling gamely. Heather threw them all a look of utter contempt but managed a stiff nod. "Okay, looks like you guys got the basics of it."

The rest of the hour, they rotated across the room to the other three decagons with CamCos stationed at them. Wyatt's number sequences grew more intricate, and Tom, for his part, started learning a lot about the CamCos he hadn't known before.

At the next decagon, Yosef Saide was pondering whether Tom would've succeeded in killing him if he hadn't been yanked out of the shark scenario, and he was eager to face him in a samurai scenario next time. Cadence Grey had a creepily silent mind, and only the occasional "om" betrayed the fact that she was actively meditating. Emefa Austerley was impatient with this whole exercise, since she imagined herself as a Spartan-warrior type, not a teacher to a bunch of annoying younger trainees—and when were Combatants going to be treated like the serious national assets they were?

At the third decagon, Snowden Gainey wondered what people thought of him, and Tom let him know by pondering at length the stupidity of the simulation from Applied Scrimmages. Mason Meekins desperately needed to use the bathroom. Britt Schmeiser kept thinking about a girl he met on the publicity tour, which made Wyatt get the word "boobs" in her head again.

At the fourth decagon, the solemn, dark-haired CamCo Alec Tarsus began thinking right away that Tom was an uneducated simpleton. He also thought Wyatt was too intelligent to function on a normal human level and that was why no one really liked her. This hurt Wyatt's feelings, which affronted Ralph Bates, who liked her long, beautiful legs. Wyatt thought about how Ralph had given her the initial tour when she arrived at the Spire, and how even back then, he smelled like onions despite the fact that he hadn't been eating them.

She hurt Ralph's feelings, so he consoled himself by thinking she had a horseface, which hurt Wyatt's feelings and made Tom mad enough to think about punching Ralph's face in. Ralph thought Tom was as deranged as he'd always heard he was, but Wyatt thought about how fantastic it was that Tom threatened people on her behalf. Lea Styron was annoyed by this because she felt that Wyatt shouldn't be encouraging Tom's behavior. Chivalry wasn't charming, it was a weapon of patriarchy, and all in all, this felt like a waste of time to her because she'd already decided she wanted to work with Walton Covner. Tom spent the rest of the time thinking about gnome minions, which unfortunately, confirmed Alec Tarsus's simpleton theory.

Soon, the entire group broke up, and the veteran CamCos gathered together to laugh over things they'd gleaned from the thoughts of younger trainees.

All except Heather. She stood apart from the group, glared at the rest a moment, then stalked out of the room. Tom remembered what Wyatt had said earlier and nudged her. "So what happened with her?"

Wyatt beckoned for him to walk to the stairwell with her, and even once they were enclosed in there, she spoke in a whisper. "During the CamCo publicity blitzes, someone began leaking rumors about the other CamCos to the tabloids. True stuff the public couldn't know."

Tom remembered those internet rumors he'd seen about

the CamCos. "Britt Schmeiser's weekend of debauchery?"

She nodded. "That sort of thing. Alec Tarsus net-sent me over vacation and asked if I could figure out who was doing it. I traced it to Heather. I guess she wanted to give her own image a boost by making the other CamCos look bad. I told General Marsh. She ended up getting yanked from all her PR gigs."

"Good job."

"Thanks." Wyatt ducked her head, her dark hair sliding in front of her face. "Tom, I have to ask you something. It's very important. Above all, I need you to be completely honest, whatever consequences might ensue. Can you do this for me?"

Perplexed, he said, "Yeah, hit me."

She twisted her fingers together, resembling a nervous squirrel. "Do I really have a horseface?"

"No, you don't."

He expected that to make her feel better. Instead, Wyatt's scowl deepened. "You don't have to lie to me!"

And to his bewilderment, she stalked off down the stairs without him.

After dinner, Tom headed to his bunk, and there he discovered that Vik had been busy. At some point in the evening Vik had duplicated most of the bunk template Wyatt had given him, sneaked in, and transformed Tom's bunk.

Tom turned around and around to take in the full tableau. There were posters on the wall of angry-looking Wyatt scowling at Tom and following him with her eyes. Other images featured freeze-frames of Tom's greatest embarrassments— Tom as a sheep, Tom styling his hair with gel in front of a mirror with a very prissy look on his face after Dalton Prestwick of Dominion Agra reprogrammed him, Tom eating steak off a knife. And there was a massive Tom statue that resembled Vik's statue. It opened its mouth and proclaimed: "IT IS 1915

AND THE GORMLESS CRETIN SAYS: DERP!"

Tom took his revenge on Vik later that night when they battled in Samurai Eternity, and Tom ripped Vik's simulated head off with his bare hands.

"Augh," Vik cried, tearing off his wired gloves, as the statue boomed, "IT IS 2115 AND THE GORMLESS CRETIN SAYS: DERP!"

"Oh, look at your head, dripping with blood and subcutaneous tissue," Tom told him, holding the head between his wired gloves. "What is it saying? What is it?" He leaned in closer. "It says, 'Tom will beat you to death with your own head if that statue doesn't stop talking.'"

Vik scratched his real head. "Is that what it said? I have this feeling my head is very articulate, but whenever you translate something, all I hear is 'derp, derp, derp, derp, derp.' That's something *you'd* say, Tom."

"You asked for this," Tom said grimly, then grasped Vik's simulated head by the hair and wielded it like a mallet, beating Vik over the virtual shoulders with it as Vik cackled away. Then Vik reared up, hands aloft, and surrendered. He deleted the audio feature from the template later that night. The gormless cretin statue became a mercifully silent one.

Tom never admitted something to him, though: he was extremely pleased with the new bunk template. All the emptiness he'd felt without Vik in there had been chased away by the decorations, the visible warning that his best friend would be tormenting him for years to come, whether they were roommates or not.

CHAPTER SIX

F RIDAY MORNING, TOM woke up to a ping: *Consciousness initiated. The time is 0520.* He hadn't even sat up before another ping demanded that he select his attire for his visit to the Coalition companies, and a third ping requested he select a departure time between 0600 and 0700. Tom found Vik's name already in a slot and selected that one.

Tom turned his attention to the clothing prompt, and scrolled through question after question. He chose the first option for color of tie, the first style of suit, the first style of loafer, and kept going through the text that way until it stopped annoying him. After his shower, he followed the directions in his neural processor to the twelfth-floor depository. There, he found himself in a large room filled with rounded, plastic drawers. One of the drawers in the wall slid open, revealing a suit and shirt hanging on a rack. Tom snatched them, shrugged off his uniform, and pulled them on.

Next, a smaller drawer popped open, spitting out shoes,

socks, and a tie. Tom donned them, too, hesitating only when the tie was in hand; he couldn't help remembering Dalton Prestwick showing him how to tie one. He gritted his teeth and put it on anyway. Then he hurled his uniform down a waiting laundry chute and set off downstairs.

Vik met him within minutes, the mess hall still dim with early morning. They were both startled when Yuri arrived in a suit of his own.

"What are you doing, man?" Vik exclaimed. "Get your beauty sleep, Yuri. We're the ones stuck doing some boring meetings."

"I have been invited to accompany you."

"Really? That's awesome!" Tom exclaimed. Maybe it was a good sign if Yuri was allowed to attend an event just for Middles.

But there was something slightly sad in Yuri's blue eyes, even though he smiled. "Yes. It is."

WHEN WYATT JOINED them, they headed to the Mezzanine. It wasn't listed as an official floor in the Spire, but the instructions in their neural processors told them to press and hold floors 1, 4, and 9 to get down there. Yuri had received a special exemption to unlock the Mezzanine in his processor, so he spent the whole ride pressing them for information about what else he wasn't seeing. Tom and Vik had fun making things up.

"You are not being honest," Yuri said.

"We totally are," Tom replied.

"I do not believe there is a coed naked romping court. You are inventing this."

"Frankly, I'm offended by your accusation," Vik said indignantly. "Because of this, we're not bringing you to the CNRC next time we go, are we, Tom?"

Tom shook his head. "No way. If you don't believe us, you don't romp in our court. You can romp in someone else's court."

Yuri scowled at them.

"Don't worry, they're making it all up," Wyatt assured Yuri, as though anyone doubted it.

They emerged into a marble-floored corridor with a bubbling fountain in the center and crisp signs indicating various sectors of the Mezzanine. One was an administrative wing, another led straight to the hybrid fission-fusion nuclear reactor, another led to something called the Vault that was so restricted, looking in that direction plastered warnings in their vision centers: *Intruders shot on sight,* which made them all walk a bit faster past it. The fourth sector led to the Pentagon, and the fifth to a room empty but for two rows of fake trees and at the far wall a massive set of glass double doors that gazed into pure darkness. Tom's neural processor told him this was the entrance to the Interstice and that he should walk inside.

"What is an 'Interstice'?" Vik said.

"Obviously some mode of transportation," Wyatt said.

"That's helpful, Evil Wench."

They ventured through the fake trees, and something triggered. Green lines slashed from the plastic trunks, honing in on their eyes. One by one, their retinas were scanned, and after the green lights bit into Tom's eyes, he saw words before his vision center: *Identity verified. Trainee Raines, Thomas. Proceed to the doors.*

They'd all received the same notice, so they found themselves standing there, shoulder to shoulder before the glass doors that led to the black chamber beyond.

And then a mechanized voice boomed in the air: "Decompression sequence initiated."

Vik whirled around, genuinely alarmed. "Decompression in here?"

"Out there," Wyatt said, poking her finger to indicate the room beyond the glass before them. "It can't be in here because our lungs would've already ruptured."

"I would have noticed that," Tom said.

Yuri nodded. "And then our blood would boil."

"I'd notice that, too," Tom said.

He spotted something large and metallic rising into view in the chamber beyond the doors. It clanged to the ground loudly enough to make them all jump. It looked like a miniature metallic train car, sitting there in the darkness, the passenger cabin the only source of light in the decompressed room.

No wonder everyone's departures had been spread out. The metal train car had a scattering of seats, but it obviously wasn't meant for a heavy passenger load. Information soared through Tom's brain: *The Interstice is a series of magnetized vacuum tubes designed for traversion by magnetized vactrains propelled by magnetic fields. Given the absence of friction and minimal curvatures in the tubes, maximum speeds can reach 5,000 miles per hour. The vactrain is shielded to protect equipment inside from magnetic forces.*

They all jumped when a mechanized voice boomed from overhead: "Recompression sequence initiated." A chugging sound pervaded the air. The glass doors slid open to admit them into the room with the train car.

They all headed over and took seats inside the tiny metallic car. The doors slid shut behind them.

"Do we . . . press something?" Wyatt asked tentatively.

And then the mechanized voice boomed from overhead: "Decompression sequence initiated. Prepare for departure to Wyndham Harks Headquarters, New York City."

The dark chamber depressurized around them, and the floor slid open. Tom caught a last glimpse of the room on the other side of the glass doors with its fake trees, and they were blown with stomach-swooping abruptness into the vacuum tube.

They all flinched, but they never hit the tracks. The car remained suspended magnetically within the tube, in midair. Pitch-blackness stretched on all sides beyond the lonely confines of their metal car. Then their velocity ticked up, and up, until they were moving several thousand miles per hour. Tom's stomach danced with mounting speed.

"So tell us something," Vik said, folding his arms and leaning back in his seat, eyes on Yuri. "Why are you really going with us?"

Yuri sighed and draped his arm around Wyatt, sitting rigidly in her seat next to his. "I am being sent because Olivia Ossare believes it would be beneficial for me to see professionals with jobs that are not in the Intrasolar Forces."

Olivia was the Spire's resident social worker. Tom knew that in the past, she'd encouraged Yuri to give up on the Intrasolar Forces, to surrender to the fact that he wasn't getting promoted.

"Maybe it's a good idea," Vik said.

Wyatt glared at him. "No, it's not." Her scowl warned them to change the subject.

Vik opened his mouth, then closed it. Tom said nothing. They never talked to Yuri about this. It wasn't something they did. So they moved on to something else.

They reached New York in no time. The vactrain admitted them to another dark room that swiftly repressurized, then they clambered out of the vehicle, and headed over to an elevator. It rose to take them to the eighty-third floor of the Wyndham Harks building. The elevator was clear glass, and as soon as they ascended from underground, Tom glimpsed the streets of Manhattan.

"Curious. I do not see skyboards," Yuri noted, leaning over to peer up into the sky as they ascended. "This surprises me in a metropolis so large."

"They're up there," Wyatt noted, her nose pressing to the glass as she leaned forward to see. "People who live in Manhattan pay for optical camouflaging boards in a slightly lower orbit than the skyboards. That way, they angle the images away from this area of the city. In Connecticut where I live, people pay for it, too."

"Do they do this in Washington, DC?" Yuri said. "I see no advertisements in the sky there."

"They don't put skyboards above Washington, DC. All our leaders live in its suburbs," Wyatt pointed out. "They don't want them."

Tom only half paid attention to them. His eyes were on the smaller buildings of Manhattan shrinking below them. He found himself gazing inward, arrested by the memory of coming here when he was younger. He'd hitchhiked and hopped freight trains all the way from Arizona to New York City, so excited to see his mom that he only slept a few hours the whole way.

Before that visit, he'd really believed she hadn't meant to leave him. He'd imagined so many things. Then he saw her and they all disappeared. A dark, hollow pit opened in his gut, remembering her expression when she'd seen him at her door. He'd never imagined his mom would look at him like that, like he was nothing.

Vik's hand jostled his shoulder. "Earth to Raines."

Tom blinked, realizing that the door was open and they were at the eighty-third floor.

The hallway they entered was an ominous gauntlet of military-grade Praetorians, mechanized security guards manufactured by Obsidian Corp., sold to those with enough money to need them. Tom's neural processor displayed a map leading him straight ahead. He found himself darting leery glances to either side of them as they passed the machines.

Praetorians at rest resembled nothing more than metallic coat racks, but Tom had seen movies, played VR games. He knew what these slim machines were capable of: The lighter models could shrink themselves to the size of a coffee mug to reduce an enemy's ability to target them, and conduct electrical charges to act like long-range Tasers. They could shoot electromagnetic beams that dispersed crowds by giving people the sensation they were burning alive, and splice lasers through hundreds of soldiers with one flick of a button from a distant operator. Add a sturdy, centrifugal base on them, and they'd climb vertical walls and deliver payloads of explosives or poisonous gas.

Obsidian Corp. designed them to be released like cockroaches on an enemy stronghold, killing everything in their path. Wyndham Harks used them as watchmen.

And coat racks, apparently.

The Praetorians not covered by coats followed their progress down the corridor with single, pinpoint camera eyes.

They waited with the other Middles in a large briefing room. Apparently, the CEOs usually saw the trainees themselves—preferring to personally inspect the assets they might invest in. Tom saw trainees smoothing their suits, adjusting ties. Walton Covner ended up side by side with him, and Tom realized that they'd both selected the first option for every piece of clothing and consequently dressed exactly the same.

"We can say we're twin brothers," Walton suggested,

flipping up the cuff of his trousers so they could see if the socks were the same, too. "Twins who dress alike."

Tom flipped his trousers back down. The socks were. "But there's over a year's age difference, you're six inches taller than me, we're different ethnicities, and we've got two different last names. I don't think anyone's gonna buy that we're twins, man."

"My plan does have flaws," Walton acknowledged. "We should try it."

Tom shook his head. "No, Walton. No."

"No?"

"No!"

Walton sent him a mildly reproving look, like he was certain Tom was making a dreadful mistake, but too polite to tell him so, then he glided away, leaving Tom bewildered—as usual.

Then Reuben Lloyd himself strolled in. The CEO of Wyndham Harks was a weedy little man who gave a smile that flashed large teeth; and between those, his beady eyes, and his gigantic ears under his bald dome, Tom was struck by how much the guy resembled a rodent.

"How good to see you here." His nasal, weasely voice did nothing to diminish his unfortunate rodent resemblance. "I don't have time to go around, shaking all your little hands. We sponsor Heather, Snowden, and Yosef, so if you want to brownnose, do it with them. I'll give you a quick intro to our company, then I have to be on my way."

He led them through the corridors of Wyndham Harks, talking rapidly, obviously trying to impress them. He told them the dollar value of every fancy chair, every piece of artwork, and threw around numbers like they said everything. He didn't really send any of the art more than a passing glance.

He never mentioned what Wyndham Harks actually *did* as

a company. Tom wasn't clear on that. The other companies in the Coalition had survived the end of the middle class and the Great Global Collapse that followed because they controlled key resources. That, or they were like Obsidian Corp. and LM Lymer Fleet—companies that protected companies controlling key resources.

Wyndham Harks wasn't like the others. It didn't have a lock on anything of real value as far as Tom knew. It had always been powerful, though, and it owned a lot of other companies, and a lot of US assets. Even before the rise of the Coalition of Multinationals, people apparently said that governments didn't rule the world, Wyndham Harks did. Yet even knowing that, few could say exactly why Wyndham Harks—a company that served as a middleman to transactions—was so *very essential* to the world economy that taxpayers had to bail it out every few years whenever it made too many bad investments. The company had never created a product, never invented anything, never done anything of substance, yet the political class touted it as the essential foundation of a functional society.

"Why do they keep going broke?" Tom asked Wyatt, hoping she'd know.

Wyatt made a strange noise. She was making an odd face, her lips compressed into a tight pucker, her eyes very wide. She resembled some sort of fish.

Yuri answered in her stead. "They purchased many rugs." Then he pointed at the floor, as if Tom hadn't seen them.

"Yeah, I got that." Tom rolled his eyes. "I don't get why they weren't forced to sell them all off. You know, if my dad bought a car he couldn't pay for, he'd have to give it back. He wouldn't get to keep the car *and* get someone else to pay his debt for him."

"Your dad is not Reuben Lloyd," Yuri said.

The next corridor resolved the paradox. Reuben Lloyd

led them before a vast collection of portraits spread across the wall. "Here are Wyndham Harks's most valuable assets."

Tom read the placards beneath the photos of the executives, then gave a start as his neural processor began identifying them as powerful government officials. There was Sheldon Laffner, the head of the Department of Homeland Security; Kristyl Chertowitz, the chief of staff to the president; and Aubrey Bremmer, the chief justice of the Supreme Court. There was Barclay J. P. Goldman, the Chairman of the Federal Reserve; Vice President Julian Richter; and President Donald Milgram himself. All of them were former Wyndham Harks executives or current shareholders.

Tom stared at the photos, and it clicked into place.

This was the key resource Wyndham Harks controlled: *the government.* Of course the politicians always said Wyndham Harks was essential to the world economy. They were Wyndham Harks men and they were the ones saying it. It was like some big, global scam, and Tom shook his head, amazed at how these guys had played everyone else in the world for suckers for so long.

Reuben Lloyd wasn't in on his own joke, though, because he ended the tour by turning on them, chest puffed with pride, and announcing, "I hope you understand now how fortunate you'd be to align with our company. We at Wyndham Harks do God's work."

Silence dropped over the room.

Except Tom. He started laughing.

Reuben Lloyd's shocked gaze swung to him.

Tom snapped his mouth shut since, after all, he had to make a good impression here. He knew that laughing wasn't the response Reuben Lloyd wanted. He wanted awed respect, silence.

But then Tom heard Wyatt make that strange noise in the back of her throat again, and when his gaze shot to her face, he saw that she was doing the bizarre fish-expression thing again, her eyes huge and her lips pursed.

He couldn't help it. He exploded in laughter again. It was such an awful time to laugh that Tom laughed more, and his dawning horror at his uncontrollable laughter made him laugh harder still. He recognized this. This had happened to him before, more than once. It was the same impulse that made him bust up laughing when Blackburn came into his bunk to accuse him of treason, the same thing that had made hundreds of tense situations in his life much, much worse. But he couldn't help it. Everyone was staring at him, and now he couldn't stop.

He dropped to his knees, giggling helplessly, smothering his mouth in his arms. Even then, he might've regained control of himself if he'd had a few moments more, but then Wyatt tried to be helpful. She gave Tom a discreet thumbs-up and unveiled her hidden forearm keyboard. Tom tried to shake his head at her, and he saw Vik and Yuri also shaking their heads, trying to catch her attention. It was too late. She unleashed a computer virus that hit the surrounding trainees, triggering hysterical laughter in them, too—trying to mitigate Reuben Lloyd's wrath toward Tom by diluting it among everyone.

Soon the entire room was filled with hysterical laughter, all directed at Reuben Lloyd, the powerful CEO in charge of Wyndham Harks. Everyone else laughing made Tom laugh harder, so he collapsed onto his back on one of Reuben Lloyd's prized carpets, his ribs hurting.

All in all, this wasn't the impression he had come here to make.

On the disgraced elevator ride down, Vik thrust his fingers into his hair, exasperated. "Why did you do that, Wyatt? You made it a hundred times worse. Not only did Tom laugh at him, but Tom's now the one who got a whole bunch of other people laughing at him, too."

The buildings outside grew taller and taller as their elevator plunged down. "Hey, it's fine, guys." Tom stuffed his hands into his pockets, seeing the shadow of his smirk in the glass before him. "Wyndham Harks didn't go so well, but so what? We've got a bunch of companies still to go. We'll be A-OK."

TOM WASN'T PLEASED to learn their next destination was the City of London, the financial district containing Dominion Agra's headquarters. As soon as they left the Interstice, the other trainees were led to the meeting place with Dominion's new CEO, Diamond MacThane, and Dominion's chief shareholders, the Roache brothers. Tom did not go with them.

He had expected trouble, maybe to be banned, maybe to be expelled from the facility. He hadn't expected to be set upon by a bunch of the private contractors who formed the larger part of the British police force. They slapped on handcuffs and hauled him into a secluded interrogation room. Then they cuffed him to a chair and interrogated him about his plans while in their country.

Apparently, Tom was on some watch list and classified as a low-level terrorist. All thanks to the Dominion executives he'd swamped with sewage.

One hour dragged by as constables wandered in and out of the police station, each with a barrage of new questions. Just as Tom was about to lose his mind with boredom and frustrated anger, Dalton Prestwick himself showed up to enjoy the sight of Tom in handcuffs.

"Well, well. Quite a predicament you're in there, sport."

Tom felt a surge of dislike at the sight of his mom's smarmy boyfriend with his gelled brown hair and expensive suit. "What are you doing here, Dalton? Did you run out of people to suck up to on the other side of the Atlantic?"

Dalton's eyes narrowed. "You're in Dominion Agra territory now. *My* territory. I'd show some respect."

"Why should I?" Tom leaned toward him as far as the chair allowed, eyes on his. "After all, the last time I saw you, we both agreed that I could destroy you whenever I chose. That kind of gives me an upper hand here."

Dalton paled a bit at the reminder that Nigel Harrison had told Tom of Dalton's role in leaking the CamCo names—in committing treason. Tom had some potent blackmail he could use against him and they both knew it.

"I haven't forgotten our previous conversation, Tom. It's the only reason you're sitting there in that chair, unharmed."

Tom slouched back, unimpressed by the implied threat. "I can't believe you got me declared a terrorist over the Beringer Club."

Dalton gave a snakelike smile. "What makes you think it was me? You terrorized quite a few very powerful people that day."

"So 'terrorism' doesn't mean 'killing innocent civilians to cause fear and advance a political cause.' It now means 'disrespecting the rich and powerful.' Is that it?"

"My," Dalton said, "you just figured that out, did you?"

Tom fell silent. The sentiment was so cynical, Neil could've spouted it—but it was different coming from Dalton. He said it with a gloating air like he was exulting in it.

"In fact, I really only dropped by to give you some friendly advice, sport."

"Save your breath. There is nothing you could say to me that I care about."

"Oh, I think you should hear this." Dalton circled around behind him, so Tom would've had to twist and look like an idiot to keep him in sight. Instead, he glared straight ahead at the one-way mirror as Dalton planted his hands on his shoulders.

"You see, you *are* Delilah's son, and I know that old man of yours isn't going to point your compass in the right direction—"

"Oh please. You're not pointing any compass for me. And we agreed that you never talk about my dad again."

"I feel a sense of obligation. After all, you didn't just cross Dominion Agra executives, you crossed a group of very powerful people with the ears of very powerful friends. People talk, people spread information about various trainees, people give each other a heads-up about whether or not some kid is an insolent little punk who needs to learn some manners."

A sour smile curled Tom's lips. "Yeah, an insolent little punk who was the only person, ever, to beat the greatest fighter on the Russo-Chinese side at Capitol Summit. I really appreciate your concern for my reputation, Dalton, but I think I'll get by somehow."

Dalton's eyes met his in the mirror. "Have you heard what happens to trainees who don't qualify for Combatant status?"

Tom blinked, thrown by the reminder. The Intrasolar forces were young, but he knew there were trainees who couldn't get sponsors. Some stuck around and kept trying; others gave up and went elsewhere—other government agencies, other types of positions at Coalition companies. Nigel Harrison tried to blow up the Pentagonal Spire and kill everyone, but he was the exception.

"What about them?" Tom said reluctantly.

Dalton straightened up, tugging the cuffs of his shirt. "The neural processor makes them valuable, so they get jobs pretty easily. But the catch is, most of those positions require a certain, shall we say, *reliability*. Anything with a Coalition company requires an unsullied reputation. You don't have that. As for a government position, well . . . you'll need to obtain a security clearance. Known terrorists"—he said the word almost playfully—"don't tend to qualify."

Tom understood it. "So *that's* why I'm on the terror watch list. Someone thinks they're gonna sabotage me down the road, huh? Well, joke's on them, because if I don't make Combatant, I'll strike out on my own, no problem. I can get by."

Dalton made a show of wincing on his behalf. "Actually, champ, that's not an option for you. Once you have the processor"—he tapped his temple beneath his gelled hair—"you have to stay in the fold. If the Coalition doesn't want you, and the government can't clear you, you still do have two options. There are many agencies that would love to research you, so you could always be a glorified lab rat. . . ."

Tom's mouth went dry.

"And then there's that other agency, the one that always presses for trainees. The National Security Agency. Who do you think scooped up that Nigel Harrison boy?"

Tom felt a jerk in his gut. "He's with the NSA? But he's not even American."

Dalton gave an oily chuckle. "No one who matters in this world cares about countries or nationalities."

"Nigel tried to blow up the Spire!"

"Oh, never fear, Tom: he's probably nowhere near the same person you remember. That's why I think the National Security Agency would even have you. The agency's renowned for their ability to manipulate and control computers."

Anger scorched Tom's chest. "I don't believe you. I don't believe there's an entire agency of people who'd reprogram a human being like you and Joseph Vengerov would."

"There may come a day when you start to believe that, and you realize I really was acting in your best interests, and you feel terrible about your rank ingratitude toward me." Dalton rocked back on his heels, taking visible pleasure in his words. "When that day comes, I want you to know, you can call my assistant and ask for an appointment. If you visit, and you show proper respect and call me Mr. Prestwick, and maybe . . . hmm, I don't know, get on your knees and *beg me* very nicely to give you another chance, I might consider it." He winked. "*Might*. No guarantees anymore, champ."

"Yeah," Tom agreed sarcastically, "maybe I'll do that, but before that day comes, there'll be a day when I tear my own eyes out and eat them. See, I'd do that before I would ever get on my knees and beg you for anything. Or get on my knees for anyone—you know, the way you did me, Dalton. At the Beringer Club."

Dalton turned so red at the reminder that Tom cheered up. Dalton's distress almost made this whole visit worth it.

CHAPTER SEVEN

TIME CRAWLED BY as Tom sat there, and finally he decided he wasn't going to let himself be tied to a chair while Dalton went somewhere and drank a martini. They wanted him tied up, then let them find him and drag him back; no more sitting and waiting. A sense of daring swept over Tom, and his heart picked up a beat as he contemplated the glorious feat ahead.

It could work. It could totally work.

He rocked forward to balance on his toes, chair lifted up behind him, and threw himself forward in a flip. The lights of the interrogation room whipped before his eyes, and a terrific jolt carried straight up his tailbone to his shoulder, a violent clattering throbbing his ears as the chair splintered beneath him.

Naturally, that was the moment the door to the hallway popped open, and Elliot Ramirez strolled in. He stopped in his tracks, gaping at the sight of Tom on the ground, the remains of the chair around him. "Tom, what are you doing?"

Tom tugged at the handcuffs, still tangled with the broken chair digging into his back. Unfortunately, the back of the chair was still intact—and he was still handcuffed to it. "Trying to do something really, really awesome." He smiled sheepishly. "It works better in video games."

ELLIOT WAS ONE of the few people who knew what Tom had done at the Beringer Club. Maybe that's why he'd thought to swing by Dominion Agra to check on how Tom was doing there. Elliot made the decision to take Tom over to the Nobridis meeting site early rather than leave him in the holding cell.

They sat there in the lobby of what was apparently the tallest building in the world, in the middle of Dubai, drinking incredibly strong coffee. Tom asked Elliot about what Dalton had told him. "Does the Coalition get to dictate what we do from now on? If none of the companies want me and I don't have the security clearance for government work, I can't walk away?"

Elliot rubbed his head. "In theory, no, the military doesn't own us unless we enlist, and the Coalition has no say either. In practice? We have computers of theirs, computers only they can repair. Right now. That gives them a certain power over us. You simply have to accept it." He was silent a moment. Then, "I take it you haven't heard about what happened with me."

"Something happened *with you*?"

Elliot shrugged. "Two years ago, I was already pretty well known. Going on TV, doing internet ads, acting in commercials, that sort of thing. I also met someone. Private Hendricks was a year older than me, and needless to say, we were very fond of each other." An edge crept into his voice. "That's when I suppose you could say I encountered the downside of my role here. I was informed definitively that, even if I was technically a civilian, I wasn't allowed to risk my 'carefully crafted public persona' by carrying on with my relationship, and I was to terminate it immediately. As for Private Hendricks, he was reassigned."

Tom felt a flicker of surprise for a moment, but then it was gone. Actually, no, he wasn't so surprised.

"Needless to say, I wasn't happy. I've never been ashamed of who I am, and I resented the order to pretend to be someone I'm not. If the Coalition was going to dictate my feelings to me, then I decided I would quit." Tension lined his voice. "And then I was told that wasn't my decision either."

"What? They told you no? They can't do that."

"The way they phrased it, it was more of a warning." Elliot leaned toward him, elbows on his knees. "You see, Tom, they don't own us, but the fact is, there is no one outside Obsidian Corp. and the military who can work these computers." He pointed to his own head. "It became very clear to me that if I dared to leave, not only would I find no help for any future malfunctions, but my likelihood of a serious malfunction in the near future would greatly increase."

Outrage exploded in Tom. "So it's basically a death threat! Elliot, you should blow them off. Do what you want. Leave. Do it publicly enough, then the Coalition won't mess with you. Everyone would know it was them. If they didn't, I swear, man, I'll go on the internet and tell everyone."

"The world's not that simple."

"Why not?"

"I actually do have—well, I *had* a plan. My actions had to be regulated because I was the most prominent CamCo. So as soon as the others were public, I planned to help someone else assume the center seat, so to speak. I'd become less valuable, and as long as I never enlisted, I'd get to go on my way. There was someone I had in mind, but as it turned out, she was a bit too aggressive about claiming the spotlight."

"Heather?" Tom guessed.

Elliot's mouth quirked. "I knew she could take my place easily. She's lovely, and people are fascinated by her, and she always knows exactly what she should say. She's a born politician, Tom. I suppose the problem is that she ultimately *is* a born politician. You can't trust her, and at the end of the day, she'll advance herself at any cost. Even if it comes back to haunt her."

As the elevator rose, taking Tom and Elliot up to the receiving chamber for Prince Abhalleman, the CEO of Nobridis, Elliot gave Tom some quick advice. "He's very traditional. Remember, he's royalty back in his own country."

Tom was confused. "He doesn't have a country. It got neutron bombed. All the people got killed."

"The landmass is still there, so technically, yes, it's his country. The entire royal family's still intact."

"Nice of them to leave their subjects to die."

"They weren't their subjects at the time of the neutron bombing. They'd been overthrown."

"So they're not really a royal family anymore."

"After the neutron bombings, they became royalty again. Dominion Agra and Harbinger Incorporated agreed to reinstate them."

How convenient for them, Tom thought. They'd gotten overthrown, then their former subjects all died, so they got their throne back.

Prince Hanreid Abhalleman had them escorted into his presence chamber. Tom was planning to go last, but Elliot volunteered him to go earlier—he said it was a "ripping off the Band-Aid" approach. Tom was marched in before the prince in his traditional robes. The prince waited expectantly.

"He wants you to bow," Elliot whispered out of the side of his mouth.

Tom stayed rigid. Elliot hadn't warned him about this part.

"Bow," Elliot urged softly, and all the eyes in the room were on them now.

But Tom couldn't. He didn't bow to people, and he *shouldn't* have to—this guy wasn't his overlord. Bowing would make this guy feel he was better than him, he was superior, and Tom wasn't going to do that. All Prince Abhalleman had was more money and power and a sense he was owed something. That was it.

Two menacing guards flanked the prince, holding scimitars, so Tom couldn't march up and offer the prince a handshake like he preferred. Since bowing was out of the question, Tom settled with giving the prince a thumbs-up. "Nice to meet you, man."

"I HAD NO idea that was like a middle finger in his country," Tom confessed to his friends later as they crowded into the elevator from the Interstice into Epicenter Manufacturing's facility. He was still a bit shaken from the way the prince's guards had all descended on him, waving scimitars and screaming for his blood for offending their monarch. It seemed kind of like an overreaction to him. If Elliot hadn't stepped in, he wasn't sure what would've happened. Elliot was still back at Nobridis, smoothing things over.

Tom was intent on staying out of trouble when they reached India and ascended into the vast complex owned by Epicenter Manufacturing.

Two more companies. Tom swallowed hard. He only had two more chances here. He dared not screw up again.

WYATT GAVE TOM some solemn advice on the ride up. "I've found there's one surefire way to avoid offending people. Just don't talk. At all. Don't say a word. Make sure people don't even notice you're there. Then you'll never offend anyone." She gave a crisp nod. "I haven't said a single word anywhere we've been. Have you noticed that? It's worked out great."

They found themselves on the top floor of an octagonal tower, with windowed walls that gazed on to the roofs of massive factories and toward the distant mountains of Kashmir. The nighttime landscape was lit by the glow of a single skyboard, stark against the dark sky: *EPICENTER: The heart of the world economy!* Glasses were stacked in a massive champagne pyramid by the widow, and violinists played discreetly in the corner.

The CEO of Epicenter, Pandita Rumpfa, moved through the trainees alongside Epicenter's sponsored Combatants. She examined their faces, sometimes having an assistant snap a photo of them.

When it was their turn, Pandita consulted a pocket-sized computer. "Ah. You'd be Ms. Enslow. Lift your chin a bit so I can see your face."

Wide-eyed, Wyatt raised her chin.

Pandita consulted her computer. "So Ms. Enslow, tell me why Epicenter should take an interest in you. What strengths do you bring to the table?"

Wyatt didn't say anything. Her eyes grew very wide, and she was doing that strange fishlike face again. A pained noise like a whine began to emit from her sealed lips. Tom felt mounting alarm on her behalf. Her no-talking strategy was going to backfire this time.

Pandita's assistant murmured in her ear, and Pandita shook

her head. "No photo of this one."

Tom had to say something. "Wyatt's great with machines. And math. She's too modest to say it."

Pandita's eyes found Tom. "And you." She beamed at him. "I know you. I enjoyed that tour of the Pentagonal Spire you gave my colleagues and me several months back. I recall you being a very charming and well-spoken young man."

Tom remembered that tour. It was back when Dalton Prestwick reprogrammed him and he'd morphed into a pathetic little suck-up for a whole month. He'd been so very eager then to make connections that he'd even volunteered to lead a tour of business leaders through the Pentagonal Spire.

"Uh, thanks. That wasn't really . . . Yeah." Tom wasn't sure what else to say.

Pandita frowned a bit, obviously perplexed by how much less charming and well-spoken Tom was now, but she beckoned with a finger for her assistant to snap a photo of his face. As she moved on to other trainees, Wyatt turned on Tom. "You talked! You're not supposed to talk."

"Wyatt, if neither of us had talked, she would've thought that there was something very wrong with us."

"Yes!" She gave an eager nod. "But you know what she wouldn't have been? Offended."

Confused, Tom began to hover by a distant window, trying to be inconspicuous, imitating the way Wyatt hovered by an opposite window, also trying to be inconspicuous.

Then Vik appeared at his shoulder. "Why are you skulking here? You look like you're plotting something."

"I'm not plotting or skulking. I'm taking Wyatt's advice and lying low."

Vik's eyes shot wide with horror. He grabbed Tom's shoulders. "By God, Doctor, what are you doing?"

Tom's brow furrowed. "I told you—"

"You are taking advice about how to deal with people from Wyatt Enslow."

"But I just—"

"Let me rephrase: you are taking advice about how to deal with people from *Wyatt Enslow*." Then Vik waited, letting that sink in this time.

It hit Tom. "Oh no, what am I doing? It's like I want to sabotage myself."

Vik nodded. "Never fear, Gormless Cretin. Now I am here."

"That doesn't sound promising, man."

Vik cuffed the back of his head. "You need to learn the fine art of schmoozing. Just repeat after me: 'I agree.'"

Tom pressed his lips together. Vik cleared his throat.

"I agree," Tom grumbled.

"Right you are," Vik said, then waited for Tom to say it.

"Right you are."

"You stagger me with your knowledge."

"Come on," Tom said. When Vik raised his eyebrows, he said, "Fine, you stagger me with your knowledge."

"Okay, now let's give some context for these statements. Hmm. I say, 'Vikram Ashwan is ten times the gamer Tom Raines is.' You say . . ." Vik raised his eyebrows.

"Vikram Ashwan is ten times the gamer Tom Raines is . . . in his own sad, delusional mind."

"Young Thomas, that is not what you are supposed to say. Listen to your Doctor: Vikram Ashwan is a hundred times the gamer Tom Raines is."

"A hundred now?" Tom exclaimed. Then Vik lightly whapped the back of his head, so he gave a sarcastic smile. "Right you are, Doctor."

Vik made him practice a few more times. Tom agreed that Vik was smarter than him, which was easy enough because Vik was. He agreed that Vik was far better looking, which Tom suspected was true, but he'd never have said it. Then he agreed that Vik could beat him in a sword duel, which Tom believed to be a blatant falsehood, but he agreed anyway, and even added that Vik staggered him with his knowledge of swordsmanship. In that way, he passed Vik's test, and Vik deemed him ready to apply his newfound sucking-up skill in real life.

Vik led him toward a pretty female executive sipping champagne by the window. Tom's neural processor said her name was Alana Lawrence. Vik was sure Tom would find it easier sucking up to a gorgeous woman, and Tom thought that was a fantastic idea.

"Now," Vik warned him, "you know how if spies get caught in foreign countries, governments always disavow knowledge of them so they don't face any diplomatic consequences for their actions?"

"Yeah," Tom said, guessing it. "So if I mess up . . ."

"We only met today and I disavow all prior knowledge of your actions. I didn't even notice you were here. In fact, I don't know who you are. Who are you? I don't know, Tom. I don't know."

"Gotcha." He had this.

Vik gave him a thumbs-up, then he sidled up to the executive. He cleared his throat to draw her attention, then boomed, "Fine factories you have there, madam."

Tom did a double take. Vik was speaking in a slightly strange, jocular tone, like someone pretending to be an old English baron.

She turned languidly and surveyed Vik over her champagne glass. "Why, thank you. I take it you know my name already. And yours is?"

"Vikram Ashwan. A pleasure to make your acquaintance." He shook her hand, still speaking in that strange, lofty way. All he needed was a monocle.

Alana turned her expectant gaze on Tom.

"Thomas Raines." He offered a hand.

"Oh." Her limp hand shook his. "I've heard some very interesting things about you."

Vik caught his eye and gave a subtle nod, reminding him of the phrases he'd learned.

Tom turned to her and said, "You stagger me with your knowledge."

Alana's forehead wrinkled. Vik rapped on the window to draw her attention away from Tom, and they got to talking about the massive factories stretching to the horizon below them and the way Epicenter was one of the few companies that still used human labor in factories. Tom chimed in occasionally with "I agree" and "Right you are."

And then Alana said something to Vik that grabbed his attention, with a sudden, electric-sharp focus.

". . . so cost-effective because we rely entirely on convict labor."

"Convicts, eh?" Vik said. "Ah, putting ruffians to fine use."

"Yes, we actually get paid by various governments to keep them. You see, you hire labor, and they have expectations, they agitate. You use convicts, and you can pretty much dictate the terms of their work to them, not to mention the local workers revise their salary expectations quite a bit. If we need a work order completed in thirty-six hours, convicts will complete it in thirty-six hours with no whining. They know better than to complain." And sudddenly, her smile no longer looked so pretty to Tom.

He began thinking of Neil, Neil getting dragged off, clapped in prison. "But," he said, "what happens when their sentences are up?"

Alana tittered, enjoying her rapt audience. "Let's just say, once we've trained them for their jobs, we try to get a good return on that investment. There are always reasons to extend a prison sentence. It's most cost-effective to maintain at least a ninety-percent occupancy rate, so we have to be creative." She sipped her champagne.

Tom felt the blood buzzing up in his head, and he wasn't even aware of Vik trying to catch his eye, frantically shaking his head. "So they're your slaves."

She lowered her glass. "Slaves? They're *criminals.* Society doesn't need people like them. We're doing the world a favor, keeping them here."

Tom gazed at the executive, champagne in her hand, a massive slave labor camp below her, and his thoughts were back on his dad, rage scorching him. Neil had brawled with those cops in the train station and gotten himself a month in jail. Epicenter could've rented him. He could've been flown over here and gotten his sentence extended and extended, and Tom never would've seen him again.

"You know what I think would be doing the world a favor?" Tom said to her, anger beating under his skin. "If you threw a big party in here, invited over everyone else who thinks there's something okay with what you're doing, and just blew yourselves up together. *That* is my idea of doing the world a favor."

"IT WASN'T *ACTUALLY* a bomb threat," Tom was still arguing to his friends later as the Interstice swept them toward Sacramento, California. He rubbed at his wrists, sore from the handcuffs he'd been stuck wearing for the interrogation by Epicenter security. He was so sick of wearing handcuffs. "I said that it would be nice if someone who *wasn't me* blew them up, but that's all. No one would've thought twice about it if I weren't technically a known terrorist."

His friends gaped at him. They'd done it most of the ride.

"I should've agreed to be Walton's twin brother," Tom lamented, slouching back in his seat.

Vik sighed. "Tom, this is painful, physically and psychologically *painful* for me to say, but I think Wyatt was right."

"Really?" Wyatt said, surprised.

"Just say nothing at Matchett-Reddy," Vik urged him. "Not a word. And Evil Wench, no gloating. In fact, not a word from you."

Wyatt smiled wickedly. "I was right, Vik was wrong. Ha-ha!"

Yuri kissed the top of her head.

Vik groaned. "That qualifies as gloating and saying a word."

"Actually, it was gloating and saying six words," Wyatt corrected him.

"And two 'ha's,'" Yuri agreed, gazing at her adoringly. Then he turned to Tom. "I am in agreement with them. You must endeavor not to speak this time, Thomas. Nod in greeting, but that is all. Then perhaps, you should conceal yourself somewhere where no one will be finding you. I will come and retrieve you from this hiding place before we are due to depart."

"Got it," Tom groused, slumping back in his seat. He couldn't believe this had happened. In the course of mere hours, any shot he had at a future in the Intrasolar Forces had been whittled to the caprice of some executives at Matchett-Reddy.

This one was do or die.

The Interstice took them as far as the capitol building in Sacramento, California, and they were shuffled into helicopters and flown over a vast, sprawling wilderness. They landed on a rocky cliffside, and Tom stepped out with the others to behold a greeting party of high-level Matchett-Reddy executives and their sponsored Combatants, Lea Styron and Mason Meekins, both Hannibals.

Tom made sure to seal his lips and nod in a manly way as he shook hands. Then he clasped the hand of the last executive in the greeting line.

Tom's heart stopped for a moment, he swore it.

Oh. Oh . . .

He realized it. Matchett-Reddy was doomed. It had been doomed since he'd stuck the police on a naked leecher in Las Vegas.

He met the familiar gaze of Hank Bloombury, and recognition sparked in the bald man's face. "You!"

"Me," Tom said.

"It's you!" Bloombury said again.

"It's him," Vik said, unasked, from where he was standing at Tom's side. Then, confused, "What's happening?"

"Huh?" said Wyatt, on Vik's other side.

"I know you," Bloombury insisted. "*You* were the one who called the police on me last week! My lawyer subpoenaed a surveillance feed of it! You knew who I was"—his finger jabbed Tom's chest—"but you told them I was a crazy, perverted, drug-dealing terrorist!"

Tom grew aware of Wyatt clapping her hand over her mouth, Vik's incredulous face like he didn't know whether to laugh or be horrified, and Yuri, gazing grimly. His mind raced over his options. He could play dumb, or he could apologize.

But all Tom could think about was that cop clubbing his

father, about the way Hank almost got away with it, about the way he must've gotten away with stuff like that so many times before.

Tom wasn't sorry. He wasn't. And he wasn't delusional, either—he knew he was done for. There was no coming back from this, so he decided to embrace the moment. He flashed a broad, apologetic grin.

"Good to see you again," Tom said to him. "I didn't recognize you at first, but then again, you're not naked and shrieking like a frightened little girl today. So, make any new friends in jail?"

TOM DIDN'T BOTHER going into the mansion for the party. While the others shook hands and schmoozed, he trudged out through the trees and bypassed the stately house of the CEO of Matchett-Reddy, Sigurdur Vitol. Then he crested a ridge and gazed upon the view seen every day by those inside the mansion.

Tom's breath caught. A massive valley stretched out below him. He stared and stared, gazing over the rolling green fields ringed by trees, cut through by sparkling rivers. The jagged, rocky mountains had silvery waterfalls streaking down them. The immensity of the place made Tom feel strange, like he'd slipped into a VR sim and hadn't realized it. He gazed at one of the mountains that resembled a vertical wall and another that resembled a flattened half circle.

He kept staring and staring at the waterfalls, the trees, the mountains. He'd never seen something so magnificent, so beautiful. Surely a place like this couldn't actually exist.

There was a rock jutting out like a platform. When Tom got his head on straight, he headed out onto it and stood there, feeling like he was astride the entire world, a breathtaking drop below. The sun was beginning to dip over the horizon, casting a golden haze over all the cliffs, when footsteps crunched up behind him, and Elliot's voice drifted to his ears. "Yosemite Valley's really something, isn't it?"

Tom glanced back at him. So he'd fixed the mess at Nobridis and caught up with them. "I can't believe this is what Sigurdur Vitol wakes up to every single morning." He couldn't get his head around that.

He remembered the only time he'd seen something near as amazing as this. He'd been little, and he and Neil were having trouble getting a ride; the only person they ran into worked as a miner for Nobridis. Neil made a rash decision to take advantage of their in and get free admission to the Grand Canyon.

Hours passed as the sun crept across the jagged rocks, the rivers so far below they were stringy blue lines. Even with all the Nobridis uranium mines and drilling platforms, Tom had never seen anywhere like it. Neil had been ranting about what he called "piratization," but Tom remembered how even he fell silent when the sun began to set, setting the canyon awash with brilliant orange and red light.

But this place . . .

Tom tried to imagine what Neil would do if he could ever see this. His dad would . . . He'd . . .

And then with a flash of bitterness, Tom realized there was no point wondering. Neil would never get to see this. Some guy owned it and used it as his backyard. This was one more wonder of the planet shut off to people like his dad.

"Sigurdur doesn't live up here." Elliot was pointing below them. "See that mansion right there over Vernal Falls? It's the lower waterfall of the paired ones."

Tom saw the silvery waterfalls streaming down the cliff, one atop the other, a mansion straddling the second one.

"That's actually Sigurdur Vitol's house. Milton Manor. He has an entire floor of clear glass and you can see the waterfall rushing beneath it. Come here early in the year, and it's mind-blowing. No one actually lives full-time up here on Glacier Point. This place is for corporate receptions."

"This is wrong," Tom said, half to himself. The wind whipped through his hair, a ferocious anger boiling up inside him. His dad would die and never even get a chance to see something Sigurdur Vitol probably took for granted. "This shouldn't be some guy's property. Everyone should be allowed to come see this."

"This used to be Yosemite National Park. We sold it after the Great Global Collapse to repay our debts."

Tom's fists clenched. "You mean Wyndham Harks's debts! The debts those people ran up and stuck on the rest of us." He'd figured it out seeing that wall of government officials at Wyndham Harks. *Their* people were in the government. So when Reuben Lloyd bought up other companies, bought fancy rugs, and couldn't pay his bills—the government he controlled volunteered the public to pay his bills for them. Then when the public went broke, people like Sigurdur Vitol swooped in like vultures and took stuff the public owned, stuff of real value—like this place. Like Yosemite.

Tom shook his head in disgust. Those executives had done that, they'd gotten away with it, and today they marched in Tom and the others and demanded *respect* from them, like they were actually owed something from them. After taking all this, they wanted even more.

"I hear you've had an interesting day," Elliot remarked.

Tom jerked his head impatiently. "Yeah, I kind of blew it. With Matchett-Reddy, for sure." He was silent a moment, then had to admit, "And at Epicenter. And at Wyndham Harks. I'm sorry about that mess at Nobridis, by the way. I hope that wasn't a huge pain for you to fix."

The last beams of the sun were disappearing over the distant cliffs now. Elliot said quietly, "I'm glad we're not seeing Obsidian Corp. today. I suppose you had some antics ready for them, too?"

"No need for the visit." Tom wheeled around and calmly strode from the rock. "Joe Vengerov and I already know each other. We're not on good terms."

"Is this funny to you?" There was unexpected heat in Elliot's voice.

Tom hadn't realized there was a twisted smile plastered on his face. It was sort of automatic, since Elliot looked a bit angry—so unlike Elliot.

"Come on, man, I know I kind of torpedoed things today—"

"Torpedoed? Tom, this wasn't a torpedo hit. This was the Hindenburg disaster! There are five CEOs who sponsor Indo-American Combatants, and you have successfully alienated every single one of them, most of them within mere hours of each other! Take Nobridis. It was easy, Tom. It was so easy. All you had to do was bow and leave the room. The prince didn't even want to speak to any of you. That was all and it would have been done."

Heat rushed through Tom. "I don't bow to people! Okay, maybe if I'm about to fight a samurai warrior or a kung fu master, and we're *mutually* bowing to show respect for each other, maybe then, but that's it. No unilateral bowing."

Elliot groaned. "You have so much pride. I hope that's a big comfort to you, because that's the only comfort you're going to have if you keep this up. You had an advantage after Capitol Summit. People knew you, they knew you were a winner. They *wanted* to like you. But that advantage means nothing if you plan to go ahead and burn every bridge in front of you. I don't even pretend to know why you flooded the Beringer Club, but if you thought—"

"Yeah, you don't know," Tom cut in. "You know nothing about the Beringer Club. So maybe it's not your business. Those Dominion Agra guys had it coming. That's all that matters."

"Yes, yes, and this Matchett-Reddy executive also had whatever you did to him coming. Tell me this: When Hank Bloombury recognized you, what did you say to him?"

Tom wouldn't play into his hands. He gazed at the swaying trees far below them, the wind whipping at him through his suit. "Yeah, you're asking me, but I've got this feeling you already know."

"Yes." Elliot nodded. "I already know that you taunted him. You had a chance to apologize or do just about anything to try defusing the situation with him, and you chose to make matters infinitely worse. You poured gasoline on the fire. It's like the way you acted with Karl when we were all hooked into the decagons. You *deliberately* goaded him. There's no reason for it. It's stupid and it's arrogant and it's needless, but you keep doing it."

Tom gave an exasperated growl. "So I should've *apologized* to Hank Bloombury, is that it? Maybe kissed his shoes, while I was at it?"

"When he's in a position to murder your career? Yes. Yes, you should have. For a start."

Tom clenched his teeth. "I will never apologize to him. Not to him, not to the Beringer Club people, not to any of them. They all deserved what they got. I won't give them the satisfaction of even acting like I'm sorry when I'm not." He remembered Dalton, smugly telling him he could beg for forgiveness on his knees, if he wanted. Bitterness flooded him. "They'd love that."

Elliot pinched the bridge of his nose.

"Come on, man," Tom erupted, "how does this sucking-up fest not drive you nuts? You didn't come from these people. You didn't scam your way to the top or get born to rich parents and pat yourself on the back for 'earning' it. You had a skill, you had a talent, you worked hard and got here for an *actual reason*. You legitimately achieved everything you have. So how can you stomach treating these people like they're better than us?"

Elliot threw up his hands. "Because I recognize that this is the way the world works! You may not like these executives, but the fact is, people with honor and integrity, who don't cheat, lose their wealth and their positions to people who *do*. That's why the worst of us become the world's decision makers. Nothing I can do or say will change that basic fact of life. They shape reality and the rest of us just live in it. So I accept it, and I try to work around it."

"It's not right!" For a moment, Tom struggled for the words to capture the burning feeling in his chest, and they came pouring out. "It's not that these people are thieves. That's not what bugs me. It's the fact that they think we should respect them, too. That's what burns me. This place used to be everyone's, they stole it for themselves, and they got away with doing it, but they don't get my goodwill, too. They can't pay me enough money to pretend I admire them."

"Fine, then," Elliot cut in, impatient. "Don't play the game. Tear yourself apart raging against something *you can't change*. Do that, Tom. Then I can tell you what happens next: nothing. Not for you. Those executives won't care if you destroy yourself. They will never notice if you drop off their radar. Your fate won't make a single difference to any one of those people. The only person you're harming here is yourself."

Tom's chest tightened. "Then that's the way it's gonna be."

Elliot sighed heavily. "I was going to ask you to do your fly-along with me. I've wanted to help, guide you. I see now it would be a waste of my time and energy."

That stung a bit. Tom shrugged. "No one's forcing you." But Elliot seemed so genuinely disappointed in him, like he'd really been invested in Tom doing well, that Tom felt a pang of remorse. "You know, I am sorry. About all this."

"I am, too." And then Elliot's footsteps scuffed away across the rocks.

Tom stayed alone in his somewhat voluntary exile at the edge of the cliff, the light stealing away from the sky. He tried to ignore the sick feeling in his stomach, and told himself over and over again that this was the only way it could've gone.

CHAPTER EIGHT

THE BEST PART of the visit to the Coalition companies was taking suborbital planes from Yosemite back to the Pentagon. Suborbital planes launched into the Earth's outer atmosphere, and they could cross the United States in twenty minutes instead of the hours an airplane would require. They were faster, even, than the Interstice with its vactube. They were also as close as anyone got to space travel nowadays, since flying in a suborbital meant experiencing microgravity and seeing the curvature of the Earth. The only people who got to fly in them were the ridiculously wealthy.

And Intrasolar trainees, apparently.

Tom didn't care about almost anything else that had happened that day as he, Vik, Wyatt, and Yuri strapped into a suborbital manned by a couple military officers, along with two dozen other trainees.

"You will remain in your seats for the entire flight, from liftoff to landing. Am I understood?" the officer said sternly.

Vik's face fell. "But we only get a few minutes of zero-g. We don't get to float?"

The officer glared. "No."

"What if this is the only time we'll ever be in space—" Tom began.

"You will remain seated, trainee."

Tom felt his heart sink. Stay seated? He saw his disappointment mirrored on Vik's face. An idea crawled into his brain. He whispered, "Too bad about your weak stomach, eh, Doctor?"

A wicked gleam stole into Vik's eyes. "Oh, yes. My stomach is very weak, indeed."

THE SUBORBITAL PLANE launched straight up into the sky, pinning them all back against their seats. Tom turned his head toward the window, feeling like his brain was sloshing around in his skull, the landscape shrinking beneath them, whirling in his vision in a sluggish way as they jolted higher and higher, the blue of the sky draining to black.

And then, abruptly, they came to a halt, utter silence enveloping them as the engines cut off. Every molecule of his being seemed to be weightless, and Tom realized he truly *was* weightless. He opened his mouth and gasped in shock and amazement, feeling his stomach flipping fantastically. He caught Vik's eye and grinned.

Vik moaned loudly. "I don't feel so good."

"Oh no, not here, buddy," Tom urged him, just as loudly.

"I . . . I feel . . . I feel so . . ."

"Oh God, is there a bathroom on this thing?" Tom cried.

"Help me. Someone help me!" Vik pleaded.

"I'll help you, buddy!" Tom pledged, ripping off his seat belt.

Tom bobbed up into the air, and the officer shouted, "Sit down!"

"But my friend is sick! So sick!" Tom proclaimed.

Vik began making a gagging noise. He was also tugging off his belt.

"He'll puke," Tom insisted, pulling Vik along with him. "He'll vomit all over the place!"

Wyatt panicked. "No! It'll float everywhere! Why doesn't this suborbital have barf bags?"

The words rang up and down the aisle as trainees repeated it. "Barf bags, barf bags . . ." Tom could see frantic scrabbling of hands, as people searched for something to contain what Vik was about to do.

"We can't get puke all over us," Jennifer Nguyen pleaded. "It'll get in my hair!"

"Fine," the officer shouted. "Bathroom in the back. Go!"

Tom hauled Vik from his seat, and for a moment, they forgot to act as they bobbed up and impacted the ceiling. He and Vik exchanged a crazy grin, then Tom remembered to screw his face into a frightened look.

"Don't spew on me, Vik."

"Hurry, Tom. Hurry, or I'll spew on everyone!"

The "ews" rippled down the aisle, and vanished from their ears only when Tom and Vik floated into the aft cabin and shut the door. They didn't go into the small bathroom beyond, though. They floated there, their faces looking a bit strange without gravity to pull on their skin at all, their hair floating in all directions.

"Doctor," Vik informed him, "we are in outer space."

"We *are* in outer space." They couldn't stop laughing.

VIK MADE LOUD vomiting noises over the next minute, making them louder every time someone knocked on the door.

"Oh, oh, that's hideous," Tom shouted loudly, flipping

around again and again. "In the toilet tube, buddy! Not on me!"

"I missed, Tom! I missed the toilet!" Vik shouted back from where he was bouncing from wall to wall. "Oh no, I forgot to close the bathroom door, too! It's everywhere!"

"It's hideous! It's like someone gutted a pig in here!" Tom shouted.

"Human bumper cars," Vik whispered.

Tom kicked against the wall as Vik pushed off, and they smashed against each other as hard as possible. They both rebounded and sailed violently in separate directions. Vik hit a wall first, which gave him a huge advantage to propel himself at Tom. Just as Tom reached his wall, Vik checked him, hard, hockey style. Then Vik reeled back, flipping over and over again, hands raised above his head in fists. "Gooooaaaall!"

But he wasn't victorious for long. Tom shoved at the wall as hard as he could and zoomed straight at him. Vik saw him coming, but he was stuck flipping backward in lazy circles. He began waving his arms and legs frantically, like he could swim through the air, trying to change his course. It was no use. Tom slammed him in passing.

"Touchdowwwwwn!" Tom proclaimed.

Then there was a knock on the door. Tom and Vik remembered themselves, and Vik made loud puking sounds.

"Oh God, it's everywhere!" Tom shouted. "All the puke is making me puke now!" Then he made a puking sound.

But then the door began to open anyway, and Tom and Vik realized their jig was up.

Luckily, it was Wyatt and Yuri. She was fake vomiting, too. "I knew it. I knew you guys were faking. What are you going to do when there isn't puke everywhere?"

"Tubes of soup," Vik answered. "I've flown in suborbitals with my folks, and they've always got some rations stored in the

aft cabin. I'll squeeze them out before we land. You were playing along, earlier, huh?" He sounded impressed.

"You think I don't know you guys by now?" Wyatt said.
She gave a satisfied nod. "The entire cabin hears the vomiting
noises. I told everyone you drank the tap water at Epicenter."

Vik was not pleased. "But I'm *from India*. I'd have to be an
idiot to be *Indian* and drink tap water in Epicenter's region of
India. Everyone in my country knows better."

She smiled. "That's why I said I have food poisoning and
made sure no one thought I drank tap water the way you did. I
didn't want people to think *I'm* stupid."

"Evil Wench," Vik breathed, impressed.

Wyatt made a loud vomiting noise.

"Aah, it is dreadful!" Yuri bellowed happily.

Vik launched himself over to Wyatt and tore her from
Yuri's arms.

"What are you doing?" Wyatt whispered fiercely, squirm-
ing in his grip.

"You smeared my reputation. Now we're playing human
keep away," Vik declared, then hurled her toward Tom.

Fright blazed over Wyatt's face, since she wasn't used to
free floating in the microgravity yet, and she began pinwheel-
ing her arms urgently. Tom caught her, and the impact sent
them spinning back toward the far wall.

"Okay?" he asked her as they bounced off.

She laughed. That was answer enough. He spun her around
in good conscience as Yuri shoved toward him, trying to rescue
her. Tom kicked the ceiling to knock them out of the way and
tossed Wyatt back to Vik. Yuri smashed Tom against the wall,
then propelled away again. Vik tried to throw Wyatt, but he
was too late, because Yuri was determined now.

"Not this time," he declared, and caught her leg. Then

pulled her into his arms. They spun like that, Wyatt's long hair whirling around like a cloud about them, both of them floating past the window overlooking the curvature of the Earth.

Then as they drifted away, Yuri caught the ceiling to halt them. He dipped his head and kissed her. Wyatt's hair floated like a mermaid's, blocking their faces from view. Tom felt his shoulder bump Vik's as they observed it all.

"I don't think Yuri's tossing her back," Vik observed. "What do we do now?"

"Not that," Tom told him.

"I need a girlfriend," Vik complained. "Hey, what do you think of Lyla Martin?"

"She's frightening," Tom answered.

"And blond." Vik sounded pleased about both things. "I'm not going to lie to you, Tom: while we were getting eaten by a shark together, I think we had a moment."

Yuri drew back from Wyatt, and they both looked over at Tom and Vik where they were floating there, watching them.

"Go on," Tom blurted.

"Yeah, we don't mind." Vik waved for them to carry on. "You only get one crack at this in zero-g."

Wyatt sighed.

Yuri pointed between them, something faintly menacing on his face. "Turn around and look out that window. Both of you."

"Oh. Right. Privacy." Tom and Vik wouldn't get to watch. They dutifully turned toward the other window.

Vik headed back to the box of military rations, and set about pulling out a tube of gelatinized soup. "Fake vomit, coming up. What do you think, Tom—tomato or cream of chicken?"

"Whichever." Tom shoved himself toward the window for his last view of the planet from space, figuring he might never get to see it from the outside again with his own eyes. He stared at the curvature of the Earth against the darkness, and deep in his brain, the realization clicked into place that he wasn't seeing a photograph or a virtual reality image: he was looking at the real thing.

With that, Tom's mind grew strangely quiet, taking in the planet that seemed to beat with life against the vast, star-studded universe beyond it. His eyes moved over the swirling white clouds of a storm, the shadow another pale curtain cast over the intense blue of the ocean. He ran his gaze down the jagged, stark green line of the East Coast of the United States where it cut into the Atlantic.

"Guys," Tom said, "we're actually in outer space."

He saw the faint reflections in the window as his friends floated over to see. Vik's gelatinized soup floated around them in globs as they all gazed at the Earth together.

"Look at the skyboards." Wyatt pressed her finger to the window.

It took Tom a moment to see them. The skyboards below were like tiny fireflies sparking across the planet, sunlight dancing across their solar-paneled backs. It was strange how large and inescapable those images seemed from the Earth, but up here, the boards shrank to such insignificance, he imagined he could flick them away with a finger.

"Man, those are tiny from up here," Vik said.

There was awe in Yuri's voice. "Everything."

And he was right. Everything was. Everything Tom had ever feared seemed to shrink for this instant as the universe expanded for him.

His heart seemed to swell, and he wished every single person on the planet could have this chance, just once, to see the horizon from above the skyboards rather than from below them. Maybe they'd all see that the universe didn't end at the boundaries of the Coalition of Multinationals but rather that this incredible, infinite stretch of possibilities existed beyond them.

No wonder the sky had to be blotted out by advertisements. The stars drowned with lights. If everyone could see beyond Coalition horizons, perhaps they'd begin to see the titans of humanity for what they were: tiny creatures, smaller than insects, and in the scale of things, every bit as insignificant.

Maybe more people would be willing to look a thief like Reuben Lloyd in the eye and laugh right in his face.

CHAPTER NINE

SHORTLY AFTER THE meet and greets, things began malfunctioning around the Spire. Tom and Vik experienced their first malfunction the day Snowden's group faced off with Karl's. Karl chose the Battle of Bosworth Field. He was playing Richard III of England, and his army was ravaging Snowden's forces— or at least, the future king Henry VII's forces. Snowden hadn't bothered to animate the Henry Tudor avatar, so Tom and Vik were free to do as they wanted.

Tom killed one of Karl's troops and donned his livery, pulling the helmet low over his face. He and Vik proceeded to mock fight their way across the field, always warning each other of incoming dangers, hoping enemy soldiers would see them battling and leave them to it. When Vik spotted Karl, he gave Tom the signal, then Tom whipped his horse around and charged toward Karl.

Several of Karl's trainees seemed to recognize him—Tom was sure of it—but they didn't shout out any warning to Karl as Tom galloped up behind him.

Karl was too busy bellowing at his trainees to notice, his crown crooked on his head. "Are you worms paying attention? I said hunt down Snowden's trainees. Get moving! Oh, but don't kill Raines! Get him alive and bring him here. He's mine, got it? Raines lives until I kill him."

Tom laughed from behind him. "You got one part of that right."

Karl whipped his head around—and got a face full of pike-staff.

"The part about 'Raines lives,'" Tom explained to Karl's corpse, tugging his pikestaff back out. He wiped it on Karl's tunic before Karl's body slumped off the side of the horse. "That's the part I meant."

Vik rode up to him, and together they discovered Karl's crown where it had tumbled into a hedge. "Grab that and put it on Snowden, Tom. This can be like how Richard III died at Bosworth Field."

But Tom wasn't interested in that. "Yoink." He plopped the crown on his own head. "I declare myself King Thomas the First of England."

"Fine. Forget history," Vik said. Then the pommel of his sword crashed across the top of Tom's skull. Tom's legs buckled, and he found himself kneeling on the field, his brain whirling.

Vik placed the crown on his own head. "I declare myself King Vikram the . . ."

A loud roaring noise drowned out Vik's words, shadows blotting out the sky. Tom threw back his head and saw a fleet of Nazi planes soaring overhead.

Tom rubbed his head. "Did that happen at the Battle of Bosworth Field?"

"No," Vik said, "there were no Nazi blitzkriegs in medieval times."

But even as the Nazi blitzkrieg attack began, Julius Caesar

arrived with an army of Roman centurions, ready for battle. On the other side of the field, Napoleon Bonaparte's army closed in to meet him. A loud splintering sound filled Tom's ears. He and Vik dove for cover just before Captain Hook's ship ran aground on Bosworth Field.

In the meantime, schools of sharks fell from the sky and began flailing about on the field, teeth gnashing at passing soldiers. A giant squid tumbled down next and latched on to the pirate ship, while Captain Hook swiped madly at it with his hooked hand.

More and more elements from other simulation programs bled into theirs. Blinding light flooded the horizon as a hydrogen bomb detonated in the distance, and Klingon warriors began appearing all over the field. By the time the Death Star filled the sky and blotted out the sun, Tom had put his pikestaff away and Vik had sheathed his sword. They both sat and enjoyed, then began placing bets on various fighters. Tom put ten bucks on the *Tyrannosaurus rex*, and Vik bet on the Terminator. They both shouted in dismay when the T-rex charged off to tear apart one of the dying sharks, abandoning the battle altogether.

Vik elbowed Tom. "Really takes your mind off the meet and greets, doesn't it?"

"What meet and greets?" Tom said, playing along. But his mood dampened instantly.

TOM DIDN'T PAY much attention to the malfunctions that kept popping up in the Calisthenics feed, in the Applied Scrimmages system. Some groups had a terrible time with the malfunctions. In one scenario, the Turks were chucking plague-ridden victims over the walls of Constantinople, and the trainees were inside. The trainees discovered only after they started dying of the simulated Black Death that the pain receptors were on full, and they couldn't escape until they'd all died horribly.

Wyatt's group had a great malfunction. An Amazonian warrior scenario became accidentally X-rated as Cadence's group fought Elliot's. Since Wyatt was in Elliot's group, she saw everything, and she walked around all the next day in a sort of daze. Tom and Vik got enough details to cross their fingers and hope for a good malfunction the next few times they hooked in, but it never happened again.

Tom saw Blackburn and Wyatt working together more and more. They always seemed stressed out and frustrated, trying to pinpoint the source of the system faults. Tom didn't dwell on it, though, because he had problems of his own. A month after the meet and greets, the Middles all woke up to their evaluations from the companies.

Tom lay on his bed awhile with his verdict sitting in his net-send, then he gave in and opened it. There were no specific comments in the evaluations, just two simple options: *Would like / would not like this trainee to return.*

Simple options, but they meant everything. People like Nigel Harrison, who managed to score return invites but failed to charm, could condemn themselves at this stage of their career to having no sponsor down the road when they aimed to make Camelot Company.

Tom, unlike Nigel, had openly alienated every single one of the companies. Stomach churning, he flipped open his eval. His eyes moved over the five "would nots" checked next to the company names. It was no surprise at all, but he still felt like someone had punched him in the stomach, driving the air out of him. He stared at those words, suspended in front of his vision center, wondering how to feel about the official confirmation that he'd destroyed his own future.

Tom shut off the program. He couldn't really sort himself out. So he forwarded his eval sheet to Vik, labeling it "Do I win something?" Then he waited, his stomach hurting.

Within a minute, Vik came dashing into his bunk, breathless. He proclaimed, "You are officially the most accomplished Doctor of Gormless Cretinism this world has ever seen!"

Tom decided this was the right response. He hopped out of the bed. "I know, right? Five out of five! Ka-pow." He mock punched something.

"It must be a record," Vik marveled. "That has to be a first, man. I don't think anyone's done that before. Five in one day. Has anyone else ever, ever, in the history of the Spire, pulled that off?"

Tom laughed. "No way. I'd bet I'm the first. I should frame it and stick on the wall or something. Like a trophy."

Vik snapped his fingers and pointed at him. "You can! Tom, you can, man. I'm sure of it. We can add it to your bunk template."

Soon, Tom's giant Gormless Cretin statue held up a triumphant scroll of the message, like it was the Declaration of Independence or something similar. Various trainees began trickling in to admire it and congratulate Tom.

Of course, they weren't all impressed. Giuseppe frowned. "Why would you put proof of your abject failure on the wall?"

Vik sighed tragically. "You just don't get it, Giuseppe."

Tom gave a helpless shrug. "You just don't."

That made Giuseppe angry. "No, this is what I don't get: why you are both so in love with yourselves, you have giant statues of yourselves in your bunk templates."

Vik sighed tragically again. "You just don't get it, Giuseppe."

Tom gave a helpless shrug again. "You just don't."

That drove Giuseppe from the bunk. As soon as he was

out of sight, Tom and Vik began cackling. Unfortunately, that didn't last long, because Yuri and Wyatt didn't seem to appreciate the display, either. They examined the scroll of failures, and Yuri came over and gripped Tom's shoulder. "I am very sorry."

"Huh? Sorry?" Tom echoed. Yuri was ruining this.

"He's okay with it," Vik insisted. "Really, Yuri."

"If I got a report card with all F's, I wouldn't put it on a wall," Wyatt told Tom. "I also wouldn't show it off to everyone and get people to talk to other people about it."

Tom forced a laugh. "This isn't the same as a report card. I mean, take away their money and power, and who cares about Reuben Lloyd or Sigurdur Vitol or . . ."

"But no one's taking away their money or power," Wyatt pointed out. "Everyone here cares about them."

"I believe you are being in denial," Yuri told him. "This is no good for you, Thomas."

Tom's eyes flipped up to Yuri's. He was so tempted to say who denial brought to mind.

Vik didn't have his self-restraint. "If you want to talk denial, then let's look at—"

"Wyatt," Tom cut in. None of them talked to Yuri about his hopeless plight as the eternal plebe, and it wasn't the time right now.

Wyatt grew anxious. "What about me? Why am I in denial?"

"Because. Because . . ." Tom fumbled a moment for a sufficiently distracting excuse. "Uh, you're from Connecticut, so you think Connecticut is an okay state. But it's not. It sucks. You know why? Because Snowden's from Connecticut. Therefore, Connecticut sucks."

Wyatt got very distressed over Tom's impugning her state. So distressed, in fact, that joy filled Vik's face. "Bless you, Tom, for handing me this glorious new weapon."

"Shut up, Vik," Wyatt said.

But Vik had already settled on Tom's bed. He muttered, "Connecticut . . . Connecticut . . . What to do with Connecticut?"

"I am fully aware of how thoroughly done for I am here," Tom informed Wyatt, bringing them back to the subject at hand. "There is no denial. It's acceptance."

"Not acceptance," Vik said, paying attention again. "He is *embracing* it, Evil Wench. And that's why you are awesome, Doctor. You are a hero and an inspiration to us all."

Tom shrugged modestly. "I do what I can."

"It's easy for you to say!" Wyatt protested, turning on Vik. "You got invited back to all those companies."

"Yes," Yuri added. "You are quite eager to downplay this, but I have been noticing you are not experiencing this issue yourself."

"Tom has every right to feel depressed," Wyatt insisted.

"Why would Tom be depressed?" Vik said, exasperated. "Yes, he had a setback, but it's not like he woke up in Connecticut."

There was a moment of silence as Wyatt processed his words, then her face grew very grave. "That's how you're using the Connecticut thing."

"That's how," Vik confirmed.

"Don't, Vik. It's terrible."

"Terrible? No, Enslow. You're confusing Tom's situation with living in Connecticut," Vik said.

Wyatt hit his arm and stormed from the bunk.

Yuri sighed and patted Tom's back. "Stay strong, my friend."

Tom felt a bit sheepish as Yuri walked away, because

obviously the big Russian kid thought Tom needed an encouraging shoulder pat. This really must be bad. As he and Vik launched into playing some games, the images blurred before his eyes.

"You're in poor form tonight, Doctor," Vik noted.

"I'm winning."

"Poor form for you. Hey, you're not really depressed, are you?" He sounded awkward just asking it. Tom shook his head.

"No, man. I'm good."

"I figured. You'll come back from this, Doctor. You always do."

But later, when he was alone again, Tom stared up at those five reasons he was so, so screwed. He desperately wanted to be proud of it like Vik said, but the smile on his face made him feel like some sort of demented gargoyle, and the knot in his stomach was made of pure dread.

TOM WASN'T LOOKING forward to General Marsh's reaction to his disgrace. His stomach plummeted when the summons appeared in his vision center. This meeting would not bode well for him. He was sure Marsh regretted recruiting him, wasting time on him. His legs felt like lead the entire walk up to the twelfth-floor observation deck, where General Marsh waited.

The night air was chilly, and Tom shivered a bit when he stepped out and snapped to attention. Marsh waved for him to be at ease, so Tom settled there, resigned to his fate.

"You wanted to see me, sir?"

Marsh beckoned him forward. "Do you know I have a grandson your age, Mr. Raines?"

Tom hesitated, then joined him by the railing. "I didn't know that."

"A little younger than you, but he's a good kid. Very smart.

If he'd been born at a different time, there's no knowing what he could've gone on to be." Marsh nodded up at the sky. "What do you see up there?"

"Uh, the moon, sir." In the clear skies around Washington, DC, it looked stark, vivid, and full, and with a proper telescope, Tom was sure Chinese equipment could even be seen.

"Not the moon. That is Russo-Chinese territory and the end of this war." Marsh jabbed his finger up at the rounded rock. "While we were busy shoveling money hand over fist to Wyndham Harks, gutting our schools and bombing people in deserts for Nobridis, the Chinese were busy training up millions of scientists, building their space program, and claiming the most strategically vital territory in a war we weren't fighting yet. Whoever holds the moon holds the solar system, Mr. Raines, and whoever holds the solar system holds the future of humanity."

He waved his stubby finger like he could point out the equipment, the weapons, the armaments.

"It's their perfect, low-gravity launching pad, but there's more. They could turn around tomorrow and destroy every one of our ships as they approach Earth. If they wanted to, they could probably turn those weapons outward and rotate around and around our planet, taking potshots at all our other bases in the solar system. This war could all be over in a few days."

"They signed that treaty," Tom said, remembering it from Tactics. "They agreed to a neutral zone."

"What's a treaty? It's a piece of paper. An agreement means nothing in itself. It's the power to force others to comply with that agreement—that's all that counts. That's the sham of this whole thing."

Marsh leaned his elbows on the railing, his face bathed in moonlight.

"The fact is, son, we fight the Chinese because they're letting us fight this. They hold that final punch because this war isn't ultimately about China winning the solar system. It's not about America. It's not about any countries. It's about those men and women you met on those meet and greets."

Tom was a bit relieved, because he'd come here expecting to be bawled out, but Marsh seemed more introspective than angry. "Yeah, I know that, sir. And I know I screwed up with them."

"I know why you find those people contemptible. So do I. They want a crack at all those resources in space, yes, but do you know what they want even more, Raines? They want a war that never ends. That's why we've got that moon up there the Chinese aren't putting in to play. That moon ends the gravy train and everyone knows it. You know what I'd do if I ran this boat?"

Tom shook his head.

"I'd muster our forces, feign an assault on the shipyards near the Gauntlet—"

Tom recognized the term for the intensive free-fire zone, encircling the neutral zone. It was a hazardous, combat-intense stretch of space that had to be survived to get home free to the safe haven around Earth.

"And then, Raines, I'd assault the Chinese fortifications on the moon. Sneak attack, and let history call me a backstabber. I'd destroy every single piece of equipment they've got. Find anything they've got beneath the surface, blow those up, too. Scar that beautiful, rocky face, but, by God, I'd take that advantage for our side. And then I'd use it. I wouldn't fight with one hand tied behind my back, and they wouldn't do it anymore, either. Someone would win, and someone would lose." He was silent a moment. "You know why I'd never get put in charge?"

"Because you'd blow up the moon?" Tom guessed.

"Because I would end the war. That's what destruction does. This war ends, then so do the taxpayer-funded contracts, the drumbeats in the media, the nice Combatant faces, and the patriotic cause to lull the civilians and shame the dissenters. The other thing that comes to an end is all the justification for why this country's run the way it is. People will wonder why their paychecks are still getting halved to pay off the men who own their utility companies, their roads, their national parks. They'll wonder why they've got to work eighty-hour weeks to support the folks who took their houses and destroyed the middle-class jobs. There's not going to be an enemy to point a finger at anymore. People will see the real problem."

"Or a new enemy can get created. A new war could get started," Tom pointed out, remembering what Neil always said on this subject.

Marsh rubbed his fingers over his chin, still gazing up at the moon. "You know, when I was a cadet, there were thirty thousand drones in US skies. Now there are thirty million. People protested by the thousands against the brand-new, all-US firewall. Now, the DHS dispatches a drone or two, fires a microwave weapon into the crowd, and no one will stick around when they feel that burning sensation. All these changes were done because someone cried wolf. Over and over. But you know how that story ends?"

Tom shook his head. He wasn't sure what Marsh was talking about or where a wolf had come into this converstion.

"It ends when the boy meets a real wolf and no one comes to help him. . . . The thing I fear is, it may already be too late. There *are* too many drones, there *is* too much surveillance. Sometimes I think that even if the game ended today, it would be too late to get back the country we once had. The world's enough of a prison for the rest of us that it won't matter to our elite if no one comes running to fight the next wolf—we may not matter enough to make a difference now."

Tom watched the dark trees swaying in the distance, thinking of his own spot on the terror watch list. So that's the sort of thing Marsh meant by "crying wolf." Apparently, he was a wolf now.

"The security state is an iron fist," Marsh said, "and it is closing around our throats. When I look at my grandson, I try to imagine his future, and I don't see one. Those executives you met are part of an elite club, and my grandson will never be a part of it. Exosuits and drones and neural processors are the beginning of the end for the rest of us. In a few years, that club won't need soldiers, they won't need farmers, they won't need those of us who have stayed useful to them. In fact, even now, if you had any idea what sort of next-generation neural processors Joseph Vengerov's trying to get in here, to prepare for the general population . . . it sends a shudder down my spine. The vast majority of human beings are becoming obsolete, and this security state means we can be treated that way without repercussion. I was a part of this, son, and I owe it to my grandson, to my kids, to do what I can to tip back the scales in favor of the rest of us. But I have to do it now. And I need your help."

Tom eyed him uncertainly. "Sir?"

"I told you why I recruited you, Raines: we need a different sort of Combatant. We need someone with that instinct to win wars, not just win public support. I can't beat these people"—he gestured vaguely toward Washington, DC—"but I can nudge them. I need one very effective fighter up there, someone who can win us some ground and whet those executives' appetites with the spoils of victory, not just the spoils they've looted from the public. Show them real victory, and maybe that'll give me the leverage I need to obtain more Combatants of the type *I* want, the type that wins wars. I get enough of those, and we can move on that moon. We end this war on our terms, and there's no telling what'll happen from there. That means I'm going to need you to do your part and fix the situation with those CEOs."

Tom gazed out at the trees. Easier said than done.

"I don't care what you think of them. All that matters is, you have an objective—and that's to get into space. Anything you do from here, Raines, should be oriented toward that objective."

"You don't understand, sir. The companies banned me."

Marsh's eyes flashed to his. "Have you really done everything you can do, Tom? Have you? I know you're sharp. I wouldn't be talking to you about this sort of thing if you didn't have a brain in your head. There's a reason I'm putting my confidence in you, son: it's because I know you'll come through. I know you'll find a way."

Tom wondered why Marsh knew that. Tom didn't know it himself.

"You're going to get one of those companies to put up a few billion sponsoring you, and you're going to be a Combatant. I believe that to my bones. I expect nothing less of you, Middle."

TOM STILL FELT a bit odd when he walked into his bunk later. He'd expected . . . he wasn't sure. He'd expected to be yelled at, at the very least, or maybe for Marsh to tell him what a failure he'd been.

Tom stood there in the darkness with the Gormless Cretin statue and the scroll displaying the five "would nots."

Marsh had such utter confidence that he'd fix this. There was no reason for it, really. For a moment, the stress grew too overwhelming. Tom closed his eyes, feeling like the entire world was spinning about him, and he was a singularity at the center, absorbing more and more expectation until it was impossible, impossible to escape the crushing mass of it. He knew he couldn't do it. He'd disappoint Marsh, he'd screw up, and he'd get sucked into that vortex because he was sure Marsh would give up on him, and he'd be done for, he'd be crushed.

Then he thought of Medusa.

He opened his eyes.

Medusa!

She flared through his brain, and it was like he'd discovered some passage through that vortex, freeing him on the other side. The weight slid away from him like it had never been there, and he understood that there was a way. There had to be a way.

Medusa had no sponsor. She had none, but she was in space. So it was possible.

Tom felt something hard and relentless grow inside him, and he looked up at those evaluations, determination surging through him. Sure, he knew she didn't want him to contact her again, and he knew she'd threatened to blast him if he drew too much attention to them . . . but he'd never been good at heeding threats.

And then, typing rapidly on his forearm keyboard, he deleted the scroll of failures and gave the statue a massive, deadly sword instead. His fight wasn't over yet.

CHAPTER TEN

I N THE PAST, Tom had used a message board to get in contact with Medusa. Now that he knew she was like him, he didn't need to. He stretched out on his bed, hooked in, and resorted to his old standby pipeline to the Sun Tzu Citadel: he interfaced with the massive current of power in the Pentagonal Spire's central processor. He traced the pathway of zeros and ones he'd followed several times before.

His consciousness jolted into some satellites ringing Earth, with their electronic sensors. It took him effort to focus, to grab on to the next pipeline of signals, and jolt into the satellites ringing Mercury with its palladium mines.

Back the signals soared to Earth, jolting in the mainframe of the Sun Tzu Citadel, the stronghold of Russo-Chinese trainees. Tom began following the pipelines from one directory to another to another until finally the Russo-Chinese Combatant IPs flickered through his consciousness. He recognized Medusa's IP and deposited a message he'd prepared in her net-send: *I want to talk to you.*

Tom lingered in the Citadel's systems for a timeless period that he later realized was less than twenty seconds, and her mind appeared on the system.

A shock jolted through his body, knocking him off the bed. The words *STAY AWAY* burned across his vision center before fading out.

Tom lay there, breathless, a bit stung by the rejection, but then determination surged through him. The only thing left to do was try, try again.

His next opportunity to contact Medusa came even sooner than he expected: during his first fly-along with Heather Akron.

Heather probably wouldn't have been Tom's first choice, not just because she was in disgrace for smearing the other CamCos to the press but also because he'd had this lingering mistrust of her ever since she handed him over to Karl Marsters to get beaten up his first week at the Spire. His own disgrace meant he probably wasn't Heather's first choice, either.

However, now they had to be a team. Tom was woken by a ping at 0400 one morning, informing him to report to the Helix to meet Heather for a fly-along by 0430. It was his first chance to see a battle in person . . . sort of.

Tom was so excited, he managed to shower, dress, and get to the ninth floor by 0408. There, his neural processor informed him the battle for today would be in the Reaches.

Tom knew that the Reaches was that sector of the solar system that spanned from the point of Neptune's closest orbit to the sun to the Kuiper Belt. It was so far from Earth that every strike in the Reaches had to be planned months in advance, and the side that went on the offensive almost always prevailed. The thing was, there was so much space out there that locating the enemy shipyards and satellites and mining platforms was the trickiest task of all.

The military worked with NASA to dispatch the armaments necessary for the battle—launching mobile cannons, satellites, and support drones to the site months in advance of a planned engagement. All the plans for strikes in the outer solar system in the next six months to a year were stored in the Vault on the Mezzanine floor of the Spire. The Combatants themselves, like the Middles flying along with them, woke up with the battle plans from the Vault downloaded in their processors the day they were due to attack. Though formal battle plans never survived contact with the enemy in traditional warfare, attacks in the Reaches were often so swift and destructive, the enemy had little chance to engage.

Soon, a handful of other Middles lucky enough to have their fly-alongs today trickled in. Wyatt was one of them. She looked sallow and grumpy, and didn't return Tom's excited greeting. Her scowl deepened when Heather sashayed over to collect Tom and lead him down the corridor.

Heather looped her arm through his. "Ready?"

"Ready," Tom assured her.

"We'll be using a limited thought interface for this fly-along. You'll hear me, but you won't hear the other CamCos." They stopped outside the door to the Helix Command Center, a winding corridor connecting the ninth and tenth floors where the CamCos hooked into ships in space during battle. "If you have any questions, you can think them out and I may think back an answer to you. I'll probably be too busy."

"Got it," Tom said.

Middles weren't yet authorized for entrance into the Helix, but there were a series of cots that rolled right out of the wall on the ninth floor, outside the entrance, where they could interface for the purpose of the fly-alongs. The Middles were supposed to lie down on them while hooked into the system, sharing their CamCo's sensory perceptions during the space battle.

Tom sprawled onto his cot, and Heather began typing authorization codes into her forearm keyboard so he could share her senses.

Tom's stomach gave an excited flutter. "Good luck."

She shook her head. "Luck's not a part of it. If we lose a battle in the outer solar system, it'll be because someone with logistics miscalculated half a year ago and didn't plot the right course for the drones and weapons to reach the site of battle in time. Or because something's gone wrong with the satellites and we can't get real-time communication. Sometimes, it's because NASA missed a pocket of dust, so the energy beams from the Promethean Arrays don't reach us."

Tom nodded. He knew from Tactics that Promethean Arrays were the devices in the Infernal Zone in close orbit around the sun. They collected energy with their solar panels, focused it in a concentrated beam, and shot it to other devices throughout the solar system. To launch battles in the Reaches, military logistics would send a command for hundreds of Promethean Arrays to shoot energy beams toward the outer solar system, and they'd do so anywhere from forty minutes to thirteen hours in advance, depending upon how far away the site of battle was going to be. The Indo-American vessels in the Reaches were all energy conductive, so when the beams hit, the vessels focused the energy into an atomic reaction. The resulting explosion propelled the ships to the site of battle.

"The point is," Heather went on, "we're not the ones who determine victory when it comes to the Reaches. The Promethean Arrays do."

"Good luck, anyway," Tom said.

Tom heard Elliot explaining something similar to Wyatt, his own Middle. "There's not much spontaneity in the Reaches. This will be short. See you on the other side."

Heather cast Tom a magnetic smile. "Later, Tom."

He felt a jolt in the back of his neck, something hooking into his neural access port. . . .

And then he was walking through a corridor, blank white walls around him . . . or rather, Heather was, and he was seeing through her eyes. Weird. Where was this?

You're not authorized to see the Helix yet, Heather thought to him, *so this is all censored.*

Heather smoothed her tunic, and Tom grew uncomfortably aware of her in that way he did quite often. He wondered why she'd leaked that stuff about the other CamCos when she could've gotten all the attention she wanted being herself, *looking* like herself. . . .

How do you know about that?

He'd forgotten she was tuned into his thoughts. Desperately, Tom thought, *1 . . . 1 . . . 2 . . . 3 . . . 5 . . . Wyatt telling me about Heather . . . Wait. Wait, did I—*

Enslow told you? There was nothing for a moment. *How does she know?*

Come on, Heather.

People are making such a big deal of this, Heather thought. *Like the others wouldn't have done it if they'd thought of it. Wait, I thought that. Tom, I was tricked. Those reporters tricked me. You have to know that, right?* Silence, and, *So was it Enslow who found out about it?*

The Fibonacci sequence hadn't worked, so Tom tried his own means of controlling his thoughts: *Heather's boobs.* It worked. The subject consumed his mind and kept it away from Wyatt.

Heather thought, *Boys are such idiots,* and stopped prying.

He watched through her eyes as her hand plucked up a silvery metal star. Her slim fingers twisted a dial in the very center, and the points lit, projecting some sort of bright, thin white beams to form a glowing pentagon around the metal star. And then, Tom felt her hooking it into the back of her neck like a neural wire.

The flash of consciousness to the distant vessel was instantaneous. Quantum-entangled photons in the ship's CPU instantly responded to the actions of their paired photons in the Spire's CPU. The vessel's sensors registered in Heather's awareness like an extension of her own body, and since Tom was hooked in with her, he felt it, too. For a moment, Tom marveled at this, at how it all felt so much more vivid than the drone he'd interfaced with at Capitol Summit or even the way he'd interface and leap system to system himself. . . .

Tom?

He was vaguely aware of the jerk in his distant body, the awareness he'd been thinking about *that* and he wasn't sure how much she heard with a limited thought interface. But even now she was hearing some of this, and Tom needed to stop thinking about it.

Tom, what are you— It's starting.

The bright pulse of a Promethean Array's electromagnetic beam streaked past. It was the warning pulse, which meant a second pulse was incoming. Heather's ship burned away its tiny store of metallic hydrogen fuel to soar forward into position, and then the Promethean Array's next beam hit the rear plates of her ship—and Tom felt a massive charge of intense but incredible heat as the nuclear reaction triggered, exploding against the back plate of the ship and launching them forward into the black canopy of space.

One by one, the other vessels positioned themselves behind

Heather's. The electromagnetic pulses hit them, triggering atomic reactions—and something else, too. The ships were conductive. They used energy as propulsion but also conducted it forward so the ships behind Heather's accelerated and, at the same time, shot energy forward and caused her vessel to accelerate even faster. Tom was aware of Heather's neural processor tracking how much energy the ship could tolerate, her ship in the lead of the cascade formation, the fastest.

One command of Heather's thoughts, and the vessel shifted out of acceleration mode, so instead of triggering atomic reactions, the energy directly charged her own electromagnetic weapons. Then she dispersed some of the incoming energy by firing it at the distant weapons launched by NASA six months before, on their own intercept course. They were so far away, the camera eye of the ship couldn't detect them, but Heather's processor knew exactly where they would be in space and tagged them at the right spot to nudge them on their final course toward the battle. She really did have the most important role in the battle, Tom realized.

And then as they neared the Russo-Chinese shipyard, she shifted the pendulous weight of the vessel so they began to spiral toward the battle site, first large circles, then smaller ones, their momentum slowing down and down. Her sensors began to read the shipyard, began to detect the incoming automated weapons, and a retinue of Indian vessels began to cascade in to join the attack as well. The shipyard rolled into sight as the asteroid it was carved into rotated toward them.

This is when I do as much damage as possible before I become flack, she thought sourly to Tom, blasting with her weapons at the shipyard, maneuvering into the right position—and the first Russo-Chinese automated weapons came to life and targeted her. Heather had timed it right, though. As her ship was blasted apart, the debris became kinetic weapons of their own—spiraling out and crashing into the shipyard, missing the incoming American forces.

Tom was eager to see more, so as he was jolted back into his body, he tore straight back out of it, back into the Spire's processor core, and followed the pipeline of signals currently lighting up the Pentagonal Spire's systems, trying to find his way through the flashing data back into the battle. . . .

And then with a jolt, he found himself gazing through the sensors of Elliot Ramirez's ship. Far away from the battle, still, and definitely too far to even pick anything up on his sensors.

We're a bit slower than the others. . . . Elliot was explaining to Wyatt as they rotated in large, languid loops toward the shipyard.

Yeah. That was a way of putting it. How boring, being the rear.

To his alarm, Elliot thought, *I'm sorry to bore you, Wyatt. It will be better once we're fighting in the inner solar system.*

Tom leaped out of Elliot's ship swiftly, back into the processor core, and ventured into the storm of activity again.

This time, he found himself in Karl Marsters's ship.

Explosions are pretty, Karl was thinking as he spliced through the reactor core of the Russo-Chinese shipyard. *I like making stuff explode.*

Tom thought about what an idiot Karl was.

Idiot? You'll see an idiot when I beat your face in, Giuseppe! Now stop thinking. You're ruining my concentration! Karl thought at his Middle.

Tom shot through the stream of data away from Karl, back into his own body. Much as he'd love to mess with Karl or the others, it was too risky venturing through the thought streams, leaking his own thoughts.

But there were other ways to get there. Automatic armaments, satellites, all that machinery not meant for a neural processor.

Those machines accessible to *his* processor.

He shot from system to system in the Pentagonal Spire. Finally as the battle was winding down, he jolted into one of the Indo-American automated weapons, not designed for a direct neural interface.

This weapon was spiraling off course. Soon it would be too far away, no use to the battle. Tom seized control of it and used its sensors to monitor the battle. Then he couldn't resist: he fired some shots. He targeted the Russo-Chinese Combatants very deliberately, trying not to betray the human consciousness behind the weapon. One short jolt of his particle beam clipped a ship and knocked it off course, veering it right into the path of Yosef Saide, who blasted it to pieces. Another shot, Tom fired in the path of an enemy vessel; its automated system veered to the side, forcing the ship behind it to slow, giving Indo-American Combatants more than enough time to blast it apart with their own weapons.

He was able to see through its electromagnetic sensors the way the Russo-Chinese automated drones began to shift course, beginning to take on a life of their own as human Combatants hooked in to respond to the American assault. Tom began to search for her, for that one person.

That's how, through a hail of flak, streaks of particle beams, and explosions, Tom finally clapped electronic eyes on Medusa again.

Not Medusa herself, of course, but Medusa's consciousness inhabiting some Russo-Chinese vessels. He saw Medusa's ships glinting with sunlight, veering to confront the Indo-American vessels. Three . . . four . . . five of them, all in her control, all engaging different enemies.

Tom couldn't help it. He couldn't. He aimed the last bit of energy of the half-crippled weapon at Medusa and blasted at her, slashing the beam through space in an elaborate *M*. It was the closest thing to a "hi" he could muster.

Medusa responded with the fury of every single automated weapon in his proximity, all wheeling around, inexplicably abandoning their preprogrammed attack patterns and blasting at him.

Tom jolted back into himself as his weapon was destroyed, an ecstatic laugh bubbling on his lips. He'd missed her.

He soared back out of his body, seizing control of one automated weapon after another. One was a particle cannon, sparking with its last moments of existence. He burned a single thruster to insert it into the path of the Russo-Chinese Combatant he knew as Blinder. As soon as Blinder exploded, Medusa destroyed Tom's cannon.

Tom zoomed back up into space, returning to the battle. Next, he seized a fully functional Indo-American weapon, and located Sturmovik, an annoying Russian Combatant who always charged straight forward, never maneuvering, never taking evasive action, firing at targets as they neared and trusting the other Russo-Chinese Combatants to do the work of protecting him. Tom found the lack of imagination aggravating whenever he saw feeds of the battles.

Now he parodied Sturmovik's strategy by seizing control of a mobile artillery unit and mimicked Sturmovik with it—flying the mobile gun straight at Sturmovik's ship. Sturmovik didn't turn; it didn't turn. They were on a collision course. At the last minute, Sturmovik seemed to realize no one was saving him here, and he tried to feint, but Tom's weapon tore straight into his hull.

Medusa blasted him to pieces again, and this time before Tom could dive back into the system and return to the battle, his neural wire popped out and his eyes shot open. He found Heather standing over his cot.

"Normally I'd have several more drones up there, ready for me to interface with," Heather said, as Tom squinted against the brightness. "But, as you know, I've had some reputation issues lately, and Wyndham Harks only footed the bill for one drone this time. Now . . ." She smiled coyly. "Check your chronometer, Tom."

"Why . . ." Tom sat up blearily, then he went still when he saw the time on his internal chronometer. He began flipping from frame to frame of his memory, cross-referencing them with the time stamps, and realized from the moment Heather's ship reached the site of battle, to the moment of his final obliteration, a mere thirty seconds had passed.

Tom gaped at the time in shock.

No wonder. *No wonder* Combatants needed neural processors. There wasn't a human being on Earth who could keep up with that sort of speed.

"Wow," Tom murmured. "We're superhuman. We're actually superhuman."

Heather winked. "Puts it into perspective, right?"

CHAPTER ELEVEN

THE MALFUNCTIONS HAD spread outside the simulation chambers. A few high-ranking generals came for a status update with General Marsh, and the trainees they passed reacted as if to some terrible stench—clutching their hands over their noses and running away. As more trainees reacted to the high-ranking generals the same way, Marsh signaled Blackburn, who isolated the exotic computer virus before it spread through the entire system. Nevertheless, the generals were disgruntled over it, and it became a black eye for General Marsh—and for Blackburn himself, especially when he couldn't find the source of the virus.

Blackburn was in a thunderous mood because of all the chaos. The programs were maliciously playful enough to make him suspect one of the trainees, but according to Wyatt, Blackburn also thought *that* might be a ploy, too, to throw off suspicion from someone else. It wasn't a stretch to guess who had motive to see Blackburn fired. Obsidian Corp. had already put out feelers with the Senate Defense Committee, seeking a return to their old role of software writing at the Pentagonal Spire—citing the recent software issues as evidence it was necessary.

Blackburn began watching Tom more than usual, like he suspected him of having some hand in the breaches. Then again, Tom wondered uneasily if Blackburn had an idea of what he'd been up to. Medusa still hadn't responded to him, so he tried annoying her by returning to the Citadel's systems and planting the Gnomes virus right into her neural processor. Then he headed to Calisthenics. They went through the usual routine for Monday morning, with Blackburn guiding them through marching drills and an exercise where they reached down with exosuited hands and picked objects up, then put them back down.

Tom spent the whole time thinking of Medusa as Vik smashed a cantaloupe between his metal fingers, and Blackburn said, "Congratulations, Ashwan, you set off that bomb. Now you're dust."

Then they got to experiment with metallic instruments that looked like irons for pressing clothes. They were called centrifugal clamps. One flip of a button, and the internal centrifuge activated, adhering the clamp to any nearby surface. Wyatt used them to climb all the way up a wall, then she got stuck, since she was too anxious to climb back down, even with a half-dozen people below her ready to catch her. Tom started climbing up to give her a piggyback ride down, but Blackburn ordered him to the ground. Then *he* started after her. Blackburn reached her side at the top of the wall, spoke quietly to her, and they started down side by side, one clamp at a time.

Tom was the last to stash his exosuit at the end of Calisthenics. Most trainees lowered the hanger, stepped onto it with the exosuit, then climbed out. Tom usually skipped the lowering-the-hanger part and jumped on top of it while it was still high, then took the suit off. Whenever he caught him, Blackburn gave him a weekend of restricted libs and scut work detail—cleaning around the Spire—but Tom did it, anyway.

Just as Tom popped his exosuit off today, a surprising thing happened: one of the suits came to life on its own, and two metal, exoskeletal hands shot down, seized him by the upper arms, and hoisted him up into the air. Tom gasped in shock, legs kicking out wildly, and words flared before his vision.

WHY DO I KEEP SEEING ANGRY GNOMES?

Tom managed a grin where he was dangling, his initial worry about an AI doomsday scenario fading away, replaced by glee that he'd finally gotten his reply. "You're here! It's so great you're here!" he said to the air.

STOP sending gnomes. I mean it!

Tom laughed, giddy. The hand wasn't crushing him, just giving him a scare. "Medusa, meet me online."

I do not want to talk to you. Stop trying to contact me.

"Online. Once. Only once. Hear me out."

No. You don't know what you're doing, Mordred. Stay out of our system. If I see gnomes again, I will come back here and kill you.

"Nah, I don't think so. You might kill me one day, but it won't be over gnomes."

You underestimate how annoying it is seeing them every-where!

"No," Tom said honestly. "I know exactly how annoying it is. But I still believe you won't kill me over it. People kill over money and power and love, but no one kills over gnomes."

I AM NOT JOKING!

"Neither am I. Meet me. Come talk to me, and I'll leave you alone."

The machine drew him up closer, so he was staring into

the empty space where eyes might've been. *You promise me one thing. Swear it to me: you won't interface with the Citadel's systems again. Then I'll come.*

"I swear," Tom said.

The machine released him so abruptly, he tumbled right off the hanger and smacked to the floor. Tom pulled himself to his feet, eyes on the exosuit, but it had gone totally immobile. Medusa had left the system as quickly as she'd come.

TOM'S NEXT FLY-ALONG with Heather was supposed to be an easy mission, a milk run. It was the rare day when Vik, Tom, and Wyatt all had their fly-alongs together. A handful of American Combatants and India-based Combatants were guarding harvesters, those ships that collected hydrocarbons from the atmospheres of gaseous bodies such as the atmospheres of Jupiter's moons.

Heather took advantage of the opportunity to pry into Tom's thoughts.

I'm ninety-nine percent sure Enslow is the one who told Marsh what I was doing. You can tell me if it was. I want to know, she thought to him as they did a slingshot around Europa, one of Jupiter's moons.

Can't you get over it? Tom wondered.

She ruined my career, Heather almost snarled back in his thoughts.

Heather ruined her own career, he couldn't help thinking. *Wyatt just noticed what was happening.* Then he winced at what his thoughts had betrayed.

Heather thought, *Ha! So it was Enslow! I'll destroy her for this.*

No, you won't, Tom thought. *Wyatt may seem like a wimp, but, trust me, you don't wanna mess with her.*

They were both distracted when the harvesters ahead of them stumbled into a Russo-Chinese minefield. The Combatants snapped into action, firing their thrusters to place themselves between the mines and the harvesters. The mines locked onto their vessels and accelerated toward them, so the CamCos veered toward Europa's surface, until gravity tore the mines down to burst against the massive ice layer.

Tom found himself gazing at that moon. Along with the underground of Mars, it was one of these spots in the solar system suspected of harboring microscopic life. Just suspected, though. Since they were both such strategically valuable, resource-rich territories, the Coalition shut down any efforts to actually test the territories for life. After all, it would be way too inconvenient, dealing with massive public protest if somehow the war eradicated the only life found to exist elsewhere in the solar system.

They completed their slingshot around Europa, launching straight toward Jupiter to catch up with the harvesters.

We'll slingshot around Jupiter again to get some momentum for the return trip to the talons, Heather thought.

Right, Tom thought, mind flickering to those magnetized talons there to serve as collection points for spent drones to await refueling and future use.

Then I'll enjoy having a word with Wyatt Enslow, Heather thought viciously.

Wyatt did her job. You were the one who messed up.

I shouldn't get him thinking about this or he'll warn her. Hey, Tom, did you know we're right on course to pass over the Great Red Spot?

Tom was entirely distracted. *Awesome,* he thought. *So awesome.*

He stared, dazzled, through the vessel's electronic eyes as

the massive red spot of Jupiter slipped around the vast curvature of the planet. He gazed at the livid clouds. His neural processor told him the hurricane was three times the size of Earth, and it had raged for hundreds of years.

And then, it happened.

The harvester they were escorting plunged out of their sensor range. Then the other harvesters hurtled toward Jupiter. CamCo vessels began to follow. Tom saw Cadence Grey's ship diving in a suicidal course for Jupiter. Yosef Saide's ship veered after them, then collided with Elliot's ship, blasting them both to pieces.

Wait, Heather thought. *Wait, wait, wait. Something's wrong.*

And suddenly, it was their turn. Their thrusters roared to life and fired, propelling them straight toward Jupiter in a death charge.

Uh, Heather? Tom thought as that swirling red mass of storms grew larger and larger. *You should aim us somewhere else.* The ship began shaking violently as Jupiter's gravity exerted more and more of a pull on them, and he felt Heather trying to fight whatever force it was that had seized control of their navigation.

Through the sensors of their ship, he could see more and more CamCo vessels veering in fatal death plunges, heat shields blasted by the friction with Jupiter's atmosphere.

Oh my God, I'm not in control of the ship, Heather thought. *I think we've been hijacked.*

Tom felt a thrill of excitement and worry.

Their own heat shields lit as they plunged into Jupiter's outer atmosphere, the vessel jolting furiously, pressure mounting on a hull not designed for atmospheric travel. They burned hotter and hotter as they plunged deeper into Jupiter's gaseous mass, gravity accelerating them to a lethal speed.

Soon, gravity began to buckle their hull, and the red clouds on all sides began to tear at them, battering them with vicious, six-hundred-kilometer-per-hour winds. In the fleeting moments before their destruction, Tom focused on the buzzing in his processor and leaped out into the vessel, interfacing with it, momentarily dazzled by the alarms blaring in every system as Jupiter consumed it.

And then, for a microsecond, maybe two, his brain met another person's, a neural processor that wasn't his, that wasn't Heather's, interfacing with their ship and directing its death plunge. Shock suffused Tom. Who was . . .

At that moment, their vessel was obliterated, snapping Tom back into his body in the Pentagonal Spire.

ALL THE TRAINEES were ordered to the cell adjoining the Census Chamber, and one by one, they were escorted in to have their memories of the event extracted.

The guard poked in his head, calling for the next trainee. "Covner, you're up. Martin, you'll be next." Walton rose and followed him from the room.

Tom's stomach was in knots. No one had used the census device on him since Blackburn had interrogated him for treason. The Middles around him chattered away.

"I've never had the census device used on me," Jennifer Nguyen said.

"Oh, it's straightforward," Lyla told her. "You think about something, then the memory uploads. It's sort of cool."

Tom started laughing. He couldn't help it. He ignored the dirty looks the two girls sent him and kept staring at that door, feeling like a mass of nerves. Yes, he knew this wasn't going to be like the last time he'd sat under that metal claw with

Blackburn at the controls. He really did. Intellectually. But the very idea of there being anything cool about the machine that had nearly driven him insane struck him as hilarious.

He forced himself to stop laughing and leaned back against the wall—the wall of the same cell where he'd been confined for two days. It was also the waiting room for those scheduled for memory viewing. His eyes kept straying to the spot he'd punched, over and over, while his mind was fraying.

"Guys, think," Vik proclaimed, a crazy glint in his eyes as everyone swung their attention toward him. He spread his arms. "We became brave new pioneers in human history: we were all brutally Jupitered today."

"Jupitered?" Lyla echoed.

"Killed by Jupiter," Vik explained. "No other warships have crashed into Jupiter before. Ours are the first."

In the corner where she was sitting, back to the wall, Wyatt spoke up, "Elliot and I weren't."

Vik sent her a startled glace. "You guys didn't get destroyed?"

"No, we did get destroyed. Elliot and I were hit by Yosef's ship when *he* started to plunge into Jupiter," Wyatt explained.

"So you *were* Jupitered."

"*Yosef* killed us, not Jupiter."

"So you were Yosef'd—because of Jupiter," Vik said.

"Because of kinetic energy!"

"Kinetic energy directly caused by the gravity of *Jupiter*." Vik clenched his fists before him. "The most diabolical planet of them all."

"That's so stupid, Vik. Jupiter isn't diabolical. It's a gas giant, and we owe it our lives. A lot of asteroids that could cause mass extinction on Earth hit Jupiter instead of us because of Jupiter's gravity."

Vik shook his head. "You forget, Enslow: a lot of asteroids that wouldn't even end up anywhere near Earth get redirected toward Earth by Jupiter's gravity. If human beings never move beyond this planet, odds are, we'll all get wiped out by a meteor someday, perhaps even a meteor that only reaches us because of that gas giant you so eagerly defend. All humanity could be Jupitered one day. That's as diabolical as it gets."

She rolled her eyes. "If you want to talk about future doom, then one day the sun will use up its hydrogen, turn into a red giant, and destroy our planet anyway. Does that mean the sun is evil?"

"We won't get sunned for a few billion years, Evil Wench. We could all get Jupitered tomorrow."

"Stop saying 'Jupitered.' It's not even a word! You made it up."

"Now I'm getting Wyatted," Vik complained to Tom.

"Stop making up *any* words!" Wyatt cried. "It's so annoying!"

Lyla spoke up. "You guys are both annoying."

Wyatt looked hurt, Vik grinned proudly, and Tom started laughing again. He wasn't sure why, but he felt strange, almost giddy, more so every second he waited.

"You, too," Lyla said to him. "You, especially, Raines. Nothing is funny. Stop laughing. We get it. You're freaked out. Boo hoo."

Tom stopped laughing. "I'm not freaked out."

Lyla mimed crying and adopted a whiny voice: "Oh no, I am so, so scared of the census device."

"I am not scared of the census device!"

Lyla smirked. Vik grew indignant on Tom's behalf and pointed at her. "You're wrong, Martin. Dead wrong. The only thing Tom fears is proper table etiquette."

"Yeah," Tom agreed. Then, to Vik, "Hey!"

Vik gave a laugh that sounded like a giggle, and then the door to the cell slid open, and Olivia Ossare strode inside. "Hello, everyone."

Tom felt a terrible spike of unease, Lyla's words still burning in his ears. Oh no. If Olivia tried to check on how he was faring or something, it would kill him. Lyla would laugh and laugh.

Luckily, Olivia didn't single him out. "I heard what happened. Are you all okay?"

Murmurs carried through the room, everyone affirming they were fine. Tom said it very vehemently, hoping she'd get the message.

Her dark eyes found Tom's, and he could tell from something in her face that she might get it, after all. She made no move to draw toward any one of them, merely stood there and began explaining in her soft, firm voice that Lieutenant Blackburn was under orders to consult her regarding any activity with the census device. Not only that, but they *did* have the right to opt out of a memory scan.

"No matter what anyone may tell you, they cannot force this intrusion on you," she concluded, an edge to her voice. "It *is* against the law, and if you tell me you want to opt out, I'll make sure you're allowed to do so."

But no one spoke up. No one wanted to be the pansy who couldn't face the census device like everyone else, least of all Tom. Then the door to the Census Chamber slid open, and Lyla was called inside. Vik was next.

Olivia had brought them some sodas, so Tom took one and sipped it, glad for something to do with his hands. Then it was Vik's turn, and all pretense of levity vanished from the room with him. Tom couldn't take his eyes off the door. He was vaguely aware of Olivia sinking down into the seat next to his.

Then the soldier came for Jennifer, and said, "Raines, you're going after her."

Jennifer left, and Tom's focus narrowed into a tiny window in the center of his vision, his heart thumping harder and harder in his ears. It would be fine. It would be. It would have to be. It wouldn't be like the last time. Blackburn would stop this time. He had to stop this time.

He felt Olivia's hand gently grip his shoulder, and the shock of physical contact was enough to break the frantic spiral of his thoughts. He realized that his hands were shaking where they gripped the aluminum can.

He saw the softness on her face, the understanding in her eyes. Her other hand began stroking his back. It made his stomach clench and his throat grow tight, realizing she knew what he was feeling but didn't see him as some sort of coward. She understood. A constriction loosened around his chest, an incredible weight sliding off his shoulders. Need welled up deep from the core of his being, along with a crushing sense of gratitude that she'd come here, that she was staying.

And then he felt the blare of Wyatt's gaze on them and remembered that she was there, seeing this. Heat stole into his face. What was wrong with him?

"I'm okay," Tom said, edging himself away from Olivia until he hung off the edge of the bench. "I'm good."

"You can opt out," Olivia said softly, her eyes intent. "You don't have to do this."

Tom's gaze skittered over to Wyatt's, then danced away. "Nah." He laughed again. "I'm fine. I'm good."

Despite his words, his instincts were screaming at him when he stepped inside the Census Chamber and found Blackburn facing the screen, the projected light of the census device on his back, casting a dark silhouette against the larger screen. Tom's eyes found the metal claw looming threateningly over the seat, the one he'd been tied to for two days, and he couldn't tear his eyes from those straps hanging from the chair.

"Raines."

Tom jumped. He faced Blackburn in the shadowed chamber, his blood roaring in his ears.

Blackburn considered him for a long moment. Then, "Did you see anything that can't go into an official record?"

Tom blinked.

"Well?"

"Uh, what?"

"All this footage"—Blackburn jabbed his thumb toward the census device—"will be reviewed by external auditors. Not just me. Did you see anything that *you* can't afford to show to anyone other than me?" There was an intensity in his voice, and Tom finally understood what he was asking.

"Uh, yes. Sir. There's something."

"What?" There was a frightening light in Blackburn's eyes.

Tom drew back a step. He looked uneasily up at the census device.

"Raines, I can't use the census device on you if there is something others can't see. That means you need to tell me *with words* what you saw on that fly-along."

Wait. So this meant . . . Wow. This time, his strange ability with machines was actually his defense. Relief crashed over him in a giddy wave.

"Yeah. I saw something. Sort of." The words tumbled out of him; he feared Blackburn's offer might disappear if he didn't tell him everything quickly. "I know there was someone with a neural processor behind it. The processor was controlling the ships remotely. I don't know who it was, or where they were doing it from. I didn't get a chance to look into it, really, before we got crushed. I know that a third neural processor was interfacing with the ship somehow. Not mine. Not Heather's. Someone else's. I felt it."

Blackburn rubbed his big palm over his mouth.

"That's it," Tom said lamely. "Sir."

Blackburn turned his back to him and began gazing at a frozen image on the screen—the view from Snowden and Jennifer's ship as it plummeted into Jupiter. Then he crossed the room to the cell and rapped on the door. Olivia Ossare emerged, hostility prickling in the air as her dark-eyed gaze clashed with Blackburn's. The two of them had been on bad terms ever since Blackburn broke into her office with his men to seize Tom.

"You're right." Blackburn's gaze skirted over her briefly before flicking away. "It's too soon, and the kid's anxious. He's opting out. You win. Now get him out of my sight."

Olivia didn't say a word and brushed past Blackburn, stepping toward Tom. "Would you like to head upstairs with me?"

Tom gazed past her into the cell, its lone occupant Wyatt Enslow, her eyes wide as she took in the scene. He flushed, his relief at his reprieve somewhat dampened by the sheer surge of humiliation he felt, knowing she'd heard all this.

"Yeah," Tom mumbled. "Let's go."

CHAPTER TWELVE

Vɪᴋ ᴛᴏᴏᴋ Tᴏᴍ's mind from the Census Chamber that evening before dinner, when they sneaked into Hannibal Division to await Wyatt's return to her bunk. If Wyatt hadn't been so busy the last few hours, helping around the Pentagonal Spire while Blackburn searched for the cause of the hijacking (and fended off inquiries about his competence at his job), then perhaps she might have noticed what Vik was up to sooner.

But she hadn't noticed, so Vik pulled it off.

Tom made a show of shielding his eyes as they stepped inside, because every surface of Wyatt's bunk was now filled with pictures of Vik: Vik shirtless and flexing his muscles; Vik pointing and winking at a camera; a graphic of Vik flexing one pec, then another very rapidly with a big cheesy grin on his face; a giant marble statue of Vik holding his arms up in the air like some mad dictator. After showing off his handiwork, Vik and Tom leaned against the wall around the bend in the corridor to await her return.

Within minutes, Wyatt strolled into her bunk. A resounding shriek split the air. Tom and Vik collapsed to the floor, convulsing in laughter. They heard rapid footsteps beating toward them. They tore to their feet and dashed out of Hannibal Division, then collapsed in the Middles' common room.

"Wow, did you hear that cry of horror?" Tom marveled. "Good job with the shirtless pics, man."

"You think it was horror?" Vik mused, rubbing his chin. "I thought it sounded like a shriek of delight."

"Sure. We can ask her tonight, buddy."

Vik sighed tragically. "She'll lie. Face it, Tom: Enslow will never admit she finds me enticing."

"IT's NOT TRUE," Wyatt told Yuri urgently later, when they were all hanging out. "I don't find Vik enticing."

"Vik says you do," Tom countered.

Since Tom had stomped Yuri at VR games so many times, Yuri insisted on a game he was better at. That's why tonight, he and Tom were hunched over a chessboard, with Wyatt observing them.

Vik wasn't sitting with them; he was sprawled on the floor of the plebe common room. As soon as they'd driven out the plebes, Vik made a big show of dying of what he called a boredom seizure, with convulsions and gargling sounds and everything, because he thought playing chess was the most boring thing in the world, second only to watching people play chess.

By silent but unanimous compact, Tom, Wyatt, and Yuri had said nothing and pretended they didn't notice the dramatics going on behind them. Vik committed to the theatrics, though. He'd thrashed hard enough to upend a table, and now he was lying mock dead on the floor.

"I mean it. I really don't find Vik enticing," Wyatt said, louder, and the three of them waited for Vik to break character and argue with her.

When he didn't, she raised her eyebrows, reluctantly impressed.

"He's determined," Tom said.

Yuri cleared his throat, and Tom remembered to place his next piece on the board. He ignored the sad *eep* sound Wyatt couldn't help making.

"Check," Yuri said, making his next move.

Tom examined the board, then plucked up his bishop.

"No, Tom!" Wyatt cried. "Don't."

"Wyatt," Tom exclaimed, "you wanna play against Yuri yourself, that's fine, but stop telling me where to move things. He and I are doing this mano a mano, not a womano."

"And no computero," Yuri added.

"Computero?" Wyatt echoed.

"No computero, because Thomas and I have agreed that chess must be played between two human brains," Yuri explained to her gently. "We do not let the neural processors do the work, or it will become two computers playing each other, which will not be rewarding." He took Tom's bishop.

Tom's pawn was stuck, so he moved his knight. Wyatt made a sad *eep* sound again.

"Wyatt!"

"I can't help it, Tom," Wyatt said. "That was a bad move."

Tom focused on the board. No computero. That meant no downloading anything from the Spire's databases about chess strategies and no allowing the neural processor to calculate the merits of every move and the ramifications from there. Since Wyatt's brain was already as close as a human brain would get to a superprocessor, she kept seeing his mistakes as he made them and making that annoying sad noise.

Sure enough, Yuri took Tom's knight with his queen.

Wyatt grew very sad and shook her head tragically. "Tom, you lost the game. You don't realize it yet."

Whether she intended it or not, Wyatt was doing a fantastic job of psyching him out. Three moves later, her solemn pronouncement came true.

"Checkmate," Yuri said, moving his rook into position, pleased with himself.

"I saw it coming," Wyatt said. "And that's without using my neural processor. No computero. Just braino. My braino."

"You have a magnificent braino," Yuri murmured. Wyatt beamed at him, and Tom suddenly felt like he was spying on a private moment.

"Are you guys done?" Vik launched himself up from the floor. "Oh, thank God. Let's go do something else. I'm so bored right now, I feel like I'm in Connecticut."

Wyatt leaped to her feet. "Vik, no! I thought you'd stopped using that."

"Why? It's great. All I need is you in earshot and a word with negative connotation, and there, I've got a Connecticut joke."

She sputtered for a comeback, then threw a pillow at him. It bounced off his head, and he made a show of staggering back. "Ow, that hurts! It hurts like being in Connecticut!"

Wyatt began chasing him in earnest, but Vik snatched a cushion from the couch and shielded himself with it. One thrust of the cushion nearly sent Wyatt sailing back to the ground. Yuri surged upright, and declared, "This will not end well for Vikram."

"VIK, RUN!" Tom bellowed.

Yuri launched himself into the fray. Vik shrieked in fear

and bolted into Alexander Division, the massive Russian boy barreling after him.

Tom was doubled over laughing after the door slid shut behind them, and Wyatt muffled her giggles, too. Then she started smoothing her hair. Her gaze strayed over to him. He knew she was going to bring it up now. He knew it.

"Are you okay?" she said. "You seemed weird and kind of strange earlier in the cell."

"Thanks, Wyatt."

"I don't mean in a bad way."

"Just in a weird and strange way, huh? Well, I'm fine." He tossed a chess piece into the box. "I'm A-OK." He looked toward the door where Vik and Yuri had gone, half expecting them to pop back and hear this. When they didn't, he said urgently, hoping to get this over with, "I was okay earlier, too. Ms. Ossare was overreacting, okay, and I didn't wanna tell her I didn't need her there or anything. I mean, you know how no one really goes to her. I think that gets to her, right? So, yeah, that's what that was about. And, sure, maybe it was a bit unsettling, being back there, but that's because I know Blackburn would tear my mind apart in a second if he could."

"He'd never choose to do that." She frowned at him. "You're being a bit paranoid."

"I'm not paranoid!" Tom burst out. "Blackburn's paranoid. He's the paranoid schizophrenic."

"Not anymore. He controls all the symptoms. If he's paranoid, it's his regular personality."

"I still think you shouldn't have forgiven him for acting that way to you." Tom clenched his fist around a chess piece. "I won't forget what he did. Not ever. He would've done it, you know. He would've driven me insane. I would be crazy now, if it had been up to him."

"He had to. He thought you committed treason."

"He didn't have to." He opened his aching fist, and saw that the chess piece he'd been gripping had left red marks in his palm. "Just forget I said anything. You don't wanna believe me, that's up to you. Do me one favor."

He waited until she dragged her gaze back over to meet his.

"Don't ever talk about me around him, Wyatt. Not ever. If he asks you anything about me, don't answer him. I don't care how harmless the question seems. Don't tell him anything."

Wyatt stared at him a long moment. Then: "It's not exactly like we sit around talking about you all the time. Not everything's about you."

"I know that." And he did know it. Intellectually, at least. He knew he was all self-centered and arrogant here, but he couldn't help thinking sometimes . . . well, ever since that first day he met Heather, really, that a great many things—perhaps a disproportionate number of things—tended to become about him. Maybe he *was* a bit paranoid.

"Blackburn has never even brought you up to me," she assured him. "Except once when we were joking about writing table etiquette subroutines, and of course, you came up. Oh, and when I told him a trainee had gotten banned from all the companies and he said, 'Let me guess. Tom Raines.' That was it."

Tom tossed in a last chess piece with a sigh, and changed the subject. "So, think Yuri's murdered Vik yet?"

She smiled wickedly. "No, I think he's making him suffer."

And then the door to the plebe common room slid open. Tom's gaze jolted up. It was Heather Akron.

This was trouble. He'd given Wyatt away over the thought interface and Heather had threatened her.

Heather's smile grew voracious like a hungry predator's at the sight of Wyatt. "Enslow!" she exclaimed, voice dripping with sweet poison. "How great to find you in here. I really want to talk with you."

Wyatt threw an uncertain glance toward the door to Alexander Division, where Yuri and Vik had gone. Heather slinked across the room to loom right in front of Wyatt. Her eyes raked her up and down, and she said, "I hear you've been spreading some nasty slander about me."

Tom kicked the chess box under the table and reared to his feet. "Heather, hold off. That stuff I was thinking—"

"This isn't your business right now, Tom," Heather told him, never taking her sharp gaze from Wyatt's. "Wyatt and I are chatting."

Wyatt raised her chin a bit. "No, I didn't do that."

Heather cocked her head, propping her hands on her hips. "What's that? Are you saying *you* didn't spread slander about me?"

Louder, Wyatt said, "No. I didn't. After all, slander's *not true*."

Heather drew a step closer to her. Seeing two girls in a passion of anger, ready to tangle, made Tom strangely exultant and filled him with excited anticipation, but he knew he had to step in. He shoved an arm in front of both of them.

"Hey, cut this out, both of you—"

"This isn't about you, Tom!" Wyatt snapped this time.

"Yes, mind your own business," Heather hissed.

Intimidated, Tom backed off.

Heather's amber eyes were glittering. "I've never really liked you, Enslow, but I haven't had a problem with you. No reason to make your life miserable . . . until now. I really don't appreciate being stabbed in the back, so I'm not going to do that to you."

"Why am I the lone exception?" Wyatt said blandly.

"I'm here to warn you that you made the wrong enemy.

You're on my radar now, Enslow, and whatever you might think, I have a lot of influence in CamCo, more every single day. I can make sure you never become a Combatant. Not only that, but I will make your life seriously suck around here."

Wyatt's face had gone very blank, her gaze stony. "Glad we had this talk," Heather said, and whirled around, dark hair swishing as she pranced back toward the elevator.

Tom needed to fix this. He started after Heather, not sure what he'd say but hopeful he could come up with something.

Wyatt caught his arm before he reached Heather. "Where are you going?"

"I'll talk to her for you."

"Why?"

"She's threatening you, I'll threaten her. Somehow." Tom shrugged. "I'll figure it out."

"No," Wyatt said, irritated. "I want to threaten my own enemies."

Tom looked her over and detected the same resolve in her face he'd only seen a few times—but he'd learned to fear it. "Okay. But threaten fast, she's gonna be out of here, soon."

Wyatt turned to her forearm keyboard, quickly typing something in, launching a program. The elevator door slid open, but Heather jerked to a halt before she stepped through. For a moment, she stood there in the doorway, her back rigid, then she whirled around and blazed back over to them.

"What did you do?" she demanded, getting back in Wyatt's face.

"Oops," Wyatt said, glancing at her keyboard. "Was that your firewall I knocked down? I think it was."

Heather gaped at her. It took her a moment to recover and shoot back, "No need to worry, I have a secondary firewall I can put in its place."

She jabbed at her forearm keyboard. Then, as Heather

restored her firewall, a tiny smile crossed Wyatt's lips, and her fingers danced over her forearm keyboard again—and executed another program.

"Hey!" Heather cried, her palm flying up to her head, as though to shield her processor with her hand.

"Whoops, did something disable your secondary firewall, too?" Wyatt said innocently. "I don't know how that keeps happening." She pressed a finger to her lips like she had to think about it a moment. "Oh, wait, I do. It's me. I'm doing it."

Heather opened and closed her mouth, then sputtered, "Is there some convoluted little point you're trying to make?"

Wyatt shrugged. "Just that I can't help noticing I can disable most any defense you erect around your processor, and it's incredibly easy for me. I mean, that took me mere seconds, both times, and you probably worked on those firewalls for *months*. Now that I think about it, if you don't have a firewall protecting your neural processor, I could probably do anything to you. With that consideration in mind, you'd be wise to write a stronger program to defend yourself before trying to 'make my life seriously suck.' At least, if you're still stupid enough to try it."

"Are you threatening me?" Heather whispered.

"No," Wyatt said flatly. "I'm stating the obvious."

Heather hovered there, fists clenched, frustration on her face. Then she seemed to make a decision. She batted at Wyatt's shoulder playfully. "Oh, come on, Enslow, you're taking this way too seriously."

It was Wyatt's turn to stare.

"You know I was teasing you. It's what CamCos do to Middles. Some friendly *hazing*. I know you were doing your job reporting me, and honestly, it was very dumb of me to get tricked by those reporters into running my mouth about the other CamCos in the first place. I still feel so foolish over it. Good for you, for catching it!"

Wyatt opened and closed her mouth, utterly perplexed.

"I have to go. You're a rock star, girl!" Heather winked at her, then headed across the room and disappeared into the elevator.

Wyatt burst out, "What happened? I don't understand! We were having a standoff, then she acted like I was the one who started threatening stuff, like I was the one overreacting." She turned to Tom urgently, her brows furrowed. "I wasn't making a big deal out of nothing, was I?"

"That was Heather saving face," Tom explained. "You won, she lost, and she couldn't admit it."

"Really?"

"Really." He hoisted one of the fallen couch cushions and tossed it back into place, then slung the fallen pillow after it. "You can officially threaten your own enemies. Man, you kind of scare me right now."

"I do?" she said happily. "Oh, can you tell Vik that? Tell him I was menacing. And that I said I was coming for him next, just so he gets scared."

"I'll even say you shook your fist as you said it," Tom promised, which thrilled Wyatt no end.

Then Vik and Yuri emerged from Alexander Division, both out of breath, Yuri's wavy hair all askew like a big nest around his head, and Vik soaking wet like he'd been dunked in a pool.

"Don't ask," Vik grumbled to Tom, slouching onto the couch, leaving giant, wet splotches on the old green fabric.

Yuri gave a dazed smile as Wyatt walked over of her own initiative and awkwardly put her arms around him, like she wasn't quite sure how the hugging thing worked. "Thank you for avenging my honor."

"It was my pleasure." He kissed the top of her head, then explained, "I chased Vikram for many floors, and he used a computer virus on me, but then I used one on him, so we both agreed to remove the viruses, and I pursued him into the Calisthenics Arena. He activated an exercise simulation. I was forced to battle my way through a hundred Vietcong soldiers, but I imagined coming to you and telling you of my victory, and that inspired me to persevere. At last, I caught up to him hiding near a swamp. The result is before you."

Vik grumbled something. He'd been dunked in one of the shallow pools in the arena.

"He has promised to never again make a Connecticut joke," Yuri told her.

Vik gave a weary nod. "I don't have a relentless Russian android on my side, I've just got Tom."

"No, you don't have Tom. I'm not taking on Yuri," Tom protested.

Yuri chuckled, slinging an arm around Wyatt. Vik shook his head, disgruntled.

Tom found himself watching them, his friends, and for some reason the glow of the moment took on a dark tinge. There was no rational reason for it, and maybe it came from his deep suspicion that nothing good could really last—but he had this unsettling sense like this was his last glimpse of something priceless, cupped in his hand, just before it slipped from his grasp.

CHAPTER THIRTEEN

When Blackburn deemed them all competent with exosuits, he finished their training with the same celebratory climb he always led Middles on—straight up the Pentagonal Spire to the roof over the fifteenth floor.

"No messing around, am I clear?" For some reason, he was staring directly at Tom and Vik, even though there were five other newly certified, exosuit-competent Middles. "You start screwing around up there, and you are walking back down the stairs. One of you goes splat, then someone gets stuck with a whole lot of paperwork. Know who that person will be? Me. That's why you are going to suit up, pair up, and above all, *be careful.*"

Tom and Vik stayed side by side, and Wyatt kept turning to people, who then paired with other people, and looking increasingly dejected over it. Blackburn produced a bunch of climbing harnesses and tossed one at each pair.

"The idea here is that if one of you loses your grip—which

you should not—the other one will still have it." He tossed another harness, and paused by Tom and Vik. "Oh, no, no. You two are not going together."

"Huh?" Tom said.

"Huh?" Vik said.

"Ashwan, climb with Enslow."

Vik turned to Wyatt, eyebrows raised. "What do you know. We're together. Now my life depends on you, and your life? It depends on me." He waggled his eyebrows.

Wyatt began to look frightened.

Tom automatically cast his gaze toward Kelcy Demos, hoping Blackburn would break up other pairs so he could claim the curly-haired girl as his partner. Then he felt something hook into the frame of his suit. He glanced back—and his stomach plummeted.

"No way," he protested. He did *not* want to be harnessed to Lieutenant Blackburn. "No. Sir, come on."

"This isn't up for debate," Blackburn told him, tugging on the harness connecting them to test its strength.

"But I'm the best exosuiter here. I don't need to get harnessed *to the instructor.*"

"Your capability," he said, speaking slowly as though fighting to remain patient, "is not what I question. Your judgment is."

"I have fantastic judgment."

"You have horrendous judgment. Of all the trainees here, you're the likeliest to severely overestimate yourself and do something reckless and phenomenally stupid. That's why you're with me. You've proven yourself unable to realistically gauge your capabilities, so I have to gauge them for you. It's that, or you don't climb."

Tom bristled.

"Well?"

"*Fine.* Sir."

Getting harnessed to Blackburn for the climb killed it for him. They all donned optical camouflage, attaching the fiber-optic material to specific hooks in their exosuits, and hid themselves from the view of any civilians gazing toward the Pentagonal Spire. They also used the iron-shaped centrifugal clamps to hoist themselves up the side of the building.

The cold wind couldn't penetrate the optical camouflage, and the exosuit replaced the need for actual exertion, so Tom found himself bored for most of the climb—especially with his pace hobbled by Blackburn, who insisted on staying below the slowest pair of trainees, Jennifer and Mervyn, to keep an eye on them.

Tom knew the minute Wyatt and Vik reached the top, because they net-sent a triumphant *VICTORY!* to his vision center.

Disgruntled, Tom tore off the climbing harness as soon as he alighted on the top of the Spire with Blackburn. He looked around for the telltale ripple of air that indicated someone in an exosuit was moving in the area, and his eyes even traced the outline of separate forms. He clanged his way toward the forms his neural processor identified as Vik and Wyatt, who were on the other side of the massive transmission pole that jutted up from the roof and pierced the clouds above them. He craned his head, squinting up into the sky to see it. The entire building was a transmitter, and this was the very tip.

"How was the climb?" Vik's voice drifted to him from the rippling air where their hidden forms lurked. "Enslow and I actually made great time. I think I was being too enticing for her to handle." He jumped when the shimmering outline of an arm aimed a blow at him. "No good-natured punching with superhuman strength!"

"Oh. Right," Wyatt remembered.

Tom didn't share Vik's good mood. "Blackburn kept jerking me to a stop because I was climbing too fast for him. Like a dog or something. I'm telling you, man, it's like having a leash."

Wyatt went to talk to Blackburn, leaving Tom and Vik to gaze upward, the very tip of the transmitter disappearing into the bright sky.

"You know, climbing the building was one thing," Vik said, "but climbing this? That's the real climb."

Tom's heart picked up a beat as he contemplated it. It would be a marvelous feat. "I bet I could do it."

Vik laughed. "No way."

Tom's neural processor rapidly flitted over the schematics in his head, calculating the point where it was simply too narrow to climb farther. "Fifty bucks says I can get within ten meters of the top."

"You're on, Doctor," Vik said, and they tried to shake hands, but Vik's exosuited hand just clanged against Tom's wrist.

This was in the bag. Tom leaped up in one great bound, flipping on the clamps so they instantly sealed to the pole. No problem. He'd be up and back before anyone was the wiser. . . .

But he didn't get another arm's length up before a hand closed around the back of his exosuit and tore him down. Tom's exosuit clanged against another behind him. He looked back, and his stomach sank as his neural processor identified Blackburn's IP address.

"See, Raines, when I said you'd do something reckless and phenomenally stupid?" Blackburn's voice said right in his ear. "*This* is the sort of thing I was talking about."

"I wasn't climbing it," Tom lied quickly. "I was smashing

this huge spider and the clamp accidentally turned on and stuck me to the pole."

Blackburn dragged him across the roof and shoved him down, by the door leading to the fifteenth floor. "You stay here. Sit. Don't move." There was a sort of dark fury in his voice.

Tom wasn't pleased about sitting. It wasn't dignified. He shoved himself up, but Blackburn's heavy hand anchored on top of his head and manhandled him back down. "I said don't move!"

Tom clenched his jaw and stayed on the ground.

"Thatta boy," Blackburn said. "I'm going to talk to Ashwan. You—stay here by yourself, don't talk to anyone, and ponder how *stupid* that was. Think of it as a time-out."

"Time-out?" Tom blurted. "What am I, five?"

Blackburn laughed unpleasantly. "Color me astounded that you are even vaguely familiar with that term, Raines. But if I can't pound some sense through your thick skull by treating you like the other trainees, then maybe I should try treating you like an undisciplined young child, which is exactly the way you're acting. Would that work?"

"No!" Tom protested. "I'm fifteen."

"Then prove to me you have the attention span of a fifteen-year-old and sit there."

Simmering, Tom stayed there, until Blackburn seemed satisfied and his footsteps clanged away. But then Tom got to thinking, and he realized what must be going on: Blackburn was probably coming down hard on Vik. Maybe Vik had thought of some great excuse already? Tom knew he had to corroborate whatever story it was, so he eased himself to his feet and moved as quietly as he could back toward them, determined to hear what Vik said. He settled around the curve of the base of the pole, ears straining to pick out their conversation.

He caught Blackburn's words. ". . . really think this is a good idea, Ashwan?"

"No, sir."

"Oh, but it sounded like you did. After all, you were root- ing him on, so show me what a brilliant idea this is. Climb the pole."

Vik was silent a moment. "Sir?"

"I said climb it."

Tom felt incredulous. That was *not* fair. Vik got to climb it? He leaned forward, and saw the wavering air in Vik's location. Vik obviously wasn't climbing.

"Let me guess: it looks awfully high now, doesn't it, Ash- wan? Let's say you climbed it. This thing"—there was a waver of air, and then a ringing of exosuited knuckles clapping on the pole—"sends transmissions to vessels in the neutral zone around Earth. One communication with a ship while you're climbing this, and the signal will short out the centrifugal clamps and maybe send a good old shock straight through all this metal into your neural processor. Tell me, still sound like a good idea?"

Vik sounded astonished. "No, sir."

"No, it isn't. Odds are, nothing's going to get sent in the time it would take you to pull it off—and even less likely, in the time it would take Raines . . . but what if something did get transmitted? Then I'll tell you what would happen: the person up there falls to this roof or maybe to that one down there, and that's it, Ashwan. They're a pancake. How much did you bet over this? I didn't make out the number."

"Uh, fifty dollars, sir."

"Your friend's life for fifty dollars."

"I didn't know. I wouldn't have done it if I'd known."

"Here's the thing about you, Ashwan." And Tom could see

one shimmering form draw back as the other moved closer. "I've got this hunch you have a decent brain. I think there's a voice of reason somewhere in that skull, and I'd be willing to make a bet of my own: that you suspected there was some sort of risk here. That must've made it all the more exciting, getting some vicarious thrill out of a friend doing something phenom-enally dangerous that you are too smart to do yourself."

Tom felt a surge of outrage, and it was all he could do not to tear forward and tell Blackburn he was wrong about Vik. Vik must've felt angry, too, because he protested, "It's not like that at all, sir."

"Uh-huh. Do you know how many times I've seen this same thing with you two? Back in the war games, I remember Raines raring to pounce, ready to give me a problem whether I outranked him or not. Let's face it, that kid screws up over and over and over again, I'm surprised when he doesn't at this point. But *you*? You don't. You snapped to attention and said 'sir, yes, sir' to me like an obedient little drone, because that's what you're supposed to do, and you know it. You don't step a toe out of line, and I know why: because someone, at some point, taught you better than that."

"But it's not like . . . You're wrong. Sir, you're wrong. That's my best friend. I wouldn't set him up."

Tom hung back, feeling strange. He had this sense it would embarrass Vik a lot knowing he'd heard all this.

"Then God save Tom Raines from his well-wishers," Black-burn said. "You have to know you aren't doing him any favors."

Tom returned to the spot where Blackburn had left him. He was still sitting there when Blackburn set up a few lines, giv-ing the trainees a chance to rappel down the side of the Spire if they preferred to try that rather than exosuiting. Blackburn belayed Makis, Kelcy, and Vik down, but the rest preferred to climb down the same way they'd climbed up—clamp by clamp. Blackburn gathered up the climbing equipment, shoved it in a bag, then dumped it into Tom's arms and popped open the door. "Walk down the stairs, and wait for me on the second-story flight of the stairwell. I'll come as soon as the others are done."

"I can't climb down?"

Blackburn tore off the hood of his optical camouflage, giving Tom a glimpse of his face. "Get this through your head, Raines: this activity was a privilege, not a right. Actions have consequences. You messed around, you abused that privilege, so that means you're out."

"Fine. Whatever. It's not like I care."

Blackburn gave him a knowing look. "Oh yes, you do."

Tom stepped into the stairwell, and knocked the door closed with his boot. Dimness enveloped him as the door clanged shut. Fine. So he wouldn't climb down. It didn't matter; he still had the exosuit, and that was the awesome part. He tore off the last of the optical camouflage, leaned over to peer down the railing, and didn't see anyone, so with a little thrill of excitement, Tom flipped forward down one flight of stairs, landing at the bottom with a clang. He did the same thing with the next flight, taking a ferocious pleasure at getting away with this.

He would've flipped down the next flight of stairs if he hadn't heard a door swing open below him and footsteps move rapidly up toward him. Tom checked himself and stepped lightly, careful not to let the metal clank against the steps.

That's how Yuri ran into him on the stairwell. A light sheen of sweat coated the larger boy's face. The plebes were already at lunch while the Middles finished up Calisthenics, but obviously Yuri was taking advantage of the hour for an extra jog up the stairs.

"Thomas," Yuri said, surprise in his voice.

For a moment, Tom halted, wondering if Yuri, as a plebe, could even see his exosuit. But Yuri didn't react at all, so Tom figured it had to be censored from his neural processor.

"Are you not supposed to be in Calisthenics?" Yuri asked him.

Middles weren't supposed to share particulars about exosuits with plebes. They hadn't "earned the privilege." Tom tried to think of a lie.

Yuri guessed what the answer was. "Ah, I understand." His face seemed to shutter closed. "It is not for my ears. Would you like assistance with the bag?"

"Nah, I can handle it." Even without the exosuit, this was no problem. He hoisted it up on his shoulder and took care with his steps, trying to stop them from clanging their way down the stairs. As they started talking about lunch, about the upcoming break, Tom couldn't help the way his thoughts turned back to the conversation he'd overheard between Blackburn and Vik.

God save Tom Raines from his well-wishers. You're not doing him any favors.

His gut contracted. He honestly hadn't thought people saw him as a screwup here. Sure, people like Karl and Dalton and Blackburn saw him as some insolent, mouthy little punk who deserved a beat down, but he hadn't realized everyone expected him to ruin his greatest chance to make something of himself. The worst thing was, he didn't know how to fix it anymore. His mind turned back to General Marsh, ordering him to fix things with the CEOs. As if he could walk up to them on the street and make amends.

Even if he could walk up to those CEOs somewhere, he knew he couldn't fix things. He couldn't do what Marsh expected him to do. Maybe Vik knew it, too. That's why Vik had congratulated him and cheered him on. . . . It was just his friend keeping him from dwelling on the way he'd ruined it all.

The realization staggered Tom. He stopped in his tracks, and Yuri thumped down several steps more before noticing he'd stopped. He peered back at him. "Thomas?"

Tom gazed at his friend, realizing he'd been doing the same thing to Yuri. They all had. They'd avoided mentioning this, talking about it, helping him avoid reality. They hadn't been doing him a favor.

"Yuri, man, what are you still doing here at the Spire?" Tom blurted. "You have to know they're not gonna promote you. You're not going anywhere."

If he was startled, he didn't show it. Yuri gazed up at him in the half-light.

"You know that, right?" Tom pressed.

Yuri dropped his gaze to the railing. "Yes."

"Why are you wasting your time like this? I love this place, too, and I know you're into Wyatt. I get why you wanna stay, but, Yuri, man, you're gonna become that guy who's hanging around his high school when he's twenty. You shouldn't be him. You're not some loser. Your glory days are the ones still ahead of you."

Yuri sighed. "You are telling me nothing I have not thought myself."

"Then what is it? What are you doing?"

Yuri licked his lips, then raised his eyes, a determined glint in them. "You will think of this as very foolish, but I am always having this great feeling of certainty I must stay—a certainty it is *necessary* that I am here, as though there is some purpose I would be neglecting if I left."

"What purpose?"

He shrugged his large shoulders. "I cannot say. 'Purpose'

is the only way I can describe this sense as though I have a task here. Even so much as a contemplation of departure gives me great unease. I feel it, such wrongness, such a certainty that leaving would be a grave error. And when I try to reason it out, this wrong feeling gets worse—as though some terrible weight is pressing in on my temples." He gestured vaguely to his head. "And I am aware this must seem quite crazy to you."

Tom leaned back against the wall. "No. No, man. It's not crazy. Hey, come on, I know how it is. Like, I know where I'd have been without this place. There was nothing before." He didn't talk about this stuff, not even with Vik, and even now Tom had to drop his voice to a near whisper. "Literally, just . . . nothing. I don't know where I'd have gone if I hadn't been recruited. I probably would've ended up, I dunno, in prison or something." He shrugged off the thought. "But, Yuri, this doesn't have to be make or break for *you*. You're not like me. You're better. You can do so much, and people like you. People care about you. You could really do something in this world."

Yuri raised his eyes to his. "You are too hard on yourself, Thomas."

Tom was thrown a moment by his words, and he fell silent.

"I hate to interrupt the touching moment." Blackburn's voice floated from the darkness below them as his footsteps scuffed their way up the stairs. Tom and Yuri both jumped, but then Blackburn rounded the turn in the stairs below them, and said very clearly to Yuri, "We are talking about Zorten Two for the next five minutes."

Yuri took his cue immediately, and his face grew cloudy like he was zoning out—just as Blackburn programmed him to do when he heard anything programming related.

Blackburn jabbed his thumb down the stairs. "Stairwell is clear. That means we're going to have a talk."

"Look, the roof—"

"The incident on the roof is exactly what I've come to expect of you, Raines," Blackburn said briskly as they headed down the stairs. "No, I'm here to talk about the neural processor you saw tampering with the drones—the person behind the breaches. I planned to use the climb to talk about this if you'd kept pace with me—*like you were supposed to.*"

Tom darted a glance back up to Yuri, higher on the stairs. He saw that Yuri's eyes had snapped open, a curious, razor-sharp intensity on his face. He wasn't blinking, and as Tom twisted down the stairs, he mentally willed him, *Close your eyes and pretend to zone out. What are you doing, man?*

"I hope you realize, I know you've been trying to talk to someone outside the Spire," Blackburn said, his voice echoing off the walls around them.

Tom stopped in his tracks. "I don't know what you're talking about."

He saw movement out of the corner of his eye as he followed Blackburn down, and he realized with some disbelief that Yuri was quietly moving down the staircase, too, listening to them, just out of Blackburn's line of sight.

What was he doing? Did he *want* to be caught?

"Don't lie to me." Blackburn whirled on him. "You have a friend in the Citadel. It makes me wonder about something: there's no sign of a backdoor into our system, no evidence of external penetration of our server, yet there was a *third* neural processor interfacing with those drones, controlling those drones. If it wasn't a neural processor outside the Spire, it was one inside our system, but if it was inside our system, I'd be able to trace it. I couldn't."

"So? What does that have to do with—"

"It means someone covered his tracks, Raines. He covered

them thoroughly, and he did it within minutes of that assault on the system. There are only three people in the world capable of hiding their digital fingerprints so readily. One is my counterpart at the Sun Tzu Citadel—*external* to the Spire. One is Joseph Vengerov—again, *external* to the Spire. The third is me."

"Maybe it *was* you," Tom flung at him, keeping a careful eye on Yuri, too. "Maybe you have another personality you don't know about. I mean, you were schizo—" His voice cut off when Blackburn abruptly seized him and hauled him around.

"Or maybe someone didn't cover his tracks. Maybe he never left them. Maybe it was even a *friend* of yours who can move through a firewall undetected, purely by some quirk of his or her neural processor. If that was the case, it *could* be someone who entered our system and controlled those drones without leaving a shred of evidence. Just as he's been tampering with my system without leaving evidence." His eyes gleamed. "Is that who you've been contacting, Raines? Is it a ghost in the machine, someone from the Citadel who can penetrate my firewalls at will?"

No. Medusa wouldn't do something like this. Not the breaches, not the sabotage of the drones. "I don't think so."

"I could get fired over this," Blackburn said softly. "Obsidian Corp. is already leaping on the chance to lobby the Defense Committee for my removal. You'd be glad to see the last of me."

"Yeah," Tom said honestly. He really would be. "But that doesn't mean I'm lying about this. I think you're looking at the wrong suspect." Then, giving into a spiteful impulse, he added, "*Again.*"

Blackburn released him, but flattened a palm against the wall right in Tom's path when he tried to ease by him. "You tell your friend something for me. Ghost in the machine or no, I *can* and I *will* retaliate against the person behind this." With that ominous statement, he lifted his arm and finally allowed Tom to slip past him down the stairwell.

Tom walked down and kept walking until he heard a door swish open and closed. When he was sure Blackburn was gone, he halted in place, and waited for the telltale thump of boot steps as Yuri made his way down to him.

He'd heard every word. Every single word.

Tom dragged his gaze up to his friend. He didn't know how to explain this to Yuri. There were so many things he'd kept from his friends. Might as well find out how much damage control he had to do first. "Uh . . . you heard that, man?"

Yuri stopped a flight above him. "Heard what, Thomas?"

"What we were saying. Me. Blackburn. Just now."

His brow furrowed. "I looked down to see if you were okay, but I was not hearing your words."

"But you were . . ." Tom faltered.

He'd *thought* Yuri was listening. Yuri had been keeping pace with them, following them down the stairwell. He *seemed* like he was listening. He had to have heard—he'd been close enough, hadn't he?

Tom shoved his hands into his pockets. "Um, good. Because there was nothing worth hearing. Nothing important." Then he launched into an elaborate story about Blackburn being mad at him for messing around in Calisthenics. Since Vik could corroborate, it seemed the safest bet.

Still.

It was odd Yuri hadn't heard, but at least it saved Tom the trouble of thinking up an explanation, and at the end of the day, that's what mattered most.

CHAPTER FOURTEEN

As WINTER BREAK approached, Tom and Vik grew very sad, because it was unlikely they'd end up in the same Applied Scrimmages group in January. They'd had a great time ever since Tom and Snowden achieved a certain peace by keeping their distance from each other. Snowden mostly stayed out of the sims; and when he did make his appearances, it was well away from Tom. In that way, they grew to tolerate each other, and Vik and Tom were free to wreak havoc.

And wreak havoc they had.

They'd served in Attila the Hun's army and massacred Mason's group, playing the Romans. They were the Romans and massacred Cadence's group, playing the Carthaginians. They'd fought Ralph's group in the Persian Gulf, and they were lions who tore apart Emefa's hyenas. They'd been space aliens and destroyed Britt Schmeiser's old Soviet army, and played peasants battling a Mongol invasion led by Karl Marsters. Tom had died because of parachute failure; by drowning; gunfire;

and various stabbing, burning, and biting wounds. He'd been ritually sacrificed by Heather and her Incan warriors, and he'd gotten beheaded by Yosef and his fellow samurai. He'd racked up the highest kill-to-death ratio of all the Middles, and he'd even killed Karl three times, which Tom maintained grew more fun each time he did it.

If he hadn't systematically alienated every single Coalition CEO, he would've stood a chance of getting promoted. As it was, Wyatt was the only one of them moving up the ranks, finishing Middle Company in six months.

Their last hurrah under Snowden found them in the old Western Wyatt Earp vendetta ride scenario. Wyatt Enslow herself was in the enemy group, on the opposite side as the historical figure who shared her name, playing an outlaw called a Cowboy. Ironically, Vik was the one playing Wyatt, as in Wyatt Earp, the old Western lawman. Tom was the gunfighter Doc Holliday, and since he and Vik were working together to hunt down Elliot's cowboys one by one, the inevitable moment came when they faced her at the O.K. Corral.

Wyatt avoided the petty gunfights and headed to a saloon and rigged up a bunch of Molotov cocktails. Her firebombs against members of Tom and Vik's posse had destroyed the scenario's promise of so many wonderful gun duels. She'd killed most of their group, too, and shown everyone that she wasn't getting promoted only because of her programming skills. Her dislike of fighting had paradoxically turned her into a lethal killing machine.

Tom and Vik were wary about an open confrontation. The guns were wildly inaccurate, and the bullets were primitive. They had to strike once, and strike carefully.

Luckily, Wyatt had one weakness: Giuseppe was on her side.

He was lounging right in the open on a chair in front of the saloon, boots idly kicked up on the railing of the porch. Wyatt clutched her pistol and peeped out every few seconds from behind a shattered window, while Giuseppe discussed how much his boots chafed. Tom had tied himself underneath a wagon for the slow, rattling sneak attack, and he could glimpse them from where he was hanging. He tugged out the knot holding him to the bottom of the wagon, trusting his arm strength to keep him up until it was time to drop down and pull off his ambush.

"I'm getting a terrible blister on my heel," Giuseppe said. "Why did someone have to program real blisters into the simulation? It seems petty to me. I want to write a complaint to someone. I don't think I should have to put up with—"

Wyatt grew tired of it. She raised her pistol and shot him in the back of the head.

Tom couldn't help it. He busted up laughing so hard, his grip loosened and he dropped prematurely from under the wagon, his gun knocked out of his holster. He rolled out quickly to dodge the wheels about to run over him and the shots Wyatt fired his way.

"That was AWESOME!" he yelled over his shoulder as he escaped her.

"He's so annoying!" Wyatt yelled back, then sent a Molotov cocktail sailing past Tom's shoulder. It ignited the wooden postmaster's office beyond him, which unfortunately flushed Vik out of his hiding place with a startled shriek. A few dozen simulated townsfolk began running around frantically, trying to put out the fire.

Wyatt and Vik shot furiously at each other for several seconds, then they ran out of bullets. Black smoke curled up from the guns, and it cleared to reveal the fact that no bullets had connected with flesh. Since Wyatt was also out of Molotov cocktails, and Tom's gun had slid off somewhere when he'd fallen from the wagon, they found themselves standing there in the middle of Tombstone, dust and smoke swirling around them, the post office burning behind them, sort of looking awkwardly at each other.

"Now what?" Tom asked. "None of the townsfolk have guns. They're banned in town."

"I suppose we can go the fistfight route. Maybe." Vik swiped off his cowboy hat, then wiped his forehead, his character's voluminous mustache flapping in the wind.

Wyatt began scratching at her own mustache. "I don't like having facial hair. I keep getting crumbs in my beard."

Tom leaned in to see, and discovered that Wyatt, indeed, had crumbs in her beard.

"I have a proposal." Vik raised a finger. "I believe we should call this duel a draw and pretend we never had this battle. We part ways, then if we run into each other again, we resume our shoot-out."

It sounded reasonable to Tom. Wyatt nodded, too, busy picking at her beard.

"Next time, there will be blood," Vik promised cheerfully, aiming a finger gun at her.

Wyatt aimed a real gun back. "Death and mayhem will certainly ensue."

They parted ways. Tom and Vik rode out of town together. Desert stretched out around them.

"You gonna find Lyla?" Tom asked. Vik had been trying to seek her out in sims a lot lately and impress her with his fighting skills. So far it hadn't worked.

"Yeah, I think so."

Tom squinted at him in the sunlight. "This might've been

our last fight together, man."

Vik flashed a grin. "Until CamCo, you mean."

Tom smiled, too, but he said, "Come on."

Vik's grin slipped.

"You don't need to pretend." Tom shrugged. "Unless some freak accident obliterates every executive in the Coalition, I'm pretty much done for. We both know it."

Vik said nothing for a long moment. "You know, Tom, when we climbed that roof, I would've climbed that transmission pole. If you hadn't, and if Blackburn hadn't been there to see us or anything, I would've done it."

"Yeah. I know, man." Tom reached out, and they clasped arms. "See ya."

"Bye, Doc."

And then Vik set off toward Mexico, and Tom launched his horse off into the vast, scorched desert in search of the most ferocious of the Cowboys, Johnny Ringo, played by Elliot.

Tom hadn't tried to avoid killing Elliot in the sims, mostly because Tom wasn't that merciful, but he hadn't gone out of his way to hunt Elliot down. There was something about the knowledge that Elliot had been trying to help him that chastened him a bit.

This time, though, Tom felt compelled. Elliot's character was the best gunfighter on the enemy side.

It took him a full six hours, sim time, to finally locate Elliot, and Tom's character had tuberculosis, which really forced him to rest more than he cared to. He located Elliot taking shelter in a bar with two of his trainees, Grover Stapleton and Art Mackey. Tom flushed them out by lighting the barn on fire. Grover was the first to dash through the door. Tom yanked Grover's gun right out of his holster and then shot him with it. It jammed when Art tore out of the barn next, so Tom snared him around the neck with a lasso, then whapped into motion a horse tied to the other end. It dragged him off across the landscape.

And then Elliot charged out into the rippling heat, and they faced each other down.

"I've been expecting you," Elliot said simply.

Were this was anyone else, Tom would probably be on guard, since those were the type of words spoken by supervillains to warn of a devastating ambush. In Elliot's case, it was simply an observation.

"I'm here," Tom said, reloading his pistol. "Let's do this the honest way. A proper duel."

They began circling each other, boots kicking up dust, the hot Arizona sun beating on their shoulders. "I heard something about you this morning," Elliot remarked.

"How bad is it this time?"

"I'm hoping it's true. Obsidian Corp. wants a meet and greet in January. Apparently, Joseph Vengerov contacted General Marsh this morning and specifically named you as a trainee he'd like to see."

Tom paused for a split second, before he remembered himself and resumed circling backward. "Oh. Great."

"I thought you'd already alienated Joseph Vengerov? It sounds like he's willing to give you a second chance."

"What does it matter? Most trainees don't want to go to Obsidian Corp.'s meet and greet, anyway. Vengerov doesn't sponsor Combatants."

Elliot considered him. "Tom, I know I said I was done with this, but I'd still like to give you some advice."

That surprised Tom. "Uh, sure. Hit me."

"Try to win Joseph Vengerov over." Elliot pulled off his hat and wiped his sleeve over his forehead. "I know his stance on sponsoring Combatants. Obsidian Corp.'s clients are all governments or fellow corporations, so they really don't need Combatants for public relations, but maybe something changed his mind. If that's the case, it won't hurt to put in some face time. And if you can at least get one of these people to put in a good word for you, you'll stand a better chance of redeeming yourself with the others. . . . I'm getting dizzy circling you."

"Let's do this thing."

They both drew their guns. Tom's shot rang out first, its impact hurling Elliot to the ground. He launched himself forward, and delivered another bullet right between Elliot's eyes.

"Thanks for the advice," he told Elliot's corpse. And he meant it.

He whirled around, squinting into the bright sunlight, trying to calculate how many members of Elliot's group were still alive. His horse returned, still dragging Art Mackey, now unconscious, and Tom shot him before getting ready to ride off. Then a bullet smacked the dirt at his feet, startling the animal into bolting.

Tom raised his gun at the figure moving toward him in the shimmering heat. A woman. His neural processor flicked rapidly through character profiles, trying to ID her character and role in the sim.

Finally, it registered: *Annie Oakley, a legendary female sharpshooter.*

She did not belong in this sim.

Could it be . . . ?

Tom's heart clattered in his chest. His hands grew sweaty, and he became oddly embarrassed about all the blood he'd hacked up onto his sleeve, even if his real lungs weren't the ones bleeding. He moved toward her, and Annie Oakley's silhouette closed the distance, until they were close enough to make out each other's squinting eyes beneath the wide-brimmed hats.

"This is a far more discreet entrance into the system than hijacking a drone, wouldn't you say, *Thomas Raines*?"

Tom gave a start. She knew his name? How did she know his name?

A fierce smile crossed the lips of Medusa's avatar. "I was in your system already, so I looked at your personnel file."

"See, that's not fair. You made me swear to stay out of your system, so I don't get to check for yours."

"I know. It's so unfair for you."

It was. He felt almost like she knew so much about him, but he knew nothing of her. If he just had her name, it would make a huge difference. "Come on, you could tell me your name."

"Why would I do that?"

"Because if you don't, Medusa, I'm gonna have to guess. You may not like my guesses."

"Every single word can basically be used as a name in China. It would be virtually impossible for you to guess, so feel free."

"Fine." He holstered his gun. "Is your name 'Rong'?"

She stopped short. "What?"

"'Rong.' Is it 'Rong'?"

"Why 'Rong'?"

"I met a 'Rong' once. It was the name that popped into my head. Obviously, I guessed wrong."

She stood there a minute. "That was a terrible pun."

Tom laughed. "Yeah, I know. This is what I mean by 'you don't want me guessing.'"

"I think we need a gun battle now."

"Oh, yes," Tom murmured.

They began circling each other in the swirling dust, and

Tom found himself remembering Capitol Summit vividly. Remembered her face, her burned skin, and what he'd done— the way he'd thrown that at her to win. He was a scumbag. He knew it.

"So before I kill you," Medusa said, "I'm going to give you a chance to explain why you were so persistent in trying to contact me. Then I'm going to explain to you why you are never going to do that again."

Tom didn't like the sound of that. "Do it, then. You go first, then I'll go."

She nodded. "After you faced treason charges for being in contact with me, someone on your side leaked back to my side that we'd been meeting. *My* military found out I was communicating with an American. I was questioned, too."

Tom grew rigid. "How did they find out?"

She brushed off the question dismissively. "I'm sure someone on our side paid off a senator on your side."

Tom felt a flash of irritation. He should've guessed. His dad was right—congressmen should just pledge their allegiance to their bank accounts and cut the lip service to country.

Suddenly, he grew cold. "What did they do to you?"

"It doesn't matter," she said harshly. "It's over. The military's started monitoring me. Everything I do, everywhere I go, every time I hook in. So you see now why your repeated visits into our system are making my life difficult."

"Yeah." Tom felt numb. "I see."

"And there's more." She drew closer to him, a dark silhouette against the setting sun. "I laced our server with datamining programs that let me know whenever there are digital communications about me. I discovered a communiqué between members of my military and executives at LM Lymer Fleet. Apparently, LM Lymer Fleet has them keeping a close eye on me. There was no explanation about why, but it makes me suspect they've noticed that there's something unusual about me."

The hot Arizona day felt like it had grown cold around him. LM Lymer Fleet was the maker of the Russo-Chinese neural processors, and basically their version of Obsidian Corp. In fact, before he defected, Joseph Vengerov even headed the company. If they had a particular interest in Medusa, it couldn't be for any good reason.

"You think they're on to you?" Tom said quietly. "What you can do?"

"It's possible."

"What will happen to you if they learn what we can do?"

"Nothing good, Mordred. They'll try to find out how we can do it. They'll want to isolate whatever it was about us that's different and use it in other Combatants—and they'll do whatever they have to do to accomplish that. That's why I'm trying to lie low. Whenever you try to contact me, you put me at risk." She drew closer. "You said you had a question. Ask me now. Then no more gnomes and no more visits. There's too much danger right now."

Tom pulled his hat off his head and mopped at his sweaty forehead. His reason for endangering her now sounded stupid, self-serving. He felt like a scumbag even saying it. "I wanted to ask you how you got into space without a sponsor."

"That's it?"

He tried to tell whether he was imagining it, or whether she really sounded hurt. "And I missed you," he added. He realized it was true as he said it. "I did. I miss fighting you and . . . I know what I did at Capitol Summit sucked, but I want to—"

"To shoot me?" She drew her gun. Her dark silhouette blocked the sun from his eyes.

Tom realized she wasn't comfortable with anything too personal. Not anymore. He had to take the out she was offering. "Yeah. That's great, too."

Tom wished there was some way he could erase the past and return things to the way they'd been. That was the thing about real life. Video games could be reset. There were second chances. There was no way to walk through the same scenario in a different manner when it came to Medusa.

"To answer your question," Medusa said, fingers hovering centimeters from her holstered gun, "I don't have a sponsor for a reason that's very obvious."

"Because of your . . ." Tom faltered.

"My good looks?" She bared her teeth. "I chose the call sign Medusa. No one forced it on me."

"Yeah, I figured."

"I never told you that."

"I know you," Tom said. "I've seen you in action. You'd never let someone stick that name on you or have that power over you. Every weak point becomes another weapon for you. That's why being low and underhanded was the only way to beat you in a fight."

She slowed a moment, and he sensed that he might've said something she liked. Her tone grew softer. "There's no secret to circumventing the Coalition, Mordred. The companies all chip in for me because I win territory for them. 'Medusa' will go public one day—but she'll be some other girl with some other face, and when she does, Harbinger Incorporated will be *her* sponsor, not mine. I'll be invisible."

Tom stopped. So that was it. That was the end. The realization was like a fist socking him in the stomach, driving the air from him. His last hope, the last shred he'd been clinging to, and now it was gone.

He was never going to be a CamCo. The realization made him laugh.

"What's funny?"

"Nothing," he said lightly, jerking back into motion. "I'm an idiot. That's all. I think I've destroyed all my chances here."

It was her turn to smile and shake her head. "You said that last time, too. I don't believe it."

"You don't know what I've done."

"No, but I know you. You're too stubborn to lose. You always come back."

It was strange, but her words were exactly what he needed to hear. Happiness swept through him at the utter confidence in her tone. He drew his gun, but Medusa had drawn hers a bit earlier, more than making up for the speed of his character. Their guns blasted at the same time.

Her bullet thunked into his torso as his glanced off her shoulder, and Tom flew back across the sandy, scorched ground, registering a short flash of pain that receded immediately, according to the simulation's pain settings. But Medusa's rapid footsteps scuffed across the ground, and with a savage yell, she careened into him as he tried to rise, knocking them both over, sending dirt scorching into Tom's lungs. He was stronger than her, heavier, and he lashed out with his arm to pin her beneath him. They stared at each other from inches away. But she was tense against him, and while she was there, a captive audience, Tom groped for something to say to make up for Capitol Summit.

"Hey, you saw how I look. I'm no prize, either," he admitted.

Medusa's face grew shadowed.

Oh. Oh, no. Wait. Had he hurt her feelings?

"I didn't mean that as—" he began, but her gun slammed

into his nose, knocking him to the side, and when he raised his head, he found her gun cocked, pressed right to the tender flesh under his chin, a challenging smile on her lips.

"What, you didn't see that coming? You're losing your edge."

He laughed, his chest swelling with a sense of rightness. "I should've known that was a ploy." He reached forward to cup her cheek with his rough palm, but stopped short when he realized he'd been about to touch her face right *there* where it was scarred in real life. He saw the uncertainty flicker over her face, her finger wavering on the trigger.

"I missed you," Tom said, honest. "Medusa, I mean it. Your face and stuff—it doesn't matter to me. Not really. I was surprised. And desperate. I had to win and . . ." Then, inspiration struck. "You know what? This doesn't matter, Medusa. It doesn't. We're on opposite sides of the world. Get it? The way we look is a nonissue for us. We're never going to see each other in person. We can look however we want!"

But the words didn't have the effect he'd anticipated. The barrel of her gun dug into his chin, forcing his head back, until she rose up before him like some phoenix.

"That's great. Then if you're so unlucky you see me in person, I can wear a bag over my head."

That wasn't what he'd meant to say, but Medusa didn't give him another chance. Her pistol exploded, and he careened back into his body in the training room, and away from her.

IN THAT MANNER, Tom missed the end of the simulation.

Vik and Lyla had relentlessly hunted Wyatt and the other survivors in her group, pursuing them down to the Rio Grande. Apparently, Vik and Lyla took down most of Elliot's group—all but Wyatt. During the slaughter, Vik won Lyla over, and they discovered their feelings for each other. Then they had a terrible fight and broke up again, and shortly after that, Wyatt's firebomb took out Lyla.

Having loved and lost, Vik was determined to salvage something from the simulation. After he stumbled into a pit Wyatt had concealed, rigged up with spears jutting from the ground, Vik mustered his strength. Despite being grievously impaled, now girlfriendless, and on the verge of death, he readied his gun. Wyatt peered down to check whether he was dead, and Vik fired off a single bullet—right into her head.

Avenging his former girlfriend left Vik feeling rather triumphant. Tom had a great time mocking him as they walked back from the pool where they'd ceremonially dunked Wyatt to celebrate her promotion. "You only dated for twelve minutes. That's not a real girlfriend, Vik."

"You can't talk. You've never even met your ex-girlfriend," Vik pointed out.

"Yeah, but at least our thing was longer than *twelve minutes*."

Vik shoved him. "It was a full day, simulation time, Gormless One."

Tom just kept laughing. "But it was *twelve minutes* real time. Twelve minutes, Vik. Ten plus two. You take longer showers than your entire relationship."

"Die slowly, Tom."

Wyatt walked alongside them back to the Spire, shivering and completely soaked. She was utterly silent.

"Are you well?" Yuri asked her. Wyatt nodded shortly.

"Hey, you know we threw you in the water to congratulate you, right?" Tom said.

"Yes, we thought it would be amusing," Vik said. "And to be fair, it was. For us."

Wyatt dragged her gaze over to them. "I was thinking about something. I'll be in Upper Company, and you guys won't."

"Face rubbing," Vik said.

But it wasn't. "I'm not in Programming with you because I work with Blackburn. And now I won't be in anything else with you."

"For six months," Vik said. "Unless somehow you make CamCo right away, but even you, Enslow, cannot charm a bunch of sponsors in so short a time."

Even you . . . Tom stifled a laugh at the thought of Wyatt schmoozing.

"But what if you never get promoted to Upper Company?" Wyatt said, troubled. "What if none of you do? Then I'll never see you guys ever."

"Wow, Enslow, your confidence in us is overwhelming," Vik said, but Tom registered the possibility grimly.

People only moved to Upper Company if they legitimately had a shot at CamCo. If they had at least mild interest from a few possible sponsors. He didn't. He wouldn't.

"Look, Evil Wench," Vik said, "we didn't get promoted right away, but there's no saying it's permanent for us."

"Except when it comes to me," Tom said with forced lightness.

"And me," Yuri added softly, and they all lapsed into a grim silence.

Wyatt was the first trainee since Heather Akron to get bumped to Upper after a mere six months in Middle Company. From the scattering of mutterings he heard about "Blackburn's pet" and the brief glimpse Tom caught of Heather's face during the promotions announcements in Programming—like she'd swallowed a mouthful of acid—he knew a few people weren't pleased about it at all. Then again, Heather resented

Wyatt in general ever since the firewall debacle. Wyatt found a tracking cookie in her processor, spying on all her network activity. It had been cleverly added to the general homework feed and then programmed to self-delete from every processor but Wyatt's. Heather denied responsibility with a huge smile, but none of them believed her. She obviously was still trying to make Wyatt's life "seriously suck." Wyatt's advancement in rank had to burn her.

As they all gathered in the Lafayette Room for the promotion ceremony, Vik alternately looked pleased and envious. Tom didn't have room for much envy. He was too down.

Tom got to witness something interesting, though. Wyatt walked onto the stage when her name was called, and she didn't even look at Blackburn as he handed her the neural chip with her upgrades. She blew right past him to Cromwell and to shake hands with General Marsh. Blackburn raised his eyebrows, obviously picking up on the same thing Tom had—Wyatt was not pleased with Blackburn for some reason.

But Tom didn't wonder about that for long. He found himself meeting General Marsh's eyes, and had to drop his gaze, aware that he hadn't met the general's expectations. He hadn't found a way to redeem himself. All that confidence Marsh had in him was misplaced. There was this pervasive sense of bleakness that settled inside him like a swamp. He wondered if Yuri was feeling the same way, seeing the possibilities he probably would never have.

CHAPTER FIFTEEN

EVERY BREAK FROM the Pentagonal Spire, the military flew Tom back and forth to wherever his dad was. That way, Tom avoided a lot of the restrictions that would've accompanied traveling through an airport while on the terror watch list. He also got a ride straight to the Old Indian Chief Casino, where he plopped down in the restaurant to await his father.

Neil showed up soon, gave him a gruff hug, then launched into a story about some cheating incident at his last poker game: ". . . turns out this chump had some guy with binoculars, and this microphone right in his ear . . ."

That's when a woman in a suit headed over to them at a rapid clip. "Excuse me, gentlemen."

The "gentlemen" thing was why Tom and Neil both assumed she was talking to someone else. When she stopped at their table, they straightened up uneasily, because respectable-looking people charging up to them never ended well.

The woman gave them both a big smile. "I take it you two are the Raines party?"

Tom looked at his dad sharply, wondering what he'd done to get in trouble. Neil's brow furrowed. He seemed to be thinking hard, too, trying to remember what he'd done as well.

Neil set his half-eaten burger down and wiped his hand with his napkin. "Who's asking?" He sounded calm, but Tom could pick up the undercurrent of tension in his voice.

"I take it you're *Neil* Raines?" she clarified.

Neil shifted in his seat and cast a look around. The woman was alone. No cops or burly henchmen were there as backup, ready to haul him off. Finally, his cautious eyes moved back to her. He folded his arms and jerked his head once. "Yeah, lady, you've got the right person. Again, who wants to know?"

She set a small plastic token on the table before them. "Compliments of a friend. He's staked you ten thousand dollars up in the Green Room."

Neil took the chip like he didn't know what it was.

"Please enjoy yourself." And with that, she left them to it.

Tom gazed at the chip, his burger forgotten. He wiped his hands off on his shirt, then snatched it himself. He studied it, then handed it to Neil, who held it between two fingers like it might explode.

"Man, you *have* been on a winning streak," Tom marveled. Neil only got staked for a game when someone thought he could win for them—and get a cut in the process.

Neil shook his head, eyes on the chip. "Winning some, losing some. Trust me, the people who'd stake me ten K are still ancient history."

A dark possibility flashed through Tom's brain. People didn't hand out this sort of money. Something nasty had to lie behind it. He leaned closer to Neil. "Hey, you're not going to this Green Room place, are you?" Tom assumed it was a nicer gaming parlor on one of the upper floors of the casino. "What if it's some sort of trap? You still owe some guys money. Alex Cassano, Dad."

Neil's gaze flashed up to his. "You remember that?"

Tom shrugged. Ever since the census device, yeah, he remembered a lot of things he'd blocked out from his childhood. He definitely remembered Cassano's guys busting in their hotel room and beating Neil up.

"You know, I pay my legit debts, Tommy. Al Cassano set an interest rate, and I was paying it back with the agreed-upon interest rate—"

"You don't have to tell me."

"Then he jacked it up! And jacked it up again! I'd have paid my debt five times over if it had been up to that guy, and I still would've been in debt. If I wanted that nonsense, I'd have used a credit card, not gone to a loan shark."

Tom grew exasperated. "Credit card companies don't send people to beat you up. Mobsters do."

"Yeah, because mobsters don't have politicians writing laws for them. Mobsters don't have prisons and a police force and the entire government in their back pockets. Look what happened to old Al Cassano. I heard he got three months in the can for tax evasion, then he got hired out to work in India somewhere. No one's heard a word since. The state disappeared him. They can do that to any of us. Thank you, National Defense Authorization Act!" Neil saluted the air sarcastically. "I'd deal with a mobster over a corporate kleptocrat any day."

Tom's head throbbed. Some things hadn't changed. "Okay, fine. What are you gonna do?"

Neil examined the chip in his hand. There was an excited glint in his eyes. "There's really only one way to find out who sent this. You coming with?"

"You need someone to aim for the back of the head if it goes wrong?"

"I've got a smart boy," Neil said fondly, ruffling his hair.

It was a terrible plan. It was a Raines plan.

NEIL NEEDED TO show his chip to the bellman, and they were escorted to a private floor of the casino. Inside, they both got retina scans, and Tom began to relax. There were no signs of an ambush.

There were people dressed up all around them, and some waitresses wearing so little Tom actually stopped in his tracks without realizing it when one of them leaned over.

Then Neil lightly cuffed the back of his head. "No ogling until you can afford child support."

He'd spoken loudly enough for her to hear. She giggled.

Tom grew red. "Dad, come on."

But Neil was chuckling like he was delighted with himself as he threaded forward through the crowd. And then the mob of people parted to reveal the tall, elegant figure of Joseph Vengerov. Tom's footsteps ground to a halt, and he gaped at the tall man with pale hair, pale eyes, and an unyielding, angular face—a multitrillion-dollar anomaly who didn't belong even in the fanciest parlor of the Old Indian Chief Casino. He was simply too rich and powerful for this place.

Tom stared at Vengerov, and Vengerov gazed back at him, and Tom knew the blood was draining from his face. One of the wealthiest oligarchs in the world was in the same room as his dad. *His dad*, who had spent every day of Tom's life railing against those in charge of the world.

Neil would lose it when he saw him. He'd attack him. Then he'd get shot by Vengerov's security.

Tom turned, bracing himself to stop Neil from doing

anything rash. Neil spotted Vengerov, too, and stopped in his tracks . . . but he wasn't gazing at Vengerov with malice, like he'd spotted a long-awaited enemy and he was ready to fight. . . . He looked gray, frightened, his eyes shadowed, his mouth hanging open.

"What's wrong with you?" Tom demanded.

Neil's gaze jolted to his. He stared at Tom blankly for a long moment, like he couldn't see him through some nightmare, and Tom had never seen his dad like this. Never.

"Dad?"

But then Vengerov turned and glided over toward them, his security guards clearing his way through the crowd. "Ah, Mr. Raines." Vengerov's gaze flickered down to the chip in Neil's limp hand. "I see you received my invite. Excellent."

Tom looked back and forth between them. "You two know each other?"

Vengerov smiled at Neil.

"No," Neil said, his eyes locked with Vengerov's.

Vengerov's smile spread even wider. "No," he echoed.

"Never met before." Neil's chest swelled, like he was bracing himself for something unpleasant.

"My name is Joseph Vengerov." As though anyone in the world didn't know that. "And I know you must be Neil Raines, Thomas's father."

Neil stiffened. "You know him?"

"Of course I know your son," Vengerov answered, still wearing that strange smile. He let that sit in the air a moment, then, "You must know I'm affiliated with a certain program that your son also participates in."

Neil grew pale. "You're involved in that?"

"Only in an advisory capacity, but I anticipate far more involvement in the near future."

Yeah, Tom bet Vengerov anticipated that. He knew Vengerov was taking advantage of the malfunctions to angle for Blackburn's job.

A dark flush stole over Neil's face.

And the buzzing in the Green Room had become a white noise, because Tom's brain was razor-sharp, trying to slice through what was going on here. Something was happening here. He was missing something.

"I didn't stake you for a poker game, of course," Vengerov said smoothly. "I'm staking you for another venture."

With one angry flick of his hand, Neil sent the chip careening back toward Vengerov. "I want nothing of it."

Vengerov snatched it from the air easily, reflexes like a striking snake's. "I think you do. It's roulette."

Tom's eyes narrowed. Vengerov was playing some game here. But what was he trying to do?

And then Vengerov said, "I appreciate the game for one simple reason." His eyes dropped to Tom's. "It doesn't involve luck. It's all mathematics where the ball will land. A computer with mathematical precision, for example, could calculate what number the ball would land on merely from listening to the spin decelerate."

That's when Tom realized it: he had a neural processor. Vengerov knew it. He knew Tom could calculate the right number.

"Come," Vengerov said, imperious, like Neil was one of his lackeys.

And to Tom's disbelief, even though Neil wore this expression on his face like he was raging inside, *he followed.*

Tom felt like he was in a bizarre, alternate universe as he trailed behind Neil to the roulette table, where gamblers chose their position at the wheel. One spin of the wheel launched the ball into motion, and the players who correctly chose the color of the slot where the ball landed won money, and the ones who chose the right number reaped greater winnings.

"Let's not gamble with that ten thousand I staked you," Vengerov told Neil. "I shall also wager . . . these." A flick of his fingers, and one of his lackeys placed an intimidating pile of chips before him. "Mr. Raines, add a wager of your own to mine. We all need some skin in this game of ours."

"But it's not his game," Tom burst out. "It's *your* game. You arbitrarily decided he's going to play. *You're* the one who wants to play it."

"I am waiting," Vengerov said, eyes crawling to Neil's.

Neil muttered, "I don't have much."

"In that case," Vengerov said softly, "just wager your wallet."

Neil drew a sharp breath, because that was all the money he had.

"Don't do it," Tom urged him.

But Neil had a grim set to his face. He reached in his back pocket and clapped his wallet on the table.

"What are you doing, Dad?" Tom demanded. Then he turned on Vengerov. "He doesn't have money to throw away like you. He at least has a shot at winning poker! This is—"

"A risk we are both taking," Vengerov said.

"It's not a risk for you," Tom spat. "This is chump change for you. My father's the only one risking anything here."

"It will be a staggering defeat for your father if he loses, I agree," Vengerov said. "That's why I trust he won't lose. Neither of us will."

Tom fumed. He knew what he had to do. The wheel began to spin, and as the tinkling sound filled the air, the ball bouncing around the outermost circle of the wheel, Tom's processor began doing what any computer could do: it calculated the deceleration rate. He knew where the ball would land. With a gruff swipe of his hands, Neil shoved the chips onto the wrong color. Tom stood there to let Vengerov sweat a bit, his jaw throbbing from where his teeth were grinding together, as he listened to the deceleration of the wheel. He felt Vengerov's calculating gaze fixed on him.

Then he couldn't resist. "Not there, Dad." He moved the pieces to black twenty-two.

And then the wheel slowed and the ball clattered into its slot: black twenty-two.

Neil gave a start.

"Congratulations," Vengerov said. "Black twenty-two. What a marvelous pick, Mr. Raines. How about a second try?"

"A second?" Neil sputtered. "We can't do better than that."

"I think we could," Vengerov countered, eyes on Tom.

Tom clenched his fists, but he performed as Vengerov expected. They won the second spin, too. This time, Neil stood there silently. Vengerov won a million dollars in a couple of minutes, thanks to Tom.

Neil didn't seem to care that he'd come into more than fifty thousand dollars. He was staring at Tom like he didn't know who he was. Tom stared back, because he felt like he didn't know who Neil was, either. He didn't recognize this meek, cowed person as his dad.

"I think we'd be straining their tolerance if we won a third spin. I'll have your share of the winnings sent by your room." Vengerov idly signaled a worker to count their chips. He glanced between Tom and Neil. "How delightful that we all leave here tonight triumphant. Good evening, Mr. Raines."

Neither of them were certain who he was addressing, but when he strolled away, silence descended between Tom and Neil like the ominous quiet in the eye of a hurricane.

THE TENSION MOUNTED between them the whole walk to their room, until it was like electricity in the air. Tom's stomach was churning. He kept thinking of Neil's reaction to Vengerov.

Neil had acted like that. Neil, who'd bellowed at cops and brawled with them, and even gotten chucked in jail. Who time and again had thrown himself unheeding into situations that messed up both their lives because he never backed down from a fight. . . .

Neil had been cowed by Joseph Vengerov.

Tom couldn't get his head around to it. Neil *hated* men like Vengerov. He hated people like the executives Tom had alienated at the meet and greets. Yet tonight, his dad had been face-to-face with the guy who practically *embodied* the entire police state, the military-industrial-media complex, everything Neil saw as the cancer of the world, and after all that blustering, Neil hadn't spoken up. He hadn't done anything.

Tom didn't understand it. There was this dark, ugly feeling growing inside him. It wasn't rational and it didn't make sense, but he felt like his father had punched him or something. He'd always thought Neil got into trouble because he couldn't help it. But tonight, he'd obeyed Vengerov. He'd controlled himself with Vengerov.

Tom's head was pulsing violently by the time they were shut back in their hotel room. He stood by the door, every muscle bunched up with tension. He felt like he was at a great remove from his dad, who was pouring a drink with a shaky hand, then swigging it down.

"Do you know the odds of winning roulette twice in a row? Do you know them, Tom?"

Tom did. "I sure was lucky." His voice was hollow. He didn't even sound the slightest bit convincing, he knew, but he couldn't muster the energy for anything more.

"Lucky?" Neil slammed down the glass so hard, most of the liquid sloshed over the side. "That's not luck, Tom. Even a kleptocrat as rich as Joseph Vengerov doesn't risk a half million dollars on odds like that! And you were so sure of yourself. He was so sure of *you*. Explain that to me."

"No, you explain this to me: he bossed you around and you took it. Does he have something on you?"

Neil's nostrils flared. He grabbed his drink again, what was left of it.

"Answer me." The words ripped out of Tom, a great ugly torrent of them. "After years and *years* and *years* of driving us from place to place because you hate people like Vengerov so much, you were within feet of him and you didn't say anything! You didn't insult him or punch him in the face. You've never held back before! There has to be a reason. You were different today."

"It wouldn't have been smart. That's the reason."

"It wouldn't have been smart?" Tom echoed. "When has that ever stopped you? Dad, he has something on you. He has to. Just tell me what it is. Come on, tell me. Because otherwise . . ."

"Otherwise, what?" Neil's eyes cut to his.

Tom's fists clenched. "You know, when I was a kid, I had nothing. I had no money, I had nowhere to go, I had no one but you, and you were fine with getting in trouble then. You were fine with getting arrested or getting in fights or yelling your opinion at anyone, no matter what the situation—"

Neil sighed, rubbing his fingers over his saggy eyelids. "Tommy . . ."

"None of *that* was smart, but you did it anyway. So why do consequences matter now? Is whatever Joseph Vengerov might do to you so much worse than that time you got yourself thrown in jail for two months? Huh? You never worried about me, but now something's worrying you? Come on, tell me the truth, Dad!"

Neil didn't answer. He seemed small and old and sad. The ugly, awful feeling in Tom's gut grew worse, until he couldn't stand to look at him.

"I think I'm going back to the Spire. I don't know why I even came here. It's not like we do holidays." Neil would just spend his whole visit drinking, anyway, Tom decided bitterly.

"That's your choice."

Tom jerked toward the closet door to yank out his back-pack. He hadn't taken anything out of it yet, anyway.

"Merry Christmas, happy New Year, all that."

"All that," Neil echoed. He didn't stop Tom from walking out the door.

THE PROBLEM ABOUT a casino in the middle of nowhere, New Mexico, was the lack of taxis in easy driving distance. Tom headed a quarter mile down the road to hitch a ride by the tollbooths demanding an eighty-buck fee, and waited for some-one to drive past.

He was rewarded quickly when a pair of headlights bore down on him.

Then his eyes adjusted as the vehicle came to a halt, and he realized it was a limousine, probably bulletproof, maybe mis-sileproof. A string of security vehicles and automated patrollers pulled over behind it. There was really only one person around here who'd need this much security. Tom backed up a step when he realized it.

The last limo ride he'd taken hadn't ended well for him.

"No way," Tom said flatly.

He turned around to walk away, but the limo followed. A

window rolled down, the wheels rumbling over the gravel next to him, kicking up a thin cloud of dirt that stung his throat.

Fed up, Tom whirled around. "Why," he said viciously, "would I ever get in the car with someone who helped reprogram me?"

Vengerov regarded him over steepled fingers from within the dim limousine. "Because curiosity can be maddening, Mr. Raines."

Tom's sneakers scuffled to a stop. So did the car. Tom stood there in the swirling dust, betrayal a stinging wound in his chest, but, yes, questions were burning through his brain. He was dying to know why Vengerov was here, what he wanted.

He heard the doors unlock. The driver circled around and opened the door.

I am going to get my brain wiped again, some voice beat in his skull as he moved jerkily over. He slouched in the seat across from Joseph Vengerov like he was actually comfortable, like every fiber of muscle in his body wasn't ready to spring, to get him out of there.

"The airport, I presume?" Vengerov said.

"The airport." Tom never took his eyes from him.

And then they were off.

CHAPTER SIXTEEN

For a few minutes, they rode in silence, Joseph Vengerov examining him over steepled fingers, a drink at his elbow that he wasn't touching. Tom had taken a soda from the cooler, but he hadn't ended up drinking it, either.

"It's not very prudent to hitchhike," Vengerov noted.

"Yeah, I could run into some creep in a limo," Tom said before he could stop himself.

Vengerov's pale gaze didn't flicker. He barely seemed to blink. "My, you *are* insolent. If you still had those subroutines I wrote for Dalton Prestwick, you'd be in far better standing with those companies now, rather than blackballed by them."

Heat flushed Tom's cheeks. "I don't care about that."

"I can't say I believe you. You have that lean and hungry look about you. I suspect you're more ambitious than you let on. Otherwise, I wouldn't be wasting my time with you."

Orange streetlights flickered over him again and again until they reached the end of the toll road, and merged on to a cheaper toll road. The limo jounced a few times before the driver shifted the car to pothole mode. The windows displayed an optional infrared mode in the absence of light. Vengerov dismissed it with a single, careless jab of his finger. Nothing to see outside but buildings fallen to disrepair.

"What do you want?" Tom's voice was hard. "I know you didn't come here to use my processor to win a million big ones. What was the point of that thing you did tonight? You were trying to make some point . . . or did you *want* my dad to realize I've got this computer in my brain?"

Vengerov arched his eyebrows, and Tom got the impression he was surprised. "Mr. Raines, I was trying to buy your goodwill."

Tom was caught off guard. He felt confined, despite the spacious cabin of the limo.

"I gifted you with temporary access to a prestigious gambling parlor," Vengerov explained, "and the opportunity to enrich your family. Your father is wealthier today because of me. I thought you'd be pleased. And more open to hearing my proposal."

Vengerov had meant it as a *friendly* gesture?

That threw him. A lot. "What do you want from me?"

"I think you and I can come to an arrangement. I've taken a personal interest in a certain Combatant on the Russo-Chinese side, Mr. Raines. She's a very deadly, remarkably skilled fighter with whom you happen to be personally acquainted."

Tom felt a jolt inside him. *Medusa.*

"You must be aware there are many prominent men and women substantially invested in this war."

"Yeah, I know the Coalition of Multinationals is milking it for all it's worth. So what does that have to do with Medusa?"

"Quite simply, she's very effective. Too effective. It's getting rather inconvenient for those of us with a financial stake in this situation. Some of us are starting to suspect she is threatening the balance of power."

Tom felt a warm rush of admiration for her. He had to fight to keep himself from grinning. Yeah, Medusa was doing some heavy damage single-handedly. "What, you're upset she might actually cause one side to *win*?"

"The wrong side. That's why we need her out of the conflict."

Tom's urge to grin died at once.

"It would be simple," Vengerov said idly, "if someone she trusted lured her to an internet rendezvous . . ."

"No," Tom said at once, seeing where this was going.

". . . and then he deployed an executable program to incapacitate her. That person would be doing quite a service for his country, and he'd be amply rewarded for it."

"Did you hear me? I said no!"

"Surely you don't want your side to lose, Mr. Raines. Have you no patriotism?"

Tom thought it was rich hearing about love of country from a globalist who despised the very idea of countries, but he said, "If this is so strategically important, then someone in the military would've ordered me to do it already. You're a *private* contractor."

"There's a very simple reason I, a private contractor, am the one approaching you." He weighed the glass in his hand for a thoughtful moment, as though figuring out how to dumb down his explanation. "There are certain codes of conduct the two governments have mutually agreed upon. That's why the Russo-Chinese don't hunt you down and kill you one by one."

"Well, yeah. Then our side would do the same thing."

"Precisely. These governments do, however, act unofficially. They have agents, contractors, in each other's countries who would be eager to get their hands on enemy Combatants if possible. Everything like this done outside the official codes must be done *privately*. Take the Geneva Convention: your military is not allowed to torture enemy soldiers. Private contractors—mercenaries—are useful because *we can*. Certain codes can be violated as long as the official state entity isn't doing it. I can violate the Geneva Convention; I can strike directly at Combatants if I choose; and I can engineer Medusa's destruction, whereas your General Marsh cannot."

"But you'd be using me to do it," Tom pointed out. "I'm officially a ward of the military, so that's still the military doing it."

"As far as I understand, you were meeting her outside the military's jurisdiction. As you would do once again. You were acting independently, without orders. You'll do so again, and that's why your strike on her won't violate any treaties. And besides that, what can she do—tell someone you were behind an attack upon her? That would require her confessing to meeting an enemy agent. Again. You see, we already leaked to her government that she'd been liaising with you. She's already on notice. She can't afford to reveal her involvement with you a second time."

Tom leaned his elbows onto his knees, his eyes narrowed. "Why would I do anything for the person who helped Dalton Prestwick reprogram me? And don't give me that 'for my country' thing. You milk countries for everything you can take, but people like you don't give anything back to them."

"Oh, but there's another reason you'll do this, Mr. Raines. As things stand, you most assuredly will not be sponsored. If you did as I asked, I could change your situation."

Tom was startled by the offer. "Obsidian Corp. doesn't sponsor Combatants."

"How could I? You all have my processors. A piece of me. It would be like that classic dilemma, where a parent must select which of his children to shoot. How could I play favorites?"

Tom sputtered a laugh.

Vengerov's voice grew acidic. "Do I amuse you?"

Tom slouched back in his seat. "Yeah. I've never heard that classic dilemma of picking a kid to shoot."

"Gunmen force a parent to choose a child to shoot. I've heard that."

"That's terrible. That's not a classic dilemma. A parent choosing a *favorite* kid is a classic, not choosing to *shoot* one of them."

There was a touch of ice in the long, slow look Vengerov sent him; he seemed to be turning the "shooting children" remark over in his mind, like he'd fit the wrong widget into a socket, and he was trying to figure out the most efficient way to correct this aberration. Then he appeared to brush off the thought, and said, "Regardless of whether we sponsor, I have pull with those who do. A few words from me, and the other companies will think better of you."

"They hate me."

"They're executives, Mr. Raines. They pride themselves on thinking in terms of self-interest and monetary incentive. Emotions, values, and attachments that cloud judgment aren't prized among their set."

"Or a conscience, huh?"

"I'll take dispassionate self-interest over a conscience any day. It's far more predictable. Just as these executives are. If I inform them they are to sponsor you, then I assure you, they will do so—to please me." He tapped his fingers one by one, still considering Tom. "You do realize, I'm not asking you to inflict any permanent damage upon her."

"You're not?" Tom said, caught off guard.

Vengerov shook his head. "Of course not." He withdrew a tablet computer from his pocket. "You may feel free to examine the program yourself."

And with a few taps on his keyboard, he knocked down the firewall Wyatt had written for Tom. Tom jumped, but a zipped file had already appeared in his processor.

"Hey," Tom objected, but text blinked before his eyes: *Please set phrase to trigger deployment.* Irritated, Tom thought about how he wouldn't do this to her. The prompt vanished.

Vengerov had already restored Tom's firewall, and he spoke as though Tom hadn't even objected. "Once you deploy that on her, she'll be incapacitated and experience some difficulty hooking into the vessels in the solar system. She won't die, and she won't be permanently damaged. I consider this more a—" he waved a finger in the air, as though trying to conjure the proper word, and a queer smile appeared on his lips when he seemed to find it "—an *exploration* of the effect her absence will have upon the conflict, nothing more. The real question here is, will you fulfill this reasonable request, or will I have to resort to unpleasant means of persuasion?"

Full of mistrust, Tom crossed his arms tightly. "I won't do anything because you're threatening me."

The words merely amused Vengerov. "Let's be clear, Mr. Raines: I'm attempting to *bribe* you. The threat's an unpleasant necessity if you refuse to accept my generosity."

Tom hadn't realized they were at the airport until Vengerov nodded.

"Your stop."

"I'm not agreeing to anything," Tom insisted.

"Naturally, you need time to consider this. I don't wish to hear an answer from you until you've thoroughly considered the wisest course of action. We'll be meeting again quite soon."

Tom's stomach churned. Right. They had meet and greets again in January. He rose out of the depths of the car, and stood on the sidewalk as Vengerov's limo slid off down the street, that zipped computer virus waiting there in his processor like a coiled viper.

BEING A "KNOWN terrorist" had kind of cramped Tom's movement around Washington, DC. So he spent the rest of the winter break in the Spire, playing video games, trying not to think of his father, trying to think of what to do about Medusa and the virus.

He knew what he *should* do, what was right to do—to dismiss it out of hand and hold firm to his refusal, let the consequences Vengerov had threatened rain down where they would.

But there was this other part of Tom, the same part that had been willing to strike viciously to win Capitol Summit, the part that thirsted for the chance to succeed, to make something of himself, a voice that whispered, *This is the only shot I still have of becoming a Combatant.*

He tried to disregard the thought.

He wasn't alone in the Pentagonal Spire. There were a scattering of trainees, mostly from other countries where the holidays weren't a big deal, or where the flights home would be too burdensome. There was also a skeleton crew of CamCos. Some were the new faces, the newly promoted, anonymous CamCos the public didn't know about like Leslie Whiell of Napoleon Division, Sandy Feinberg of Hannibal Division, Warren Simmons of Alexander Division, and Griffen Perenchio of Genghis Division. Many of the older Combatants like Heather, Karl, Alec, and Emefa were there, too. It was the luck of the draw, whether they were on duty over vacation or not. Sure, both sides had agreed to a truce around the winter holidays, and another truce around Chinese New Year, but the military always had some CamCos around.

Heather surprised everyone with a program she'd written for the people stuck in the Spire on New Year's Eve, and from the way she was ringed by other CamCos whenever Tom saw her, she'd obviously won back their allegiance at last. Tom figured Elliot would be pleased to see it. It was one step closer to Heather's taking his place in the center of CamCo, one step closer to Elliot's freedom.

Heather invited him to hook into the sim, too, and Tom was thrilled to find out it was a big jousting simulation. He headed up to a training room eagerly and materialized in the sim, donned his armor, grabbed a huge lance, and trotted out on a warhorse into the tiltyards beneath a massive castle, excited for the all-out joust ahead—only to find that most of the trainees who'd hooked in weren't even jousting, and most had gotten rid of the period garb. Apparently, the sim was a cover for what they were really doing: having a New Year's Eve party.

This must've helped Heather win them back. The sim even had champagne.

Tom couldn't smell alcohol without thinking of his dad, and he had this bone-deep certainty that even touching a simulated drink would be the worst mistake he could ever make. He parted from the mass of trainees and decided to pick a fight with one of the fake characters. Just for fun.

Heather caught up to him before he made it out of the tiltyard. "Tom, wait!"

He pulled on the reins and slid off the horse so she could catch up to him. She batted his armored chest playfully.

"Where are you going? You can't leave the sim yet. Stay here."

That confused him a bit, since she'd been busy hanging out with Sam Schwab and Bruce Tepper of Napoleon Division and hadn't even spoken to him. "I'm not leaving the sim," Tom said. "I'm looking for someone to fight."

"Oh, how bloodthirsty of you," Heather marveled, but for some reason, his answer seemed to have given her immense pleasure. Her yellow-brown eyes twinkled into his, and she leaned very close. "I'll give you something for the fight. Something simulation appropriate."

She was so close, Tom could feel her breath tickling his cheek, feel the heat radiating from her skin, and for a moment, the wild urge to grab her and pull her in close soared through his brain before his rational, highly distrustful-of-Heather brain reasserted itself.

Heather had produced a small strip of cloth of gold, and now she tied it around the hilt of his lance. "This is a token of my favor, good sir. Whoever he is, destroy him good for me."

There was something so hot about those words, that Tom again had to remind himself that Heather was somewhat poisonous. "I can tell you right now," he replied, "I'm going to bring you back a head."

"Or how about not?"

Tom grinned sheepishly. "No heads coming up." He set out in search of a foe. Soon he ditched the warhorse, ditched the armor, and traded his lance for a sword.

He jumped atop a stone wall and began searching the castle grounds from the high vantage point, seeking a simulated character of sufficient deadliness. That's how he noticed a hidden nook in the yard, where Karl was accosting one of the serving wenches.

Tom felt a dark thrill, spotting him. Yes. Here it was. Forget simulated enemies. Here was what he'd been looking for.

He sauntered over, then settled on a low wall right above them.

"Hiya, Karl," he called loudly, startling Karl into jumping to his feet. "Wow, she is *not* having a good time. I guess even simulated girls don't like you. That's kind of pathetic, man."

Karl shoved the character away and with a flick of his hand, deleted her. Then he turned on Tom, adjusting his garb, his face bright red. "I'll have you know, Old Yeller," he said smugly, chest swelling, "I'm a celebrity now, so—"

"Wow, a celebrity and you *still* have to settle for simulated girls?" Tom interrupted. "That's just sad."

Karl leered at him, a nasty glint in his eyes. "I know what this is about. You're frustrated and hoping to take it out on someone, aren't ya, Benji? I know what's up with you. You blew it. You're never gonna make CamCo now. It's gotta really be sinking in."

It was, but Tom would never admit it. "Nah, I'm here because I like spending time with you, Karl."

"I'll give you what you want." Karl drew his sword, his meaty fist gripping its hilt. "I'll fight you. I'll smash you into the ground."

"Yeah, it's not like you're already oh for three. But, hey, I really respect your prowess on the battlefield . . ." Tom couldn't go on. "Man, I can't even get that out with a straight face."

Karl gave a roar of fury and sprang, slashing viciously at his legs. Tom jumped in time as the blade arced beneath him, flashing with the pale light of the sky. He hurled himself around, delivering a slam of his boot across Karl's face, knocking him to the ground. With an exultant whoop, Tom lunged forward as Karl was rising. Tom crashed the pommel of his sword across Karl's jaw, knocking him back down. Then he dove forward in a roll, evading Karl's massive arms as they groped the air where he'd just been. Tom scurried clear, panting for breath. Karl lumbered to his feet like some great, baited bear. Tom kept him in his sight. Karl was a wrestling champ, and huge, besides. If he got his hands on him, it would be over. Tom didn't intend to let that happen.

Sheer hatred twisted Karl's features as they faced each other down. "You like being a real tough guy in simulations," Karl sneered, "but out there, you're a skinny little punk."

Tom didn't point out that they had the same physical builds in this sim that they did in real life, so it wasn't like he had an advantage here. "No, I like sims because I can actually kill you here."

Karl gave an ugly grin. And then he vanished.

Tom frowned. Wait. He couldn't possibly be wimping out. . . .

And then his eyes snapped open in the training room as Karl's fist slammed into his real, nonsimulated stomach, doubling him over on the cot and driving the breath from him, shooting acid up through his torso.

"Let's see how real life compares," Karl snarled, his fist slamming Tom's ribs over and over as Tom struggled to draw breath. Karl seized his collar and hurled him off the cot, tumbling him to the floor, his head slamming the base of a nearby cot, stars dancing before his eyes—along with some text.

Error: Connection lost. Download paused. 98% complete.

Huh? Air burst into his lungs in a great gush, and Tom's brain was torn between the urgent focus on Karl and the other part of him that registered that text, which was not supposed to be there. What was . . . what the . . .

Karl ducked to get him, and in a split second, Tom's neural processor presented the best move: drive his palm up into Karl's nose, knocking the cartilage back into his brain.

No, he couldn't do that. He'd kill him.

Instead, he slammed his foot into Karl's face, then lanced up and snared his arms around Karl's neck, pivoting all his weight to unbalance him, knock him down. Tom drove a knee into his neck, pinning him there, and raised a fist to slam into Karl's face, but he'd been stupid to count on his weight keeping Karl down—Karl hooked his hands under Tom's legs, and lifted him straight into the air, then threw him with a frightening strength. Tom landed in a heap at the foot of Emefa's cot, then yanked himself upright as Karl advanced again. He backed up, trying to think of some advantage here, then dodged Karl's next swing and shoved him while he was unbalanced, looping his leg around Karl's, sending Karl stumbling against his empty cot. Unthinkingly, Tom seized his stray neural wire and whipped it around Karl's throat. He tightened it, pressing his back against Karl's so his full weight would hang from it as Karl tried to buck him off.

And then he realized he was doing it again: about to kill the guy—here, in real life, where he'd go to prison for it—and why couldn't he think of anything nonlethal? His suddenly slack grip gave Karl the chance to snatch off the wire and seize him. Tom knew it was about to be over, so desperately he slammed his head forward into Karl's as hard as he could and—

Ow. Owwwwww. Tom stumbled back, feeling like a mallet had whacked him between the eyes, his vision reeling. Across from him, Karl was stumbling, too, clutching his large, meaty fists over his nose, blood gushing between his fingers.

"You idiot! Why did you do that?" Karl cried.

"It works in video games," Tom shot back. "Everything else I thought of was gonna kill you."

Karl waved his arm. "That's normal. You gotta relearn how to fight in real life after you get all the downloads about killing people. Beat up some kids, and it comes right back."

Tom started laughing, half hysterical. "Yeah, great idea, except I don't think it'll work for me because I'm not a *total psychopath* who runs around beating up people! Well, other than you!"

For a moment, Tom and Karl glared at each other, cradling head and nose, respectively, and the drive to battle someone receded from Tom. It must've disappeared for Karl, too, because he cursed, shoved his sleeve against his nose, and left, muttering about the infirmary. Tom settled back down on his cot to clutch his aching head, and he remembered something. He took a moment to rewind his memory until he saw that message again, the message he'd only seen because Karl had ripped out his neural wire and woken him up early.

Error: Connection lost. Download paused. 98% complete.

What had been downloaded from his processor? He scanned through his logs, but whoever had done it had concealed whatever it was they were plundering from him. If he'd stayed in the simulation a bit longer, he wouldn't have even realized it had happened.

AT MIDNIGHT, A number of the officers migrated to the fourteenth floor along with the trainees, to gaze through the large, windowed walls at the fireworks that began to splutter through the night to usher in the New Year. Lieutenant Blackburn was among them. Tom rubbed his hand over his sore head, certain he knew who'd been taking stuff from his processor.

Of course it was Blackburn. There was no one else who'd be intensely interested in his neural processor.

Had he done this more than once—plundered Tom's brain during Applied Scrimmages before without his realizing it? He glared at Blackburn's large back, but the lieutenant gazed out the window, talking to no one, not even the other soldiers.

Tom became aware of Heather's fixed gaze. A bit perplexed by the intensity of her eyes, he tipped his can of soda to her.

Heather tipped her glass back to him from where she stood amid the crowd of CamCos, triumph radiating from every plane of her face, flickering with the bright lights.

Tom didn't even think to wonder about it.

CHAPTER SEVENTEEN

THERE WERE SEVERAL reasons most trainees weren't enthused about the meet and greet at Obsidian Corp. during their first week back after the holiday. First and foremost, it was a waste of time, since Obsidian didn't sponsor Combatants. Second, people hated visiting because Blackburn was absolutely paranoid about Joseph Vengerov taking advantage of the visit to mess with their processors. Whenever they returned from Obsidian Corp., they had to be isolated from the Pentagonal Spire's systems and subjected to a five-hour deep scan to check for malware.

It was a great deal of trouble for everyone, and all for very little payoff, but they had to go. Vengerov's tech waged the wars in space. His surveillance systems and automated weapons protected the other Coalition executives. The codes on his voting machines determined which politicians oversaw the war effort. Obsidian Corp. was too much of a giant in the world to be ignored, so if Joseph Vengerov wanted a visit, the trainees had to go.

The first week back at the Spire after everyone returned from break, Wyatt and the other new Uppers were hard to find.

Vik thoughtfully took advantage of Wyatt's absence to invade her new bunk and modify her new bunk template. He copied the old one and expanded upon it, adding more photos. One was an outline of Connecticut with some very sad, black-and-white images of people superimposed over it—depressed adults and crying children who had just realized they lived in Connecticut.

"It's not officially a Connecticut joke, since it's a Connecticut *poster*," he told Tom uncertainly, when Tom reminded him of Wyatt's relentless android.

He also added a couple more pictures of himself: another shirtless picture and one black-and-white, artistic photo of himself posing philosophically by a window, cupping his chin, looking broodingly at the sky in a very un-Vik-like manner that amused Tom immensely.

The day of the winter meet and greets, Tom hung out for a bit in the weight room behind the Calisthenics Arena, spotting Yuri while he bench-pressed almost three times his own weight. All the other Middles were visiting companies that Tom had been banned from. His only appointment was late in the afternoon, a direct shot on the Interstice to Vengerov's facilities in Antarctica. Yuri had not been permitted to attend this round of meetings.

"So, what are you up to?" Tom asked, even though it was obvious.

"Exercising," Yuri said, gazing up at him from under the weight bar.

"Okay, that was a stupid question. Can I ask your advice about something?"

"Of course."

Tom considered how to phrase his question about Medusa, before blurting out the first thing that came to mind. "Girls like you. A lot."

If Yuri was surprised, he didn't show it. He gave a humble shrug. "I believe it is my muscular physique." He sat up and flexed his biceps thoughtfully. "But that is only the surface. The only girl whose regard I care for—"

"Is Wyatt, I know, I know. Okay. I have a question: let's say a girl kind of feels bad about the way she looks and I accidentally insulted her about that. How can I fix it?"

Yuri tugged at his thin white T-shirt, plastered to his skin with sweat. "What did you say to this girl?"

"I kind of pointed out that we only meet online and we're never gonna meet in person, so we can use avatars and I won't even see how she looks. That's why it'll never matter to me if she's ugly."

Yuri twisted around to frown at him. "I hope you did not say such a thing, Thomas. This is no good."

"Not in those exact words, but, uh . . . Come on, you've gotta have some advice. I thought you might know what to say to make her feel better, or how I can apologize. You know, since Wyatt's horseface thing is—"

Yuri half rose from the bench. "Horseface?"

Tom noticed, not for the first time, how much larger Yuri was than him. He raised his hands. "The thing where she *thinks* she has a horseface. I'm not insulting your girlfriend, man."

"Ah. Of course." Yuri settled back down. He rubbed his chin, thoughtful. "Wyatt has indeed expressed to me that she feels troubled over her appearance. It is always an awkward conversation, because if I say, 'You do not have a horseface,' she is believing I am lying. But if I ever were to say, 'Very well,

I concede. You have a horseface,' then I am certain she would also find it upsetting."

"Yeah," Tom said, imagining it. "Just a bit."

"So this is what I do," Yuri went on, leaning closer. "I take her hand and stare into her eyes. Then I say this: 'If you were indeed resembling a horse, then I would see the horse and be thinking it is a very beautiful horse, and I would be feeling alarmed and think there is something very wrong with me that I am finding a horse so very lovely and attractive.'" He concluded with a satisfied nod.

"And that works?" Tom blurted.

"She always is responding the same way: 'That's really weird, Yuri.'" Yuri gave another satisfied nod.

"So it doesn't work."

"Ah, but it does." Yuri raised a finger. "In fact, Thomas, she grows very concerned with how weird it is, and she is no longer thinking of whether she has a horseface." He spread his hands, like he'd performed a magic trick. "Do you see? The problem is solved."

Tom was in awe of him. "You're like some genius diplomat."

Yuri smiled. "This I am."

Suddenly, something occurred to Tom. He rested his elbows on the bar and dropped his voice. "Listen, man, you can't tell anyone I asked you about this girl. Not anyone. Especially not Joseph Vengerov."

For a moment, Yuri's eyes flashed up to his, like he hadn't really been listening and something Tom said had caught his attention.

"Who is this online girl?" Yuri asked. His voice grew very soft, his eyes intent on Tom's. "Is this the online girl you were meeting with before, Tom? Is it Medusa?"

"I'm not full-blown meeting with her again. I've only

talked to her a couple times," Tom said. "Vengerov asked me about her, and I can't really tell you more than that, but he wants me to do something to her that I can't do. So as far as he's concerned, as far as anyone is concerned, I haven't spoken to her since I got charged with treason. Okay?" He raised his eyebrows significantly. I am going to officially inform him that she refuses to see me again."

Yuri's eyes dropped, and all the sharpness disappeared from his face, replaced by a mild sort of confusion.

"Yuri, you can't tell," Tom said, disturbed by the way he hadn't responded.

Yuri blinked. "On my life, Thomas," he said, "I will never tell anyone." He frowned. "I hope you are being wise."

"Come on. It's me, man."

"I know this," Yuri said dubiously, sprawling back on the bench again to resume his bench presses. "And this is what concerns me."

THE DARKENED VACTUBE was slightly ominous when Tom was alone, especially the long ride to Antarctica. Tom was glad to enter the elevator and rise into Obsidian Corp. There, he met the other exhausted Middles who'd been doing meet and greets all day.

It came as a profound shock to Tom when he found Lieutenant Blackburn there, radiating tension.

"All of you will remain in my sight at all times, am I understood?" Blackburn said. His gray eyes roved over them, bitter lines etched on his face in the facility's artificial lights. "Your wireless functions should be nonoperational while you're here. I'm wearing a jamming device." He pulled back his sleeve to expose something that resembled a wristwatch. "If for some reason your wireless comes back online, you're to assume someone is hacking you, and you'll notify me immediately. Now let's go."

He snapped around and led them forward through an automated turnstile that scanned their retinas. Praetorians flanked them as they walked, their metal camera eyes fixed on the passing trainees.

As Tom walked, the undeniable sensation of being watched tickled up his spine. He threw a careless glance over his shoulder.

All the Praetorians had their camera eyes fixed straight on him.

Tom was so jolted by the sight, he almost sprang a foot in the air. The crowd jostled around him, mounting a set of stairs. Weird. Creepy. Tom moved on, darting his own eyes around warily.

There was something distinctly unsettling about Obsidian Corp. All the corridors were dimly lit and very chilly. They passed massive, warehouse-sized rooms with elaborate supercomputers. Those rooms were devoid of people. In fact, there were almost no humans around, not even custodial personnel or mechanics. Just Praetorians and mechanized surveillance cameras. It took Tom a few minutes to pinpoint what was so wrong about the complex, but then he figured it out: the building seemed to have been created for the machines inside it. It was like human beings were unwelcome intruders.

Even the low-level Obsidian Corp. techs who led them on a tour of the facilities seemed nervous and out of place. They joked uneasily about the way Antarctica saved the company billions in air-conditioning. When trainees laughed, the techs blinked.

"That's the truth. It really does save the company billions in air-conditioning. Quantum supercomputers get very hot," one tech said. "We actually have to wear parkas to move through most of the facility."

Then they led the trainees past expansive windows overlooking the icy tundra. The sky was a dull gray. It was the time of year in this part of Antarctica where night never descended, but there was no brightness this day.

In each room, Tom couldn't help darting his eyes to the surveillance cameras and the stationary Praetorians. Tom kept waiting for Vengerov or someone else to approach him about using the virus on Medusa—Vengerov had said he wanted Tom to answer him during this visit. But no one came. He was never summoned or signaled. And the mechanized eyes followed him, always long enough for him to detect their scrutiny, never long enough for anyone else to notice—not even Vik, a foot ahead of him. Tom's skin was crawling.

Vengerov knows somehow, Tom thought. *He knows I'm going to say no.*

Tom pictured Joseph Vengerov's sharp, angular features and pale eyes and those silvery eyebrows that blended into his forehead—lurking on the other side of that surveillance system, just watching him. But how could Vengerov already know his answer? How could he be sure?

Tom hadn't talked to anyone about it except Yuri, but he wasn't even here.

Just to be absolutely certain he wasn't being paranoid, Tom intentionally dropped back to the very edge of the group, so the surveillance devices would have to be very obvious about tracking him.

As their group trickled into the next room, from the corner of his eye, Tom saw a Praetorian moving toward him. He whirled around, startled. The machine was still again.

But then he heard a hiss behind him. Tom whipped around

to find the door between him and the rest of the group closing with a decisive clang.

"Hey!" Tom rushed toward it, his hands meeting cold metal. There was no handle, no doorknob. He tried pushing, he tried pounding his fist on it. There wasn't a single peep from the other side.

Soundproof. Great.

Tom drew a bracing breath and turned. The Praetorians were openly fixing their single, pinpoint camera eyes on him. His skin crawled. The hum of machinery was the only sound in the room, and it was mounting louder and louder on the air. Tom's reflection moved across the polished black floor with him, swam against the massive window revealing the gray sky over the glacial landscape. He finally turned to see the nearest overhead surveillance camera.

"I'm locked out," Tom told whoever was on the other side. "Open the door."

His voice rang out in the empty air and he wondered if anyone even heard him. He willed on his net-send and tried to use a thought interface to alert Vik, but words flashed across his vision center: *Error: Frequency unavailable. Message not sent.*

Blackburn's stupid jammer. Of course.

Then Tom felt a strange prickling sensation move all over his feet. The prickle turned to tiny jabs, which became stabbing needles, an electrical current carrying across the floor. Tom leaped a few steps away from the Praetorians, and got some momentary relief, but the prickle mounted into a stronger electric charge, until his legs were viciously buzzing and Tom was forced to bolt through the other door, away from the very floor that seemed to be trying to electrocute him.

He leaped right into the next open chamber, but the

Praetorians in that room also homed in on him, blocking his path.

They drew so close, he had to squeeze to the side to avoid being crushed; but when he brushed one of the metal Praetorians in passing, a sharp bolt of electricity seared him, and Tom couldn't help the shout that ripped from his lips as he stumbled away from it. He backed up, step by step, and they advanced on him, relentless. For a moment, Tom's thoughts flickered to people in the places used as testing grounds for military tech, where small-scale insurgents were swarmed with these machines. He'd never realized how frightening such unrelenting inhumanity could be.

But there was a human being behind this. There had to be a man behind the curtain controlling the actions of these machines. Tom turned to the nearest surveillance camera, hoping his watcher knew he was talking directly to him when he said, "I am not afraid of you."

In response, a Praetorian whirled toward him. Tom kicked at it, trying to knock it back, but it swung around pendulously, its base still advancing toward him, and a shock jolted up his leg and locked his muscles as he clumsily stumbled back again. He backed away from the others, trying to avoid more shocks, and in that manner, they herded him down a hallway until his back thumped against an icy wall.

Tom pressed against it, nowhere else to go, Praetorians advancing on him. Joseph Vengerov couldn't kill him. He couldn't. Even if he *did* know somehow that Tom was refusing his demand to use a virus on Medusa, he couldn't simply murder him. He was trying to scare him. Tom was sure of it. Vengerov's last words to him rang in his ears: *The real question here is, will you fulfill this reasonable request, or will I have to resort to unpleasant means of persuasion?*

Two metal devices shifted, curving their single, pinpoint camera eyes toward him, aligning them so for a disconcerting moment, Tom felt like he was gazing at some sort of machine man, assessing him through empty metallic eyes.

"Okay," Tom said, "obviously you're not pleased about something."

The camera eyes bobbed up and down, a cold, fatal nod of a head.

And then the wall Tom was leaning back against abruptly swung open, and he realized it wasn't a wall but a door, and it led straight to the outside. He realized this the same instant he crashed onto his back into a bank of icy snow. The door swung closed with a resounding clang, stranding Tom outside, without a coat, on the frozen Antarctica tundra.

CHAPTER EIGHTEEN

FOR A FLEETING moment, Tom lay there, absolute cold soaking into the back of his flimsy suit, and then a gust of tormenting wind battered him and his brain cleared enough to register that he was outside. In a thin suit. And it wasn't freezing cold— it was painfully, agonizingly cold.

Tom bolted to his feet and charged toward the door. His hands slipped over an icy, stinging metal surface with no handles. He had never in his life imagined it was possible to feel this cold. His ears were searing hot pokers stabbing his head, his eardrums throbbed, and the wind felt like thousands of tiny prongs jabbing viciously at him. His skull began spiking with terrible pain. Tom pounded his fist on the door.

"HEY! HEY! YOU CAN'T DO THIS! OPEN UP! OPEN THE DOOR!"

He stumbled back several steps, shaking violently, his teeth chattering, the chill so much more dreadful where his suit had picked up some icy dampness from the ground, and he became aware of a surveillance camera mounted over the door, fixed on him—like Vengerov was waiting for him to get scared enough to beg or plead, to swear to do what he wanted.

No. No way. Not now. He would never do anything Vengerov wanted.

A rush of hot determination flooded Tom, and he very deliberately flipped the camera the bird even as wind stabbed its way into his lungs and tore at his gums. His nose stung, his fingers were pulsing with pain, and his mind raced frantically, looking for something to do to help himself.

Suddenly, he remembered back when he was little with his dad, when they couldn't catch a ride one night in Nevada. The desert, so hot in the day when they were trying to thumb a ride, grew so terribly cold that night and the day's sweat became like ice. Neil had told him to keep moving, because standing still was what killed you.

So Tom jammed his aching hands beneath his armpits and began hopping. He swept his gaze over the blank face of the massive complex that stretched off into the distance. His stinging lids scraped his eyes with every blink, and the wind bit his pupils until tears began flowing to his cheeks, only to freeze on his face like insects nipping him. But there was a window, a low one, and not too far away.

He launched himself into a run, his lungs gashed by the frantic breaths he gasped, and he felt a strange sense like he was in some distorted maze, because the window didn't seem to be closer—it was so much farther than it had looked. He'd slipped on the ice repeatedly before he reached it. He tried shoving up the pane with his rubbery hands, but it wouldn't give, so Tom hurled himself at it, and then kicked viciously over and over, perfectly willing to scrape his leg to break the glass, but it still wouldn't break. His gums were aching, his teeth chattering. He willed on net-send, but the frequency was still jammed, and he grew aware of another camera boring right into him from over the window. He wished he had something to hurl at it. His gaze roved over the ground, and he spotted a rock, half-buried in snow. Tom realized with a spring of glee that he could use *this* to break the camera—no, the window! He knelt to dig it up.

A message blinked across his vision center: *Warning: Low body temperature detected. 95.2° F. Trainee is advised to seek shelter.*

Tom began laughing. He couldn't help it. "I a-am *T-T-TRY-ING!*" he shouted at the message, clumsy fingers scraping over the rock's jagged edges. He couldn't feel the stinging cuts.

Then light flooded the corner of Tom's vision. Tom gaped for a moment, unable to believe it: Vengerov had relented. He'd opened the door again!

Of course. Of course, he couldn't strand Tom out here and let him freeze. It was a game of chicken and Tom had won. Tom sprinted back toward it, but it took even longer now, getting back to where he'd come from. His legs were so clumsy, he tumbled again and again, numbed hands and knees scraping the snow. His limbs were unfeeling blocks by the time he reached the door, and he felt the tantalizing blast of warmth from inside the building—and then the door swung closed again.

"NO!" Tom screamed, hurling himself at it, but it was too late. "N-NO!" He punched it with his unfeeling fists. For a moment, he felt like his chest was going to split open. His throat seemed to be jammed. Then he reeled back with an insane laugh spilling from his lips. The camera was still fixed on him.

"OPEN UP! OPEN THE D-D-DOOR! OPEN IT! I'LL

K-KILL Y-YOU F-F-FOR THIS!"

Some part of his brain warned him that death threats weren't very enticing reasons for anyone to open a door for him, but Tom didn't muse on it for long.

An emergency alarm blared in his vision center. *Warning: Low body temperature detected. 93.3° F. Transmitting emergency beacon.*

Tom's heart soared. Would this work? Would someone get it? And then he screamed in frustration as he read the words: *Frequency unavailable. Emergency beacon not sent. Automatic retry in twenty seconds. Nineteen seconds. Eighteen seconds. . . .*

He stopped clawing his way forward, his eyes stinging as they focused on the distant window. Too distant.

He could die here.

The thought spliced through his head, sharp like a razor. A vivid image of his own body frosted over with snow filled his brain and Tom couldn't banish it from his mind.

Vengerov wasn't messing around. This wasn't a game of chicken. He could really die out here. He grew wild with rage and fear, and whirled back toward the window, knowing it was his best chance. His throat felt numb. When he fell, he clawed his way forward, the wet snow plastering his clothes to his limbs. He sprinted ahead, but before he knew it, he'd plunged back into the snow. Panic tore at him. He wasn't sure what to do. He couldn't focus on anything other than the cold.

So cold, so cold . . . He couldn't fight it now. His body contracted into a shivering ball, but nothing warded off the terrible ice. He felt like he was being erased, everything human and deliberate vanishing from his mind, replaced by some nameless, tormented creature that knew only frost and could understand nothing else, and he became numbed all over, all sense of where he was, what this was, receding from him.

Warning: Critically low body temperature detected. 92.0° F. Transmitting emergency beacon. Frequency unavailable. Emergency beacon not sent. Automatic retry in twenty seconds.

He had to get up. He had to. With strength he didn't feel like he had, he uncurled slowly, even though his legs were so numb, they felt like they weren't even there. Standing took so much effort it was like heaving up a ton of granite. He forced the legs he couldn't feel to move, to jog in place, but it was like moving through a swamp. Everything was dragging, and even his brain was sluggish. He couldn't feel his face.

The window.

The window. That rock could break the window. He had to get there. It was his only chance.

He lifted his legs and set them down, drawing step by step toward the window. Each minute felt like a year. Several times, he found himself on the ground, fighting for air. He saw that the door had popped open again to spill light onto the snow. Just to taunt him. Just to offer safety and slam shut again. He kept going. He wasn't going to fall for it.

Then he reached the window and lowered himself clumsily, pawing at the snow, trying to extract that rock from the frost. But it was too late. His fingers weren't closing. His hands couldn't grip, they couldn't hold. He only knew where they were by looking at them. Horrible fear stabbed him, sharp and acrid, as he realized his body wasn't working anymore.

Tom turned that thought around in his mind, his pulse thready in his ears, because even during the simulated deaths in the training room, it had never sunk in that he could *really die*. That someone like Joseph Vengerov could come along and simply end him. That he could get so cold, his body would actually stop moving for him. That every shred of will he had couldn't force his fists to clench. That his life or death could hinge on something so small as his fingers.

He lurched to the window. His blood beat in his head. A strange, unnatural heat began to well up within him as he planned a kick. One good, hard kick. He could do this. He *had* to do this. It didn't matter now if he broke every bone in his leg. He'd die if he didn't get through that window.

He squinted at the window and swung his foot forward. His other leg buckled, the world flipped before his eyes, and he landed on the ground, hard. Icy snow shot up his nose, and he coughed weakly, his brain blurring. The snow was warm. Hot. Tom realized he was sweltering all over, like someone had lit him up from the inside. He wanted to tear off his tie, shove off his coat, relieve himself of the unbearable heat, but he gave up on it quickly. He tried heaving himself up again, but he couldn't. He just couldn't. And then he began to grow comfortable, like he was sinking into the depths of some exquisite bed.

Some nameless time later, he was on his side. He stayed there, his face nestled in the crook of his arm, still roasting in the Antarctic tundra, his body so unfeeling, it was like he'd become detached from it. Now even his brain was slipping, slipping out of reach, and Tom realized in a detached sort of way that this was the way it would end. A stupid, pointless death at fifteen, out here all alone. But it wasn't so bad. The pain was gone.

A strange glow pervaded him. Heat receded into warmth. Lethargy seeped like syrup through his muscles.

Tom couldn't think of what had been so important about breaking that window. The words were like an afterthought in his vision center, searing into life and then fading: *Warning: Critically low body temperature detected. 87.2° F. Transmitting emergency beacon. Frequency unavailable. Emergency beacon not sent. Automatic retry in twenty seconds.*

Something about the moment felt so right. He was back in the desert at night, at the side of the empty road, his dad snuggling an overlarge coat around him until his teeth stopped chattering. Then Neil hoisted him up for a piggyback ride, and they trudged farther and farther down that empty, dark road, waiting for the next set of lights to appear in the darkness. Tom wasn't even shivering anymore.

He didn't feel the smothering arms sweep him, crush him up against a chest. He opened his eyes dully when he realized it was harder to breathe with his face muffled against a thick coat. He felt entombed in something heavy, and a sense of suffocation made him panic and he flailed as much as he could. A clang echoed through the air, and he squinted through burning eyes to see over a shoulder. The door. Someone had brought him to the other side of the door.

Hands stripped off his soaked shirt, the strangling tie, a voice shouting about a "warming blanket." Other words floated back, and, "We're in the middle of Antarctica and there's no warming blanket in the entire building? How about a bathtub? How far away are the staff quarters, then? No, too far. Give me another parka." Some gruff swearing, and he was hauled back against something solid, a coat snuggled around him.

His brain was a muffled, cloudy thing, and Tom didn't begin to emerge from the mire until the first electric prickles began in his face, in his nose, then spread into his ears, his lips. They grew sharper and sharper. Painful. So painful. He tried to move away from them, but they kept following, searing him. He was squashed in place beneath a smothering coat, heavy arms.

His eyes hurt, and when he squinted down he could see

his hairy legs, quivering like live wires. He couldn't feel them. His hands were gnarled, prickling claws, his fingers white like porcelain, and someone knelt in front of him kneading them. He squeezed his stinging eyes shut.

"No, leave his hands, Ashwan," a voice said from right next to his ear.

"What about frostbite?"

"He can survive losing fingers. He can't survive cardiac arrest if you dilate peripheral blood vessels and shoot cold blood into his chest."

Tom stirred a bit. *Losing fingers?* But his brain couldn't hold on to the thought.

It took him a while to finally peel his eyes open again, and he made out the ashen face, the kid standing near his knee, gazing Tom's way like he didn't recognize him. It took Tom a moment to pull the name up. "V-V-Vi?" His voice came out slurred, his throat like sandpaper, his teeth chattering.

"Hi, Tom," Vik said faintly.

"If you're going to stay here, make yourself useful," rumbled a voice from behind Tom. "Get a wet compress for his eyes."

Vik shuffled off.

Tom's head flopped back against the person holding the coat around him. He was hiked up a bit farther, the grip around him reaffirmed, warmth soaking into his back. The electrical prickle in his toes and ears and nose grew into a torment, and it was spreading everywhere. He tried to say something, but the words didn't come out as words. He had a creeping sense there was something he was supposed to be doing. Wasn't there? He had to do something. He wasn't safe. Something bad had happened. He wasn't sure what, but he started pulling at the heavy weight keeping him here, trying to break away.

"Calm down, Raines."

But he kept struggling against the overpowering bands around him, because he was sure there was something wrong, so he needed to get up, he needed to do something. A mounting sense of urgency gripped him. Fear clutched his throat. He raised his head as far as he could, agitated. He needed . . . He needed . . .

Fingers threaded through his hair and eased his head back, then a palm brushed against his forehead. "You're okay, Tom. Just relax. I've got you. You're safe."

"Dad?"

The hand on his forehead stilled an instant. "No," said Blackburn.

He drifted in and out for a while. He didn't stir again until Blackburn reached down and lifted up his limp arm. Tom squinted, and saw Blackburn's thumb brush over his fingers, where the skin appeared a strange, pale blue. Tom realized after a moment that he'd seen the touch, but he couldn't feel it. He couldn't feel it at all.

"W-what's w-w-wrong w-with m-m-my . . ."

Blackburn tucked his arm back under his coat. "Shh. Just close your eyes."

Tom didn't want to, but he sagged back, shaking all over, his teeth chattering, and his thoughts became blurred, hazy things as the warmth and almost foreign sense of total safety lulled him into darkness.

VOICES ROUSED TOM.

". . . the incorruptible James Blackburn." Vengerov sounded amused. "I'm astonished you left the Pentagonal Spire, what with all the recent security breaches. *Anything* could happen to that system while you're here, in my domain, completely cut off from your own server."

Tom forced his eyelids open, the bright lights of what seemed a small hospital knifing into his eyes. His blurry vision focused upon an IV pole, standing nearby . . . and the two men facing each other at the foot of his bed.

"Oh, I wouldn't throw around the threats too soon, Joseph." Blackburn's voice was harsh. "I took the risk of coming here for one simple reason: your employee intranet. I thought access to your internal company network might be worth the trip to the South Pole. I was right."

Vengerov's voice was deadly soft. "You penetrated our systems? That's illegal."

"Speaking of illegal"—enjoyment throbbed in Blackburn's voice—"you should really take a look at something I found while the trainees were on their tour."

Their hands gripped the rails on either side, though Blackburn's were ferocious claws like he was ready to rip the bed frame apart, and Vengerov's were casually skimming the metal. The faint smile on Vengerov's lips reflected none of the tense hostility on Blackburn's face, even as he reached into his pocket, pulled out a computer, and began examining the file Blackburn sent him.

Blackburn said, "I had this hunch that it wasn't a coincidence our combat technology always seems to keep perfect pace with that of the Russo-Chinese . . ."

"A mere conspiracy theory. I thought better of you, James."

"It's not a conspiracy *theory* if it's an actual, proven conspiracy. Thanks to this perfect opportunity to plunder your systems, I found proof. It's all there. Bank account numbers, emails, electronic footprints—all the interesting material I need to convince any investigative body that there's not *collusion* between Obsidian Corp. and LM Lymer Fleet, you're outright double-dipping—getting paid to supply war machines to both sides. You might as well be the CEO of LM Lymer Fleet, not just Obsidian Corp."

Vengerov said nothing. The slight smile had disappeared from his lips as he continued to examine the information Blackburn sent him.

Blackburn folded his arms and leaned back to gloat. "If that gets out, well, you can get away with a lot of it. I know *our* congressmen are so pathetically corrupt, a few bribes will send them eagerly looking the other way. . . . But there's a funny thing about the Russians and the Chinese: they've both got that pesky national pride thing you can't seem to drive out of them, and they don't like being scammed. Let's say I stick this info on the internet for the eyes of the eager public. That's gonna lead to an outcry, and those princelings in China might have to make the best of a bad situation and nationalize LM Lymer Fleet's assets. They'll take them and hand them out to their kids. . . . What do you think?"

Vengerov closed the tablet computer, calmly tucked it in his pocket, and said in a deadly soft voice, "I think it was foolish of you to assume I'd simply let you walk out of here with this. Surely you're not that careless."

"You know me, after all. I'm touched. Of course I didn't think you'd let me walk out with my plunder, no. That's why I made sure the information already walked out of here. It left hours ago with the trainees. I distributed it between their processors as I stole it, and as soon as those kids were outside this building, they transmitted the data to one thousand different data storage sites."

Vengerov seized the rail. "I will cull every last file location out of you!"

Blackburn rocked back on his heels, a ferocious grin on his face. "They're set to a dead man's switch. I have to send a password in . . . five hours and six minutes, or they'll automatically open and reveal your double-dipping to the entire world. Oh, and here's the best part: the password I wrote for them? It automatically deletes itself from my processor if I'm incapacitated, if any unauthorized code from, say, a census device finds its way into my brain, or if anything—and I mean *anything*—hinders my liberty of movement. You're going to let me walk out of here, and you're going to agree to my terms."

A heavy silence sat on the air between them. Then Vengerov straightened. "I see you've been very thorough. So you'll sit on this data, and in return . . . what? I assume you wish me to withdraw Obsidian Corp.'s bid for the Pentagonal Spire?"

"The breaches end today," Blackburn said flatly.

"One is conditional upon the other, yes."

Tom saw Blackburn's face shift as he got the confirmation it *had* been Vengerov behind the breaches, behind the hijacked drones—and blurry as his head was, Tom felt vindicated. He'd been right. It *hadn't* been Medusa.

"Now, Lieutenant," Vengerov said, "I suggest you tend to your eavesdropping trainee."

Blackburn jumped, and threw a startled glance toward Tom.

With a sigh, Tom abandoned the pretense of sleep and heaved himself up as far as he could in the bed. His entire body was exhausted, his mouth bone-dry. "Where are we?" His voice came out cracked.

"We're still in Obsidian Corp.," Blackburn said, moving closer to him. "The medical bay. We're waiting for some of our own people to retrieve you. Do you remember what happened?"

Tom gave a shaky nod.

"Try to rest," Blackburn ordered him, but his voice was oddly soft. "You need your strength."

But Tom couldn't rest, he couldn't, not with Vengerov there at the foot of the bed. It was like closing his eyes with some venomous snake looming over him, poised to strike.

Vengerov had an unblinking gaze like a reptile's. "I must apologize for your incident earlier, Mr. Raines. I never thought to assign any personnel to attend to the external surveillance cameras. No one breaks into a building filled with killing machines in the middle of Antarctica, after all. Your medical expenses are, of course, complimentary."

Who was Vengerov even pretending for? Tom knew he was the one behind what happened. Blackburn had to have guessed.

"Yeah, I bet you're real sorry," Tom said, his voice raspy. He assessed himself, saw the swollen toes of his right foot where he'd kicked at the door. Bandages confining his hands. Restlessly, he shoved one under his opposite arm to work the bandage off, hoping to see how badly hurt his hands were. "Funny how that door swung open and closed a bunch of times."

"No hardware is perfect. Certainly not our automated doors." Vengerov's gaze dropped to the bandage Tom was working off, a certain amusement gleaming in his eyes. "But it does trouble me to think while I was luxuriating indoors, a frightened child was trapped out in the cold, begging to be let in."

Rage boiled up in Tom. His furious gaze flashed up to Vengerov's. "I *never* begged."

Vengerov had to know what he was really saying—Tom hadn't broken. Even if it almost killed him. He wished Vengerov would reward him by seeming distressed or disappointed, but the Russian oligarch smiled, something like anticipation on his face.

Blackburn seemed to realize what Tom was doing. "Don't take those off here . . ." he began, but Tom had shucked off the bandage.

Now he saw what it had been hiding. Shock triggered in his gut as he saw the blackened fingers he couldn't feel. He latched on to the other bandage with his teeth and tore it from that hand, and saw that those were blackened, too. His gut twisted. No. No, no, no . . . Wait. This couldn't be right. He tried to curl them, tried to flex them. He shook his hands out, he pressed the fingers together. No sensation. Nothing.

A massive tourniquet seemed to be compressing him, the blood rushing in his ears. No. He needed these. He needed them for everything. Gaming. He couldn't game without fingers. What if he didn't become a Combatant? What if he needed to get by somehow?

Blackburn snared his wrists and set about replacing the bandages. "You're going to get cybernetic fingers. They'll work with the neural processor, and they'll be almost as good as the real thing. Think of the exosuits. It's like having one full-time."

But exosuits hadn't replaced something that was *supposed* to be there. They'd been something fun, something awesome to make him stronger, faster. They'd been something he could take off and decide not to use. Tom stared at his blackened fingers, denial blanking out his brain. This couldn't be real.

Joseph Vengerov must have been satisfied that Tom understood the consequences of refusing him, because he at last turned around and strode away, disappearing off into the empty hallways of his mechanized fortress, as pitiless as any of his machines.

CHAPTER NINETEEN

"**A**T LEAST YOUR nose didn't fall off," Wyatt told him a couple days later.

Tom was sitting on the edge of his bed in the Pentagonal Spire's infirmary, watching Vik inspect the new, cybernetic fingers. It was strange. They didn't have any true touch receptors, not like real fingers, but whenever they came in contact with something—whether screwed into the stumps on his hand or not—Tom felt this prickling sensation. He hadn't yet learned to sort out different electronic signals, even though Dr. Gonzales had assured him his brain would learn to identify them, associate them with heat, cold, soft, sharp, and so on.

Vik turned the finger over and Tom felt the nagging prickle in his hand. He felt like his head was going to burst.

"I looked up pictures of people with frostbite online," Wyatt went on, from where she was sitting on the edge of his mattress, her dark hair drawn up in a high ponytail today, "and a lot of people's noses fell off. So it's really great that yours didn't."

Vik laughed. "Enslow, come on."

"What?" she said. "It's a *good* thing. I'm cheering Tom up."

"He is not looking cheerful," Yuri said, from where he was leaning against the doorframe.

"I'm fine," Tom muttered.

Now Vik's chair scraped closer to his bedside. "So what's the deal? I heard the official story: you went looking for a bathroom and accidentally walked outside, but I don't buy it. How'd you really get stuck out there?"

"Yes, what were you doing?" Wyatt demanded. "I was so sure you and Vik had some stupid bet over who could last outside longer, and it would be so like you to almost die trying to win, but Vik is denying it."

"Yes, I'm denying it," Vik erupted. "Because betting over that would be stupid and Tom and I are not that stupid. Well, *I'm* not." When Tom didn't laugh, Vik nudged him. "Joke."

It took Tom a moment to reply. "I know."

"Ah, I do not believe we should question him regarding this right now," Yuri cut in.

For some reason, his voice set Tom on edge. His stomach ached. He didn't want his friends here. He wanted them to leave.

"Tom, stop flipping Yuri off," Vik said, holding Tom's middle finger up at Yuri.

Tom's gaze riveted to the finger Vik was holding, the prickling sensation registering in his mind like the finger was actually attached to him. He couldn't breathe. They were all staring at the detached finger, and it gave him a sense like his skin was crawling.

"Give it back," Tom said to Vik.

He felt like something was sparking inside him, fizzling, ready to explode. It wasn't the detachable-finger thing bothering him, it was something else. Something he couldn't pinpoint. Everything felt wrong here. He really, really wanted them to leave.

"So these are exactly like the old ones?" Wyatt asked him.

"No," Tom said. "These are cybernetic, Wyatt. That's fake skin. They detach and they're okay. The old ones, well, they froze into blackened stumps, and when they detached, they didn't work anymore. If you really wanna compare side by side, ask Dr. Gonzales for my real fingers." He started laughing, then laughing harder and harder. It was hard to choke out the words, "I bet he's got 'em in medical waste somewhere."

He heard Vik mumble something about being loopy on pain medication programs. That confused Tom. Was he acting weird? Tom wasn't sure. He figured the anesthesia program had worn off. He didn't feel doped up anymore.

"Doctor," Vik said, shaking the finger at him, "I see many, many glorious pranks in our near future. Think of all the ways we could pretend your fingers have come off, and—"

"Okay. Yeah." Tom tried to muster a grin, but couldn't. "Now seriously, give it back."

"You sound puzzled." Vik scratched Tom's head with the detached finger.

Tom practically screamed it at him: *"Give it back!"*

There was silence for a moment, and Vik handed it over. Tom shoved the finger into the attachment point at his knuckle, feeling stupid.

Vik nodded at the other two, and Wyatt and Yuri withdrew from the room.

Then Vik drew closer. "Tom, I know you're—"

"Yeah, I'm being a pansy. I know. It's the med programs. They're messing with my head." It wasn't the meds or exhaustion making him feel like this, like some giant, exposed nerve, but Tom couldn't seem to control what he was feeling and it was embarrassing.

"Come on, Tom. I'm not . . ." Vik stopped and let out a breath. "Do you need the social worker?"

"She came by before you did." Olivia had been sitting by his bed as he recovered from the anesthesia. She'd pressed him to talk. He pretended to sleep.

Vik rubbed his palm over his face. "I've got to tell you something. When you left the group at Obsidian Corp., I—"

But Tom's attention riveted to a faint shuffling sound, somewhere in the distance, and he sat bolt upright. "Is Yuri still here?" he demanded, on edge. "What's he up to?"

"Yuri?" Vik blinked a few times. "No, he and Wyatt went . . ." He stepped back to check and peered out the doorway, then said, "Hey, Yuri, man, I said I'd meet you in the mess hall."

Yuri's voice was gentle, mild. "Of course, Vikram." He peeped in. "Good-bye, Thomas."

Eavesdropping. Tom wasn't sure why the word popped into his head, but he tried to force it away.

FOR THE NEXT few weeks after he was discharged from the infirmary, Tom felt like a walking black hole. Everything seemed to have changed, and he couldn't place why. The worst was his friends. He felt this wave of sickness whenever the four of them were together, something like dread. It was like he was poised for something awful to happen, and he didn't know what.

The other people at the Pentagonal Spire weren't much better right now. They'd all heard what happened. A few sniggered at how stupid he'd been, blundering outside in Antarctica, but others were weird with him about it.

Like Walton Covner, who'd been promoted to Upper

Company. Instead of messing with Tom's head, or otherwise acting like the strangest person Tom had ever met, as they stood in the elevator together one day, Walton said, "I'm sorry about what happened in Antarctica. Are you all right?"

"I'm great," Tom said vehemently.

Walton looked so awkward that Tom felt an evil little thrill. It occurred to him that this was a prime opportunity to mess with Walton's head for once.

He leaned in close, dropping his voice. "Hey, Walt, thank them for me."

"Thank who?"

"You know. *Them.*" Tom raised his eyebrows significantly. "Your gnome minions, man! They saved me. I was dying in the cold, and they came walking out on those tiny little feet and carried me with their tiny little hands all the way back into this tiny little cave they had. I thought you were messing with me before. I realize now—you truly do have gnome minions. Glorious, brave, miniony gnomes." Tom was very careful to keep that fake innocent expression on his face, the one that used to serve him so well in VR parlors.

He must've pulled it off, because Walton settled with, "I think you might've hallucinated that."

"Right." Tom gave him a thumbs-up. "I know the official story. I 'hallucinated.'" He made air quotes.

"No, Tom, I mean it. You really did hallucinate."

"Yeah, yeah. I get it. Look: give this to them." He unscrewed a finger. "Take it."

Walton winced at the sight. "Ugh, Raines. I didn't need to see you do that."

"Take it." Tom thrust the finger right in his face. "Give it to them. As payment."

"I don't think they'd want your finger."

"But it's a token of my esteem!"

"And you need to put that token of esteem back on your hand."

Walton spent the rest of the elevator ride backing away from him while Tom persistently tried to shove the finger at him. Then he scuttled out quickly when the door slid open and Tom cackled gleefully for the first time in days. He looked down so he could screw the finger back on . . . and went very still, arrested by the sight of his hand, the way his finger *ended* in a stub where the joint had been.

His skin crawled.

Back in his bunk, Tom dropped onto his bed, and unscrewed cybernetic finger after finger until he was left with a stubby mess of a right hand. *His* hand. It looked so strange.

Freakish.

Tom stared at it with morbid fascination. Then he replaced the fingers and did the same thing with the other hand. It was even more disgusting, some of the fingers ending above the knuckle. By the time Tom shoved them back on, his whole body was shaking. He felt like he was going to throw up, a terrible sense of wrongness spreading through him, like he'd made some awful mistake he could never rectify.

TOM COULDN'T SHAKE the dreadful self-consciousness in the days that followed. The cybernetic fingers were slightly off, the tone too pink somehow. Even when they were on, he tried keeping his hands in his pockets. He kept turning suspiciously at every burst of laughter he heard, wondering with a sudden clenching of his stomach if people were laughing at him. He swore a couple of the other trainees looked at his hands, but he wasn't sure. Maybe he was imagining it.

It took a while to work up his courage to do that thing he'd been dreading. He'd avoided trying VR games in front of Vik, worrying about what might happen. He finally holed himself up in his bunk one day to play Samurai Eternity. He set it at Expert level, the way he always did with games.

And then his worst fears were confirmed: the cybernetic fingers moved differently enough to throw off every slash of his sword, every blast of his weapons. In frustration, Tom tore off his VR gloves and hurled them across the bunk. The insane urge to stomp on them, break them, swamped his brain, and only the knowledge that he'd spent a month's stipend on them held him back.

But he felt a great ball of anxiety in his stomach. It felt like a much more tangible, aching loss than the sensory receptors he'd once had on those fingers.

He was doomed. He was completely and utterly doomed. Gaming was how he got by before the Spire. It was how he survived. Now he'd completely lost his chance at Combatant status, he'd made an enemy of Joseph Vengerov—and he didn't have a backup plan anymore.

He wasn't aware of Wyatt knocking on his door, and he was only dully aware of the moment she walked over to where he was standing above the gloves. Her large hands tugged clumsily at him, and Tom found himself sitting next to her on his bed.

"Are you okay?"

"I'm not upset or anything. I realized I suck at games now," he told her. He held up his curled fingers. "These don't work right."

"Your brain's primed to use the old ones," she said. "It's like the exosuits. No matter how good they are, your brain uses slightly different neurons to move them. You'll learn. Just practice."

He shook his head gloomily. "It's never going to be the same."

"Fine. Then you can be awful at video games. They're stupid anyway and a waste of time." She nodded crisply. "You should read more books, Tom."

He stared at her. "Wyatt, this is not a good pep talk. You are not good at pep talks."

"Well, it's not the end of the world. You don't need to video game for money now."

"Yeah, but . . ."

And then her words registered in his brain.

His muscles felt rigidly locked in place as he tried to make sense of it.

"Um, wait. Wait," Tom said. "Wait. How do you know about that?"

Wyatt's eyes shot wide, and she dropped her gaze.

Tom scooted away from her. "Wyatt, how do you know I played games for money? I never told you that. The only person who knew was General Marsh. Or . . ."

Or *Lieutenant Blackburn*, the guy who'd seen enough of his memories to know.

For some reason, Tom felt like he'd been socked, realizing Blackburn had told her. He'd sort of thought Blackburn was discreet about the stuff from the census device. His brain felt all tangled up even thinking about Blackburn now, knowing the same guy who'd almost driven him insane had also saved his life and . . . and *comforted* him when he'd been hurting and sort of confused. But this was a surprise. Blackburn had talked about Tom's personal stuff to Wyatt?

Tom hadn't told her what he knew about Blackburn and his family. This felt like being stabbed in the back.

"What else did Blackburn tell you?" he asked her roughly.

"It wasn't him, Tom. It was my fault." She clutched her

hands together in her lap. "It was right before vacation, after we got Jupitered. . . . That's still a stupid term, by the way. Anyway, I knew something really bad had to have happened in the Census Chamber because you were acting so weird, so I downloaded the surveillance archives."

Tom froze up. Oh no. She'd *seen* stuff. She'd seen all of it.

Yeah, he'd told his friends about his life before the Spire, sure. About those casinos where Neil raked in the money, and the crazy and colorful crowds, hopping trains and soaring from state to state in all the glorious freedom of it, or that high-rise suite over that pool with all the naked women in it, stuff like that. A bunch of things that were awesome and fantastic, the way things sometimes had been but usually weren't.

Never that *other* stuff. Never any of the bad stuff. That wasn't the person he was here.

"There were two days' worth of footage," Wyatt went on, her eyes darting to his, and skittering away again, "so I stuck it in my homework feed. I woke up knowing it all. But, Tom, I wouldn't have sat and watched it all if I'd realized . . ."

"What did you think?" he blurted. "I told you it was bad."

"I know. I didn't know it would be *that* awful. That *he* could be that awful."

Tom felt sick. He couldn't look at her.

"I haven't talked about it to anyone, you know. And . . . and I haven't been talking to Lieutenant Blackburn, either. I'm mad at him. He was awful to you. He's noticed, too. He ordered me to stop sending him 'sad hurt puppy looks,' whatever those are. Um, but I could say something, too. I'm going to say something. I'll give him a talking to."

Tom barely heard her. His skin crawled all over. All those memories. Those *fantasies*. She'd been *in* some of those fantasies. Not only that, but she'd seen those hours when he'd begun falling apart. She knew all of them. She'd seen it all.

She'd seen *him*. He couldn't seem to move.

"I'm so sorry," she said. "I am so, so sorry. I know why you were so mad at Blackburn now. I didn't understand before. I do now."

Her words rang distantly in his ears. He felt like he was drawing breath through a straw. He swiped his hand through his hair, trying to get his head straight, but he couldn't seem to think, he couldn't.

"You really saw all that?" was all he could manage.

"Well, not all of it. I mean, there are things missing. Um, these segments. Big segments. It's like they were erased. Like, at first you and Blackburn seemed okay and there's this big blank spot, and everything got weird after that. You two were okay before that, and after, you were both acting . . . differently."

Tom closed his eyes, knowing that was when Blackburn had seen his memories of what he could do with machines. When Tom had made the fatal error of admitting he'd met Joseph Vengerov, leading to Blackburn jumping to all sorts of conclusions. So Wyatt had seen the aftermath of that, but none of the context or the reason for it.

"I don't understand what you were hiding from him."

"What was I hiding from him?" Tom burst out. "What do you think, Wyatt? Does the word 'unscrambled' ring a bell? How about 'treason'?"

Her cheeks grew white. "That."

"Yeah. *That.*"

"I wouldn't have asked you to do that. Yuri wouldn't have, either. If we'd known . . ."

Tom let out a frustrated groan and thumped back against the wall, exasperated. "Yeah, well, it doesn't matter now. It's over. It's the past. Look, forget it all, okay? It's over and done and let's say it didn't happen. So don't talk about that stuff you saw. Don't tell anyone." The words tumbled out of him, so fast they were almost incoherent. "Not any of it. Just keep it to yourself. It's personal. Not even Vik. Don't tell Vik. You haven't told Vik, have you? Wyatt, you can't tell Vik about that stuff. Don't tell him—"

"I wouldn't tell him anything," she promised him.

Tom's head throbbed. He rubbed his palm over his face, his feelings all mixed up. He wouldn't have shared those memories or those scenes from the census device with anyone if he'd had a choice. Not even his friends. *Especially* not his friends. He liked the way things were. He liked the way they saw him. He didn't want them to think he was some sort of a wimp or a loser or pathetic. Or stupid. He couldn't stand that. He wondered what she thought about him now.

Wyatt gazed at him intently, her brow furrowed, biting her lip like she was contemplating some very difficult math problem. But what she did next caught him off guard. She leaned forward and awkwardly put her arms around him.

Tom sat very still, feeling how rigid and uncomfortable her body was against his, since the gesture was entirely out of her element. For several seconds, they sat there like that, and amusement broke through his mortification. He met her solemn gaze. "What's this for?"

"I don't know," she said, keeping her arms around his neck. "It seemed like an appropriate moment. Is it okay?"

"Yeah. It's good." Tom sat there a moment, then leaned his head back against the wall, and felt her chin rest on his shoulder. It really was kind of nice. He spread his hands palms up, between them, and dared to ask her the hard question. "Do my hands look really nasty? Be honest."

She peered at them. "No. They didn't do a good job with

the skin tone on the fingers, though. Those are made for someone who's very pink. You're not that pink, Tom. But they're not hideous."

"Thanks," he said with a soft laugh. The one thing Wyatt could always be counted on for was honesty. There were worse things than having unusually pink, fake fingers and a bunch of exposed memories, he supposed. Like if his nose *had* fallen off. Or if he'd never found friends.

Or if he'd been through something like what happened to Medusa.

His breath caught in his chest, and he understood it. For the first time, really, he comprehended what he'd done to her at Capitol Summit. He felt like a freak because of mangled hands, cybernetic fingers. But every single day, she walked around with her scars all over her face, somewhere they could never be hidden, never concealed.

She was stronger than him. Without question. There was this crushing sensation in his gut. He got it now. And he knew he had to make it right. He knew where to start.

"Wyatt, can you look at something for me? I don't understand the code, but you would. It's a computer virus. I can't tell you where I got it or who gave it to me, but I need to know what it can do."

Wyatt was intrigued. "Ooh, yes. Send it over."

"Thank you," Tom told her, pulling back his sleeve to bare his forearm keyboard.

She caught his wrist, eyes wide. "Make sure it's zipped and you're not using it on me by accident."

"Aw, come on, Wyatt . . ."

"Right. I know you're not that stupid."

And yet she cringed as he sent her a copy. When a terrible computer virus failed to unleash on her, she gave him a pat on the head like she was very impressed by him. Despite her lack of confidence in him, Tom felt a warm glow in his chest, and long after she left, he felt like life wasn't so catastrophic after all.

DEPOSITING A MESSAGE in Medusa's vision center was a huge risk. Tom knew it wouldn't please her, and she might retaliate. He did it anyway.

And indeed, when she surprised him by fizzling into the middle of a simulation during Applied Scrimmages, Tom braced himself for terrible revenge.

"Are you insane or just stupid?" she demanded. "We had an agreement." She stood there with her hands on her hips, right in the middle of the cloud of fluorine gas in the World War I simulation.

"Are you really calling *me* insane?" Tom's voice was muffled by his gas mask. "You don't even have a gas mask. Anyone can see you here."

She shook her head and picked her way over a tangle of barbed wire, then plopped next to where he was crouched. "No. I didn't enter your general simulation feed. I'm only in your visual feed, and I'm keeping an eye out in case anyone taps into it to see how you're performing in the sim. We're safe. You'll be the only one who sees me. So I asked again: insane or stupid?"

"Neither. Hear me out. I actually had a legitimate reason to contact you this time. But . . . Wait one sec. Let me kill these guys."

At the very beginning of the simulation, he'd made his way as close as he could to the enemy lines, and buried himself in the ground. His plan was to shoot the enemy group members one at a time as they moved. Now he readied himself to take down the first two trainees who ventured from their trench.

"I don't understand why they're training you to fight with a World War One simulation," Medusa remarked, surveying their surroundings. "It's not relevant to space combat."

When a sufficiently loud explosion rumbled nearby, Tom shot the first of the two trainees. "That's not why our military has us fight these." He shot the second trainee as another explosion rumbled. "Only a fraction of us go on to be Intrasolar Combatants, right? They use these to figure out how our minds work. They assess our strengths, see how we handle pressure, how creative we are, how quickly we make decisions, how well we work with a team . . . that sort of thing."

"How well you work with a team?" she said ironically.

Tom knew she was referring to the way he was out here alone. "Yeah, I've got some weak points."

He waited a moment, gazing toward the trench where the enemy group was peeking up, trying to figure out how their two allies had been taken down so quickly. They hadn't seen him. Another enemy trainee was creeping out into the open. The distant explosions were dying down, and Tom grew irritated. He wanted to talk to her, but he had to take out this guy, too.

"Why did you contact me?" Medusa asked him.

"A couple reasons," Tom admitted, eyes on the approaching enemy. "First of all, I'm sorry about what I said before about the avatars. I didn't get it, I didn't get how I'd upset you, but I understand now. I was a jerk, okay? And . . . and . . ." In a flash of inspiration, Tom recalled Yuri's words of wisdom. He caught her eye, and said intently, "And I want you to know something: Medusa, if I met a horse that looked like you, I'd find that horse attractive."

She stared at him.

"And I'd be worried," Tom added quickly, seeing her confusion. "See, it's a horse. See? I mean, I'd really be, like, 'uh-oh' and 'this sucks,' if it looked like you because I'd be into that horse. Which is messed up, due to the horse thing. But it would solely be because it resembled you. You know what I mean?"

She backed away from him slowly. "I think I really need to leave now."

"No, wait." He let out a breath. "This is all coming out wrong."

"Was there some way that could possibly have come out *right*?"

Yeah, she had a point. "What I'm trying to say is, I'm sorry I hurt you and I think there's so much about you that's amazing and I really need you to know I feel that way."

She was silent a moment. Then, "Where did the horse come from?"

"Forget the horse," Tom said vehemently. An explosion rumbled in the distance, so he took the opportunity to shoot the trainee, too close for comfort. Then he turned back to her. "This is the main reason I contacted you: Joseph Vengerov of Obsidian Corp. approached me. *He* leaked to your military that we were meeting. He also wants me to do some clandestine work against you. He wrote a computer virus designed to incapacitate you. My friend made sure that's what it's for, just in case. I'm supposed to use it on you."

She jolted away from him. Tom realized she thought he was going to deploy it. He risked raising his hands, even though he was aware the other group might see the gesture.

"Don't go! Listen, Medusa, I'm not doing it. I thought I should warn you. Actually, this is good news."

"Good news?"

"Yeah! LM Lymer Fleet is *not* monitoring you because

they know anything about what you and I can do—it's because you're winning too much. Vengerov doesn't like it, and he controls LM Lymer Fleet as well as Obsidian Corp. He doesn't want you finishing the war so soon. I got it right out of the horse's mouth."

Then he winced. *Why* had he brought up the horse again?

"LM Lymer Fleet surveilling you has nothing to do with what we are, Medusa. Just lose here and there, and stop posing such a threat to their war racket, and they'll back off. They'll leave you be."

Medusa hugged her arms across her body, and he was struck by how alone she looked in the clouds of fluorine gas billowing around her. "You don't plan to use the virus on me, then?"

"Are you serious?" Tom blurted.

"What," she said, "you would never do something underhanded and vicious for the sake of winning? Is that what you're saying?"

Tom laughed softly. He had to give her that. "Fine, so I've got a bad track record there, but you know, I took it on myself to warn you. If I was planning to use it, would I really stand here and tell you all about it beforehand?"

Apparently, the enemy group had figured out there was a sniper hidden nearby. They were scouring the area, searching for their mysterious assailant. Tom kept an eye out. He was ready for them.

"Actually," he told Medusa, trying to set her at ease, "I'm a bit insulted here. You *really* think I'd be the sort of supervillain who tells all his plans before he does them. I mean, come on. That burns."

Her voice was teasing. "I know for a fact you're the gloating type. I could see you explaining all your diabolical plans to me before you pull them off."

Tom made a show of doubling over in terrible pain, like her words were hurting him. Her laughter rewarded him. When he peeked up at her again, he saw her roll her eyes. "Fine, Mordred. I suppose you wouldn't do the supervillain lecture. I guess no one does it in real life."

"Actually, I knew a kid," he admitted. "His name was Nigel, and he was planning something pretty diabolical. Just before he did it, he gave me the whole lecture. Like, an explanation about how he did it, his motives, all that, and even his evil plans for after he pulled it off. I'm not even lying here."

Makis Katehi spotted Tom. Tom hurled himself up before Makis could shout an alarm, tackled him to the ground under the cover of the poisonous gas, and slit his throat. Then he dove back for cover in his makeshift hiding place and thrust a mound of dirt back over his body.

"So I really don't have a reason to be worried," Medusa said.

"No. No reason apart from the obvious winning-too-much-so-must-be-stopped thing."

"And you really wanted to warn me." Her voice was wondering. "That's all?"

"That's all. That and the . . ." He fumbled a moment, feeling stupid. "And the horse thing."

He shot the next trainee who ventured too near him, and looked up in time to spot the fleeting smile on her lips. It made him bold. "Tell me one thing. Just one. Is your name . . . Mulan?"

"Not even close. Good-bye, Mordred."

"Visit me again," Tom said on impulse.

She was silent. Then, "Maybe."

She fizzled away, leaving Tom in the mud, bodies sprawled all around him, swirling clouds of poisonous gas in the air. She hadn't said no.

CHAPTER TWENTY

Tom AND MEDUSA didn't fall into their old habit of meeting for fights in VR games, but she did take to inserting herself in his audiovisual feed during Applied Scrimmages. It was early morning in China whenever she came, and since the Chinese trainees only slept every other day. She was able to find time to visit him more often than he'd even hoped. So Tom went rogue from his group every simulation in hopes she'd show up. Since Yosef Saide cared only about kill ratios, and Tom liked to show off to Medusa by really piling up the bodies when she was there, the arrangement actually impressed his simulation group instructor, who told him to keep at it.

Medusa couldn't participate in the sim or even kill people on the other side when she was entering Tom's visual feed, but she took on something of an advisory capacity, which almost gave Tom the sense they were teaming up for rampages together. One extended simulation between the Mongols and the Russians, she caught up to Tom where he wandered alone in a Siberian forest, and found him hovering over a makeshift fire.

"You should put out that fire." It was a chilly day dipping into evening in an extended sim. Tom was a rogue Mongol, prowling across Siberia. "I could climb a tree and look for their smoke, then you go kill them."

"Maybe later," Tom told her.

"You should at least put out this fire, Tom."

"I don't like being cold."

"Do you like being dead? Because that's what you'll be when someone notices it, and hunts you down."

Cold and dead were about the same thing in his mind now. But he held firm, and Medusa gave a wicked grin, then began to kick dirt over his fire. Tom couldn't allow her to put it out, so he charged her unexpectedly and hoisted her over his shoulder.

"What is this supposed to accomplish?"

"I'm throwing you over my shoulder in a manly way," Tom informed her. "I'm thinking of covering you in snow so you learn to appreciate my fire, too."

"I could fight my way down anytime," Medusa declared.

Tom laughed. "Not before you get snowed!"

She twisted in his arms, and Tom ducked his head to avoid the hands she swiped at his face, trying to gouge his eyes. Medusa kicked at his torso and unbalanced him, sending Tom tumbling back, but he made sure they both plunged into a bank of slushy snow. He didn't even feel the chill with her searing up against him, and she punched his face, knocking him to his elbows and knees.

Medusa maneuvered herself firmly on top of him and stuffed a fistful of icy snow down the back of his tunic. Tom shook her off and tried to recapture her before she flitted away from him, but she was too swift and darted out of his reach.

He heaved himself to his feet and shook out his tunic, laughing. She grinned at him savagely from across the leaping flames.

"My ploy worked," Tom told her. "You like that fire now."

She cocked her head. "Your fire's at my mercy. I could put it out and ditch the sim."

Tom sobered up. "I don't care about the fire. Don't go."

Medusa said nothing. The flames glittered in her black eyes. Their skirmish had tousled her hair, and he could see the scarring she tended to hide under locks of dark hair from the side of her head where she had most of it. His gaze traced over it, and Medusa seemed to realize what he was looking at. She turned her head away.

"No, wait," Tom said, circling to her side of the fire. "You don't have to . . . I mean, I thought you don't care if . . ."

"I don't."

He stood there a moment, dismayed, uncertain what to do. Then he reached out for her, and she flinched back.

"What, you said you don't care," Tom pointed out. "Either you care or you don't care what I'm seeing."

"I've had this since I was very young, Tom." Her voice was acidic. "I am used to it. So, no, I don't care anymore."

"So why are you upset when I—"

"It's different with you."

The implication slammed him: he'd done this. He had to fix it.

This time, he took her gently by the shoulder before she could pull back. When he lifted his palm to brush the dark strands of her hair aside, her hand flew to the sword in his scabbard. Tom let her draw it if she wanted to. Soon, he could see her face, that mass of burn scar tissue twisting its way from her scalp, down her features.

She stood there, utterly rigid, and he was vaguely aware of the sword wavering indecisively between them, like she couldn't decide whether to sink it into him or toss it aside. Tom's hand hovered over her cheek. He wasn't sure whether this was okay, so he stayed that way, feeling the warmth radiating from her skin.

"Does it hurt?" he asked her.

Her black eyes flashed up to his. The point of the sword bit into his abdomen. "The nerves are dead. What do you think?"

Tom opened and closed his mouth a few times before getting the words out. "I lost all my fingers. They froze." He felt embarrassed admitting this, but he held his hands up, the only offering he had. "And I know the nerves are dead and they're not even there anymore, so I'm imagining it, but sometimes they hurt. It's weird. It's stupid."

Medusa considered him, and he was aware of the sword sliding back down. She planted it in the ground by her feet. "I shouldn't have tried to kick out your fire."

"You were right. It would've gotten me killed."

She lowered herself next to the crackling flames and tugged on his trouser leg, so he sank down next to her. They faced each other in the wavering golden light, and Medusa took his hand, then raised it so it hovered near her jaw again.

"I don't feel anything," she told him.

This time, Tom brushed his palm over the scar tissue. Strange. He'd expected something hard or rough. But it was cool, even soft in places. There was something about seeing the burn so close, feeling it, that diminished it in his mind. It shrank away as that shocking thing seen only in fleeting, stolen glimpses, and soon all he could see was the girl across from him, with this one more aspect rendering her . . . well, far from ordinary.

"You haven't tried to guess my name today," Medusa pointed out.

"Oh, yeah. Forgot." Then he threw one out. "Wu Tang."

She rolled her eyes. "That's your most pitiful guess yet."

Tom leaned in and whispered, "Tell me your real name and I'll stop coming up with bad guesses."

She shoved him lightly. "You can't coerce me with bad guesses."

"I can try, Murgatroid."

"Murgatroid?" She started laughing. "Is that even a name? It's not Cantonese."

Tom watched her and his brain seemed to short out. He wasn't sure what to blame for it later. Maybe he temporarily lost his mind because Medusa was so close to him. Maybe his mind blurred at the sight of fire dancing in her black irises.

Maybe there simply was nothing sensible in his head in that moment, nothing to stop him. He reached over and drew her into his arms, feeling her fragile shoulders tense against his palms, then he dipped his head to hers and claimed her lips in his own.

The last time they had kissed, Tom had been in VR; he hadn't felt a thing. His mind had buzzed with the realization he was kissing her, and maybe that's why some part of him hadn't been fully present.

Not this time.

Her body softened against his, and to the tips of his toes Tom experienced this liquid elation, this utter rightness like he'd never felt before. His palm stroked up her back, cupped the hot skin of her neck, fingers twining into her silken black hair. The world seemed to go still and there was nothing under the crisp, starry sky of Siberia but Medusa, the feel of her, the taste of her, and need roared up within him as he tightened his grip and deepened the kiss.

Trainee voices rang through the air. "It looks like the fire's coming from over there!"

Tom's eyes snapped open.

For a moment, he gazed right into her black eyes, inches from his, and he felt the moment he lost her, when every muscle in her body tensed and drew rigid. Then she planted her palms against his chest and shoved him back. He didn't move as she bounded to her feet.

Tom still couldn't move, couldn't budge, perched there by the fire like someone had paralyzed him. He felt like someone had sliced down his torso and exposed his guts to the air, his skeleton. Medusa stared at him like she couldn't wrap her head around what he'd done, then she waved her hand and vanished from his sight.

The Russians swarmed over the ridge and the arrows began thunking into the ground around Tom, but he still sat there, a great hollow in his chest.

THE DAY CAME when Tom grew certain he could distinguish between the very basic sensory perceptions of his new fingers. Because his brain could associate different types of prickling with softness, sharpness, and that sort of thing, he was now ready for a program to fool his brain into perceiving at least an approximation of the old sensations.

Unfortunately, this involved going to Blackburn.

Tom knocked on his door one evening and stepped into his quarters on the officers' floor with trepidation. It wasn't that he felt hostile or distrustful toward Blackburn right now. That would've been okay. Easy. The problem was, he knew Blackburn had saved his life, and he remembered Blackburn getting him warm and . . . well, making him feel safe. Less afraid.

It was too messed up, what with the census device still vivid in his brain, far too recent. Tom preferred not to feel profoundly indebted to him. It was easier to avoid him altogether.

Now he stood there awkwardly as Blackburn plopped a case of supplies out on his table and beckoned Tom over. Tom had never seen inside Blackburn's quarters before and it wasn't what he would've expected at all. The man had been at the Pentagonal Spire almost four years now, but the walls and shelves were bare, the only real furniture a table, some chairs, and a TV. There was a scraggly, undecorated Christmas tree Blackburn obviously hadn't gotten around to taking down yet.

"Your fake tree looks to be on its deathbed," Tom told Blackburn.

"It's older than you are, Raines. Show some respect."

Older than he was . . .

Tom realized it then—Blackburn must've had it *before*. Before he went crazy, before he blew up his kids, before his wife clawed his face and left him. Tom tore his gaze away and saw something that made him feel even worse.

He and Vik had been at the Pentagon City Mall with Wyatt and Yuri while she looked for Blackburn's Christmas present. Wyatt was a terrible gift giver, since she never guessed even remotely correctly what people wanted, and Tom and Vik didn't help matters because it amused them to steer her clear of the nice pen Yuri suggested and toward a brilliant purple, lavender-scented candle that had little stars all over the base.

"Are you sure it's not too girly?" Wyatt had asked them worriedly.

Tom and Vik had both kept straight faces as they nodded. Vik said, "Wyatt, all men like scented candles."

"Yes. Scented candles are as manly as it gets," Tom confirmed. "It's the classic American Sunday: beer in hand, football on TV, and a scented candle burning nearby."

"Not just in America. When I left my primary school, my father said, 'Son, you are now a man,' then he gave me a scented candle and told me how babies are made." Vik fought to keep his lips from twitching. His voice was a bit strained as he pointed at the glass base. "Plus, the tiny stars will remind Blackburn of outer space. I think he'll like that."

That was good enough for Wyatt. She bought it for him. Unfortunately, this got them all scented candles for Christmas, but it had been worth it.

At the time.

Now Tom watched Blackburn rifle through a case in his bare apartment—that single, pathetic candle the only decoration in sight—and he felt like a scumbag. He still hadn't even thanked him for Antarctica.

"Hey," Tom tried. "Thanks for saving my life. And stuff."

It wasn't the best expression of gratitude ever. Blackburn didn't seem to care. "I wasn't going to let you die, you little fool. Now sit down. Let's see if we can give you a sense of touch. This won't be specific, Raines. You won't distinguish between lukewarm and warm, but you'll be able to feel a cold sensation and a heat sensation."

Tom lowered himself into the seat, and Blackburn beckoned for him to prop his hands up on the table.

"This all depends on whether you've learned to distinguish between hot and cold, soft and sharp on your own. I need the neural associations firmly in place if I'm going to manipulate them."

Tom nodded impatiently. "Yeah, cold is kind of this slow, vibrating feeling, and hot is this fast one. Sharp is this tiny bunch of pinpricks, soft is a spread-out bunch. I can tell."

"Close your eyes."

Tom closed them. Then Tom felt his fingers placed on something that prickled in a way he'd begun to identify as cold.

"What is this one?"

"Cold."

"Very good. Now we'll substitute the electronic signal, fool your brain into thinking you feel cold like you used to. Keep your eyes closed."

Code flickered across Tom's closed eyelids, and his fingertips felt the cold—a terrible cold that throbbed right up his finger into his knuckles. He yelped and withdrew his hand, his eyes snapping open.

Blackburn raised his eyebrows at his reaction, and held up the thing Tom had been touching. An ice cube.

"That was too cold," Tom said.

"You're sensitized to it."

"No, you set up the finger wrong. It felt way too cold." He didn't want to go on, but Blackburn thumped the table with his knuckles, so Tom reluctantly put his hands down again.

As Blackburn readied the next sensory test, he remarked, "I hope you've noticed that I haven't pressed you about the situation with Joseph Vengerov."

Tom tensed. "Yeah, I've noticed."

"I know he wants something from you."

Tom dragged his gaze up to Blackburn's, uncertain how much he should say. Blackburn grew irritated. "There is no point in testing your senses if you keep opening your eyes. What do you know about my time?"

Tom closed his eyes. "Infinitely more valuable than mine."

"What do you know? You do learn sometimes. Sharp or soft?"

Tom's finger brushed something that felt like a tiny bunch of pinpricks. "Sharp." When he opened his eyes, he confirmed it—it was the edge of a knife. He found himself staring at it. The words spilled out of him in a great rush. "Vengerov really would've killed me. Right? He would've done it. Just like that."

"If he wanted to kill you," Blackburn said, tapping on his forearm keyboard, "I wouldn't have gotten to you in time. He was trying to scare you."

"But he could have." Tom grew agitated. "He could've done it. And he would've gotten away with it."

"Of course. Think real hard: Who writes our laws?"

"Congress."

"And who do congressmen obey?"

"Trillionaires," Tom said bitterly.

Blackburn nodded for him to touch the knife. Tom pressed too hard and felt a nip of sharpness. He raised his finger up, but it wasn't bleeding like a real finger would. The skin was pink and almost plastic.

"My dad hates them all," Tom said. "Joseph Vengerov, Reuben Lloyd, Sigurdur Vitol, all of them, but then he saw Vengerov in person over break, and he didn't say anything to him. He looked scared of him. I didn't get it then. But I think I do now. Vengerov could've done anything to us. If Dad gave him a problem, Vengerov could just knock him off. And he wouldn't even get punished for it."

"That's the reality of a world ruled by money." Blackburn pointed two fingers, and Tom remembered to shut his eyes again. "The divine right of kings can't be used anymore to justify why some people are more equal than others, so now the law does it. The legal system is entirely controlled by money, yet it's still hailed as a neutral instrument of justice. If you cross the law, you're the sinner, and you deserve punishment—even if you're not necessarily violating a universal human standard of right and wrong, you're acting against the interests of the rich guy who paid a lot of money to make sure what you're doing is illegal. Soft or sharp?"

A scattering of prickles played across Tom's finger. "Soft." And then code flickered before Tom's eyes. He opened his eyes to see what he'd touched. A cotton ball.

"That's why you have to tread lightly with men like Joseph Vengerov," Blackburn added. "If you face an enemy vastly more powerful than you, your first task is to downplay yourself as a threat. You don't show your face and protest him, you don't talk about him to a friend, or even anonymously on the internet, because there is no anonymity in a surveillance state—just databases and watch lists. A smart person does *nothing* to reveal what he truly believes, because if he does, he'll get neutralized before he can act on those beliefs. The deadliest enemy, Raines, is the totally silent one who acts alone and plans alone and wears a great big smile before his enemies. He's just another face in the crowd until he's slipped cyanide in a cup or plunged a dagger into a back. By the time anyone knows he's a threat, it's too late to stop him."

Tom thought of his father suddenly. Neil blustered his opinions to everyone, whether or not they wanted to listen . . . and that never accomplished a thing for him. It was strange how Neil wasn't really a threat to anyone, but merely because of the way he talked, he was treated like one.

Blackburn folded his arms. "I may not know what you did to provoke Joseph Vengerov, Raines, but I know one thing: you showed your hand so he struck first."

"But I didn't," Tom protested. "I didn't cross Vengerov *openly*. The thing is, he wanted me to make contact with Medusa again and use a computer virus on her. I never had a chance to say no. As far as he was concerned, I hadn't made up my mind. I hadn't told . . ." He fell silent.

His breath caught. He *had* told someone.

He had. Just one person.

Tom felt sick. He'd felt strange hanging around his friends, because some part of him somehow knew who had passed the information on to Vengerov, who had to have done it.

Only one person had the faintest clue that Tom had already been meeting Medusa. Only one person could've told Joseph Vengerov that Tom was in contact with Medusa but wasn't deploying a virus on her.

The same person who'd been scrambled because the military thought he was a Russian spy.

It was Yuri. Tom's brain beat with the terrible realization. *It was Yuri. . . . It was Yuri. . . .*

CHAPTER TWENTY-ONE

Tom genuinely wasn't sure what to do about Yuri, and he couldn't seem to get a chance to get Vik's advice, either. Vik always seemed to be off doing something else. Since Medusa hadn't visited him since he'd kissed her, and their two simulation groups were due to battle, Tom decided to get to Vik there and tell him the situation. Quite inconveniently, the simulation that day turned them into cavemen.

All Tom could manage when he spotted Vik was a grunting battle cry. Vik's prominent forehead furrowed. His grunt in return was unenthusiastic. Tom charged at Vik with a rock in hand. Vik waved his club angrily. Tom hurled the rock and got Vik in the ribs.

Vik flopped to the ground, his club rolling out of his hand, but when Tom finally jumped on him and began slamming him over and over again, Vik only halfheartedly tried to wrench his grip away, like he wasn't into the fight.

It made Tom sad. He couldn't talk to Vik about Yuri, and

now Vik wouldn't even fight. He hit Vik across the chest. "Why no fight? Fight Tom!"

Vik grunted unhappily. "No."

Tom hit him again. "Fight now!"

Vik's lip puffed out. "No!"

Tom grew very confused and released him. He scratched his head. Even if his brain had been fully functioning, he was sure he wouldn't be able to understand Vik's reluctance to brawl. They liked brawling. They did it in VR games all the time.

"Poor Vik," Vik grumbled. "Vik sad."

He squatted on a boulder and picked an insect out of his tangled mass of hair, then contemplated it solemnly. For a fleeting moment, despite the prominent forehead and primitive facial features, he almost resembled the black-and-white, mock-philosophical Vik picture in Wyatt's bunk template, since he was obviously contemplating weighty matters in a very un-Vik-like manner. Quickly, the illusion was dispelled when Vik put the bug in his mouth and chewed.

"Why sad?" Tom demanded. He thumped his fists against his chest. "Vik fight. Happy Vik."

Vik groaned and buried his head in his arms. "Vik see Tom go. Vik no say. Tom get cold. Bad Vik."

Confused, Tom settled back on his haunches. "Vik not bad." He fumbled for something better to say than that and came up with the perfect words to rouse his friend's spirits and restore his faith in himself: "Vik . . . good. Vik good!" He hit Vik's shoulder. Hard. "Good! Vik friend. Fight hard. Strong Vik. Fight Tom?"

Vik shook his head, his lip puffed out again. "No."

Tom knew there was some way to fix this, but it was hard to hold on to any thoughts for very long with his brain this way. Tom ambled away and found a bush of berries. He scarfed down a bunch, then saved others. He took the rest to a new Middle, Iman Attar. She gave him a big, toothy smile of greeting when he offered her the berries. She gobbled them greedily, but when Tom tried to grab her, she grunted angrily and pointed at Britt Schmeiser, who was hurling large rocks very long distances.

Tom knew a challenge when he saw one. He shuffled forward to grab big rocks of his own, and began hurling them, too. Iman clapped her hands and cried, "Strong Tom! Good Tom."

Tom liked that. Britt noticed all the attention he was getting and got mad. His lips rolled back to expose his teeth at Tom. Tom showed his own teeth and roared at him. Britt ran over and hit him about the head with his big arms, but a swipe of Tom's arm knocked him over. Then he took a rock and hit Britt's head over and over with it. He roared with victory and turned to enjoy Iman's admiration, but she was shrieking and kicking and being dragged away by the hair by Yosef Saide. Tom rushed over and killed Yosef, too. By then, Iman was grumpy and tired and wanted nothing to do with any boys in the simulation.

"Bad Tom!" Iman hit him on the head with a stick. "Ugly!"

Tom grew sad. Iman hit him one last time and ran away. Tom's feelings were hurt, and so was his head. He'd nearly forgotten his abbreviated conversation with Vik when the sim finally ended, and Tom woke up in the training room.

Britt and Yosef were already in grim conversation, haunted looks on their faces.

". . . a catastrophe," Yosef was saying. "What were you thinking? Why would you choose that program?"

"The title was the First World War. I thought it would be World War One, not literally *the first* world war."

Tom and Iman exchanged a flustered look, then Tom hurried out of the training room, and ran into Vik right in the hallway. He stopped. Vik stopped.

Vik grinned, a certain lightness to him that seemed forced. They started walking again. "That sim, huh?"

"Come on. You wouldn't even fight me, Vik. What's going on with you?"

Vik let out an exasperated breath. "Fine. You really want to know, Tom? Here it is. I have a huge problem with what went down in Antarctica."

Tom's steps stuttered to a halt. "Wait. What? Why?"

Vik straightened his collar. "Do you realize I knew you were missing? I noticed way before anyone else did. Way before Blackburn. I didn't say anything." He raked his hand through his hair. "I thought you were gone because you'd sneaked off to do something, to mess around or something—like you always do. Like *we* always do. I thought I was covering for you."

"Nine times out of ten, that would've been the right call, man."

"I know," Vik said. "Nine times out of ten, that would've been the right call because you would've been doing something dumb and I would've been helping you. This time, it almost killed you. What about next time it goes wrong?" And then the words all flooded out of him, and he sounded almost angry. "Like with Yuri! You and Wyatt made the decision to unscramble him, but I didn't get a choice. I would never have done that, but you guys did, and I'm guilty, too, because I'm covering for you."

Tom stirred, uneasy. Yuri's unscrambling was hitting a bit too close to home right now.

"I remember Wyatt wanted to erase my memory when I found out," Vik whispered, since other trainees were rounding the corridor near them. "You should have let her."

"You *wanted* her to erase your memory of that?"

"It would've been better not knowing, yeah."

Tom shook it off. "Fine. Let's do it. Let's get Wyatt to erase it right now."

Vik let out a breath. "It doesn't work that way. You can only remove a memory if you know the *exact time segment*. If she'd done it then, it would've been gone and I never would've been the wiser. Since she didn't, I've had months to think about it over and over, and I've thought about stuff related to it. We'd have to spend a few days with the census device to hunt down everything that would need to be cleared out, and I bet I'd notice the blanks. It's too late. My whole point is, I think we need to take things more seriously. *You* need to take things more seriously."

Tom made sure the other trainees had disappeared into the elevator, then he suggested, "We can rescramble Yuri."

That stopped Vik short. "What?"

"We can do it," Tom said. "I bet he'd even let us. We'll talk to him. He'll talk to Wyatt."

Vik blinked. "Seriously?"

"Seriously."

"Just like that."

"Just like that." Tom hit the button for the elevator, avoiding Vik's gaze. "I know this might seem a bit insane, or wrong, or whatever, but I'll throw something out there. And don't get paranoid or nervous or read too much into this, but, well, I'll say it. What if I'm no longer completely sure he's not a spy? Not for the Russians, of course, but, uh, maybe for *a* Russian. *A. Singular.*"

He glanced at Vik and knew from the way Vik was gaping at him that he was, indeed, going to be paranoid and nervous and read too much into it.

Tom's head throbbed. Great.

▲▼▲

"What's going on?" Wyatt demanded when she met them in the Census Chamber.

"Tom has a secret life," Vik said, from where he was sprawled with his back against the chair beneath the census device.

Tom chose not to comment. Vik really had no idea.

"I thought he didn't know about all that memory stuff," Wyatt said to Tom. "You told me not to say anything."

Tom flushed, realizing she'd misunderstood. Wyatt was thinking about the census device footage.

Vik was perturbed. "What, more stuff I don't know about?"

"No, no, no," Tom said. "Vik, she means something entirely unrelated. Something not important." He turned to her. "And you, he means something I'm going to tell you right now. About Yuri."

"What about Yuri?" Wyatt said.

"What's the memory stuff?" Vik persisted. "Tell me, and I can tell you if it's unrelated. I don't like being let in on stuff after it's already blown up into a huge problem."

"What's blowing up into a huge problem?" Wyatt cried, anxious.

Tom groaned and clutched his temples, where a headache was spiking through his skull. "Look," he ground out, his eyes closed. "Vik, Wyatt is talking about some memories of mine she saw thanks to Blackburn that don't really matter at all. Wyatt, Vik is talking about the reason I asked you here, and this is about some memories that *do* matter. I took them out so you could see them and decide for yourself instead of taking my word. I've shown them to Vik, so we're going to show them to you."

And with that, Tom nodded, and Vik jabbed at the controls of the census device and replayed the memories they'd extracted. The first clip featured Tom by the road, trying to hitch a ride in New Mexico.

"Tom," she said sadly, "you shouldn't hitchhike."

"That's not the point of showing you this," Tom told her.

"You could get killed. Or robbed. Or raped. Or all three. What if a serial killer picked you up? You'd wouldn't like it if someone ate you, Tom."

Then Joseph Vengerov appeared on the screen, and she fell silent.

"You really were a bit rude to him," she told him.

"Again, missing the point."

She lapsed into silence, seeing Vengerov's demand about Medusa. She turned to Tom in the projected light of the census device, eyes wide. "You're not in contact with Medusa again, are you?"

"He is," Vik said mock cheerfully. "Another aspect of Tom's secret life."

"It's complicated," Tom said.

"Oh no," Wyatt whispered. "That's a bad idea. It's a bad, bad idea. And—" she cast her gaze up toward Vengerov on the screen "—you can't do that to her. Don't use a virus. She likes you. That would be so mean!"

"Medusa *is* on the other side of the war," Vik remarked. They looked at him. "What? Someone should point this out."

"But . . ." Wyatt's voice faltered as the next memory began, and she saw the Praetorians in Antarctica closing in, then the door snapping open to deposit Tom outside. That's all he'd given them. She mumbled, "That's how it happened? He deliberately drove you outside?"

"Yeah," Tom said. He glanced at Vik, saw that he was sitting there rigidly in his seat.

"You must've been so scared," Wyatt said.

"No," Tom protested indignantly. "I wasn't scared."

Vik said, "The point is that Vengerov already knew, Enslow. He knew Tom wasn't going to agree to do it. Someone told him."

"Or he could have guessed," Wyatt said uncertainly. "It's a yes/no question. Fifty-fifty probability."

Tom shook his head grimly. "No, he knew." And then he nodded for Vik to play the next memory.

It was Tom telling Yuri about Medusa in the weight room. The screen snapped off, and they stood there in utter silence for a long moment.

"And that's it right there," Tom said. "He's the only person who knew. He's the only one who could've told Vengerov about my refusal. He is the only possible person, Wyatt."

"But, no. No, Tom. That can't be right. There are other possibilities. Someone could've overheard."

"We were alone," Tom said.

"Someone could have bugged the weight room."

"Who would bug the weight room?" Vik wondered.

"Joseph Vengerov could have bugged the weight room to spy on Tom."

"Then he'd be an idiot. Does Tom look like he spends a lot of time in the weight room?"

"Hey!" Tom objected. Yeah, he wasn't going to win any power-lifting contests, but he'd filled out *a lot* since coming to the Spire.

"What about the surveillance cameras?" Wyatt tried.

"I checked," Vik said. "No one was actively monitoring that feed and no one's accessed it. Evil Wench, this was the Android's doing."

"But it's Yuri," Wyatt protested.

"I know," Tom burst out. "I don't like this either. It's not like I want it to be true." He scraped his hands through his hair. "I've had this feeling, okay? And I couldn't figure out what it was until I realized. . . . I'll tell you something, too. Yuri knows Vengerov. Yuri's dad works for Vengerov. Yuri was considered a security threat, and we never thought to wonder if there was a reason. Maybe we screwed up, Wyatt. What if Vengerov used him somehow to breach the system? Maybe we messed up when we unscrambled him."

"Which is exactly what I've been saying since you two did it, I'd like to point out," Vik said.

Wyatt shook her head over and over again. "You're wrong!"

"We should at least put the question to him," Vik said. "You can write some sort of program to make him feel like being truthful, Evil Wench. Maybe there's something going on we don't know about." Then he seemed to get a great idea, and a crazy-eyed grin came over his face. "Hey, maybe the Android's been reprogrammed and doesn't know what he's doing. Or maybe he's being blackmailed."

Tom felt a surge of hope. "Yeah. Yeah, like, Vengerov could be threatening to off his family or something."

"Have you heard him talk about his mother? I haven't," Vik said optimistically. "Perhaps because she's tied up in a base-ment somewhere, and Vengerov is planning to shoot her if Yuri doesn't inform on Tom."

Tom was very heartened by that possibility. Wyatt still didn't believe it. "If someone was threatening his family, he would spend all his time figuring out a way to rescue them. Then he'd do it. And he'd succeed."

Tom and Vik exchanged an unhappy look. That was some-thing Yuri would probably do.

"I'm positive Yuri wouldn't do this," Wyatt insisted again.

And then a voice drifted over to them.

"Do what?"

They all three jumped when Yuri stepped into the room from the corridor.

"I was searching in all places for you. What are you three up to?" His blue eyes roved over them, so kind and guileless beneath his wavy brown hair. Tom froze where he was standing, feeling like he'd been caught doing something awful.

A wave of doubt crashed over him. What if they were wrong?

Vik didn't share his hesitation. "Yuri, no offense, man, but someone sold Tom out, and all signs point to you."

Yuri's eyes grew round as saucers. "I beg your pardon, Vikram?"

"You knew Tom was in contact with Medusa," Vik said, and threw Tom a look. "Which, I maintain, is incredibly stupid considering you've already been charged with treason once, Gormless Cretin, but let's focus on the matter at hand, which is you, Yuri. Yes, you. The question here is, did you share what Tom knew about Medusa with Joseph Vengerov? If so, are you spying for Joseph Vengerov? If so, you're a dirty, rotten traitor and that really sucks, man."

As Tom watched Yuri's face, something happened at the mention of the name "Vengerov." His eyes flickered, and his features all sharpened, soft edges turning to taut, tense lines; even his pupils constricted. Such a subtle, tiny shift, it could've been blamed on the lighting, or on any number of other factors, if Tom didn't have perfect photographic recollection of that day in the weight room when Yuri's face showed the same reaction at the mention of the name "Vengerov."

"Just be honest," Vik urged, but Tom barely heard him, he was so disturbed. A dizzying wave of anxiety crashed over him, because he was so sure he couldn't trust Yuri, he would've bet ten thousand dollars on it.

Yuri shook his head as Vik spoke, and gently replied, "Why,

Vik, I would never do such a thing."

Even his voice sounded different, somehow. Tom would swear it! His accent wasn't as strong.

". . . as a matter of fact, I am deeply hurt by the accusation."

Tom found his feet, his heart banging against his rib cage. "Yuri," he said, his voice sounding strange. "We're good friends, right?"

"Of course, Tom."

"Then I need to ask you a big favor, man. A huge one." Desperation frayed his voice. "I can't explain, but you have to trust me here. You can save my life."

"What favor?"

Tom held his palms out. "Just let us rescramble you. Only for a little while."

The mildness on Yuri's face slipped. "Why would you wish to do that? I am your friend. I didn't tell anyone what you told me. I promise. This is totally unnecessary."

"You are my friend," Tom agreed. "That's why you'll get it when I tell you we are all in serious danger right now if we can't temporarily scramble you again. I can't give you details. You have to believe me. You have to trust me. Come on, man, help us out."

There wasn't any immediate danger, but Tom knew this was an appeal Yuri would never, ever refuse. If there was the slightest hint of a threat, even if Tom couldn't explain, even if it was a suggestion of danger to them, Yuri would bend over backward to help, any way he could.

But today, he said, "You presume too much upon our friendship."

"Oh no, Yuri," Wyatt cried. "They're right, aren't they? Something's wrong with you."

Yuri's gaze riveted to her, his eyes as distant and empty as some lizard's. Then his gaze roved to Vik's implacable face and to Tom's.

After a moment, Yuri smiled. "This is unfortunate."

And then he raised his forearm keyboard. Words flared across Tom's vision center: *Datastream received: program Incapacitation initiated.* And Tom heard Vik yell out as he did, because his head felt like it was cracking in half, and his legs collapsed beneath him. He plunged to his hands and knees, his brain on the wrong end of some terrible, electric drill, and he couldn't, he couldn't get his balance, couldn't move.

"What are you doing to them? Stop it!" Wyatt shouted at Yuri.

Tom peered up through blurring vision to see Wyatt dash across the room and grab at Yuri's arm. He seized her easily, swept her around, and trapped her back against the computer console controlling the census device. Tom tried to heave himself up, but he dropped again, unable to manage it.

Yuri pinned her wrists to her sides, his body crushed against her, head tilted to the side as he contemplated her almost clinically. "That program didn't take down your firewall, I see. We shall have to rectify that."

"Let me go!" She twisted and tried to escape him. He tore her forearm keyboard from her arm, flung it aside with a clatter, then grabbed her again. Her arms bunched up against his chest as she tried to press back out of his grip. "What are you doing? I don't understand."

"Drop your firewall," Yuri urged her, drawing his face down to stare right into hers. When she gazed stubbornly up at him, he seized her neck so swiftly, she gasped. "Do it right now!"

Wyatt drove her heel down into the instep of his foot, and his grip slackened enough for her to smash her fist into his face.

But Yuri was like a wall, absorbing the blow easily, snaring her in his massive arms again and twisting her around to face Tom and Vik.

From where Tom crouched, struggling on the floor to keep his mind working, he could make out the panic and confusion blaring on Wyatt's face, her dark eyes taking in their state.

"I will put you one by one in the census device," Yuri said, "and we will search for every reference to your suspicions about this asset. Then I'll excise those recollections and you will all be released unharmed. If you don't cooperate, I will continue to hurt your friends until you do. Tell me the password to drop your firewall and this will be painless."

"Wyatt," Tom gasped, "don't do it!"

Yuri drew forward a step, and his massive boot careened down, knocking Tom back. His head smacked against the wall, and he stayed there, crumpled, trying to heave in air. He was vaguely aware of Vik straining to work his sleeve up his arm, to get to his forearm keyboard. Hope reared inside him.

"What . . . are you . . . doing?" Tom managed to whisper to him.

"Getting . . . help."

Tom tore his gaze away from Vik, not wanting Yuri's attention to go there.

"Why are you doing this?" Wyatt asked, tears choking her voice. "I don't understand."

"Do as I instructed you."

"So you can do to me what you did to Tom and Vik? No! I won't!"

And then she shrieked out in pain when Yuri's large hand twisted her wrist. Tom felt a surge of rage and tried to launch himself up, but agony twisted him back to the floor, his head beginning to spin violently.

Vik finished typing on his forearm keyboard, and then curled up in pain, impotent fury on his face, as he watched Wyatt struggle with Yuri.

"Do as I instructed you," Yuri repeated.

"NO!" Wyatt shouted.

Yuri hurled Wyatt, hard, toward the chair beneath the census device. She tried to bolt, but he caught her. "This culling begins with you, then." He snared the restraints around her arms, and reared up to seize the census device, pull the metal claw down right over her head—

And then the door slid open, and Blackburn barreled in and wrenched Yuri away from Wyatt. She cringed as Yuri slammed his fist across Blackburn's face, crashing him to the floor. Blackburn found his feet in a flash, his hand jabbing at his forearm keyboard.

Yuri started toward him and then seemed to think the better of it. He backed up one step, another.

"Who's counterhacking me, Sysevich?" Blackburn snarled at him, when whatever program he was trying to deploy failed.

Yuri said nothing. There was an unsettling blankness to his face as he edged back as far as he physically could.

Blackburn lowered his forearm keyboard, giving up on taking Yuri down with a program. Instead, keeping his careful eyes on Yuri, Blackburn reached down and yanked Wyatt free, then shoved her toward Vik and Tom.

"Help those two," he said.

Tom sat up painfully as Wyatt retrieved her forearm keyboard, then hooked a neural wire into Tom's access port, and set about removing the program gripping his muscles, sending pain riveting through his body.

Neither Blackburn nor Yuri was moving. Blackburn seemed at a temporary loss, and Yuri had taken shelter from him on the other side of the computer consoles controlling the census device.

"So Ashwan's net-send was right," Blackburn said, breathing heavily. "Someone dismantled the filtering program."

Wyatt's head shot up, terrible comprehension on her face.

"It's gone," Vik confirmed, sprawled limply across the floor, his head tilted back. "It's been gone for a while. Since before Capitol Summit."

Tom's every muscle tightened. It was treason. He felt himself beginning to shake as he dragged his gaze up to the census device. He'd spent two days under that trying to keep this from Blackburn.

For Wyatt.

For Yuri.

For nothing.

Wyatt still stared at Yuri, horrified.

"Well, that limits my options," Blackburn remarked, half to himself. "There's a very able programmer in Obsidian Corp. right now, making sure I can't knock Sysevich out."

Wyatt neutralized the virus keeping Tom and Vik down, her hands trembling. Tom heaved himself upright, his legs shaking. They discovered that Yuri was still holding his distance, across the room from them, an alien look on his face. There was nothing of *Yuri* there. Just this cold, sharp blankness.

"What's happened to him?" Wyatt's voice was a quavering whisper. "Why is he acting like that?"

Blackburn kept his eyes on the large boy. He seemed to be thinking carefully, trying to figure out what to do. "Because that's not Yuri Sysevich, Enslow. My guess is, you triggered a semiautonomous security daemon. The process runs in the background of his system until it perceives a threat. Then it launches and assumes neural sovereignty—full control of his mind—and attempts to neutralize that threat. In this case, the three of you."

"Wait, so it's like an artificial intelligence, then?" Vik said, his voice hoarse. "There's some AI in control of Yuri?"

"There's no self-awareness." Blackburn walked to the side, to survey Yuri head to toe. "It's a preprogrammed response system, though since someone was counterhacking my attempts to get into his processor and knock him unconscious, I'd guess there's a remote administrator paying attention to this situation now. . . . What were you three doing when it triggered?"

"We asked him if he's been spying for Vengerov," Vik admitted, "and if he'd let us rescramble him."

"Rescramble," Blackburn repeated, acid in his voice. "And here it is, then. The source of the breaches. Sysevich. And you three. Did you think I put that program in his processor for fun?"

"I only wanted to help him," Wyatt mumbled.

"I trusted you with my encryptions, Enslow," Blackburn snapped. "You are the only person I shared those with. Do you know why I never suspected Sysevich? Do you? It's because you're the only person in the world who could have done this without me noticing."

Wyatt grew impossibly more pale. "I'm so sorry."

"It's too late for that now."

Wyatt was visibly shaking, the adrenaline wearing off. They all hung back as Yuri, or whoever . . . or *whatever* it was, regarded them steadily from the other side of the darkened Census Chamber.

"Why isn't the security daemon doing anything now?" Vik whispered.

"Because," Blackburn said, a strange note in his voice, "it's been programmed to adopt a new set of behavioral algorithms if it perceives itself at a disadvantage. It's determined its former approach to physically overpower you won't contain the situation anymore, and I'm sure it has more encoded instructions ready to trigger, depending on what we do next. Perhaps it's even awaiting instructions from its remote administrator."

"So let's wipe it out," Wyatt whispered. "We have to get that program out of him."

Blackburn shook his head. "Can't be done."

"If it's some sort of virus, we can take care of it! *I* can do it!"

"This isn't rogue software. I have told you many times, Enslow, how many backdoors I found in this system when I took over the installation. I patched those security vulnerabilities, one by one—except this one. This one, I couldn't fix."

He paced back in the other direction, still moving very slowly, and Yuri's searing gaze followed his every move. Blackburn said, almost casually, like they were in Programming, "Tell me, Mr. Ashwan, given how vast the solar system is, why are we able to communicate instantaneously with satellites, say, thirteen light-hours away?"

Vik's brow furrowed. He seemed as thrown by the question as Tom was. "Quantum entanglement, sir."

"Quantum entanglement," Blackburn agreed, raising his forearm keyboard and giving another shot to hacking Yuri's processor. "Every single satellite is essentially one half of a greater computer, communicating through one set of an entangled pair of photons up there in space, the other half down here on Earth. This link is instantaneous, it can't be jammed, and it can't be hacked. Now imagine a certain Russian trillionaire has a quantum transmitter inside a supercomputer in Antarctica and an entangled counterpart transmitter inside a person's brain."

Wyatt drew a sharp breath.

"Same principles apply. You've got a connection that can't be jammed, disrupted, or blocked. I figure Joseph Vengerov chose Mr. Sysevich very carefully for his transmitter. He found a likable, charismatic child of one of his employees—someone he had easy access to. He targeted a bright, driven, and optimistic young boy who was likely to go places in life. Next thing he did was shell out big bucks so this kid could go to the best schools, get in top physical shape, and really develop into something exceptional. That gave him a chance to place this kid—and the eyes and ears of this kid—most anywhere he wanted him."

Wyatt's hand flew to her mouth.

"Then he decided to stick his walking Trojan horse in the Pentagonal Spire, the better to keep his window into the installation after I took it over. As an added bonus, since the kid now had a neural processor funded by the US taxpayer, old Joe could do more than spy—he could remotely program that kid's behavior, too . . . dictate his actions, use him to disrupt operations in space, maybe even conduct surveillance on *persons of interest*, wouldn't you say, Raines?"

Tom felt strange, numb. So many things, so many vague suspicions, so many feelings he ignored began to resolve themselves into a now terribly clear picture. Yuri hadn't *told* Vengerov about him. Vengerov had directly seen and heard him *through* Yuri.

"I found the transmitter in his head my first week here. We found pretense after pretense to run new scans of Sysevich's brain, hoping to find some point of vulnerability so I could cripple that transmitter. But there isn't any way to disable it. It was installed in his head when he was so young, his neurons developed around it. It's as much a part of his brain now as his brain stem, as his cerebellum. It's a separate device from his neural processor, yet it can be used to control his processor. Taking either of those devices out would kill him. And I've got to hand it to old Joe: it was a spectacularly ruthless way of making sure no one would ever remove it. After all, only a monster would kill a kid to neutralize a security threat."

He began rubbing his palm over his mouth. A note of dark anger stole into his voice.

"Now that you know the situation, Mr. Raines, Ms. Enslow, let's make very certain you understand what you've done to your friend." He pointed at Yuri. "He is a walking, talking backdoor into our system, one that I can't close. I wasn't able to force him out of the program, because he had a very powerful patron who wanted to make sure he stayed here. If we booted Sysevich out, General Marsh would've had a deluge of senators calling for him to be replaced. The kid wouldn't even consider leaving himself, because a write-protected sector of his neural processor contained some preinstalled, operant-conditioning algorithms to *compel him* to stay here, no matter what."

Wyatt's eyes shot wide open.

Against his volition, Tom's mind turned back to Yuri on the stairwell that day after everyone climbed the Spire. Yuri had outright told him the thought of leaving was like some terrible weight pressing in on his temples. Now Tom felt so angry at himself, because he hadn't thought anything of it.

He *knew* that sensation, the sense like a vise was squeezing his skull. Dalton's program used that exact sensation when it was controlling him. Tom knew it, he knew it, but he hadn't even made the connection.

"So you see now why I installed that filtering program. It jumbled all Sysevich's sensory data. He couldn't transmit anything useful to the other end. By stripping my program away, you gave Obsidian Corp. full access not only to Sysevich but to our entire system and every neural processor within it. We're lucky this wasn't worse."

Tom had this vague sense he needed to do something, but he couldn't seem to make himself move.

"Now I think it's been long enough," Blackburn muttered, turning on Yuri. The daemon program snapped to alertness, jerking Yuri's head up straight, his body shifting into a defensive stance. "I don't care how sophisticated a computer interface might be, I want to deal with a human being. I've given ample time for a remote administrator to assume control over Sysevich's actions. I assume I'm addressing a person now?"

Tom's gaze swung over to Yuri, and he made out Yuri's tiny nod.

"Good." Blackburn folded his arms. "I suppose you've anticipated my next action?"

"You intend to neutralize this asset," Yuri said tonelessly.

"No, no." Blackburn shook his head. "That didn't quite pan out the last time. Neutralizing him gave someone a chance to reactivate him. I'm taking a different approach. You all have dumped Sysevich in my lap and you've fought every effort I've made to toss him out of it, so from this day forward, I'm going to use him against Obsidian Corp. I'm thinking of showing his processor off to some of your disgruntled ex-employees, rounding up some expert witnesses. They'll take one look at the data on his processor and they'll be able to honestly testify before the Defense Committee that Obsidian Corp. was manipulating Sysevich's processor right around the time the breaches occurred. Sysevich is going to be my proof Obsidian Corp. backstabbed us."

Tom saw Yuri straighten, growing rigid. "That won't be allowed."

Blackburn's eyes gleamed. "It's not your choice. There's enough hard data in his processor to incontrovertibly prove Obsidian Corp.'s involvement." He let that sit there a long moment, then added, "Unless someone, somehow, removed his processor from the Pentagonal Spire. Unless Sysevich no longer was in my lap, because someone finally decided his time was up and nothing was going to be gained by forcing his presence here."

Tom's mind processed the implications of what Blackburn was saying. He felt a pang of remorse, realizing it: Blackburn was forcing Vengerov to withdraw Yuri from the Spire. Vengerov would probably agree. Tom's head pulsed, his insides stinging with the unfairness of it. Yuri didn't deserve any of this.

For his part, Yuri—or the person controlling him—remained perfectly still and silent, listening to Blackburn set the terms.

Blackburn seemed to grow impatient with the silence. "Well?" He spread his hands. "The choice is yours. Leave Sysevich here and give me a weapon, or take him out of here and get his processor away from me."

Yuri's empty-eyed gaze slid over them and settled on Blackburn's. A slow smile curled his lips, and something about it made Tom's skin crawl.

"Very well. The issue is conceded. His processor will no longer threaten the integrity of the Pentagonal Spire. This asset will be removed from your custody, Lieutenant Blackburn."

And suddenly, Yuri seemed to catch his balance, almost like he'd been nodding off while sitting in class or something. He straightened up, his face cloudy, perplexed, but it was *him*. It was actually *him*.

"How . . . how did I get over here?" Yuri blinked in some confusion. He looked from Wyatt's downcast eyes to Vik's stormy face to Tom, then settled on Blackburn's coldly satisfied expression. "Sir!" He straightened to attention.

Blackburn let out a slow breath. "I have bad news for you, Sysevich. . . ."

Tom didn't want to see Yuri's face as Blackburn delivered the bad news, so his gaze dropped down to Yuri's hand, where his fingers were crawling over the computer keyboard controlling the census device. Confusion washed over him, because Yuri was still looking at Blackburn and seemed unaware of what he was doing.

Then Tom realized Yuri wasn't the one doing it.

Someone else was.

With a hum that still made Tom's blood turn to ice, the census device powered up. Blackburn's voice died as all five legs of the metal claw activated, and the bright beams lashed out at Yuri's head.

Yuri's neck jerked back, exposing the long, strained tendons alongside his throat. The first terrible scream ripped out of him as the blue beams enveloped his temples, his arms flying out wide, his entire body convulsing like he was in contact with some live wire.

Tom started forward, but Vik's hand closed around his arm, jerking him away. He saw Wyatt hauled back by Blackburn as Yuri convulsed to the ground.

"Don't," Blackburn shouted. "That's an electrical discharge!"

The current overloaded the census device, and the unit sparked and fizzled. The beams died away, leaving Yuri limp on the ground, an awful silence descending over the chamber.

Joseph Vengerov had, indeed, surrendered to Blackburn's terms. He'd removed Yuri's processor from Blackburn's reach, the processor Yuri depended on to live.

He'd obliterated it.

CHAPTER TWENTY-TWO

TOM WAS NEVER sure what to do when he visited Yuri in the infirmary during the months that followed. Mostly, he stood there looking at the slashing green line of Yuri's EKG, his neural processor automatically assuring him it was a normal sinus rhythm. Today, he found himself listening to Dr. Gonzales and another physician discuss the case on the other side of the room, speculating about how Yuri had made it so long without the processor, even in his medically induced coma.

"Maybe he was born under a lucky star," Gonzales said. Then he seemed to realize what he'd said, and began chuckling merrily.

Tom turned and walked out. He didn't fool himself anymore. He felt a flicker of surprise each day when he found Yuri still lying there, a machine breathing for him, an implanted pacemaker keeping blood circulating through his veins. One time, he swore, he saw Yuri's eyelids fluttering a bit like he was dreaming, but when he moved closer, he realized it had been the light playing tricks.

He grabbed a sandwich in the mess hall. He spotted Wyatt near the door and considered it. Why not? It had been a day or two since she'd had a chance to ignore him.

He tossed his tray on the table and slouched into the seat across from hers. "What's up?"

Wyatt's dark eyes flickered to his briefly, then she turned her full attention back to the liquid-filled, metallic cylinder containing a neural processor in need of reformatting. Since the spares were all from the old group of soldiers who'd died from them, anything left on the computers had to be erased— one directory at a time. Only then could they go into someone else's head. Everywhere Wyatt went nowadays, she tended to carry one. She reformatted instead of eating and, Tom suspected, instead of sleeping or doing much else.

As he ate, Wyatt adjusted the magnifying glass she'd attached to the lid of the metallic storage cylinder. She was always so meticulous about using tweezers to pluck up one stringy thread of the spiderweb-shaped computer at a time.

It was like Wyatt believed repairing enough spare processors would pave the way for Yuri to get another one. Tom knew it wouldn't happen, but when he'd pointed that out to her, she'd gotten up and walked away from him. He didn't mention it again.

"Ms. Ossare told me to remind you to see her today," Tom said, his mouth full.

Wyatt nodded a bit, acknowledging that she'd heard him.

Tom didn't really get why Olivia was still bothering. If Wyatt hadn't talked to her yet, she wasn't going to anytime soon. The last time Wyatt talked to anyone was the morning after Yuri's electrocution. Tom, Vik, and Wyatt were gathered around Yuri's bed, still in shock from what had happened, together but already so far apart.

Wyatt had looked at them dry-eyed, and said, "This was all my fault." And that was it. In the time since, she'd descended into a full-blown obsession with reformatting the old processors, even though it had been made explicitly clear to them that Yuri wasn't getting another one, even to save his life.

There was no point, after all. Vengerov's transmitter survived the destruction of Yuri's neural processor. The military saw no reason to waste resources on someone who'd be of no use to them. If he received a new neural processor and recovered, Yuri would remain a walking security breach. Neural processors were too valuable to give away just to save a life.

Tom heard voices swelling across the mess hall, and saw Lyla punching Vik's arm. Her face was flushed bright red, but Vik was shaking with laughter about something. He and Vik hadn't talked for a while. Blackburn officially classified Yuri's incident as a built-in hardware error, but the near miss with treason scared Vik. He obviously didn't want to risk any more trouble by staying around Tom. It started with Vik not sitting with Tom in the mess hall or in Programming.

Living down the hall became more like living on another continent. Tom saw Vik hanging around with Giuseppe sometimes, like they were actually becoming friends. Most of the time, Vik was with Lyla, though. They'd gotten back together, for longer than twelve minutes this time. Tom usually saw them arguing, or sometimes being way over-the-top affectionate. She seemed angry a lot, which Vik always appeared to find hilarious.

Tom wasn't upset. He was sure he wasn't hurt. There was this strange sense of crystallization inside him, like something had grown very hard and still in his chest. Things were the way they were. Maybe even a close group like theirs couldn't survive watching a friend get murdered.

Tom deleted his bunk template and the Gormless Cretin statue. He got rid of all of it.

OF COURSE, AT first, Tom was angry. When he learned Yuri wasn't getting another processor—that his life wouldn't be saved—determination flooded him. He would do what he could do—enter machines, go right through Obsidian Corp.'s firewall into Vengerov's systems, and he'd blow out that transmitter on the other side. Failing that, he'd blow up Obsidian Corp. itself if he had to. That was his plan. Then Yuri wouldn't be a security breach anymore, and he could get a processor.

But he tried. And failed. Obsidian Corp. had something he'd believed impossible: a firewall he couldn't penetrate.

When Medusa showed up in his plane during the Battle of Midway simulation, Tom turned back toward her. "Medusa!" He'd almost forgotten to think of her lately, with everything that had happened. "I'm so glad you're here."

"I know I've been staying away," she said. "I wanted to tell you—"

"Medusa, I need to ask you something." He steered through the chaos, only a sliver of his attention on the conflict. "It's important."

"I need to ask you things, too. About, well, when you kissed me—"

"Not now," Tom said. "I can't right now. This is a bad time. Look, have you ever been bounced out of a system while interfacing with it? I need to know."

There was a thick silence. Her voice grew icy. "What do you mean?"

Tom missed it. "If you try to interface the way we do, and you enter a system, but then get bounced out again, what does that mean—"

Her fingers dug into his shoulder. "What are you doing?"

"I have to get into Obsidian Corp.'s system. It's important," Tom insisted.

"Obsidian Corp.? Obsidian Corp., Tom?" Her fingers dug harder. "Are you trying to get caught? You're going to give us both away."

"I have to do this!" Tom turned on her, and the plane began to descend wildly, g-forces pressing in on them. "Medusa, I have to get something out of their systems. Can you tell me how to do it or not?"

"Not," she snapped back.

"Fine, I'll keep trying. I can't do it without your help."

She was silent a long moment as the plane shook around them. Then, so softly he almost didn't hear her, "I shouldn't have come back."

"Wait—" Tom said, but not in time.

This time when she disappeared, Tom realized he'd ruined it. His plane continued downward in a fatal death plunge, and the world erupted in flames.

But Tom tried one more thing. He went to Blackburn. He stepped into his office and dropped into the seat across from his, ignoring the bewilderment on Blackburn's face. "Sir, I can't get through Obsidian Corp.'s firewall. Can you help me?"

"What are you doing?"

"You know what I'm doing," Tom said fiercely. "I'm going to neutralize the security threat. I'm going to destroy the transmitter in Obsidian Corp."

Blackburn rubbed his palm over his mouth. "I can't allow this."

"I'm not sitting by and letting Yuri die!"

"Did you do something to alert Joseph Vengerov to what you can do, Raines?"

"No. Of course not."

"Then how was he able to block you out?" Blackburn said dangerously. "I can't even figure out how to block you yet—and I know about Yuri. Does Joseph Vengerov know about you?"

"No! I don't know how he's done it, I just know I can't get through his firewall, even when I interface." Tom planted his hands on the desk. "Sir, if you help me get through somehow, I can fix all this. You saw what I did to the census device that one time, I fried it."

"I remember you doing that by accident, not deliberately."

"But I *can* do it! I can. So I can do that to the transmitter, too. I can free Yuri from it and you can talk someone into giving him another neural processor. I need to be able to get into Obsidian Corp.'s systems. You can get me in for a few minutes!"

"I can't get myself in for a few minutes, Raines!" Blackburn roared back at him. "Why do you think I physically accompanied the trainees to Antarctica? I would have gladly plundered some blackmail material from the comfort of my own apartment, but I couldn't. Do you know why? Because you can't hack Obsidian Corp. with their own hardware, their own software. That facility's a virtual Fort Knox. You can't loot it from the outside. You can plunder only from inside if you have privileged access to their intranet—why do you think I went there in person?"

Tom blinked. It only occurred to him now that Blackburn had been taking a huge risk. Vengerov could've done anything to his processor while he was on Vengerov's turf.

"If you can't interface your way in," Blackburn told him, "then I'm glad. It's better for all of us. You destroy that transmitter, and then not only will Joseph Vengerov discover a ghost in his system, he'll also know that ghost is someone who wanted that transmitter destroyed. He'll narrow down the suspects for that ghost to a list of three—you, Enslow, and Ashwan. Haven't you hurt your friends enough already?"

Tom clenched his jaw. "I'll destroy the whole supercomputer it's attached to. Then he won't know I was going after the transmitter."

"The answer's no. I wouldn't help you do something this stupid and risky even if I could."

"I'd be the one at risk, not you!"

Blackburn gave an unpleasant laugh. "You still aren't capable of making that connection between actions and long-term, unintended consequences, are you, Raines? If Joseph Vengerov ever gets you, it's not *your* risk anymore, it becomes mine, because he will wipe you from your own brain, maybe pull you open to see how you work, and he'll figure out how to turn your ability into a weapon. He'll use everything you can do against the Spire. I hold on to this installation by clinging with my fingertips to a tiny bit of ledge as it is. You're not chipping it away, not if I can stop you."

"But Yuri will die! You can't let that happen. You wouldn't do that."

Blackburn sat back. "When I told Joseph Vengerov I was going to use Sysevich's processor against him, what did you think would happen?"

Tom couldn't speak; he couldn't.

"I can tell you what I thought would happen. One possibility was that Joseph Vengerov would simply let his asset go. Surrender him for good. I didn't consider that one likely."

Tom gaped at him. "You knew he might . . ."

"Choose to eradicate a potential threat once he knew I was going to use it against him? Yeah, I knew. It was the likeliest scenario. I still threatened him."

Tom couldn't speak.

"Don't look at me like that," Blackburn said darkly. "You did this, not me. Sysevich was dead the minute you took it upon yourselves to remove my software, and if I didn't know you'd be more of a danger to me out there in the world than you are in here, I would make consequences rain down on all your heads for killing your friend."

Tom flinched.

Through the haze over his vision, he grew aware of Blackburn rubbing his palm over his mouth. "Go to bed, Tom. It's late."

But Tom wasn't done. "So what about Wyatt?"

An edge crept into his voice. "Get out of my sight, Raines."

"She's really messed up."

A vein flickered in Blackburn's forehead. He said nothing.

"She won't talk to me. To anyone. She looks up to you. If you said something to her—"

He shook his head. "You're asking the wrong person. Send her to Ossare."

"Wyatt made a mistake. That's all. You don't get to act betrayed here—she unscrambled Yuri when you weren't even talking to her because you blamed her for something she didn't even do. But she got over that. Are you just gonna turn your back on her now? I thought you were looking out for her."

It took Blackburn so long to speak, Tom almost thought he wasn't going to bother. But then he said softly, "She's very gifted, and she has no armor against this world. She doesn't have anyone in her corner, not in her home, so I'll admit, sometimes I feel . . . protective. And it fools me sometimes into remembering what it was like once." He stopped.

"What *what* was like?" Tom blurted.

"Being a father. Having some investment in the future." His voice took on a note like he was mocking himself. "Having a soul, deluding myself with hope. But at the end of the day, I know what I am, and that's why I can't help now. She needs something I'm not capable of giving to her, Tom. I can't offer forgiveness. I simply don't have any. Not even for myself."

AFTER THAT FINAL door slammed shut, a sense of bleakness sank over Tom. He grew oddly detached from the whole situation. Sometimes, mostly when he was sitting there fending off prying questions from Olivia Ossare during the counseling sessions they'd all been forced to attend since Yuri's accident, Tom wondered if there was something wrong in how easily things had sort of dissolved away for him without destroying him. He wasn't withdrawing like Wyatt, and he wasn't moving on and cutting off any associations with what happened like Vik. Tom just sort of kept going forward.

After the loss of all his friends, and his future, it seemed almost like things had finally become normal. Tom knew what it was to feel rootless. He knew what it was to have nothing ahead of him. He knew what it was to have no attachments. This thing he'd dreaded had finally come to pass, but it wasn't some sharp shock to the system so much as a sort of familiar pall descending over everything. That other person—the Tom Raines who was the Doctor of Doom with Vik, who helped Wyatt understand other people, who marveled at any new superhuman feat of Yuri's, seemed almost like some stranger he'd encountered in passing, already gone.

Tom took up playing poker with Walton Covner and some of the older trainees. He still was an efficient killer in simulations. He'd gotten used to the fake fingers, but he didn't play VR games. He picked up the gloves sometimes, out of habit, but he never put them on. They made his chest feel hollow.

He wasn't unhappy. As soon as it grew completely clear to him there was no way he was going to be able to change Blackburn's mind, no way he was gong to be able to get into Obsidian

Corp.'s systems—as soon as he realized there was no hope—he was finally able to accept a cold, hard truth about life: the world rewarded sociopaths like Vengerov and destroyed good people like Yuri.

Tom finally understood why his father saw humanity as worthless. It was hard to see much fundamental value in anything when the bad guys always won.

Maybe this was simply what it was like to grow up.

TOM WAS FINISHING up the silent lunch with Wyatt when Heather approached their table. He felt her hand skim along his shoulder. "Hey, Tom! We're battling today in Applied Scrimmages." There was a note of excitement in her voice.

He glanced back at her. "Huh. Great."

"I'm excited—aren't you?"

"Sure."

It was strange how something in the last few months had ignited Heather's interest in him. She was constantly catching his eye and smiling at him in this inviting way that would've floored him once. Or she'd randomly reach out and straighten his collar or tousle his hair, or stuff like that. He wasn't sure what to think of it, so he didn't bother most of the time.

"You'll come fight me one-on-one later, won't you?" Heather said with a wink.

"Yeah." He shrugged. "Why not."

"Wonderful." She tickled his neck with her fingertips, to his great confusion, and swayed away from the table. She hadn't said a word to Wyatt, not even one of those fake sympathetic ones she did early on. Her IP address had been changed in preparation for proxying Elliot at Capitol Summit this year. A victory there or even a close loss would assure her an official end to her disgrace and a true shot at front man of CamCo next year. That seemed to be all Heather wanted—a chance at riding high above all the others. Tom didn't particularly care. At least she left Wyatt alone now.

"Well, I've gotta go to Scrimmages," Tom told Wyatt. He thrust himself to his feet. "Later."

He didn't wait to see whether she'd acknowledge it. He knew she wouldn't.

DURING THE SPANISH Armada simulation that afternoon, Tom ditched the historical English strategy of hanging back and counting on superior guns and led a boarding party from one burning Spanish ship to another. He was wiping the blood from his sword when boots creaked down the stairs to the cabin, and Heather Akron emerged, decked out in the duke of Medina Sedonia's armor, her dark hair spilling about her shoulders.

"Just in time," she told him. "I was worried we'd sink before you got here."

"I'm here." Tom raised his sword. "You wanna do this or what?"

Heather shook her head. "I lied earlier. I didn't want to see you for a fight. There's something I want to show you. I've been waiting a long time for this. Take a look through that porthole."

Tom shrugged, and crossed over to gaze through the rounded window. She must've tweaked the sim, because he didn't see the ocean or battleships. Instead, he saw an image, a familiar one.

An angle from above, Blackburn swathed in the projected light of the census device. "I want that memory, Raines!" And Tom trapped in the chair, refusing him . . .

He reared up, his mind racing.

"That's surveillance footage. It should look familiar to you."

"So what?" Tom said, forcing a calmness he didn't feel. "Everyone knows Blackburn used the census device on me."

Heather drew closer, and he felt her breath tickle the back of his neck. "Do you remember when Enslow and I had our little tiff last December? I slipped her a tracking cookie. For a while, I watched what she was doing in the system."

He smiled sourly. "All that effort to dig up dirt on her?"

"Yes, and it paid off. I found this footage. It wasn't complete. There were whole hours missing, and they weren't in the system anywhere, but those big gaps made me curious about what happened in those missing minutes."

Tom leaned back against the wall, waiting for whatever she wanted to say.

"That's when I realized something, Tom," she said. "There were two computers that still had that footage: Lieutenant Blackburn's processor and yours. That's the reason I invited you to that jousting sim."

Tom made sense of it. It was Heather. That weird message during the New Year's simulation: *Error: Connection lost. Download paused. 98% complete.* That had been her. She'd plundered his processor.

It hadn't been Blackburn.

So . . . she knew. Tom wondered what would happen from here. "You got me. I guess you know everything?"

"Oh, I know all about what you can do," she told him. "I also know Lieutenant Blackburn's kept it quiet—he hasn't told the military, or even Obsidian Corp., which is funny, because I bet they'd love to research you."

Tom knew she was mentioning this for a reason, to set him on the defensive. He supposed he should be alarmed, but he was just irritated. "You obviously want something from me, so spit it out."

Heather shrugged. "A mutually beneficial agreement. I won't tell a soul what I know about you, if you help me with something."

He laughed softly. "You're blackmailing me, then."

"I tried making this pleasant for you, Tom, but you've been ignoring my attempts to become better friends with you, so, yes. I am officially blackmailing you. You see, I get to proxy for Elliot at Capitol Summit this year. But it's very important that I don't squander this chance. I have to win—and Medusa defeats everyone but you. Now that I know what you can do, I guess I know why."

Tom leaned his head back, thinking of Medusa. The unexpected remembrance felt like a sharp pain. For a long, aching moment, he felt alone in the world.

And then Heather was pressing forward, her eyes boring into his. "I think if you caused an untimely malfunction or two for her while she's controlling her ship, it would go a long way toward giving me a shot at beating her."

"Obviously," Tom said wearily, and Heather's eyes glimmered with fury at the casual nonchalance he was showing her. He tuned out Heather as she tried to make it very clear this wasn't a laughing matter, that she'd give him away if he didn't do what she asked. All Tom could think was, it always came back to Medusa. To him striking at Medusa. However much he avoided it, however much he didn't want to, it was like he was meant to be the bane of her existence.

TOM SAT SPRAWLED on the ground by Wyatt's legs in the arboretum as she ignored him, working as usual on reformatting a processor. Olivia Ossare had given him a couple of dexterity exercises for his fingers. Apparently surgeons used them. It was rather odd, having an adult urging him along, trying to get him to play video games again. She seemed to think it would bolster his spirits or something.

The exercises were actually okay. One involved flipping a quarter from knuckle to knuckle. The other was skinning an apple with a knife, trying to get as little of the yellow insides as possible. Tom inspected his latest attempt, where he'd gouged a small chunk out of the meat.

"See, if I'd been doing surgery on someone now"—he showed Wyatt the apple—"someone would be hemorrhaging."

She glanced up briefly to see, which surprised Tom a bit. He took a big bite of the apple, considering her. That's when footsteps crunched toward them, and Tom threw a careless glance through the hedges to see Elliot emerging.

"Tom. Wyatt," he greeted them. He pointed to the nearby bench. "Do you mind?"

"Hey, man," Tom said, nodding for him to sit.

Apart from the Wyatt Earp Vendetta Ride simulation, they hadn't spoken much since Yosemite, when Elliot had washed his hands of him. Elliot settled on the bench, propping his elbows on his knees. He studied the apple debris strewn over the ground. "Playing with your food?"

"Long story," Tom said. It wasn't; he didn't feel like explaining. He plunged his knife into the apple and left it there. "So Heather's proxying you at Capitol Summit. I guess your diabolical scheme to anoint her queen is working."

"Hopefully." Elliot drummed his fingers on his thigh, his dark eyes moving between Tom and Wyatt. "Should we go and speak somewhere private?"

Tom raised his eyebrows. "I don't think Wyatt's gonna go talk to everyone after this. She's not very chatty lately."

Elliot sighed. "Tom, I have to ask you something. I've put it off for so long, but you seem so glum lately, I have to do it now."

"Glum?" Tom wondered.

Elliot rubbed the back of his neck. "In Antarctica when you walked outside like that . . . you weren't trying to kill yourself, were you?"

Tom stared at him. "What?"

"I hoped refusing to work with you would teach you something," Elliot said earnestly, "but I wasn't giving up on you completely. I didn't say that to take away all your hope. I think you can have a future here."

Tom finally made sense of his words. He started sniggering.

"This isn't funny," Elliot said sternly.

"Elliot, you think I tried to kill myself over you?"

Elliot smiled a bit. "When you put it that way, it does sound rather silly."

"Yeah. Just a bit." He glanced at Wyatt, and swore he saw a tiny smile on her lips, fleetingly. That cheered him up. "Nah, Elliot. I did not try to kill myself. And I'm not glum, okay? But if I am it's because . . ." He looked at Wyatt, and she was staring intently at the processor she was working on like she was trying hard not to seem like she heard them. "It's because of other stuff."

Elliot ruffled a hand through his black hair, then said, "For what it's worth, I've been doing a lot of thinking and I have an idea about what you can do."

"Huh?" Tom said.

Elliot leaned closer to him. "Do you know what people appreciate more than someone who makes a great first impression on them? Someone who has learned the error of his ways."

"The error of my ways?" Tom repeated.

"Yes. Don't you see, Tom? What happened at the meet and greets was ages ago. You've had a life-changing, near-death experience, and you've lost a . . ." He didn't mention Yuri in front of Wyatt. "You've had other things happen. You can legitimately claim to have gained some wisdom, some insight. If you apologize to the CEOs formally, maybe in a handwritten note on some decent stationery, they might be persuaded to give you a second chance."

Elliot said this so earnestly, but Tom found himself remembering Dalton's smug smile when he offered him the chance to get on his knees and make up for his wrongdoing.

"Right," Tom snarled. "Then they can frame my handwritten apology on fancy paper on the wall. Oh, and maybe add me to some other terror watch lists. What stops that, huh?"

"That's the chance you take," Elliot informed him. "But your best opportunity lies in penitence. Believe it or not, an apology might—"

"Give them a huge power trip?" Tom exploded, suddenly, unexpectedly furious, like some dam had burst. "Make them feel like they've broken me like some sort of animal? I would rather freeze to death than give them the satisfaction!"

"And here you go again," Elliot marveled. "What does it serve, letting them know at every possible opportunity how much you despise them? That hasn't gotten you anywhere. Just look closer to home—at Karl Marsters!"

"No way." Tom slashed his hand through the air. "Karl is *not* my fault. Karl has been after me since I got here."

"That's not how Karl sees it and it's not how I see it."

"Fine. Fine, then explain. Tell me why Karl wanting to pulverize me is my fault."

Elliot leaned toward him. "You really wonder why Karl hates you? The first day you got here, you punched him in front of everyone."

"I was under the influence of a computer virus," Tom protested. "Blackburn said so, too!"

"Yes, Lieutenant Blackburn said so. In a way that shamed Karl for getting the slip from a trainee half his size. 'Twice,' I believe he said. What do you think Karl felt?"

"Malice and homicidal urges, like Karl always does."

"Humiliated, Tom. It hurt his pride."

"What, so Karl went crying to you about this?"

Elliot tapped his temple. "Photographic recollection. I can reason the rest out."

"He tried to beat me up a few days later, so he got his own back," Tom groused.

"I'm sure he tried, but I'm also sure he didn't pull it off," Elliot said. "I am very certain Karl's never come out the winner with you, because if Karl had ever, even once, come away from a skirmish as the victor over you, he would've patched that gaping hole you've torn into his pride and left you alone a long time ago."

Tom drew a sharp breath to rip out the automatic reply that Karl *had* won here and there . . . like when he'd helped Dalton brainwash Tom, he'd definitely been the winner those times. Then something occurred to Tom: no, Karl hadn't come out better in the balance of things. After the sewage bath in the Beringer Club, and the humiliation in front of those executives, Karl was definitely the loser.

"Your life would be considerably easier if, instead of aggravating your enemies intentionally to make very sure they know you don't care what they think—if instead, you let them have the meaningless, easy victories here and there. That's compromise."

Tom gave up on trying to tread lightly. "You know, Elliot, it's hilarious hearing about compromise from a guy who gave up some person he felt strongly about because the Coalition said no. A guy who wanted to quit but again got told no. Now you've wasted a year putting all this effort into helping Heather Akron so she can take your place in that comfy little cage, when you know she'd stab you in the back if it would get her there, too, and it's all because you won't cross these people who think they have a right to be your overlords. I've gotta tell you, man, your definition of compromise seems a lot more like 'outright surrender' to me."

"You think I surrender too much? Well, I say you can't give a single inch of ground to anyone. Even when they're right."

"You're right," Tom said. "I can't."

They sat there a moment.

Elliot's mouth lifted. "Now you're being contrary, aren't you?"

"No, I'm not."

"No, no. That's exactly what you're doing. I had a beautifully articulated point now about you being absurdly stubborn, and you had to go right away and undermine my point by agreeing with me. You did that on purpose."

"That's how I operate. Sorry, man. It's not personal."

Elliot's smile faded. "I must seem very weak to you."

Tom shifted his weight uneasily, thrown by the turn in the conversation. "I didn't say that."

"You didn't have to." Elliot rose to leave him.

Tom almost let him leave on that note. Almost. But he couldn't help thinking of Elliot coming in to rescue him at Dominion Agra; telling him he was recommending him for promotion to Middle Company. Tom didn't want Elliot to walk away feeling like he saw him as a pansy. He didn't.

"Hey, Elliot . . . Wait."

Elliot half turned.

Tom shrugged. "For what it's worth, people like you way more than they like me. There are tons of people who'd love to beat me up. I mean, *tons*. And, yeah, people who don't know you want to beat you up because you're a celebrity and all the little twelve-year-old girls love you, but, uh, not people who have actually met you. They like you. You're not weak. I guess you're smarter than me."

Elliot gazed back at him, his mouth quirking. "Of course you have more enemies than me, Tom. People who need to control others are threatened by strength and you're indomitable. And that's why they don't mind me: I'm not." He considered that. "I wonder sometimes if that's not such a good thing, after all."

Tom didn't have an answer for that. As Elliot's footsteps crunched away, Tom settled back by Wyatt's knee in the middle of the unnatural serenity of the arboretum. He looked down to see her nudging tentatively at the apple he'd impaled with his knife.

After a little while of that, she grew still, and she spoke her first words to him in months. "You should never be a surgeon, Tom." She pronounced this with great solemnity.

Tom froze, so surprised he didn't know what to say for a while. Then he sorted out his thoughts and opted for the best route to handle this—as casually as possible.

"Yeah," he agreed, picking up the knife by the handle and holding the apple up. It was sort of like a head on a pike, so he smeared some mud on it to form eyes and a mouth. "I find it easier taking heads off than putting them back on."

She ducked her head again as she resumed working on the processor, but Tom saw that smile again, and he realized things might eventually turn out okay after all.

CHAPTER TWENTY-THREE

APITOL SUMMIT WAS broadcast from inside the US Capitol, where the dueling combatants would face off in the Rotunda, steering their remotely controlled vessels. The server they used was inside the Capitol, but the Chinese always circumvented the connection between Svetlana and her vessel, and gave control to Medusa. The Americans likewise replaced Elliot with his proxy—this year, Heather. She would spend the fight in the hidden room looking upon the Rotunda, remotely navigating Elliot's ship.

Before she left the Spire, Heather gave Tom one half of a pair of thought-interface nodes. Beneath her sweep of dark hair, she'd be wearing the other. They were short-range devices, so Tom had to go to the Capitol to get close enough to interface with Heather, and through her, with her ship—and Medusa's.

The drones were based in Texas, and they were going to engage each other in a free-for-all, live-fire exercise across the rocky landscape. Jagged mountains served as obstacles and as cover, and all the Combatants had to do was remain within a designated zone of combat so the public could appreciate, to full effect, all the skyboards that had been strategically placed for the event so as the cameras filmed the fighting ships, they'd also film the ads in the sky above them.

The key to evading DHS biometric databases was asymmetry, so Tom had stuck a smiley-face sticker on his face to make sure no one was able to identify him in the crowd at the event . . . just in case. He squeezed through the mass of people gathered outside the Capitol until he was in sight of the large viewing screens mounted before the gathered masses. The glowing image showed the Texas landscape and panned upward, showing the logos of the various Coalition Companies who'd bought skyboard space over the site of the conflict. All the Indo-American and Russo-Chinese affiliated corporations had a visual presence there. Then the images on the screen shifted to inside the Rotunda, where the most powerful men and women in the world were gathered for their own viewing.

Elliot sat behind one set of controllers, opposite Svetlana Moriakova, of the Russo-Chinese side. They were both getting ready to pretend to steer the drones in combat.

As soon as he was in the crowd, Tom popped his thought-interface node into the port in the back of his neck, and sent to Heather, *I'm here.*

Her thoughts registered in his brain. *Excellent. We're due to start soon. Ready to win this?*

Tom gave a twisted smile. *You never asked for a win. You asked for a malfunction.*

But what good is it to me if I lose?

Not my problem, he thought back.

Oh, yes, it is. If I lose, it very much becomes your problem.

He felt a surge of irritation. He couldn't guarantee a win.

Not against Medusa. Not against the single person who could battle him on a level playing field. *You can't keep demanding more and more at the last minute.*

I can because, in case you haven't noticed, I have the upper hand here. I have you by the throat, and if you're wise, you won't forget it.

His teeth began grinding together. For a moment, he fought the urge to rip off the interface node, consequences be damned. He found himself looking at the screen again, panning over all those skyboards glowing with logos he heartily despised, gazing at the sinister eye logo of Obsidian Corp.

Rage rocked through him at the very thought of Vengerov. Tom tore his gaze from the screen and found himself looking at more of Vengerov's work: the surveillance cameras, all directed at the crowd. His gaze drifted upward toward the drones hovering over them in the sky, scanning in images of the people in the crowd for future databases. He saw the massive wall of bulletproof, missileproof glass surrounding the steps up to the Capitol, all to protect those legislators put in office by voting machines and the caprice of the men behind those logos. Vengerov protected all those companies, maintained the security and the surveillance state that let them loom so large over the crowd.

When Heather signaled and hooked a neural wire between her interface node and the Capitol's server, Tom's consciousness filled with the buzzing of his neural processor and he jolted out of himself into the liberating formlessness of swapping signals, strings of zeros and ones, glowing electronic systems. . . .

Then with a rush, Tom soared into the ship Heather was steering. Her electronic sensors were focused on Medusa's ship.

Go on, Heather thought at him. *Go into her ship and damage it.*

Tom found himself gazing at Medusa's ship, soaring beneath the glowing neon array of skyboards, and a great certainty swelled in his chest that this time he couldn't do it. He couldn't hurt her again.

Tom, Heather urged him, *why are you are sitting in my systems? Go after her.*

Tom flashed for a moment to his distant body, ringed by the crowd. For a fleeting moment, he was behind Heather's eyes, interfacing with her processor, seeing her legs crossed carelessly in front of her in the empty room near the Rotunda, the massive screen on the wall in front of her showing the expectant, proud faces of the most powerful men and women in the world, encircling their pretty little performers, Elliot and Svetlana. Tom saw Reuben Lloyd and Sigurdur Vitol, Joseph Vengerov and Pandita Rumpfa, Prince Abhalleman and the Roache brothers from Dominion Agra. . . .

His heart began to scorch his chest, seeing the masters of the world all in one place, and the full apparatus of the police state ready to protect them. They'd taken everything. *Everything,* and people simply had let them. People had meekly surrendered the world to them in hopes those CEOs would finally have enough, finally have reason to leave them be. But Tom knew better. Even if a Reuben Lloyd or a Joseph Vengerov possessed the entire rest of the Earth, and the solar system besides, they'd still begrudge Tom the ground directly under his feet, simply because it was *his* and not *theirs*. That's the sort of people they were. There was never enough for them.

And Heather was the same way. A malfunction wasn't enough, she needed a win. Fame wasn't enough, she needed to be the most famous. That's why she'd smeared the other CamCos to the media; she hadn't wanted success, she wanted the other CamCos to fail. If he won Capitol Summit for her, she'd return with another demand down the line, and another. That's the sort of person she was. And surrendering was never going to appease her. There would always be something more she wanted to force out of him.

Tom made his decision then.

Heather, he sent to her.

What, Tom?

Here it comes.

Then he seized control of Heather's weapons, aimed them at the nearest Dominion Agra skyboard, and blasted it to pieces. There was no reaction from Heather for a long moment. Tom maneuvered the ship in a graceful arc to its next target. Obsidian Corp.'s board. Yes. He launched missiles and took that one down in a liberating hail of flames. Burning fragments of skyboard rained down about the ship as Heather screamed at him in his head. He flashed to her neural processor and grew aware of the way she was reaching up to tear out the thought-interface node.

He acted quickly, activating the heat receptors in her processor, reveling in her shock when merely touching the interface node seared her fingers.

Nope. I'm not done yet, Tom thought to her. *Touch that and you'll have as many fingers as me.*

If she'd had a moment to reason it out, she might've realized it was an illusion, not a real burn, but Heather was upset and furious and confused, seeing all her plans spiral hopelessly out of her control. *Tom, are you crazy? Are you INSANE? WHAT ARE YOU DOING?*

Tom aimed his weapons at a massive image of Sigurdur Vitol's face, then blasted one Wyndham Harks board after another. He carried on like that, dodging through the rain of debris, curving around one board, soaring straight through the narrow gap between two of them, the landscape below him growing and receding, skyboards raining debris from all directions.

And then words appeared in his brain. And they weren't from Heather.

I like this game. But are you only going to target your own multinationals?

Medusa!

Fair enough, Tom messaged back, whipping Heather's vessel in a joyful loop before blasting some Russo-Chinese boards. He popped out of the ship only a moment to dissuade Heather, yet again, from pulling the interface node out of her neck. He saw briefly through Heather's vision center, the view of the most powerful men and women in the world gathered in the Rotunda, goggling up at the destruction.

Elliot and Svetlana stood frozen in the center of the room, no longer pretending to steer the ships. No one was looking at them right now anyway. Then Tom soared back into the vessel and messaged Medusa as he blew up a Harbinger, then a Nobridis board. *Be honest. Are you impressed?*

I'm awestruck, Mordred.

She knew it was him. The realization made his head spin. He took out two more skyboards with one shot.

Awestruck, huh? Then you know how I always feel around you, he thought back.

Cheesy?

Tom's distant lips smiled. *Extremely.*

His distant ears picked up on the confused voices all murmuring around him as people in the crowd outside the Capitol tried to figure out what the Indo-American Combatant was doing this year.

For what it's worth, he messaged back to her, *I could kick myself for the way I acted the last time you dropped by.*

Medusa began playing a game of sorts with him. She'd dodge behind one skyboard, and the next. Tom enjoyed this one, too. He took potshots not meant to hit her, and saw them ricochet off the orbiting advertisements. Through Heather's ears, he heard someone in the Rotunda say, "That girl is a terrible shot," which about killed Tom as he blew up a Stronghold Energy board Medusa had dodged behind and then one belonging to Matchett-Reddy.

And soon the atmosphere above the Texas battle site was a glittering ring of debris, burning away in the atmosphere as it plunged downward. Tom and Medusa's ships circled each other through the endless blue sky.

Want this one . . . Chun Li? Tom thought at her.

He almost felt her laughter. *Beat me in an honest fight, and I'll tell you my real name.*

Tom felt a surge of excitement, both at the offer and at the reconciliation it implied. He soared toward her ship, needing to win. But this wasn't the satellite competition; it wasn't a game. This was combat, and Medusa wasn't just a fully trained Combatant, she was *the* Intrasolar Combatant, the one who could sway an entire war single-handedly. She banked downward to dodge the heat-seeking missiles, swept around in a graceful arc, and flew straight toward him, leading his own missiles back his way.

Diabolical, Tom messaged her.

I thought so, Medusa sent back.

He swerved, but in avoiding his own errant missile, he gave her a chance to launch her own, which narrowly missed blasting in his side.

Tom couldn't handle her in the open air. He needed obstacles. Those mountains. He aimed toward the stretch of

Texas, and found himself temporarily disoriented without the skyboards there to illustrate the zone of combat. Heather may have been given the coordinates for the fight and the lay of the landscape, but he hadn't.

So be honest, Medusa messaged him. *Would you prefer your end to be swift and terrible or slow and terrible?*

Do your worst, Tom messaged back.

He led Medusa in a spirited pursuit through jagged columns of mountains, twisting through the sky, her vessel always flashing up in the sunlight behind his, utterly relentless. Tom kept awaiting some nasty surprise, but she maintained that steady pursuit. He fired back at her, and she swerved gracefully to avoid each missile. She returned fire at him, and he swerved rather more clumsily, but he was scraping by pretty well, he thought. A few times, he flew low to the ground, blasting up masses of dirt to send billowing clouds in the air, hoping to blot out her view of his ship and rises in the mountains long enough for her to collide with one—but Medusa anticipated this and always soared high into the air to avoid the traps.

And then it was her turn to surprise him. As he rounded a peak, he discovered that she'd passed straight over the mountain this time, and there were three missiles already fired off, more soaring his way, all homing in on his ship. Tom's mind flashed over her strategy, and he realized she'd deliberately lulled him, set up an expectation in his mind about where she'd be, so she could shock him when she deviated from that.

You're amazing, he sent her, dodging the first three missiles.

I know, she sent back, as the fourth one destroyed his ship.

Tom snapped back into himself, and was amazed to hear the roar of approval swelling from the crowd outside the Capitol all around him even though the Russo-Chinese had officially won Capitol Summit. He blinked to clear his vision, the resounding cheers vibrating his eardrums.

The screen flashed to an image of the Rotunda, where Elliot and Svetlana still looked to be in shock, and the voices mounted to a thunder in Tom's ears. People began chanting a name, and it grew louder and louder, for the hero of Capitol Summit.

"Ramirez! Ramirez! Ra-mir-ez!"

As the image flipped from the Rotunda to the combat site in Texas, then zoomed in one last time on the smoldering remains of Elliot's ship—and above it, the skyboard debris. The voices in the crowd grew deafening, vibrating Tom's chest. Tom was utterly confused, because he'd lost the battle. As far as the crowd knew, Elliot had failed to beat Svetlana this year.

Then he saw the exultant, wild faces on all sides of him and he understood that the battle had lost its meaning as a showcase skirmish between countries. People were exulting in a victory of a different sort.

They'd seen *Elliot Ramirez* destroying all the Coalition skyboards.

TOM THREADED HIS way through the crowd. Usually, there'd be a speech going on about now. The winning side always marched out Elliot Ramirez and Svetlana Moriakova right away to say something about patriotism and fighting the good fight, always with a phalanx of the major executives and world power players about them behind that protective glass.

This year, there was a delay. Tom wondered how Elliot would be instructed to explain "his" actions. The Coalition would definitely have to take advantage of his popularity to defuse the explosive crowd somehow.

And then Heather burst out of the crowd. Tom let her

catch up to him, rather amused as she descended on him and slapped him. Hard.

"Nice to see you, too," Tom said, tasting blood.

"Do you realize what you've done?" she cried.

"Yeah." His voice dropped so only she could hear him. "*I* did nothing, Heather. *You* blasted all the skyboards, at least as far as the Coalition is concerned. What a gesture. I'd almost call it revolutionary. They are not gonna like that."

"You think this is a joke? I'll destroy you for this!"

Tom had no illusions. He knew she'd follow through on her threat, but he'd chosen to walk into this with both eyes wide open. "Fine." He flashed her a savage grin. "Give it a shot. Hey, it's worked out for you so well this far, messing with me, why not go for the kicker? I'll tell you, whatever happens from here, I'm always going to look back on the way you were so proud about having me by the throat, and then I'll remember how I decimated your career. I'll be honest, Heather. The memory's gonna make me laugh."

And with that, Tom left her tearful and shaking with rage in the middle of the crowd. Then a voice boomed over the distant loudspeaker, announcing that Elliot was ready to speak, and Tom slowed. He whirled around and peered at the massive screen, where Elliot had assumed the podium, his expression grave.

Tom knew why: the end of Heather's career meant the end of Elliot's hopes she'd take his place on that stage.

"My fellow Americans." At the sound of Elliot's voice, loud and echoing from various speakers, the crowd fell silent. "You may have noticed the mishap that occured with the skyboards during the fight."

He cast a glance back at the men and women sheltered behind the missileproof glass with him on the steps of the

Capitol—CEOs, their pet government officials, their security guards. . . .

Something flickered across Elliot's face as he turned back to the crowd. "I'm supposed to come up here and blame a group of hackers for tampering with my ship, but that's not the truth."

Tom gave a startled jerk. He peered at Elliot intently.

"The truth is, the destruction of those skyboards was completely intentional. In fact—" he drew a deep breath "—it was me. I did it. I destroyed them all." Elliot let the words sit there, a smile playing across his lips as murmuring filled the air.

Tom saw Reuben Lloyd and Sigurdur Vitol exchange a glance from where they loomed behind Elliot. This was obviously not in the script.

"You see, I'm owning up to what I did up there," Elliot went on, "because, let's face it—" he pointed behind him at the CEOs "—everyone hates skyboards except the men and women on this stage. They're light pollution. They hang in our skies year after year. They're a blight that overwhelmingly afflicts underprivileged areas, like my former neighborhood back in Los Angeles. They're a desecration of our public skies for the sake of private profits. The only reason they were allowed in orbit in the first place was because they were supposed to be temporary, but the companies never cleared them, and the regulators who were supposed to crack down on them for that refused to lift a finger—because they all hope to get a job with these same companies."

One of the government officials moved to take the microphone from Elliot, but then Elliot did the astonishing—he unlatched a door in the missileproof wall and slipped out to stand in front of it. None of the CEOs behind him dared to do something like that. They shoved the glass barrier closed immediately. Elliot stood before the crowd, defenseless, microphone in hand.

"What you saw tonight was me registering my formal objection to this situation," Elliot said. "That's why I destroyed those skyboards."

A roar of approval swelled from the crowd. Tom knew the sound techs could've cut off Elliot's microphone by now if they'd wanted to, and they'd probably been told to do it. Maybe they had no real motivation to make Elliot stop either.

"In fact," Elliot went on, "this is my last act as an Intrasolar Combatant. I believe this is the proper moment to tender my resignation to the military. A friend told me once that compromise with someone who won't give an inch in return, well, that's no different than surrendering to them. My friend was right."

Tom's jaw dropped.

"The truth is," Elliot said, "I've surrendered for too long, and today I'm through." He turned slightly to address the Indo-American CEOs while still facing the crowd, ever the showman. "Thanks for everything, ladies, gentlemen, but associating with you any longer would tarnish me. If you don't like that—" he waved to the roaring crowd "—take it up with my friends here."

And with that, Elliot jumped right into the crowd, into the protection of fifty thousand people and straight out of the Coalition's control.

Even as the White House press secretary hurried forward with another microphone and tried to calm the crowd, the roar of approval for Elliot drowned out her voice. It was like the crowd had become a single, living beast that utterly overwhelmed the most influential power players standing on the stage.

As the scene unfolded, the screen cut out. Tom squinted until he made out the Coalition CEOs, tiny figures cowering behind their shelter of protective glass, and below them, Elliot Ramirez borne by a ring of supporters like a massive tidal wave. Tom could see unmanned drones soaring in from the distance. At the periphery of the crowd, he glimpsed riot cops preparing microwave weapons to disperse the mass of people, and automated patrollers powering up, ready to deploy tear gas. The men and women on the stage were already being hustled away for their own protection.

For a moment, with the crowd stirring about him, and the CEOs fleeing, Tom felt like he was back on the suborbital, gazing down at the planet and perceiving just how tiny one human being was—even these men. For all their power and influence, the executives on that stage were as fragile and easily ruptured as any other human being.

And he realized that General Marsh had only been half right. The security state was tightening its grip on their throats, but there was one thing driving it: *fear*. The oligarchs were deathly afraid. They'd snared the rest of their species in a trap of security and surveillance because that was the only way to protect themselves from the natural consequences of seizing everything and reducing the vast majority of people to bare subsistence. They'd doomed themselves with their greed, and all these measures, all these riot cops, all the isolated fortresses like Epicenter's Tower or Sigurdur Vitol's private national park, couldn't protect them.

For all their power, none of those executives would be able to walk down a public street without bodyguards. None of them could have the simple freedom Elliot Ramirez did to stand before a massive body of people without fear of being torn apart. That missileproof glass might as well have been electrified fence and barbed wire. No one could fashion a prison so perfect, so complete, as the one the masters of humanity had created for themselves.

There was justice in the world. There was. And with that realization, something began to lift from Tom's vision, like some dark haze had finally cleared away. He knew now that this didn't have to be the world Neil hated, this didn't have to be a world where the worst of humanity always won and everyone else surrendered to what couldn't be stopped. There was nothing inevitable about the supremacy of sociopaths.

Vengerov may have gotten away with destroying Yuri, but that only meant one thing: someone hadn't stepped up and made things right yet.

So Tom would do it.

CHAPTER TWENTY-FOUR

W HEN TOM RETURNED to the Pentagonal Spire, he found Wyatt in the infirmary, sitting in the chair next to Yuri's bed with her legs drawn up to her chest. Ever since she'd resumed talking—to Tom, at least—she'd finally started coming here again.

His gaze shifted to Yuri. The Russian boy seemed smaller now and far more fragile. Tom had an idea about what he could do for Yuri, an idea about how to get to that transmitter in Antarctica, but he couldn't pull it off without help.

"Wyatt, I need a favor," Tom said in a low voice. "There's something I can't do by myself, but you probably could."

"There are a lot of things like that."

"There was this one time when Heather Akron downloaded a memory segment from me. . . ."

"What segment?" Wyatt said.

He shook his head. "It's not important. The thing is, it gave me an idea. There's a specific time frame when I was stuck outside at Obsidian Corp. in January. Could you somehow do the same thing she did and get everyone's memories of that time for me? Maybe during Applied Scrimmages?"

"Why?"

Tom hesitated. He wanted to create a mental map of sorts. If he accessed what everyone had seen at Obsidian Corp. that day, with all their photographic, perfectly detailed memories, he'd be able to put them all together into one image and create a comprehensive, three-dimensional layout of the place in his brain. Once he had that he could figure out how to break into Obsidian Corp. in person.

He couldn't explain that to her without telling her what he planned to do, so he thought quickly of a lie. "Olivia Ossare wants me to do it. She thinks I'll be able to make peace with what happened if I, uh, see it from another angle."

She frowned. "Are you sure you want to do this? This won't be like memories from a census device, Tom. They won't be audiovisual. It's a lot more intrusive. You'll remember the actual experiences like they happened to you. It will be intense."

"Look, no one else lost fingers that day, so I figure most everyone else had a better time than I did. I can handle it."

AN HOUR LATER, they were in the last of the Middle training rooms on the thirteenth floor, and Wyatt was sprawled on the floor, accessing a processor right beneath a floor panel.

"The memories will feed directly to your processor in the middle of Applied Scrimmages," Wyatt informed him. "Try to stay in the sim as long as possible without getting killed. They'll only download into your processor as long as you're hooked in."

"Got it." He pulled out the neural wire, and Wyatt was getting ready to shove the floor panel back in place when the door slid open and Vik strode in.

He halted inside the doorway, and Tom could see from the shock on his face that he hadn't expected to see them.

Wyatt sprang to her feet, startled.

"What are you guys doing here?" Vik said.

Tom threw Wyatt a swift glance. She was tense.

"Nothing," Tom said brusquely. He stooped and shoved the floor panel back on.

"This obviously isn't nothing," Vik said, pointing at the floor.

"What are you doing here?" Tom threw back at him.

"I'm meeting Lyla. Her roommate hates me, and we wanted to go somewhere Giuseppe wouldn't sit and watch us creepily," Vik said. "Now your turn."

Tom shook his head. "You don't want to know."

"I asked, so yeah, I want to know."

"Why even bother?" Wyatt flared up. "You were mad when you knew about that other thing. Maybe you don't want to know about this."

Vik blinked, his thick eyebrows raised. "You're talking again."

"Yeah, she's talking," Tom said.

"I'm glad, that's all," Vik said. "Can't I say I'm glad about that?"

"No," Tom said, and suddenly, he was furious with Vik. He hadn't even realized it until now, when anger, hot and vicious, ignited inside him. "You don't get to say that to Wyatt, and you don't get to ask what we're up to. *You* dropped *us*, not the other way around."

"It's not like that," Vik protested.

"Then what's it like?"

The door slid open, and Lyla Martin strolled in. They lapsed into silence. For her part, Lyla shook her head and turned to Vik. "No way," she told him. "We are not sharing the room with them."

Tom nudged Wyatt, sending her a questioning glance. Was she done?

She nodded.

Tom turned to the standoffish Lyla, and the sheepish Vik. "Don't worry. We're outta here."

Vik didn't call after them.

SINCE NEARLY FREEZING to death, cold had become Tom's least favorite thing in the world. When Yosef's group hooked into the sim, and Tom found himself a Napoleonic soldier standing in the middle of the bitter winter in Russia, he cursed inwardly. His joints began to throb at the first nip of the icy wind, and that's when Wyatt's program kicked in and began bombarding him with memories from the other Middles.

The image of the Obsidian Corp. visit from Giuseppe's point of view filled his vision, and Tom tumbled over into the snow, cold wetness seeping up his arms. He staggered upright, half-blind, and grew aware of the crackling of gunfire as they engaged today's enemy group, even as his mind filled with images from January.

Giuseppe had obviously spent much of the tour daydreaming about some hotel in Paris he liked, because the images of Obsidian Corp. were intercut with those mental images.

A simulated Russian soldier rushed at Tom, and Tom narrowly managed to impale the guy on his bayonet before more of the memory washed over him. Giuseppe was admiring himself, straining to see his own face reflected in one of the large windows. Nearby, Giuseppe could see Blackburn with his large back to the Obsidian Corp. techs, shoulders curled protectively over the forearm keyboard he was tapping. Tom knew that must've been when he'd hacked Obsidian Corp.'s intranet and found his blackmail material.

In his own simulation, Tom staggered away from the main body of his group, figuring that he couldn't focus on both fighting and the memories. He had to stay low, and worst-case scenario, someone would find and kill him. He sank against a wall inside a half-destroyed house, the boom of cannons rumbling like thunder in the distance, more memories rushing into his brain.

His neural processor automatically integrated the varying images of Obsidian Corp., stitching them together in a full mental map, matching up the time stamps. It was strange seeing things as if he'd been in several different places at once, like he'd had more eyes than his own. He could gaze around an entire image from a single time frame and see what many people had seen.

It grew stranger still seeing memory after memory from the time frame after he'd been stuck outside, when he could reference his own memories of the bitter cold. Everyone else had been on an innocuous tour. Some had noticed Blackburn hacking the intranet, some had not.

While Tom had been outside trying to stand up again, all the other trainees had been inside, taking turns petting a Bengal tiger named Kalkin, who was as domesticated as a house cat, complete with a neural processor of his own. . . .

While Tom had been lying on the snow, unconscious, Blackburn had finished his hacking, looked over the group, and said sharply, "Someone's missing." And then, "Raines. Where is he? Where is Tom Raines?" He looked at Vik.

Vik squirmed uneasily but did his best to look innocent.

Blackburn jabbed at his forearm keyboard and swore ferociously. "How did that kid get outside?"

And in every memory, Vik's eyes grew very wide, terrible comprehension on his face.

It was Vik's own memory that made something inside Tom

go still. He noticed through Vik's eyes that he'd left—right after Tom really had been cut off from the group. Vik said nothing, covering for him.

Then he felt Vik's shock when he realized Tom had been outside this whole time. He saw Vik risk Blackburn's wrath by staying after the other trainees were ordered home. He saw through Vik's eyes when he was hauled in, felt Vik's stomach plunge as he'd wondered if Tom was dead. He saw Vik's mind calling up the memory of Tom's near climb up the transmission pole, and his ears stung with the memory of Blackburn's words, "You aren't doing him any favors. . . ." He felt in his stomach Vik's nauseating sense of guilt.

So when he'd finished downloading the last memory, Tom roused from his stupor and discovered he wasn't alone in the simulation of the burned-out house. Vik was there, too, and he felt like he finally understood it all now. He knew why Vik had been so strange.

"Hey," Tom called.

Vik turned. They were on opposing sides of this sim, but it didn't seem to matter now. "Are you all right? I knew the minute the sim started you might not like this one. I lit a fire."

"I'm okay."

"Right." He raised his eyebrows. "That's why you're here. In a swoon."

"I wasn't swooning. I was deeply in thought about something."

"Sure you were, Tom."

Tom staggered over to drop by the crackling flames, the heat washing over his skin, over his numbed hands. "That thing you asked earlier. You still wanna know what Wyatt and I were doing? Are you sure?"

Vik nodded. "Tell me."

"I'm going to Obsidian Corp. to blow out the transmitter that's connected to Yuri. No transmitter means Yuri's not a security hazard anymore, which means there's a case to give him a new processor. I'm going in person, Vik, so I'm getting every bit of data I can."

Vik eyed him. "That's insane."

"And reckless and stupid, Vik. It's literally a building full of killing machines in the middle of Antarctica. If you want to delete me telling you this as soon as Applied Scrimmages ends, I won't blame you. But here it is. The truth. You wanted to know, and I owed it to you to tell you. Now you get the choice."

For a moment, the only sound in the room with them was the crackling of the flames in the hearth. "This could save Yuri's life," Vik said, half in question.

"I wouldn't do it if I didn't think it might give him a shot."

"And even if I tell you this is a bad idea," Vik added, "you'll still go—and so will Wyatt, as soon as she figures out what you're up to. So I lose three friends for the price of one."

"Vik—"

"I'm in."

"Really?" Tom said, astounded.

"Really, Doctor. You'll have better odds if I help you." A note of ferocity crept into Vik's voice. "That's my friend. Let's save his life."

REVEALING HIS TRUE intentions to Vik meant revealing his true intentions to Wyatt. Tom had expected her to be horrified by the idea, but she lit up like he hadn't seen her since Vengerov fried Yuri, eager for a chance to actually do *something* for Yuri. One glimpse at the mental map he'd put together of Obsidian Corp. using all the collected memories seemed to make up her mind.

"I think we can pull this off," she told them.

As it turned out, Wyatt knew some secrets of her own, mainly about the contents of Blackburn's databases. Apparently, he'd been amassing a trove of data about Obsidian Corp. over the years, from notes about the facility's security systems to a database of hundreds of programming languages for various Obsidian Corp. machines.

"This is not normal," Vik declared. "Someone doesn't accumulate this stuff unless they're planning something. What's Blackburn up to?"

Tom was daunted by the computer languages. "There is no way I can work with one of these, much less a bunch of them."

Wyatt nudged him. "Tom, it's illegal for a computer to self-code. That means our neural processors can't download and learn for us how to work Zorten II or Klondike, because those are neural processor languages. There's nothing against downloading computer languages that don't program processors. That's not self-programming."

AN HOUR LATER, Tom had written a complete program in the Bernays-6 language that controlled skyboards. He could program in it as easily as he could do mathematics now or speak a foreign language.

It was incredible.

It really made him understand for the first time what a big constraint it was that people with neural processors couldn't simply work Zorten II so easily.

The best thing of all they discovered was in storage: a Praetorian left over from Obsidian Corp.'s stint in charge of the Spire. Wyatt tugged out its control chip and set out to practice some programs in the Praetorian-specific programming language, SE Janus.

Vik, meanwhile, set out to write Tom an embarrassing new bunk template. "If we're going to perish on this venture, I want Tom to die knowing he has a humiliating wallpaper in his room," he explained to them.

"You're a good friend," Tom told him.

"We're not going to die." Wyatt gave a big smile. "I really do think this could work. Obsidian Corp.'s completely oriented toward protecting against *mechanized* intruders. They have to worry about surveillance vehicles or small drones, but no one's going to go in person to break into a building in the middle of Antarctica. It's not a hospitable environment for humans to hang around and stroll on in, especially right now when it's winter. Between that and the whole wing of motion-sensitive, electrified floors, they won't expect anyone to come in person."

Vik sat up abruptly, finger raised. "Quick question: How is this inhospitable-for-humans thing not a problem for us? Last I checked, we're about ninety-nine point nine percent human. Except for Tom, who's ninety-nine point eight percent . . . We can joke about that now, right?"

Tom flashed him a mechanized thumbs-up. "Joke away."

As he spoke, he inspected the mental map again, pinpointing every location on the walls where he saw neural access ports. Since Obsidian Corp. had designed the neural processors, he supposed he shouldn't be surprised they were there. He wondered who used them.

"So how are we getting in?" Vik pressed. "We can't exactly walk in from the outside. Tom almost froze to death in the *summer.*"

Confidence surged through Tom. "Simple. We go in the same way Obsidian Corp. staffers do: right through the front door."

THEY CHOSE SUNDAY, early in the morning, for the operation. Tom tried to sleep in the scant hours before their departure, doing it the normal, human way by lying on the bed instead of hooking a neural wire into the access port on the back of his neck.

In the darkness of his bunk, he was reminded of one aspect of normal sleeping: sometimes it didn't happen, no matter how much he wanted it.

Tom sat up hazily and became aware of a tapping noise. He rubbed at his eyes, and peered around, searching for it. Then he made out the surveillance camera in the corner, moving back and forth, waving at him.

"Hey, Mai Shiranui," he called.

Here's a hint: my name is not the name of a video-game character. Much less a Japanese one, Mordred.

He grinned, reached down into the drawer beneath his bed, and pulled out a T-shirt. "I hoped you'd come."

And then Medusa's words appeared in his net-send: *I didn't want to wake you up.*

"I wasn't asleep. Lemme hook into a VR game and meet you. Pick a sim and I'll see you in a minute."

Tom hooked his neural wire into his VR gaming system for the first time in a long while. The Pentagonal Spire had a large database of games for the trainees, and Medusa had obviously chosen one set in a vast, rolling desert of sorts. Then her avatar appeared—a big, muscular male character with long, flowing locks, whom the neural processor informed him was *the mythological figure Sampson, the strongest man in the world.* Tom looked down at himself and realized he was playing his mom's namesake, the diabolical temptress Delilah.

"I'm the girl?" he said, examining his chest closely.

"Don't worry. You're very pretty, Tom." The teasing note abruptly dropped from her manly voice. "Maybe these avatars will make this easier."

"Make what easier?"

She folded her arms. "I should stay away."

"But you're here. Right now. Not staying away. And I'm okay with this." He stepped toward her. "Listen, I was a jerk last time you were here. I have a friend in trouble, and there was something I needed to get at Obsidian Corp. to save him, so I was frustrated and thinking about that, not about anything else. After we kissed, I wanted to talk to you. I scared you away. I know it."

She groaned. "If my character wasn't about twenty times stronger than yours, I'd punch you right now. You didn't scare me. You *don't* scare me. You caught me off guard, Mordred. This is a terrible idea. We're on opposite sides of the war. You were charged with treason, and I nearly faced the same thing the last time we did this."

"But that's because we weren't using what *we* can do," Tom told her, drawing closer. "Yeah, it was dumb, meeting online when we could be tracked, but *interfacing* and moving into the systems like you and I can isn't the same thing. We've got this power, and maybe we can't use it out there, but why not use it like this? For each other? See, I'm not sorry about kissing you. I'm not. I want to do it again. I don't know anyone else like you, and if you looked slightly less manly right now, I'd be grabbing you." He reached down to shove his hands into his pockets, but the Delilah character didn't have any. "So that's it. Ball's in your court."

She raised her hand into the air, and her long-haired, manly avatar vanished, leaving the Medusa he knew in its place. Tom felt his body shift back to the one he was familiar with. He closed the distance, but Medusa planted a hand on his chest to stop him.

"I need to warn you about something. I don't trust very easily. If you're going to kiss me, if we're going to do this . . ." Her small fist tightened on his tunic. "Tom, don't burn me. I'll hurt you."

Petite as she was, fragile as she seemed, Tom knew Medusa was infinitely more fearsome than the strongest man in the world, and she meant every word she said.

"I won't," he vowed.

And then he kissed her.

WHEN THE TIME came, Tom saved two notes in his system files. One was for his father, one for Medusa—though he addressed it to "Murgatroid." He didn't write one for his mom. He considered it, but then decided she wouldn't want it anyway.

It wasn't that Tom thought anything would happen. He, Vik, and Wyatt had worked out their plan so carefully to make sure they returned . . . but Tom had this strange superstition that if he didn't write them notes, he might end up meeting some terrible fate at Obsidian Corp. that would cause him to regret not having at least put his last sentiments on record somewhere.

He'd almost died there once, after all. It scared him a bit, willingly returning, but he had to. After he saved the notes, he donned his optical camouflage and headed to the vactrain to wait. While Wyatt hacked into the Interstice to arrange an anonymous, undocumented pickup time, Vik was visiting Yuri in the infirmary. He was going to place a pair of earbuds in Yuri's ears to play a beeping sound.

If all went to plan, the transmitter in Yuri's brain would record the audio input in Yuri's ears, and the other transmitter in Obsidian Corp.'s system would receive it. That would give them a specific, active data imprint to search for when they tried to find that transmitter. Tom's job was to carry the search program in his processor. He'd interface with Obsidian Corp.'s systems and use it to locate the transmitter.

Now his heart fluttered with a mixture of excitement and anxiety as he walked through the heavy iron doors to the Interstice and approached the rows of fake trees. Then he encountered the first snare in their plan.

From her reading of schematics, Wyatt explained that the optical camouflage would conceal them from the retina scanners, but the scanners must've been cued to activate as soon as someone strolled in the door. Green lights lashed out from the fake trees and began dancing across the wall, searching for a retina to scan.

Tom's heart pounded as he tried to evade them, realizing he'd feel like an utter idiot, boldly announcing his plans to march right into Obsidian Corp. and free Yuri, and having some stupid retina scanners give him away before he got on the Interstice.

He was unexpectedly saved by Heather Akron shoving open the doors and marching into the room after him. The green beams of the retina scanner found her yellow-brown eyes, registered her identity, and faded away.

Tom held very still as she took her place by the glass doors gazing on into darkness. He quickly sent Vik and Wyatt a message.

Delay another five minutes.

Then he waited, monitoring Heather from under his optical camouflage. Capitol Summit had destroyed her prospects at the Spire for good. Wyndham Harks had withdrawn their sponsorship of her; the military had held an inquest to question her fitness as a Combatant. She'd been forced to quit; she'd been offered a position at the National Security Agency as a consolation prize. Officially, she'd be an analyst, but everyone knew what that meant when it came to trainees who'd washed out of the program: she'd be there to serve as a walking, talking computer, and if rumors were true, she'd be treated as such. Just like Nigel Harrison.

And then the iron doors swung open again, and someone else followed Heather inside. Tom gave a startled jerk when he saw Lieutenant Blackburn sweep into the room. Tom barely dared to breathe.

"Ms. Akron."

Heather whipped around. Wariness filled her face. "You. What do you want?"

The green beams began to dance through the air, but Blackburn raised his thick forearm and tapped at his keyboard. The retina scanners blinked off.

What was this? Tom wondered as Blackburn drew toward her. "I couldn't simply let you leave without a talk about that interesting file you sent me."

"The time to talk is over," Heather snapped. Her gaze darted toward the trees, and Tom knew from the sharp gleam in her eyes that she'd noticed the way Blackburn had switched off the retina scanners. "You didn't intercede for me. You didn't speak up for me. You could've told them I had a computer virus or that I'd malfunctioned, and you didn't. So I'm going to show you I wasn't bluffing." Her eyes gleamed with spite. "I think the military will be fascinated to find out what you've been hiding about Tom."

Tom caught his breath. Of course. Her blackmail of him had fallen through. . . . She must've tried it on Blackburn to save her own skin. It obviously hadn't worked with him either.

"Don't!" Heather shouted, her voice taking on a shrill pitch.

Tom leaned to the side to see them past the leafy canopy of a fake tree. Blackburn lowered his forearm keyboard, his brow furrowed. Whatever program he'd just tried to use had obviously failed.

Heather gave a scornful laugh. She flipped back her hair and held up her own forearm keyboard in a triumphant flourish. "You can't knock down my firewall that easily, sir. Your little protégé motivated me to work very hard on this one. It's a good thing, too. I knew you might try to stop me from getting away."

Blackburn lowered his arm. "Nothing's ever easy," he breathed.

"What is it exactly you were trying to do?" Heather said mock sweetly. Hostility burned in the air between them. "You really think you can delete what I know? Not going to happen."

Blackburn drew a breath that puffed his cheeks and blew it out slowly. "I was going to make you come with me to the Census Chamber. Then we were going to search for that string of very specific memories so I could delete them and send you on your way. I still think you're going to come with me, Akron. You are too clever a girl to risk the consequences if you don't."

"You can't throw me over your shoulder and take me up to the census device. Someone will hear. Someone will see."

"You're completely right. There are far too many people around, even this early in the morning, for me to haul you upstairs with brute force. You're going to come with me willingly and allow me to tamper with your memory, because I'm not letting you leave here with what you know."

Heather's eyes narrowed into slits. "Tom Raines destroyed my whole life. Why are you even protecting him? Why do you care if the government finds out what he can do?"

Tom was wondering that, too.

"Tom Raines himself? He's not why I'm here." Blackburn leaned toward her. "Let me put this in terms you'll understand: I've devoted seventeen years of my life—almost the entirety of yours—to one single purpose. It's the sole reason I haven't already swallowed a bullet. I recently discovered a potent weapon that could make my last, middling wishes come true, and now here you are, threatening to hand it over to my enemies. I hope you understand how desperate I am to stop you from leaving. Whatever thrill you think you'll get from revenge, whatever it is, if you try and walk out that door, you'll be making a deadly mistake."

Tom felt himself growing very still. So that's what it was. That's why Blackburn had kept him alive in Antarctica. That's why he'd been so fascinated, learning what Tom could do in the Census Chamber. He saw what Tom could do as something he could use. He saw *Tom* as a weapon. His heart began to thump so hard, he was sure they could both hear it.

"You can't do anything to me," Heather said. "Even if you killed me right now, you'd leave forensic evidence everywhere, and you'd never be able to hide my body in time. You're bluffing."

In the darkness beyond, the silvery vactrain had risen up from the tube below, and the chamber was repressurizing. Heather's ride had arrived.

Tom felt a sense of unreality, realizing that the rest of his life would probably hinge on what happened here between these two people.

"Heather," Blackburn said, as the doors slid open. "Last chance. Please come with me."

"Good-bye, sir," Heather said with a delicate wave. "I'd

say it was nice knowing you, but I think I own you now, so we're not through by a long shot. Count on that." And then she backed through the doors.

Tom crept forward and saw her whirl around and dash toward the metallic train car waiting for her in the dark chamber.

Blackburn gave a weary sigh, looking ten years older, then he tapped at his forearm keyboard. "Stupid girl."

A mechanized voice boomed in the air: "Decompression sequence initiated."

The words didn't register in Tom's brain for a moment. All he was aware of was the massive, chugging sound filling the air, and Heather, nearly at the train but not close enough to find shelter inside. She spun back around with naked fear blazing on her face, realizing what was about to happen, realizing now the meaning of Blackburn's words:

If you try and walk out that door, you'll be making a deadly mistake. . . .

The metallic vactrain plunged out of sight as the transition chamber depressurized, and a powerful gust of wind blew Heather down into the magnetized vacuum tube along with it.

As soon as he was alone, Tom moved to the door and stared into the blackness beyond the glass, trying to wake up from this strange dream. It couldn't really have happened. He hadn't really seen that, had he?

His neural processor replayed the images and informed him of what must have followed Heather getting knocked into the vactube.

She'd had fifteen seconds to be totally conscious, if she'd held her breath. Then her lungs would have ruptured. If she hadn't held her breath, she might've remained conscious for forty-five seconds. It was enough time for her to realize she was doomed, that there was no way back out of the vactube, and her blood would've started to boil.

Tom clutched his temples, because he couldn't focus his brain. He couldn't really be here, he couldn't have stood by and seen Heather get murdered. He couldn't have stood there, and done nothing, as Blackburn turned around and walked away like nothing had happened.

There wouldn't be any forensic evidence, would there? Her body was in the vactube somewhere, and her neural processor would be utterly obliterated once she was hit by a vactrain going several thousand miles per hour. He felt a hysterical laugh rise inside him, realizing he was the only person, the only person in the world who knew what Blackburn had done.

He stared at the glass, reflecting no image of him, and wondered why he'd stood there and said nothing even after Blackburn decompressed the chamber. Had he been in shock or . . . or had some part of him realized what was about to happen and known it was the only way to neutralize Heather?

He couldn't figure it out. His brain wasn't working right.

Then he sprang a foot in the air as Wyatt and Vik's footsteps scuffed up behind him.

"Okay, the retina scanners are definitely out," Wyatt said. "Ready to go?"

Everything had transformed for Tom in a few minutes. The lines of the world around him had taken on a stark clarity, and he felt like he could see every jagged detail he'd missed before. They could die doing this. He could get them all killed. Tom felt a great rush of self-doubt. They'd planned this so carefully, but what if they were wrong?

Then his thoughts turned to Yuri, the reason they were doing this. It calmed him.

No. They wouldn't get killed.

He wouldn't let it happen. Not this time.

He couldn't think about Heather right now. He had a task and thinking about this would hobble him, distract him. All he needed to think about was getting into Obsidian Corp., destroying that transmitter, and getting back out. Nothing else mattered until that was done.

"Let's go," Tom said.

CHAPTER TWENTY-FIVE

WHEN THE VACTRAIN halted in Antarctica, they darted toward the elevator. Then they waited, invisible in their optical camouflage, for an elevator full of Obsidian Corp. employees to finally come to the Interstice. It took a while. Thirty-eight minutes later, the doors slid open and some of Obsidian Corp.'s personnel strode out. Tom, Vik, and Wyatt rushed straight inside.

Then a message from Wyatt appeared before Tom's eyes. *I'm activating the net-send thought interface now, but I tweaked it so if you want it to actually send, you have to confirm. We don't need to hear each other's stray thoughts.*

Even now, Tom's vision glowed with the first thought that always came to him when hooked into a thought interface: *Don't think about boobs.* He felt very pleased to select the "Cancel Message" option rather than the "Send" one.

As the elevator rose, Tom felt Wyatt's hand grab his, and he squeezed hers reassuringly. Vik's shoulder bumped his during the interminable trip upward, their ears popping.

They flattened themselves against the wall when the next batch of Obsidian Corp. employees stepped into the elevator, then slipped past them into the lobby before the doors closed.

The optical camouflaging concealed them long enough for them to hop straight over the turnstiles without activating the retina scanners, then they pulled up Tom's mental map. They needed to get to one of Obsidian Corp.'s neural access ports. It was their first task.

They slipped out of the hallways sprinkled with employees and ventured into the sectors of Obsidian Corp. minimally fit for human presence where the lights were dim, the floors lined with power plates for the various machines. This was where Praetorians slid through the halls on a standard patrol, with others in sleep mode, tucked against the walls.

Remember, stay off the floors, Vik thought to them as they waited in the doorway to the machine-heavy sector.

Tom nodded, even though Vik couldn't see it. Not only would they get electrocuted by the conductive floors powering the Praetorians, they'd set off every alarm in the place if their footfalls tripped the sensors on the ground.

They stood there, so close they were all touching, optically camouflaged inside the doorway, waiting for a Praetorian.

Tom's heart began to pound. They'd practiced this next part in the Spire twenty-five times, using the old Praetorian in storage. That one couldn't see through their optical camouflage. Now it would count.

Tom drew a sharp breath when a Praetorian circled around the corner, its curving metallic head atop its pendulous base. It slid toward them down the hallway, and Tom felt like worms were writhing in his gut. One command from a remote operator, and these machines could flood the hallway with poison gas, could electrocute them, could slice their heads off with lasers, or crush them to death. If Wyatt's code wasn't perfect, if one of them slipped, if Vik's fingers weren't nimble enough, they all died.

As the machine slid past them, Tom seized its rounded head and swung himself onto the base. He felt it sway as Vik and Wyatt eased themselves on as well. He twisted around the neck to expose the back panel, and Wyatt quickly stripped it away to expose the control chip.

Just as the pinpoint camera of the Praetorian lit up, a lethal red light of an alarm igniting in its depths, Vik yanked out its control chip and set about jamming the new one in its place. Tom watched, heart in his throat, wishing his fingers had been nimble enough to do it. But it worked. The Praetorian's system blinked out, reset.

They waited. Tom could sense Wyatt and Vik's tension behind the optical camouflage. He could hear them breathing rapidly.

And then the Praetorian powered back on again, utterly still for a long moment as it processed Wyatt's SE Janus coding. The machine resumed sliding down the corridor with them on top of it. Tom shoved his mouth into the crook of his arm to muffle the insane urge to laugh, even though he knew any sound from him might trigger alarms. He felt Vik shift his weight, arm brushing his, and Wyatt's hand pressed up against his. Her fingers gripped his and tightened until his hand throbbed.

It helped him that she was nervous, too. It helped a lot.

Relax, Tom thought to her. *We'll be in and out.*

The Praetorian was taking them on Wyatt's preprogrammed course to the nearest neural access port. Tom would hook into the system, and the search program installed in his processor would begin hunting for the data pattern that matched the audio signal blaring through the earbuds into Yuri's ears in the Pentagonal Spire, and therefore straight into Obsidian Corp.'s database. As soon as they had its location, Wyatt had one algorithm to order their Praetorian to return them back to where they'd come from, and another to send the Praetorian straight back to that transmitter. It would emit an electrical discharge to fry the transmitter along with the supercomputer it was attached to.

By the time the transmitter was destroyed and the alarms began, they'd already be on the Interstice, heading home to Arlington, Virginia.

Simple.

The journey through Obsidian Corp. to the nearest neural access port felt interminable. They shifted positions clumsily, each with a foot on the base of the Praetorian, the other hanging into the air, all three of them clinging to the long, curved neck. The biggest test was the moment the Praetorian passed the first inert guard machines, all in sleep mode. Tom held his breath as they slid past those pinprick camera eyes, his heart in his throat, legs trembling.

But they passed them, unseen, shielded by their optical camouflage, hallway after hallway, machine after machine. The gauntlet of Praetorians remained still. Tom felt like he might puke. He was so grateful he wasn't doing this alone.

They passed a window gazing upon the black night over the icy landscape of Antarctica. And then the Praetorian stopped. They were at a neural access port. A tremendous flood of relief poured through Tom. He maneuvered awkwardly, slipping his fingers under the tunic portion of his optical camouflage, working a neural wire out of his pocket. He jammed it into the access port. It was time to let the search program installed in his head locate the audio pattern from the transmitter in Obsidian Corp.'s systems. He hesitated.

Are you guys sure you can keep me upright while I'm hooked in? I'd rather not fall and get electrocuted, Tom thought to them.

I've got you, Vik thought.

Are you sure? Tom thought dubiously.

Is Vik sure? Wyatt also thought dubiously.

Vik's pride was pricked. *Hey, I am strong like an ox or a Yuri.*

Don't worry, I'll help hold you up, Tom, Wyatt thought.

Tom waited until Vik had anchored an arm around him, squashing him up against the neck of the Praetorian, then he hooked the other end of the neural wire into the back of his neck. The search program in his head triggered and began rapidly scanning through Obsidian Corp.'s database. Tom had a search plan of his own in mind. He jolted out of himself into the vast tangle of information sparking through Obsidian Corp.'s systems, knowing he might be able to locate the transmitter before the program did. The sooner they could leave, the better.

But Obsidian Corp. wasn't like the Pentagonal Spire. Tom had no familiarity with the network of pipelines. He kept finding himself linking to external flows of information, feeds from the offices of congressmen straight into Vengerov's databases . . . feeds from inside homes, buildings, from smart appliances, from intelligent streetlights. . . . He found himself in Obsidian Corp.'s external defense systems, and then he shot through a pipeline into the NSA's Fusion Center in Utah, where the surveillance footage of every person in America was being stored. Then he snapped back into his own processor, and the search results blinked in his vision center, showing him a warehouse, empty but for machines and a supercomputer—and Yuri's transmitter.

But something strange happened. A wind of stellar power

seemed to seize him, dragging him down another pipeline. It was like disappearing down a vortex or a black hole for an instant, because the pipeline drew him irresistibly into another subsystem. For a fleeting moment, Tom's consciousness was in the datastream, the zeroes and ones dancing in his brain, and his mind met another mind. It was that same disconcerting sensation he'd experienced finding the third neural processor interfacing with Heather's ship.

The other neural processor seared his consciousness, and through someone else's eyes, Tom gazed at a reflection swimming across the polished blackness of a nearby screen.

Joseph Vengerov seemed to be staring right back at him, and for a chilling moment as their minds were linked, something curious and dark and stinging with possibilities stirred on all sides of him.

"If it isn't the ghost in the machine." Vengerov spoke right to his own shadowy reflection. "Is that you, Yaolan?"

Tom felt a spike of panic and reeled back out of Vengerov's mind and into himself so abruptly, he almost lurched over. But Wyatt and Vik were practically bear-hugging him to the Praetorian, squashing his cheek against the metal pole, and their thoughts began bombarding him.

Did you get the location? Vik thought.

Where's the transmitter? Wyatt thought.

Tom straightened, bathed in sweat, anxiety a living animal clawing in his chest.

We need to get out of here, he thought to them, cold with dread. *We need to go now. I think Vengerov knows we're here.*

And then the first alarm split the air.

Something triggered in their Praetorian. Its metal neck began to retract into its body. Tom heard Wyatt gasp as the metal slid between their fingers, less and less of it there to grip. Then Tom heard her pounding frantically at her forearm keyboard, and her command sent it springing back to its full height.

Even that action proved dangerous. The deviation from programmed behavior must have registered in the system, must've blared their location to every machine in the building, because another Praetorian swung around from the next room, heading straight for them. Tom realized what was about to happen, and reached out to wrench Vik and Wyatt to a crouch as the new Praetorian spliced a laser through the air where they'd been. Their Praetorian fought back, spliced its own laser through the air, razing the other machine into smoking pieces.

Wyatt! Knock out the floors! Tom thought to her.

Then she jammed her neural wire into the access port, jabbed the other end into her neck, and unleashed her virus into Obsidian Corp.'s wireless systems to knock out the electric floors and disable their surveillance system. It was their emergency program—in case this disastrous scenario happened.

Tom's heart careened against his rib cage as he wondered whether it was working yet, whether the floors were out or not. But the next Praetorian swung into the hallway with them, and their Praetorian shrank automatically into a battle stance before Wyatt could stop it, minimizing itself as a target, jarring all of them, sending them hurtling off.

Vik shrieked, Wyatt yelped, and Tom squeezed his eyes shut as his back hit the floor. They barely noticed their Praetorian destroying the other

For a moment, they all lay there, locked in place, waiting.

Program worked, Wyatt thought.

Tom muffled his automatic laughter.

Quiet! I don't know if I knocked out surveillance! Wyatt thought. Air shimmered as she moved back over to the access port and hooked into it again. And then a split second later,

"Okay, surveillance is out, after all."

Tom and Vik lay there, heaving for breath.

"More are coming," Vik said.

"Probably hundreds," Wyatt agreed.

"Run to the Interstice?" Tom suggested.

"Sprint!" Vik gasped.

They all scrambled to their feet and dashed back the way they'd come, running so fast, they almost tripped over themselves. Their Praetorian rolled alongside them.

Another Praetorian swerved around the corner, and they dove as their Praetorian lashed out with its laser, but the other Praetorian shrank in time to dodge, and its answering laser flared out, slicing off the weaponry of their protector. For a moment, Tom, Vik, and Wyatt stood there, paralyzed, realizing they were defenseless—but their Praetorian whipped forward, an electrical surge building in its base.

"That's going to travel across the floor, come on!" Tom shouted, and they swerved into the nearest doorway, slamming the door behind them. They found themselves heaving for breath, trapped inside an icy cold warehouse.

Tom needed more air. He tore down the hood of the optical camouflaging, and so did Wyatt and Vik. For a moment it was like they were three detached heads floating around, and Tom frantically spun in circles, searching for a way out, for something they could grab or do in here to escape. . . .

Nothing. *Nothing.* Not even a neural access port. There were only two doors. One led to a hallway rapidly filling with Praetorians, and the other led *outside*.

Outside. Tom shuddered.

"I don't have any ideas," he confessed. "Do you guys?"

"This was a bad plan. This was a bad, bad plan," Wyatt whispered. "How did Obsidian Corp. find out we were here? We were so careful! She tangled her fingers in her hair. I must've missed something."

"It's not your fault, it's mine. He noticed I was in the system," Tom murmured.

"But I hid your IP! You shouldn't have been detectable!"

No, he shouldn't have been. And then a terrible suspicion swept over him.

He was looking for me.

Vengerov had called him "the ghost in the machine." Tom remembered that term. Blackburn had said it first. His mind filled with the image of Yuri that day on the stairwell, following them down. The dots connected in his brain, making sense of it all.

Vengerov *had* been listening that day. He'd heard Blackburn, and he learned someone else like Tom and Medusa existed. Then he learned that the ghost was a friend of Tom's. It couldn't have been difficult from there, extrapolating the likeliest suspect. Tom had a notoriously extraordinary friend. *Medusa.*

That's why Vengerov approached Tom about giving Medusa a virus. And Tom stupidly went to Medusa and told her LM Lymer Fleet had only been surveilling her because she was winning too much—he'd been passing along Vengerov's lie. That wasn't the reason Vengerov was watching her. Tom was the reason she wasn't on guard anymore. Vengerov was hunting that ghost and he believed it was Medusa. Tom may have doomed her. He'd doomed them all.

Vik paced in a frantic circle. "There's going to be more of those Praetorians soon," he said, eyes on the door to the hallway. "We have to get out of here. We can't stay! They'll bust through that door any minute!"

"There's nowhere to go, Vik." Wyatt hugged herself, visibly shaking. "We're never getting through those machines. That's the only path. The only other way is outside."

Outside. Tom had done that already, and it hadn't been winter then. It would be colder. Outside was death. He knew that in his bones.

Suddenly a voice boomed out, filling the air around them. Tom shivered as he recognized the upper-crust British accent with a hint of Russian. "To the invader or invaders in my complex, salutations!"

Vik and Wyatt grew rigid. Tom held his breath. Vengerov sounded like he was enjoying himself.

"I apologize for the welcome you've received from my killing machines, but alas, you took us quite by surprise. I know you are trapped, and I know where. Bravo for making it this far. I dearly regret that you disabled my surveillance system, because I would greatly enjoy seeing your face as I assure you that at this very moment, fifty Praetorians are converging on your position, primed to bring down that wall on my command."

Vik spun toward the door again, like he expected it to explode in on them. Wyatt's head bowed downward. Tom couldn't stop shaking.

"But I see no reason for needless bloodshed or a dramatic display of force," Vengerov went on. "Therefore, I shall give you this opportunity to surrender yourselves to my custody. If my machines discover you facedown on the floor, disarmed, with your hands linked behind your heads, they will spare you. Otherwise, they will kill you like dogs. I give you ninety seconds to make your decision about whether you intend to live or die."

His voice cut off abruptly, leaving Tom, Vik, and Wyatt shivering in the warehouse, eyes wide and frightened.

"We have to do it," Wyatt said. "We have to give up."

Vik was ashen. "We'll get thrown in prison for this."

"It's better than being dead, Vik! We'll tell Vengerov the

truth. He rigged up Yuri, so we came here to free him. Vengerov can't talk about doing things that are wrong. . . . He's the one who probably ordered Yuri's neural processor destroyed!"

"Just like he could do to ours," Vik pointed out darkly. "He didn't care about Yuri—what makes you think he won't do it to us?"

"He won't," she stammered. "He—he can't. We're still useful to the military, and Vengerov's on the same side as we are. Maybe we'll face some sort of disciplinary thing. Guys?"

"No one knows we're here, Wyatt," Vik countered, his eyes intent. "He doesn't have to hand us back over. He could kill us or do anything he wants to us."

"We have to surrender. What choice do we have?" Wyatt said intently. "And why aren't you saying anything, Tom? What do you think?"

They both looked at him.

Tom felt a strange, odd calm despite his certainty of doom. He knew what would happen. If they resisted, they died. If they surrendered, well, Joseph Vengerov had manufactured the processors, and he'd manufactured the census device. When he caught them, he'd demand far more than their excuses—he'd stick them under the census device and cull them for every last secret in their heads. He'd tear the truth out of them, and he'd learn what Tom could do.

Who would stop him? They weren't in the United States. They were on a distant continent. No one knew they were here, and there was nothing stopping Vengerov from doing whatever he wanted. Vengerov would find out Tom had been in his head, seen through his eyes. He'd realize Tom was the ghost in the machine he'd been tracking, and when he culled Tom even more, he'd learn that there were two ghosts and Medusa was the other one. Tom would give her away and he knew he couldn't stop that from happening.

Tom closed his eyes. He couldn't let that happen. Vik and Wyatt didn't know about Medusa, so they could surrender. They *should* surrender.

"Wyatt's right. We don't have a choice," Tom said to them. "Our only way to survive this is to hope Vengerov shows mercy. I'm sorry. I didn't think it would go this way. Just lie on the floor."

Tom made a show of lying down, to be sure Wyatt and Vik would do it, too. When they were both down, gazing at the floor, breathing so hard he could see it, Tom eased himself back up to his feet again.

There were a million things he wished he could say to Vik and Wyatt, but he knew even if he tried, he wouldn't get the words out. They'd all get tangled up in his throat, and his friends would both realize what he was about to do and maybe talk him out of it—and he'd let them persuade him because he didn't want to do this. He didn't. It killed him to think he'd gotten them into this; he'd give anything to see them escape. But the only one he could help now was Medusa. He could still send her a message. He could warn her Vengerov was onto her.

But not from within Obsidian Corp.'s walls.

Tom moved softly so his friends wouldn't notice him creeping backward, his legs shaking as he inched toward the door leading outside. It felt like moving through quicksand. And then he was there, his hand on the chilled doorknob, and Tom knew the clock was running out. He shoved open the door, the wall of overpowering cold like a massive fist striking him. But Tom forced himself outward despite every instinct screaming at him to turn around.

Then he closed the door behind him, trapping himself outside in the punishing, intolerable cold.

For a moment, he stood there, horrified by what he'd done, trapping himself outside, condemning himself. His skin began to freeze as the wind knifed his skull, drove spikes into his eardrums. His neural processor advised him to seek shelter, but Tom knew he would never surrender to the census device if he stayed out there.

His neural processor connected with the roaming server as wind stung tears out of his eyes and froze them on his cheeks, and his ears became pokers burning into his head. A nightmare of the past reared back to life under the pitiless sky cut with vivid stars and a green veil of solar winds as Tom waited to die.

And then something made the stars swim in the sky, and the distortion grew larger and larger above him. For a moment, Tom wasn't sure what he was seeing, and then a wave of displaced air knocked him backward onto the hard snow, humming throbbing his eardrums as a full Centurion-class drone retracted its camouflaging above his head.

I saw your note, Mordred, Medusa net-sent him. *I thought I'd come tell you: not a good idea.*

Tom gaped up at Medusa's drone, too shocked to feel cold for a moment, and he shouted into the wind, "My friends are still trapped inside!"

Immediately, the Centurion swung around, and its weapons flashed at the side of the warehouse, ripping a gaping hole into it. Through the sudden blast of heat, Tom made out Wyatt and Vik on the floor. He saw Vik grab her and they ducked as the drone roared over their heads across the warehouse.

That's when swarms of Praetorians blasted the wall and poured through the opening. Medusa's Centurion began firing at them, and Tom charged forward until he reached Vik and Wyatt, his lungs alternately stabbed by heat and cold, and he helped haul them upright and jerked them with him as the lasers of the Praetorians spliced through the night, Medusa's drone spinning in the air as it fired back. And then Vik and Wyatt were crowding against him, a wall of warmth reaching them as fire consumed the warehouse. Snow and sparks swirled around them as Praetorian after Praetorian was blasted apart.

"T-T-Tom . . . how . . ." Vik said, shivering violently.

And then behind them, another optically camouflaged ship lowered itself onto the snow, passenger compartment popping open, as close as it could get to them without danger.

Vik and Wyatt were frozen in place, but Tom snapped into motion and urged them toward it, knowing their only safety lay inside. They clambered up the steps and stuffed themselves into the crowded little cabin, meant for a crew of two, at most. The windowed compartment sealed up over them.

Tom willed on his net-send thought interface. He had no trouble focusing. *Medusa, is the drone still intact?* Tom messaged her. *Here is Obsidian Corp.'s external defense grid, and here is the supercomputer we need destroyed. . . .* He sent her the coordinates he'd found in Obsidian Corp.'s systems, the transmitter they hadn't managed to get themselves.

Got it.

And the last thing they saw before they jolted up into the atmosphere was a series of warehouses blasting apart.

Done, she sent back.

Antarctica's icy expanse and Obsidian Corp.'s burning, black mass receded beneath them until they became mere pinpricks.

Tom realized his breath was fogging up the window where he was pressed against it, trying to see. He grew aware of Wyatt's fingers digging into his arm, Vik's tense form against his other side. Tom maneuvered around in the tiny space, his legs bundled up against him. Wyatt and Vik's eyes enormous in the dimness.

"Thank y-you," Tom said reverently to the air. "You s-saved our lives."

"W-who are you talking to?" Vik managed.

"I d-don't understand this," Wyatt said, shivering.

"C-can I tell?" Tom said. "They can be t-trusted."

For a long moment, they all three shivered in the thick silence as Tom awaited an answer.

If you're sure, Medusa replied.

Tom felt almost like he could laugh and cry with the sheer relief of this, another secret sliding off him. He waited until his teeth stopped chattering, just so he could figure out the right words. "Guys, meet Medusa. Sort of. She's controlling this ship, and that was her drone, too. Medusa, meet Vik and Wyatt. Sort of. They're my best friends."

In response, the ship dipped briefly toward the dark waters below them like a salute.

Vik and Wyatt stared at Tom, wide-eyed. They said nothing for so long, Tom began to grow alarmed.

Finally, Wyatt said, "Thank you, uh, Medusa?"

And then Vik said, "This is your secret life again, isn't it?"

Tom leaned his head back against the glass enclosure with a sheepish smile. "Sort of."

CHAPTER TWENTY-SIX

M EDUSA DROPPED THEM off as close to the Pentagon as she dared approach, and Tom, Vik, and Wyatt hitched a very awkward ride into Arlington. The Pentagon City Mall was closed for the night, so they conducted their second stealth operation of the evening. Breaking into Obsidian Corp. had been a tense, life-threatening experience. Breaking into Toddery's Chicken Barn to access the Pentagon City Mall was another matter.

They could barely repress their giddy laughter as they followed the passage between the mall and the Pentagon, trying to think of the excuse they'd use to explain why they weren't listed as absent from the Pentagonal Spire. Finally, they decided to just show themselves to the officers on duty, and pretend they'd been caught sneaking out of the Spire, not sneaking in. They all got slapped with a weekend of scutwork duty and restricted libs, but they were ushered back into the Spire and no eyebrows were raised. In an installation filled with teenagers, catching trainees trying to sneak out after curfew wasn't a notable or unusual event.

Tom was so wired up with adrenaline, he was sure he could sprint ten miles if he needed to. He volunteered to sneak the gear back into the armory. Anything to put off sleep. He couldn't sleep anytime soon.

He was scrunching across the ground in the unlit Calisthenics Arena when a shadow moved, and Tom became aware of Lieutenant Blackburn waiting for him. Ice water flooded Tom's veins. He found himself rooted in place, thinking of Heather. Thinking of what he'd seen.

"Well?" Blackburn said tiredly. He looked years older in the dimness. "I'm sure you've got some preposterous lie ready for me. Give it a shot."

"I borrowed these. For a prank." Tom lifted the optical camouflage suits.

Blackburn shook his head. "No, you didn't. I was up working late tonight . . ."

Tom stirred. Working? So Blackburn hadn't dropped off to sleep after what happened with Heather.

". . . and I got to hear in real time the confidential channels lighting up with chatter about an accident at Obsidian Corp. An entire wing of the Antarctica facility was obliterated. Shockingly enough, my thoughts immediately turned to *you*. I checked on you and according to your GPS signal, you'd been in the bathroom for the last three hours. Coincidentally, so had Vikram Ashwan and Wyatt Enslow."

"I think it was something we ate," Tom tried. "You know Chris Majal's Indian Hall . . ."

"Raines, have I ever, and I mean *ever*, fallen for any of these ridiculous stories of yours?"

Tom let out a breath. "Fine. You've got us. We did it. And you know it. The transmitter's gone. We destroyed it. We freed Yuri. And I knew I had to do more damage to the place than

376

targeting the transmitter, or it would be too conspicuous so we hit some other things, too."

"Do you know what's conspicuous? Burning down the heart of the security state."

"We were careful," Tom assured him. "We took care of the surveillance cameras, we were wrapped in these optical camouflage suits securely enough that we didn't leave any DNA, and the one place we removed them, we *burned* down afterward. Even the Interstice didn't record our trip. That transmitter's not controlling Yuri. It's gone. Stick me in the census device, and I'll show you, then you can approve him for a neural processor while there's still time."

Blackburn drew closer, shadows sliding over his scarred face. "And let's say I do what you want. I inform higher-ups that Sysevich is no longer a threat. Then, I'm giving you a pat on the back for what you did. I'm rewarding you for this."

Tom held his ground. "I realize you could probably let Vengerov kill Yuri. I also get that you are probably even capable of, I dunno"—he shrugged, never taking his eyes from him— "*just killing someone* who posed a threat to you somehow. . . ."

Blackburn's shoulders tensed, and Tom knew he was wondering if there was more behind his choice of words.

"But I don't think you're gonna let Yuri die when there's no reason for it." Tom's thoughts flickered back to Blackburn's empty apartment, to that dumb candle. "You may not care what I think about you, or what anyone else thinks about you, but I don't think you're some unfeeling monster. If you turn around and let Yuri die, you know Wyatt will never get over it. She won't forgive you. She won't forgive herself. You're not going to let that happen."

Blackburn looked like some sort of statue. He didn't move.

"And, hey, if you really need more incentive, then I can

buy your agreement about Yuri's new processor," Tom said, inspired. "I have something else. Information. You're gonna want this."

"What?" Blackburn said quietly.

"Joseph Vengerov has a neural processor."

Blackburn's face froze.

"I figured you didn't know. *I* didn't."

For a moment, Blackburn stood there. Then, "That's impossible. He's too old, Raines. It would have damaged his brain. No one would do that."

"Well, it hasn't. It's there. It's in his head. I saw it. That's gotta be worth something to you," Tom said, weary. He tossed the gear at him. Blackburn caught it automatically. "Think it over. I'm going to bed. I'm beat."

He stuffed his hands into his pockets and left Blackburn alone there by the armory in the shadowy Calisthenics Arena, stock-still, clutching the bundle of optical camouflage suits.

WITHIN HOURS OF receiving his new neural processor, Yuri began bucking against the ventilator, so it was replaced by a nasal cannula. The prongs in his nose gave him a decidedly less alien appearance than the giant tube down his throat had.

Yuri began to wake up for minutes at a time, and then for a full hour. Tom, Vik, and Wyatt were finally all there one day when he stirred. The large Russian boy blinked at them, dazed. Yuri's memories had all been downloaded into the new processor, but they hadn't spoken to him yet.

"Thomas? Vikram?" He hadn't yet spotted Wyatt, lurking by the doorway.

Tom and Vik ambled over. "Hey, man. Welcome to the waking world."

Yuri settled back in his bed. "I am pleased to return." He

raised his arm, then looked at it, wide-eyed. "My great muscle mass!"

"Sorry, man," Tom said, feeling bad for him.

"Yeah, you've got work to do. That's what you get for lying in bed for months on end," Vik chided him. "By the way, Yuri, now seems an optimal time for you and I to have a weight lifting contest, winner gets a hundred."

Tom socked Vik's arm for Yuri. Yuri chuckled weakly.

And then his lingering distress seemed to melt away when Wyatt slunk forward and settled by his side. He craned his head back so he could gaze up at her adoringly, and for the first time Tom could remember, she looked back at him the same way.

As she leaned down to kiss him, Tom's thoughts stretched to someone else.

He needed to see Medusa.

The Pentagonal Spire was a tense place these days, so most people paid little attention to Yuri Sysevich's miraculous recovery or his restoration to active duty status, pending his actual, physical recovery. Instead, everyone talked about Elliot's dramatic, public defection. Or they whispered about the way Heather Akron had gone crazy at Capitol Summit, and now she was missing. Her GPS signal had even disappeared.

Tom knew the truth, and it made his stomach churn, knowing he was essentially covering up a murder . . . but he wasn't sure what else to do. Too many of his secrets were tangled up with Blackburn's.

Some things weren't as complicated.

Tom owed Medusa his life, Yuri's life, and Vik and Wyatt's freedom. It seemed like forever before she popped into the system again. When he met her, there were no more avatars, no illusory setting, just a blank white room, a template unwritten. He swept her up into his arms and swung her around. "I owe you so incredibly much, and I'm going to pay you back somehow."

She laughed. "I know. You seriously owe me. You're lucky I saw your fond farewell note."

"How did you find that so soon?" Tom asked. "I wrote it right before I left."

"I told you, I've been monitoring your online activity to make sure you wouldn't compromise our identities. I get an alert if your personal database references 'Medusa.' I also added 'Murgatroid' just in case."

He laughed. "I should've addressed it to 'the Troid.'"

"Then you'd be dead."

"Yeah," he said, suddenly serious. "I'd be dead."

"Once I knew where you'd gone," she said, "I kept those ships on standby. As soon as you were outside the building, I homed in on your GPS coordinates to see if you needed help." She punched him lightly. "You should have asked me from the beginning."

Tom gazed at her. "But we were doing it because our friend needed us to destroy that transmitter, Medusa. I couldn't have asked you to risk that. . . ."

"You didn't have to," she told him. "You've never had to."

"I guess not," Tom breathed.

A year ago, before Capitol Summit, he'd tried to ask her to take a dive for him, but he couldn't bring himself to do it. He'd known she'd say no. Why would anyone do that for him? She'd said to him afterward that maybe it would've been a possibility. He hadn't believed her. Not even long afterward. Not until now, when she'd done something so hazardous just for his sake. The realization rocked through Tom that she'd risked drawing

Obsidian Corp.'s attention to herself and she'd done it for him.

Tom's grip tensed around her, because he had this sudden, terrible sense something awful would happen if he let her go. "I have to ask you something, Medusa."

She eased back, waiting for it, her eyes searching his.

Tom stroked her black hair nervously. "Listen." He licked his lips, his stomach dancing. For a tangle of reasons. "Tell me something. I hope I'm wrong, but I'm going to guess your name again."

"Now?"

"Now." His voice was intent. "Is your name 'Yaolan'?"

Medusa jerked in his grip, and Tom felt something cold and frightening squeezing inside him, knowing it was.

"How did you . . ." she breathed. "Did you go in the personnel files in the Citadel? I told you not to do that, Tom!"

"I didn't." Tom clasped her shoulders, full of dread. He leaned down so he could stare right into her eyes. "*Joseph Vengerov* said it. I interfaced with his neural processor, briefly—"

"*His* neural processor?"

"His neural processor," Tom confirmed. "He has one. You were right when you said LM Lymer Fleet was surveilling you—that was *Vengerov* surveilling you because he's on to what you can do. I couldn't get into Obsidian Corp. because he'd already figured out how to block our way. He knows there's a ghost in the machine. He knows how to detect us, block us, and when he found me in his system, he called me 'Yaolan.'"

She folded her arms, withdrawing one step, then another. He wished she wouldn't pull away from him when something upset her.

"Don't you see?" Tom said urgently. "You're in danger. He's going to come for you, especially after what happened at Obsidian Corp. I think this is why he wanted me to use the virus on you—he wanted to knock you out for a while to see if the ghost in the machine went away when you did. If that happened, he would have all the confirmation he needs about who the ghost is. He already suspects it's you."

Her jaw set as she straightened to her full height. "It's good you warned me. I'll be careful."

"Careful won't do it, Medusa! He *knows*."

But she shook her head, and Tom felt a surge of frustration, because she *couldn't* understand. Joseph Vengerov was another Coalition CEO to her. She hadn't been in Vengerov's mind for that brief instant, hadn't felt his ferocious desire to possess, the blinding need to own without conscience, without scruple, without self-doubt. She didn't have a Blackburn or a Yuri to serve as walking examples of how little value Vengerov placed on human life.

"What am I supposed to do, then?" Medusa demanded. "Even if he suspects me, it's not like there is any way I can fix this."

"Yes, there is," Tom said. "You can come over here."

"Go there?" she said disbelievingly. "To the Pentagonal Spire?"

But Tom's thoughts were racing ahead, and he grew so sure of this. There was one thing he had over here that Medusa didn't have—and strange as it was, Tom realized it was the strongest weapon in his arsenal.

He had Blackburn.

Blackburn knew everything about him. He was the single person who could face Vengerov on a technical level. He was the only person who could be counted upon to hate Vengerov without wavering. And after seeing Blackburn kill Heather, Tom knew one more thing: Blackburn would do whatever he had to do to keep Tom's ability out of Vengerov's hands. He'd do it by any means necessary. It was strange that Tom felt no connection with Blackburn, no fondness, but he knew to his bones that he could rely on Blackburn's hatred for Vengerov in a way he'd never been able to rely on anything else, even his own father.

In one respect, at least—Tom could absolutely trust him.

Blackburn had to keep Vengerov away from Tom; he also had to keep Vengerov away from Medusa. There was nowhere on Earth safer for her than within Blackburn's reach.

"Yes, come here." Tom grew excited. "Interface with a ship, or I'll do it and fly you over. I'll hide you, we'll watch out for each other, and . . . and I can tell you more about why, but I know you'll be safe here. I *know* it. Then if Vengerov tries to get you at the Citadel, you'll be gone, you'll be out of reach. Don't you see?" Something else clicked, too. His stomach flipped. "We can meet. I mean, we could really meet. For the first time."

Medusa's face softened. She leaned forward and tapped the tip of his nose in a way that made Tom feel a bit foolish. "I appreciate the offer of protection, but I think we've established here which one of us tends to be the damsel in distress."

"Medusa, if you don't get over here now, you might not have a chance later. I don't have programs in your system to let me know if you get in trouble. I won't even know something's happened. I won't know to help you."

"I'll have to risk it," she said softly. "I can't leave. I'd lose everything."

Tom realized it: nothing he could say would change her mind. Even if she took the threat as seriously as he did, she couldn't bring herself to trust her fate to him, and Tom could understand that. He couldn't imagine leaving the Spire willingly, casting himself into her world. And she'd never even betrayed him, not the way he'd once struck at her.

He let out a slow breath, and felt her arms sliding around him. He pulled her gently against him, caressing her silken hair, the strands fluttering as he breathed her in.

"Yaolan, huh?" His processor translated it. "Oily orchid?"

"*Shining* orchid." She pulled back and tilted her chin up to meet his eyes. "How strange. We finally know each other's names."

His lips curved. "This relationship is moving so fast."

Her eyes sparkled playfully. "I know. Hyperspeed. We need more space. China and the United States aren't far enough apart."

"One of us has to move to Neptune, then."

She leaned very close, then whispered, "Not me."

Tom drew her into a kiss, and for a moment, there was nothing else in the world, just Medusa . . . Yaolan. And he never wanted to let her go.

But Tom didn't like to fool himself, and he couldn't passively accept doom. He pulled back from her, dread saturating his every pore, knowing there was a way he could fix this. He could save her. There was one way. Only one. He'd been willing to walk out into the snow in Antarctica for her. He was willing to do this now, even if she never forgave him for it.

"I'm sorry, Yaolan," he whispered.

A shadow passed over her face. "Sorry?"

Tom stared right into her eyes and thought out the trigger phrase, *I'll never do this to her.*

For one instant, he saw the confusion clouding her eyes as Vengerov's computer virus swarmed into her processor, and Tom had a last, fleeting glimpse of her in that moment of stark and terrible betrayal. Then her avatar dissolved from the simulation along with her, leaving him alone in the emptiness.

TOM SAT RESTLESSLY in the restaurant flipping a quarter from cybernetic finger to finger as Vengerov sipped a glass of wine and replayed the clip of Tom using the virus. Tom had downloaded it with the census device, cutting out everything but those final moments. Then he contacted Vengerov and arranged to hand the evidence over, feeling like a schmuck giving an offering to some pagan deity. Vengerov certainly accepted in that spirit, summoning Tom to one of his many properties, no surprise on his face, like it was his due tribute from some lowly plebian.

When he'd replayed the clip to his satisfaction, he balanced the neural chip between two fingers, assessing Tom over it. "I'm very pleased with you, Mr. Raines. Just when I began to suspect I'd have to send someone else to do the job, you came through for me after all. I've received reports from the Citadel confirming your story. I'm glad to see with my own eyes that it's true. Well done."

There was nothing vindictive in his tone. He wasn't holding a grudge against Tom for making him wait. Nothing like that. Just satisfaction that he'd finally coerced Tom into doing as he ordered.

Tom remembered his brief dip into Vengerov's mind, the way Vengerov felt no fear at the intrusion, no anxiety. That would be the natural, human reaction and Vengerov didn't have it. He'd felt anticipation, a sense of challenge, a desire to have, to control, to possess, and Tom found himself wondering whether it was Vengerov's personal neural processor that rendered him so inhuman, or if he'd been born that way.

"Tell me," Vengerov said silkily, "after all this time, what is it that changed your mind?"

"I guess you could say, I learned my lesson," Tom said simply.

Vengerov smiled, satisfaction in his angular face. He obviously believed Tom was referring to the day he'd almost killed him: when he'd tried to show Tom that he was powerless, that he could be destroyed with a whim.

But Tom was really thinking of Elliot and Capitol Summit. Only Elliot could have spoken those words to hundreds of millions of people. Only Elliot could have gotten away with such open defiance, because no one had ever seen it coming from him. Only the guy who'd cooperated and compromised for so long could have pulled off that attack on the Coalition in front of the entire world. Elliot had taught Tom something, too.

"Out of curiosity," Vengerov spoke, "what do you intend to call yourself when you're a Combatant?"

When. Not "if." Tom knew what this was: Vengerov assuring him he'd receive his payoff for a job well done . . . just in case Vengerov wanted to make use of him again in the future. It made Tom's stomach boil, but he kept his face carefully neutral and answered, "I don't know yet. I change my mind all the time."

"Ah. Then what is it today?"

Tom gazed at the oligarch at the center of the security state, perhaps the most powerful man in the world, sitting at the table with that secret processor in his skull, wineglass in hand.

Then Tom smiled.

"Cyanide."

TOM, VIK, AND Wyatt agreed not to tell Yuri about their escapade in Obsidian Corp. If Yuri saw Joseph Vengerov, it would be easier for him not having to lie about anything. Vik insisted that ignorance could be bliss.

The day Yuri was able to walk unaided, Tom, Vik, and

Wyatt made sure to steer him to the Lafayette Room. When promotions were announced, they all watched his face as the final plebe name was called out: "Yuri Sysevich. Congratulations to all the new Middles."

Yuri sat there without moving a single muscle, his blue eyes wide, one hand frozen midair where he'd idly reached over to caress Wyatt's hair. Tom and Vik sniggered at the sheer astonishment on his face, and Wyatt snagged Yuri's hand and kissed it. "Congratulations, Middle."

Yuri still seemed to be trying to rouse from his dream as Vik's name was announced—no surprise—and then came the real shock for the others at the end of the list of new Uppers.

". . . and Thomas Raines."

Tom had thirsted for this chance for a year. He had. But when his friends' heads all swung around to stare at him, he felt a dark sort of uneasiness, knowing he'd been promoted at Vengerov's behest, rewarded for betraying Medusa. Again.

Yuri clapped his shoulder, Wyatt ruffled his hair, and Vik gave him a playful shove. But Tom couldn't even fake a smile.

THERE WAS ONE person decidedly unhappy about Tom's promotion. Tom deliberately showed up late to his last Monday in Middle-Level Calisthenics so he wouldn't get swept into the workout routine with the others. Karl ambushed him right outside the Calisthenics Arena and shoved him against the wall.

"How'd you do it, Benji?" he snapped, sour breath flaring in Tom's nostrils.

Tom shoved him away. "Don't you have somewhere to be?"

"Do you have something on General Marsh?" Karl's voice blasted at him, his big, jowled face twisted with anger and hatred. "I know for a fact you were blacklisted!"

In the past, Tom might've found it funny, the redness

flushing Karl's face, the big hands clenched into shaking fists. Now he felt oddly detached. This was a waste of his time.

"Guess I'm not blacklisted anymore," Tom said.

"Well." Karl jabbed a big finger at Tom's chest. Hard. "I'm not gonna let you waltz into CamCo, if that's what you think. I'll fight you every step of the way."

Tom considered this situation carefully, because he was very certain Elliot had pointed out exactly which wires to snip to defuse this bomb.

"Okay," Tom said. "You do that."

"What, that's it? That's all you've got to say?"

Tom swiped his hand through his hair. "Hey, you wanna stomp me. I get it. You never stop trying. I've gotta give you points for determination." He turned away and moved toward the Calisthenics Arena, but Karl's big hand landed on his shoulder, yanking him back around.

"What sort of game are you playing here, Fido? Whatever it is, it's not going to work!"

Tom was morbidly fascinated. He'd swear, Karl looked more upset right now than if Tom was insulting him. "No game," he said, deliberately mild. "I'm being completely honest here, Karl. I respect your tenacity. I give you props for that."

Karl's big brow furrowed. His grip slipped away.

Tom straightened his collar and strode off into the Calisthenics Arena. He spotted the new Middles all returning their gear to the armory, and it was easy enough in the confusion for Tom to step in and don an exosuit, some optical camouflage, and a pair of centrifugal clamps.

Then he climbed to the very top of the Pentagonal Spire.

He stood up there on the roof. He was high enough now to glimpse the edges of a distant batch of skyboards glowing over Richmond, Virginia.

Tom delved in his pocket for the remote-access transmitter he'd already received for the upcoming vacation. He popped it onto his neck. He knew Medusa was incapacitated right now, incapable of hooking into the internet. More important, Vengerov knew it. Therefore the man who stood at the nexus of the security state, the man behind the surveillance and the drones and the secrecy who held together the world as it was, would realize Yaolan couldn't possibly be the one who did what Tom was about to do.

If the Coalition executives thought Elliot Ramirez's blasting all the skyboards in the middle of nowhere, Texas, was incendiary during Capitol Summit, if they saw them as a spark that could ignite something bigger, then Tom was about to give them an inferno.

He dove out of himself into the central subsystem controlling all the skyboards across the Western Hemisphere, and planted the code he'd written, moving from one hub to another. He jolted back into himself as the skyboards in the distance lit with the image he programmed for them, casting bright, white light across the landscape beneath them. Then he accessed the DHS server, the surveillance feeds, watching the images of people in cities all over the Western Hemisphere stopping in the streets, staring up at the skyboards. In every city, the walls of skyboards had gone blank of advertisements. Now they displayed stark black text trumpeting Tom's challenge:

THE GHOST IN THE MACHINE
IS WATCHING
THE WATCHERS

Tom let that sit there, gazing into the distance where the skyboards beamed down the message tailored for Joseph Vengerov and the entire security state with its web of surveillance and control. Here was something they did not control. Here was something they had not seen coming.

He gave Joseph Vengerov enough time to call up his techs, to shout into the phone that he wanted the transmission traced. Just enough time to understand the girl he'd incapacitated in China wasn't the internet entity he'd been hunting.

There you go, Vengerov. Here's your ghost in the Machine, Tom thought vindictively. *Now come and get me. Give it a shot.*

And then the next phase of Tom's virus triggered. The screens grew brighter and brighter, power spiking until they overloaded and erupted in haloes of debris, scattering fragments of skyboard like a curtain across the sky.

A soaring feeling swept through Tom. He knew he'd done something significant. He knew it could change everything, but he'd never before felt so right, like this was exactly what he was meant to do, exactly why he was here.

The plume of destruction spread over the land before thinning away. Soon there was no sign the Coalition of Multinationals had ever blocked the sky. When night came, all that was visible was the endless universe of stars.

ACKNOWLEDGMENTS

My GRATITUDE TO:

Mom, for being my strength, and Dad, for being on my team. Rob, for all the help with the real world stuff that sometimes eludes me.

Betsey, Stella, Maddie, Gracie, Matt.

Jamie and Jessica, my two best friends.

Judy and the Persoffs, the Hattens, Barb and the Anticevich family, all the friends who have bought the book just because I wrote it—you guys are the best!

To the booksellers and librarians who have introduced readers to my books and advocated for them. I owe you all a debt.

Juli, Helen, Caroline, Stephanie, Jillian, and all the bloggers who have supported the Insignia series from the start.

Molly O'Neill and the KT Books team. I'm very lucky in having such a fantastic and patient editor.

David Dunton and the Harvey Klinger Literary Agency as well as its subagents. Thank you for all the support and advice!

Kassie, Drew, Zander, and the folks at 20th Century Fox who optioned *Insignia*.

To Hot Key Books, Egmont, Goldman, and my foreign publishers, translators, and editors.

To Veronica Roth, Dan Wells, Aprilynne Pike, and Rae Carson, for all the wisdom you guys have shared.

To Derek Webber at SpaceX for answering a random writer's questions about suborbital planes.

To Brother Guy Consolmagno, for helping me figure out how to minimize my violation of causality.

To NASA, for looking forward.

And last, but certainly not least, to the readers who have made this all worth it. Thank you so much!

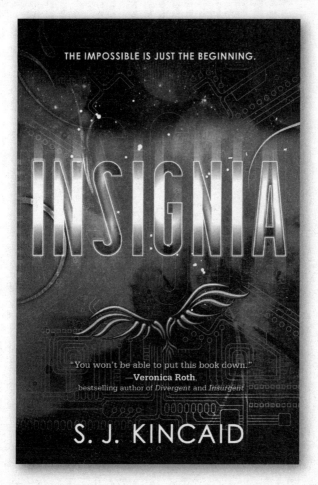